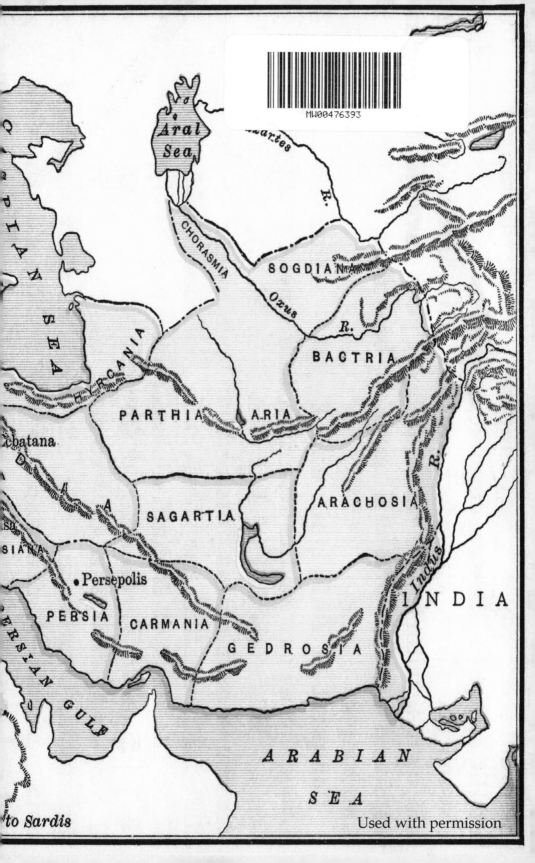

Used with permission

THE QUEEN

&

THE SPYMASTER

✖✖✖✖✖✖✖

Books by
SANDRA E. RAPOPORT

BIBLICAL SEDUCTIONS

MOSES' WOMEN
(Coauthored with Shera Aranoff Tuchman)

THE PASSIONS OF THE MATRIARCHS
(Coauthored with Shera Aranoff Tuchman)

THE QUEEN
&
THE SPYMASTER

A NOVEL BASED ON THE STORY OF ESTHER

BY
SANDRA E. RAPOPORT

KTAV PUBLISHING HOUSE

Copyright © 2018 by Sandra E. Rapoport

Library of Congress Cataloging-in-Publication Data

Names: Rapoport, Sandra E., author.
Title: The queen & the spymaster : a novel based on the story of Esther / by Sandra E. Rapoport.
Description: Brooklyn, NY : KTAV Publishing House, [2018]
Identifiers: LCCN 2017058729 (print) | LCCN 2018001511 (ebook) | ISBN 9781602802964 (ebook) | ISBN 9781602802940 (hardcover) | ISBN 9781602802957 (pbk.)
Subjects: LCSH: Esther, Queen of Persia--Fiction. | Bible. Esther--History of Biblical events--Fiction. | Women in the Bible--Fiction. | Bible fiction.
Classification: LCC PS3618.A727 (ebook) | LCC PS3618.A727 Q44 2018 (print) | DDC 813/.6--dc23
LC record available at https://lccn.loc.gov/2017058729

Published by
KTAV Publishing House
527 Empire Blvd.
Brooklyn, NY 11225
Email: orders@ktav.com
http://www.ktav.com

(718) 972-5449

This book is dedicated to my parents
Rebecca and Gabriel Sharon

INTRODUCTION

✠ ✠ ✠

This novel, inspired by the biblical story of Esther, imagines the untold story behind one of the Bible's best-loved, yet enigmatic tales.

While we know that the Scroll of Esther was the last biblical book of the Old Testament to be canonized, many mysteries still persist. No one knows for certain precisely when it was written, or by whom, or if the characters described in it ever lived, loved, struggled, wept, plotted, rose or fell. Yet the biblical story has persisted—embellished, redacted, endlessly analyzed, even retold in various cultures and religions—for over two millennia.

The global backdrop for this fast-paced story of palace intrigue is the ancient Near East of the mid-fifth-century BCE. And at the time our story commences, the world powers— Babylonia, Assyria, Persia, and Greece—have been engaged in a centuries-long battle for world domination.

Our palace drama presents a fascinating and terrifying world-within-a-world, and takes place over the course of two decades in the middle of the Achaemenid or Persian Dynasty, from approximately 486-465 BCE. The actors and action hold me by the throat: We read of the personal and political rivalries in the royal court of Persia between the king's vizier and an ambitious minister. Of two beautiful queens, one of whom dares to disobey the king and disappears without a trace, and of a second queen who is not who she pretends to be. Of a personal affront that escalates to a genocide decree. Of a people on the brink of annihilation, desperate for a hero. And through it all, we read of a king who alternately appears foolish and fierce, pandering and paranoid, manipulative and murderous.

As exciting as this plot-line is, it is the untold stories *behind* the story that fascinate me. At the biblical story's pauses and points of high suspense, and because one of its canonical rules is that nothing is as it seems, I hear whispered secrets. It is the secrets that fuel this novel. Treating the Scroll of Esther as an outline or skeleton narrative, and using my beloved *midrash*, or legend literature, as a springboard, I imagine the *back stories* of the well-known characters, answering questions that I—and surely uncounted readers before me—have pondered for years:

Why does Queen Vashti defy the king, courting death? Is she executed, or does she escape the hangman? The biblical text—never shy of recounting hangings, impalings and violent deaths in hand-to-hand combat—is strangely silent about this. Vashti simply disappears from the narrative. What happens to her?

Does Xerxes, the mercurial Persian warrior-king—the most powerful man in the Empire and possessor of a hair-trigger temper—live in a state of unrelenting fear of coup and assassination? What fuels his dangerous whims and passions?

What is the *real* reason Haman and Mordechai—vizier and minister—detest one another? The biblical story hints at a dynastic political rivalry begun centuries before, rooted in the deeply personal; each is a son of ancestral arch-enemies. But is there more? Have the two met in battle in the past? Is mutual attraction to the same woman fueling their antipathy?

What exactly is the "lot"—the *pur*—that Haman consults, setting the day for the Empire-wide massacre? Could it be an ancient Temple oracle now fallen into evil hands?

What is the true relationship between Esther and Mordechai? Are they cousins? Guardian and ward? Lovers? Husband and wife?

What is Mordechai's game? Is he a political hanger-on, an ambitious opportunist, a collaborator? Or is he someone other than what he seems?

Who is left standing at the end of the twelve months of the Persian Terror?

Naturally enough, solving these puzzles entailed layering complex motivations, subtle nuances, and historical depth onto the story's familiar characters. This, in turn, led me to create *new* characters that animate a fictional Persia operating in several dimensions: the ancestral past; an exotic and violent fifth-century-BCE present; and a parallel supernatural realm.

Familiarity with the biblical story is not necessary for the reader's enjoyment of this gripping new tale. You will be transported to the fortress city of Susa, housing the imperial palace and the royal harem, a labyrinthine hotbed of jostling factional loyalties, political intrigue, sensuality, and unrelenting tension.

You will discover a rich and intricate tale of ambition and espionage; evil and revenge; magic and love; death and survival. Here is a saga of a thousand-year vendetta. Of a century-long friendship riven by betrayal. Of survivors of extreme trauma who morph into beings with extraordinary powers. Of an orphaned girl with a gift for languages and an innate political intuition. Of brilliant political maneuverings and surprise military victories. Of a shattering and rebuilding of the lives of betrothed lovers.

This gripping novel interweaves familiar characters with those newly conceived, taking the plot in exciting and unexpected directions. *The Queen & The Spymaster* imagines *what could have happened* in the palace at Susa, and in the kingdom of Persia, twenty-five centuries ago. Reading the story of Esther through this bold and original lens, the danger, exoticism and thrill of this ancient story come to vivid life, as unforgettable, three-dimensional characters animate a sweeping new saga.

Here is a thrilling novel that, while it takes place in ancient Persia, mirrors modern historical events such as those that took place in Germany in 1938 and fomented a world war. Yet the story also resonates as fresh and as crackling as today's news bulletins of Isis and the Taliban operating out of 21st-century Iran and Afghanistan.

The Queen & The Spymaster reimagines the story of Esther, recreating it as a multilayered, multigenerational epic tale that had its origins on a bloody battlefield a thousand years before Esther, Mordechai and Haman were born, and whose ripples we are still feeling to this day.

Here is the Esther story you never knew.

Sandra E. Rapoport
New York City
December 2017

CAST OF CHARACTERS

✖ ✖ ✖

Women's Names	Character	Meaning in Pârsi (unless otherwise noted)
Atossa	Queen of Persia, Xerxes' mother, first wife of Darius the Great	a trickling well
Azam	Esther's handmaiden	greatest
Banou	Esther's handmaiden	lady
Dassi	Diminutive of "Hadassah"	
Elizeh	Esther's friend in the harem	Hebrew for "happy"
Esther	Xerxes' second queen	star; Hebrew for "hidden." In Persian, Esther is Ishtar, the Persian goddess of love and war
Farah	Mistress of the harem	cheerfulness
Fatima	Vashti's old servant	captivating
Hadassah	Esther's given name	Hebrew for "myrtle tree"
Hulda	Mordechai's operative	Hilda in Persian; strong
Maheen	Vashti's grandmother	greatest
Mihan	Esther's handmaiden	home, homeland
Poupeh	Mordechai's housekeeper	bird
Rachel	Shimon's daughter	Hebrew for "ewe lamb"
Razma	Maheen's handmaid	warrior
Samar	Vashti's mother	reward
Vashti	Xerxes' first queen	beauty, goodness
Zareen	Haman's daughter	golden
Zeresh	Haman's wife	misery

Men's Names	Character	Meaning in Pârsi (unless otherwise noted)
Abbas	Daniel's mute servant	lion
Abednego (see Azariya)	One of Daniel's three original friends	Akkadian for "servant of the god Nebo"
Ahmad	One of the royal scribes	most praiseworthy
Anoush	Vashti's steed	immortal
Artabanus	A captain of the king's bodyguard; assassin	true lord
Avichayil	Hadassah's father	Hebrew for "father of strength"
Azariya (see Abednego)	One of Daniel's three original friends	Babylonian for "guardian of Ishtar"
Ban	Master in the shadows	master
Baradari	The Amalek crime family	"brotherhood" in Tajik and Old Persian
Biktan	Palace gatekeeper	fortune
Carshena	Xerxes' First Minister	sleeping
Cyrus	Xerxes' Grandfather	sun; originally Kouroush, first king of Iran
Dalphon	Second-born son of Haman	crafty
Daniel	Old man, advisor to kings	Hebrew for "God is my judge"
Darius	Xerxes' father	rich and kingly
Darius II	Son of Xerxes and Esther	"he possesses" and rich and kingly
Eliezer	Mordechai's friend	Hebrew for "God is my help"
Gidon	Member of Sanhedrin Brotherhood	Hebrew for "one who fells"
Hadwin	Mordechai's minister-colleague	strong friend
Hafez	Member of Royal Guard	protector
Haman	Vizier to Xerxes	an Elamitic deity; alone or illustrious
Hami	Butcher's delivery boy	protector
Hananya (see Shadrach)	One of Daniel's three original friends	Hebrew for "Yahweh is gracious" or "gift of God"
Harvona	Xerxes' trusted chamberlain	the bald man

Hegai	Xerxes' chamberlain; Guardian of the virgins Keeper of the Women	separation
Hatach	Messenger and go-between for the queen and Mordechai	Hebrew for "in the middle;" Persian for "the good one"
Jalil	Minister colleague of Mordechai	great
Jamshid	Vashti's lover	shining river
Lev	Member of Sanhedrin Brotherhood	Hebrew for "heart"
Levi	Member of Sanhedrin Brotherhood	Hebrew for "one who is connected"
Majid	Minister at the King's Gate; colleague of Mordechai	honorable
Mehuman	First-advisor to Xerxes	making an uproar
Memuchan	Advisor to Xerxes	dignified
Meshach (see Mishael)	One of Daniel's three original friends	Babylonian for "shadow of the prince"
Mishael (see Meshach)	One of Daniel's three original friends	Hebrew for "He that is a strong God"
Mordechai	Esther's guardian; spymaster; Xerxes' advisor	Babylonian god; warrior
Natan	Member of the Sanhedrin Brotherhood	Hebrew for "one who is given"
Pinchas (& 6 brothers)	Member of the Sanhedrin Brotherhood	Hebrew for "serpent's mouth"
Raaz	Secret Master	secret
Salim	Xerxes' aide	safe or peace
Shaashgaz	Keeper of the Concubines	he who shears sheep
Shadrach (see Hananya)	One of Daniel's three original friends	Sumerian for "servant of sin"
Shimon	Mordechai's friend	Hebrew for "one who is heard"
Shimshai	Xerxes' chief scribe	my son
Teresh	Palace gatekeeper	severe, dry
Vafa	Vashti's old groom	loyal, faithful
Xerxes	King of Persia	righteous ruler
Yousef	Guard in Vashti's house	Hebrew for "God increases"

Esther — Alone
474 BCE
Year 12 in the Reign of King Xerxes
Year 5 in the Tenure of Queen Esther

Esther took a deep breath and uttered a silent prayer that today's sunset would not be her last.

There was no sound as she walked the marble breezeway connecting the women's compound to the king's palace. No sounds, no echoes, and no walls. The white gauze curtains hung from silver rods and draped over marble pillars fifteen feet high, pooling onto the floors. Sweeping panels of translucent fabric marked off rooms and chambers, coded by color to indicate place and station. It was a melting evening, the unrelenting Persian sun just sinking behind the palace ramparts; still, the air moving across the marble floors was mercifully cool, the lengthening charcoal shadows shifting. As she walked, Esther's own shadow appeared and disappeared on the curtain with the occasional breeze. *Like me*, she thought. *Here one moment, then who knows? Perhaps gone the next.* Her soft slippers moved along honed white and gold marble floors inlaid with emerald- and sapphire-colored mosaics. As she walked, she noted that the curtain color changed from white to blue, to, now, purple brocade of triple thickness, hanging heavily without any movement; she was nearing the Forbidden Zone.

She was wearing royal day-dress: the long chiton tunic of pale golden linen woven with iridescent threads, trimmed with turquoise braid and hanging down to her ankles, slit to show deep blue harem pants. Her slim waist was belted with a wide golden girdle. Her shining hair, loose to her waist the way Xerxes preferred it, was secured with her smaller day-crown, a jeweled *kulah*. Her arms, fingers and ear lobes were bare. Normally lissome with feminine curves, on this day, her third day of refraining from food and drink, Esther stood tall but she was reed-thin, almost disappearing beneath her glistening raiment. Her face and lips were free of enhancements, her eyes naturally shadowed, her skin parchment-pale. Her felt slippers were shot through with gold threads, and sported tassels to match her tunic's turquoise trim, but had no decorative bells. She would approach the king's Inner Court unannounced.

How strange, she thought as she walked, *that on this third day of fasting the hunger and thirst have ceased to bother me.* Esther was past hunger. Her thinking was lucid, even sharper than usual; her vision was clear. She saw the tiniest, individual dust particles floating in a horizontal stripe of waning daylight. She could hear her own breaths, feel herself blink. Time had slowed for her; she was ready to face a death sentence. Or, if she was very, very lucky and blessed by her One-God and her Persian namesake Ishtar, goddess of love and war, she would have the chance to do what she had been born and trained to do: entrance a king, set a trap, save her people.

Esther — Beginnings

A tall girl for a Persian, Esther was that rarest of young women: she was flawlessly beautiful of both face and figure. Added to her stature and erect carriage she was quite simply dazzling and distracting to the male eye. In a country where most of the women were shorter or rounder, Esther was willowy but with essential curves. Where most Persian women possessed hair as black as ebony, Esther's thick, wavy hair was a dark and natural russet-red color, reminiscent of rich mahogany touched with a pomegranate-red stain, and it hung like a velvet curtain almost to her waist. Her skin was another delight; companion to her hair color, her complexion was peach-toned rather than swarthy. Yet with all her physical uniqueness, it was her eyes that drew you in. They were large and fine and deep brown, with incongruously dark lashes and brows. They did not dart from side to side when she spoke to a man; they remained calmly fixed on his face, or lowered respectfully as was expected. Even at twenty-three years of age — five of those spent married to Xerxes, King of Persia — she still projected an aura of innocence and secrets.

But Esther also had something extra. Unbeknownst to anyone, her slow smile and pleasing nature concealed a quick and intelligent mind, and an almost photographic memory. And, unheard-of in a culture where a woman's coin was her face, her form or her ability to bear sons; where a beautiful woman could name the highest of bride-prices, Esther was without conceit.

Perhaps this was because her beginnings were humble, marked by a double tragedy: Esther, an only child, had been orphaned at birth, never knowing her mother's love. First, her father, a Persian of Israelite lineage by the name of Avichayil, a man of means and stature, had died during his wife's first pregnancy, and following soon thereafter, her mother had died giving birth to her. The hopeful midwives had named the jaundiced newborn Hadassah — from the Hebrew word *hadas*, for the evergreen and strongly rooted myrtle tree — her name, perhaps to contradict a cruel fate, a hopeful augur of the infant girl's life-force. Significantly, the myrtle tree is characterized by dense clusters of leaves that obscure its branches. The ancient Near East was a region that respected symbolism and superstition, and the girl Hadassah would come to embody the various qualities of her given name: she grew to be beautiful, strong, sought-after, and, essentially, a mystery.

As was common practice among tribal families in the ancient Near East and among the Israelites in particular — from as far back as the Patriarch Abraham taking responsibility for his orphaned niece, Sarah — the orphaned Hadassah was taken into the household of her nearest male relative, the only son of her father's brother, a first-cousin named Mordechai. Mordechai, a vital and ambitious young man in his early 20s, with no siblings or family of his own, really had no choice in the matter. The strong and family-centered Israelite social code demanded that he take responsibility for his uncle's orphaned daughter and raise her as his ward. He had the means to hire a wet nurse, who, along with a cook and housekeeper, formed the tiny girl-centered family circle that nurtured Hadassah. Unexpectedly, however, given Mordechai's age and other interests, he took his surrogate calling seriously. And as Hadassah grew, to Mordechai's credit he recognized that far from the burden he had initially expected when he agreed to raise the girl, he had inherited a treasure instead.

So Hadassah lived for fifteen years in the house of her cousin Mordechai, learning all that the household women could teach her about pleasing her guardian. She became adept at blending into the background whenever Mordechai had groups of men from the Sanhedrin Brotherhood over for his nighttime meetings. She drew the window drapes, trimmed the candles, and set out the food and wine for his guests. As she grew to young womanhood she came to recognize the men her cousin privately called Shimon, Yochanan, Eliezer and Natan, the leaders of the Jewish community of Susa. She also took as commonplace the coming and going at all hours of various turbaned, bearded, and also clean-shaven men, both young and old; some, like Mordechai and Hadassah, of royal Benjaminite blood; some clothed in humble homespun and others in rich court dress. Some were laborers, shepherds or tradesmen. Others had fathers and grandfathers who had been able to bring a portion of their wealth with them when they were led out of Judah into exile three generations earlier, to what was then Babylonia. Still others were utterly foreign to Hadassah. She memorized their dress and manners, and particularly their modes of speech. She also paid careful heed to their political discussions.

The Israelite exiles, following decades of misery and trauma, adapted well to their new king, new land, and new countrymen. Once they became resigned to the fact that their Temple was dust and their beloved Jerusalem a ruin, they had dried their tears, turned their faces to the east, and plighted their troths, first, to Babylonia, the ancient homeland of their forefather Abraham, and then, as the years passed and Babylonia's star fell and Persia's rose, to Persia. Sadly for the Israelites, living as exiles in countries not their own was something they had grown adept at doing.

The Persia of Xerxes—conqueror-king and son of Darius the Great and grandson of Cyrus—was going through an adjustment period of its own. Because their king had a ferocious nature and an insatiable drive to conquer the known world, even venturing as far north as Greece, the Persians learned to live side-by-side with conquered and exiled strangers. And people being people, over time the Persian bazaars rang with the sounds of scores of languages, and were redolent with spices from plants carried into Persia in hoarded pouches of conquered mothers and grandmothers. The Persia of Xerxes, and of Hadassah and Mordechai, was, on the surface, at least, a true blending of nationalities, cultures, languages and beliefs.

Susa

Dominating Persia's capital city of Susa—one of several capital cities in the far-flung Persian Empire; the other principal city was Persepolis, nearly 500 kilometers to the southeast—was the great stone and wood palace of the king. It housed the royal family, the king's court, and his retinue. It also contained the business side of the monarchy, with special chambers for the king's cabinet advisors, eunuchs or chamberlains, satrap governors, scribes and officers. The palace compound was, in actuality, a citadel, a walled and gated fortress, a small city. Within its thick limestone walls all the business of the king and court were conducted, and the royal family housed and cloistered. The compound contained Xerxes's Palace; the Royal Harem; the House of the Women; the king's Throne Hall, the Royal Treasury; the Council Hall, and the Apadana, or great assembly hall, ringed with one hundred marble columns thirty feet high.

It was in this teeming and exciting royal city of Susa that many of the exiled Israelite nobility rebuilt their lives and felt at home. They could blend into the multivariate Persian culture and partake in its commerce with relative ease. The diplomatic and specialized skills they possessed were in demand by the royal bureaucrats, notably their facility with languages and ciphering. Some of the descendants of the former Great Sanhedrin of Jerusalem were as facile speaking and writing in foreign languages as their fathers, grandfathers and great-grandfathers had been. This rare cosmopolitan skill allowed them to assimilate into and be valued by Persian society, even as it also stimulated some envy.

Thus, over time, the ancestral Hebrews-turned-Persians shed the outer trappings of their origins. In public they no longer wore their prayer shawls and phylacteries, their sidelocks and their special head coverings. They dressed and spoke like Persians. Even their doorpost *mezuzah*, the household amulet containing the words of the holy *Shema'*, the signal prayer proclaiming the Oneness of their God, and affixed to the street doors of their homes, was seen no longer. It was as if by common consensus that the Israelites' customs and faith persisted, if at all, only in the deepest privacy of individual hearts and secret rooms.

Mindful of blending into Persian society, Mordechai and the exiled Israelites took popular local names. Mordechai was named for Marduk, a Babylonian deity and the Persian warrior-god. His ward, Hadassah, had as yet not been assigned a Persian name, as she spent her girlhood at home in the familiar and protected circle of her cousin. *Time enough*, Mordechai thought, *to name her in a few years, when she has reached the age of betrothal and must walk outside the compound among the Persians.*

Unbeknownst to Mordechai or Hadassah, that time was nearly upon them.

Mordechai's House

Mordechai's house in Susa was constructed, as were the houses of the nobility and wealthy classes, as a square compound, laid out surrounding a central, fountained courtyard. In one wing were the private chambers, and in the other were a salon and gathering spaces. Three stories high and of golden stone, the solid old house had been his father Yair's for four decades before it passed to Mordechai. It was perfectly situated; not too distant a walk from the bazaar, and midway between the outer walls of the ramparted city and the king's palace.

Many of Mordechai's salon regulars had fathers and grandfathers who had been members of the Great Sanhedrin, the Israelites' governing body in Jerusalem. The sons and grandsons of these men—who would have been entitled to hereditary seats on the court had Jerusalem not been conquered and burned to the ground—still referred to themselves as "Sanhedrin." This despite the fact that the exalted law court had fallen into disuse a century before, with the Babylonian exile. And because old habits die hard, they felt more comfortable and trusting with one another than with anyone else.

Other than Mordechai's cook and housekeeper, Poupeh—who had been a fixture in his home when his father was alive and was trusted by and familiar to the salon's members—and a day maid, Hadassah was the only female presence in Mordechai's house. Having grown up side by side with many of Mordechai's male friends, Hadassah was treated like a daughter or sister, and was an accepted, if passive, part of the salon scene. She had the run of the house and moved unobtrusively from the cooking quarters to the dining salon, where she was an accomplished hostess, to the inner meeting rooms where business matters were discussed.

Thus, over time, undetected by the men and unnoticed by her cousin, Hadassah developed a measure of business acumen, and also picked up facility in half-a-dozen languages and dialects in addition to her native Pârsi.

By day, Mordechai and his friends enjoyed proximity and access to the Persian court, and a concomitant elevated status. The well-born or wealthy Persian/Israelites had mastered the ability to blend in. They did not make a fuss or strut about; they appreciated that their elevated status in a country that worshipped Zoroastrianism was dependent to a large extent on maintaining a dignified distance from visible practice of their One-God religion. In exchange, and not insignificantly because of the subtle power they wielded as financiers of merchant ships and armies, and as traders in silks and precious metals, they were accepted in Persian society and at court. These Jews were third-generation exiles, and so were, in their hearts and to all outward appearances, Persians.

Of course, there would always be those among the Persian people who resented all newcomer/interlopers to their thousand-year Persian culture. There were, in particular, some who held special grudges against the Israelites or Jews as a race; but during Darius' rule and before him under Cyrus' tolerant reign, these resentments remained underground. Ironically for the Israelite/Persians, the very reason they were valued by the Persian emperors sowed the seeds of resentment in the hearts of some Persian courtiers as well as ordinary citizens. Over the course of the past century there had always been a Jew whose wise counsel had been sought at the highest level of the royal court. Even interspersed as they were throughout the provinces of the Empire, the Jews remained loyal to one another and were extremely valuable to the crown as a class. The Israelite/Persians contributed more than their population share dictated to the king's treasury, giving their leaders a voice at court and sometimes access to the ear of the king himself. All reason enough for certain political factions in Susa to harbor discontent at their success, and to watch for a chance to undermine them.

If Mordechai and the Sanhedrin Brotherhood had no reason, as yet, to be fearful of Xerxes, historical experience had taught them that maintaining a measure of underlying insecurity in one's adopted land was a healthy frame-of-mind to cultivate. *Trust in no foreign king,* Mordechai's secret mentor had cautioned. *Serve him well, but know—he will turn his back on the Jew when it suits him. Always be vigilant! Always be ready!* So Mordechai and his Sanhedrin brothers, outwardly Persian but inwardly "other," watched, listened and served.

Haman Memuchan

Among the jostling and striving and ambitious courtiers in the court of Xerxes there was a thirty-eight year-old man by the name of Haman Memuchan, known as Memuchan by his elders at court. He was tall, dark-haired and trimly bearded, dressed in linens and silks to fit his station. He carried himself with arrogant confidence, and was canny in the ways of the king's court. Memuchan's prime characteristic was his enormous ambition. Memuchan was going places, though he kept his burning hunger for control a secret. He had an easily-roused temper, but was smart enough to know that a short temper was allowed only to those already in power. Desirous of moving up and acquiring power, Memuchan kept his temper leashed. Haman also wielded the dagger with expert skill, causing those who knew him to tread carefully around him.

As did most of the young nobles, Memuchan lived in a house in Susa nearby to the king's palace. He was at the King's Gate shortly after sunrise, and often did not return to his home until well into the night, when events quieted down at the palace. On days when he was not required to sit at the king's court, Memuchan spent hours in the king's outer court, or foyer, where advisors and supplicants milled and gathered informally, waiting for their turn to be heard by the king. Memuchan enjoyed bumping up against the crowds there, the better to overhear the conversations of other court advisors and also the claims of diplomats from distant provinces. By feigning concern, Memuchan befriended his fellow Persian nobles, and also established himself as a familiar face and a listening ear to the various satrapies and constituencies. By assuming an officious air and promoting a feigned familiarity with the king's guards, he intended that the outer province governors would attribute to him more power and influence than he actually possessed.

Memuchan was obsessed with knowing what issues would be presented to the king on any given day. His intent was to make himself minutely informed so that he would be ready at a moment's notice should the king ever seek his counsel. That would be his time to shine, and he would be ready to dazzle the king and the court with his brilliant grasp and analysis. Memuchan did not intend to remain in the seventh or lowliest chair of the king's advisors for long. He may have inherited his spot at court, but by Heaven he would use that spot as a stepping stone. He envisioned himself as a king; his first step toward that goal was to be Royal Vizier.

As fate would have it, Mordechai Bilshan was a courtier in the king's service at this same time as Haman Memuchan. While Memuchan was higher on the social ladder than Mordechai — Memuchan had a seat at court, while Mordechai did not — the two men could not help but be aware, peripherally, of one another. Both men were of an age — in the third year of Xerxes' reign both were in their mid- to late-thirties — they were each of them distant descendants of royal families — Haman of King Agag of the Amalekites, and Mordechai of King Saul of the Israelites. Both men were politically ambitious and brilliant; and both were intensely focused. The additional fact that they both had served in the same regiment in Darius' army seventeen years before gave an edge to their present interactions. Mordechai had won the regiment's fencing title two years running, a coveted status, and the envious Haman had developed deadly skill with his knife.

Memuchan was now a married man with numerous sons and one marriageable daughter, and Mordechai, though unmarried, had the responsibility of his young female ward, also of betrothal age.

Over the past three years in Xerxes' court the two men had had only impersonal interactions with one another, giving each other wide berth due to their vastly different personalities. There was no camaraderie between them — more an incompatibility, a low-level political rivalry — so that each avoided the other. Though inevitably, from time to time the two men found themselves drawn into wary political conversation in the courtyard of the palace.

While ostensibly all Persian nobles, whatever their origin, were equals at court—protocol dictated that one was not required to disclose his people or his origins—Memuchan, obsessed as he was with "knowing," had tried in undisguised as well as covert ways to learn of Mordechai's ancestry. To Memuchan's mind, knowledge equaled power. And since he perceived Mordechai—and every other courtier, as well—as his rival, he wished to know everything about the man's life, assuming the knowledge would one day stand him in good stead. In the past three years none of Memuchan's spies had uncovered anything unusual about Mordechai; he appeared to be a true and loyal Persian. But Memuchan suspected otherwise.

In the third year of Xerxes' reign, at the time of the king's great banquets, Haman Memuchan—all brilliance, all unscrupulousness, and all ambition—is a minor player either ignored or tolerated by the older advisors. He is as-yet undiscovered by Xerxes.

Xerxes
474 BCE
Year 12 in the Reign of King Xerxes
Year 5 in the Tenure of Queen Esther

Xerxes was bored. He leaned an elbow on the armrest of his ebony and gold throne, turned his crowned head and stole a glimpse of the evening sky through the skylight above, not wanting the diplomat from the Indus, droning on through an interpreter about taxes and roads, to realize he had lost the king's attention. The sun was already nearly at the western horizon; his afternoon court was just ending. The royal scribe was hunched conscientiously over his scroll, and the seven royal advisors, ranged below the elevated dais to the king's right and left in a broad semi-circle, shifted in their seats, restive now. All were hungry; they had been attending to business for nearly four hours. The white-clad Ethiopian serving boys had appeared at the entrance to the inner chamber as a signal that the hour of the mid-day recess had arrived.

The king gave the signal for the diplomat to end his monologue, raised an eyebrow to the First Eunuch, and within minutes cabinet ministers, courtiers and diplomats, interpreters and scribes, eunuchs and fan-boys were bowing out of his presence in reverse order of their importance. Only the king's personal guard, standing on the dais and to the king's left, his spear at the ready, and his personal fan-boy, remained.

On some days the king did not choose to leave the royal court right after his entourage. Just now, with his newly built throne room nearly empty and finally silent, Xerxes relaxed marginally. He knew that his solitude would be honored; for it was the law of the land that no one could enter the throne room unsummoned, or come before the king unbidden. The penalty for trespassing in the Forbidden Zone was death.

Xerxes — Beginnings

Beginning in the 7th century BCE, the Babylonians dominated the ancient Near East culturally and militarily for two centuries. They had conquered the vast territories of Mesopotamia, Persia, Judah, and even Egypt, and, with their unstoppable garrisons of armed foot soldiers and tens of thousands of horse-drawn chariots, they were considered invincible. The Babylonians had rolled through the known world conquering, plundering, exiling and enslaving in a pattern that seemed inevitable. So the conquest of Babylon by Cyrus the Persian, Xerxes' grandfather, in 539 BCE, ending Babylonia's "Golden Age," was a phenomenal world reversal.

Cyrus had earned his stripes by overpowering first the Medes and then the Lydians, the era's great powers, before moving successfully against Babylonia. His cylinders, those baked clay inscriptions that have survived two millennia buried beneath dry sands, proclaim his prowess: "Cyrus, King of Anshan, King of the World, King of Babylon, King of Sumer and Akkad, King of the Four Quarters." So with his conquest of Astyages, fierce overlord of Medea, Cyrus the Persian began the Achaemenid Empire, what was to be a two-centuries-long Persian domination of the greater ancient Near East, stretching from the Caucasus Mountains in the north to Egypt and the fortress of the Abu Elephantine in the south.

After Cyrus' death in 529 BCE, the Empire passed to Cambyses, Cyrus' son and named successor. But Darius, an ambitious outsider—his father was a Persian satrap from Bactria, in Hindu-Kush, and some say his mother was a high-born Jewess—and a ferocious warrior, was determined to rule Persia. He overthrew Cambyses, seized the throne and, ending a crisis of succession in 522, imposed stability on the Persian Empire. Darius consolidated his newly-won throne by marrying two of Cyrus' daughters, thus cleverly joining himself to Cyrus' royal family and strengthening his hold on the Persian royal house.

Darius I, known to all as "the Great," as was Cyrus before him, was obsessed with conquering and annexing a vast empire, and so was wary of independent or rebellious satraps governing in the far provinces. It was known that if Darius sensed that an appointed official had overstepped his authority, the fellow would face swift and extreme consequences. On one occasion, when an ambitious satrap coined his own local currency, Darius reacted brutally and swiftly, making a public example of him, treating the ambitious satrap the way he treated conquered kings and generals: Darius cut off his nose, ears and tongue, cut out one of his eyes, bound him, still alive, to the King's Gate, and displayed the man for days before impaling him on a stake. It is unsurprising that there were no successful attempts at independence among Darius's satraps.

Darius' boldness and success on the battlefield allowed him to vastly expand the boundaries of the Persian Empire in every direction. He accessioned the Indus River Valley region, known as Hindu-Kush and India to the east, expanded southwest across Libya, and marched into northeast Saharan Africa. He was similarly aggressive and victorious in Egypt to the southwest, remaining there long enough to complete the digging of a great canal from the Nile River to the Red Sea. Egyptian *stelae*, standing north of Suez, proclaimed Persian sovereignty over Egypt, arrogantly depicting Darius in Persian dress and wearing a Persian crown. Back at home, Darius likewise erected a ten-foot-tall stone statue of himself on a marble pedestal and placed it at the imposing gate of Susa.

But Darius was more than just a military machine; he also was a visionary and an adept and clever bureaucrat. He strategically organized the huge empire he had amassed, appointing scores of satraps—answerable to him—to govern its territories. He installed a unified monetary system with his profile on the coinage, and put in place a state income tax, fixing an annual tribute based on the wealth of each satrapy or province. He instituted standard weights and measures, and promoted use of an official language for the entire empire. Important for peacetime commerce as well as to facilitate troop movement in time of war, Darius built a system of all-weather roads that ribboned the now-huge Persian Empire, thus enabling Persia's speedy and reliable postal system. Darius's innovative royal courier system introduced post-houses and regular relays of horses and trained riders, so that a trip from the city of Sardis in Asia Minor to the city of Susa, which in prior years took three months, under Darius took a royal messenger only a week.

Before his death in 486, having ruled the Persian Empire for 36 years, Darius chose Xerxes to succeed him as rightful king. Darius was, at his essence, a builder. By choosing as next king of Persia his eldest son from Cyrus's daughter—born while Darius still ruled as King of Persia—Darius was ensuring an imperial Persian dynasty. And Xerxes, the new king at age 35, was no stranger to governing; he had cut his teeth by personally ruling Babylonia for the past twelve years at his father's behest. King Xerxes inherited the reigns to a vast, interconnected Empire stretching 7.5 million square kilometers and spanning three continents.

Unfortunately, with the death of Darius the Great, simmering discontents in Egypt and Babylon erupted into outright rebellions. Where Darius had spent much time personally appeasing both Egypt and Babylon for the purpose of uniting the Persian Empire, Xerxes was not his father; he ruled with a heavier, more oppressive hand. For the first two years of his reign he marched armies into Egypt ravaging the Nile Delta, and sent garrisons into Babylon, tearing down its fortresses, pillaging its temples and destroying the statues of their gods. He did away with the titles of King of Egypt and King of Babylon, arrogating to himself the all-encompassing title of King of the Persians and the Medes.

Significantly, in a serious misstep, Xerxes allowed himself to be goaded by vociferous court advisors into preparing for war against the Greeks, ostensibly to avenge his father's single humiliating defeat at Marathon. Xerxes raised troops from all the kingdom's satrapies, and built and equipped a navy to serve as his army's supply line. This was a massive, sophisticated and hugely expensive undertaking, done for no reason other than a combination of the king's once-youthful fire now sitting indolent and requiring an outlet, and his governing style of royal absolutism. Once he settled on an idea, Xerxes stuck with it for good or ill. And regarding his invasions of Greece, that country lay at the extreme edge of the Empire, and posed no threat to Persia.

Yet early in his reign Xerxes waged an unneeded war against the Greeks; a war he could ill afford, and that he was fated ultimately to lose.

After the Greek War, Xerxes settled down in his palace in Susa, where he further depleted the royal treasury by continuing his penchant for empire-wide parties and by engaging in self-aggrandizing construction projects. These included a massive *apadana* or great audience hall containing a hundred pillars and as many rooms, a personal palace, a treasury building, a harem and a colossal throne room.

Our story takes place during this latter period of Xerxes' rule; his military campaigns into Egypt and Babylon and the ill-fated Greek War comprise the background — the king's world proscenium — and inform his behavior at home in Susa. Xerxes is badly in need of reassurance, of unity within his Empire, and, not insignificantly, of an infusion of silver for his royal treasury.

Esther
Year 12 in Xerxes' Reign

Esther's personal handmaidens could not understand how the queen could plan to cross into the Forbidden Zone and present herself to the king unbidden; everyone in the kingdom knew that the penalty for such audacious behavior was death. They implored her to enhance her face, rouge her cheeks and lips, and adorn her trim arms with golden bracelets in an effort to appear charming and desirable, giving her the best chance at success.

"My Queen, won't you allow Mihan to dress your hair, and Banou to see to your face and eyes? Surely this will appeal to His Majesty better than…"

Azam did not need to finish her thought. Esther knew that her maids thought her insane or distracted by hunger and worry. *Surely a beautiful Queen will appeal to His Majesty better than a thin, weak, pale and anxious one.*

Esther laid a hand on Azam's shoulder. "Do not fret, Azam. I will dress well and the king will see me." Esther spoke more out of hopeful bravado than expectation; over these past two days and nights she had developed a plan.

The three handmaids were intimate servants of the queen, dressing and bathing her, seeing all, but keeping silent except when the queen invited their opinions or confidences. Experienced at serving royalty, they had learned to love this new young queen who spoke softly to them; in the five years of her reign she had never once raised a voice or a hand to them or to any palace slave. She was generous with coins and gifts, and commanded the kitchen staff to put aside overstocks of food, sending the packages via her personal messengers to the servants' families in greater Susa. So devoted were the maids to the young queen that they took it in turns to sleep on pallets outside Esther's royal chamber door to keep her from harm.

In the course of their duties, the queen's handmaidens went daily to and from the royal House of the Women, where the royal concubines were cloistered, so they were aware that the king had a varied and voracious sexual appetite. They also knew that he was fickle, suspicious, quick to take offense, and sometimes brutal. They had been apprentice-maids to the prior queen's personal handmaidens, and had witnessed what had happened to Vashti, Esther's predecessor, when *she* had dared to defy him. Their fortunes had risen with Esther's, and they whispered amongst themselves their fervent hope that Esther would hold the king's interest. Not just for her sake, but also for theirs.

For this reason and for Esther's own wellbeing the handmaids pressed the queen on this day to make herself both beautiful and desirable. They were acutely aware of the nocturnal doings of the queen, and so they were concerned and anxious that the king had not summoned the young queen to his bed these past thirty nights. They fretted that the king had lost his lively desire for her, perhaps spending his nights with one or several of his concubines instead. They whispered to one another that perhaps the fact that the queen had failed to fall pregnant these past five years might have discouraged the king and caused him to sow his seed elsewhere. Everyone knew that a king needed sons, and lots of them.

And more, because Esther was about to engage in the unthinkable — even the prior queen had never dared enter the Forbidden Zone on her own initiative — they encouraged Esther to enhance her appearance. Perhaps once the king glimpsed her and was reminded of her extraordinary beauty he might forgive her audacity, extend his royal scepter, and spare her life.

They appreciated that something essential and terrifyingly imminent was at stake. The young queen had told her maids that she would be denying herself food and drink for three days. Something disastrous must have befallen her or her guardian; she had been desperately sending and receiving messages from Minister Mordechai over the past several days, and after the last relay the queen, distraught, had sat on the bench in her chambers, her face in her hands, and wept. And the handmaids, in a gesture of solidarity and sympathy for the unknown danger, had promised the queen that they, too, would refrain from eating and drinking for three days. What their queen suffered, they did, as well.

But Esther had refused their pleas and ministrations. She knew precisely what she was about, having learned during her time in the House of the Women how to use her appearance to achieve her ends. And Esther intentionally did not wish to appear at peace. Alluring, yes and always; but for the first time in five years she also allowed herself to appear as wan and ill as she truly felt, and was hoping the king would notice this and be curious. Her initial plan was to pique his interest and thence his desire. If her opening gambit did not work she would never make it to implementing her strategic plan. Xerxes, paranoid of coup and assassination, had already executed a man who was found inside the Forbidden Zone uninvited.

Esther was on her own, the only agent from the secret brotherhood in the king's palace. Or was she?

Mordechai and the Sanhedrin Brotherhood

Mordechai's full name was Mordechai Bilshan, meaning "warrior with knowledge of many languages." His great, great-grandfathers had been noblemen in Jerusalem more than a century before, when the city's walls were still standing and the magnificent holy Temple was the center of Israelite life. Mordechai's ancestry traced back to King Saul, Israel's first monarch, who came from the tribe of Benjamin. King Saul's own father had been named "Kish," and subsequent generations were known as Benjaminites of the house of Kish.

With the exile of the Israelite nobles to Babylon in 597 BCE and the subsequent sacking and burning of Jerusalem eleven years later in 586 BCE, the Benjaminite family of the noble house of Kish was relocated to Babylon, and over the ensuing decades they gradually established themselves as advisors to its royal court. The ruin of their way of life had been complete, but in hasty advance of the exile decree they had packed their coins, their precious objects and their scrolls into purses, earthen jars and travel bags, and had loaded them onto wagons. Grateful their lives had been spared, they had walked and ridden for four months, overland more than 1200 kilometers through rocky wilderness and mountain passes, their Babylonian captors treating them strictly and harshly, but not brutally. They were the nobles of Jerusalem and they were accorded some basic privileges. The Babylonian king had use for these exiled Judeans.

It was known that King Nebuchadnezzar of Babylonia did not desire to utterly subjugate the noble classes of his conquered lands. As such, he allowed the exiled Israelites to settle in various towns and villages along key rivers and irrigation channels. They lived peaceably in their new communities, establishing farming enterprises, and many families prospered. The king was clever enough to realize that the Israelite exiles could be valuable to him, aiding in the governing of Babylonia's varied populations. What's more, the Israelites' knowledge of commerce, local customs, languages and laws would come in handy at court. Their practical usefulness to their captor-king, as well as their wealth, kept them alive.

Mordechai's paternal great-grandfather had been a member of the Sanhedrin or Great Assembly back in Judah. This gave Mordechai a literate, multi-lingual, politically sophisticated ancestry. Nearly one century after Darius' conquest of Babylonia, born into Persian exile and named for a Babylonian-Persian warrior-god, Mordechai grew up an only child in a privileged house in Susa under Darius the Great, Xerxes' father.

At age eighteen Mordechai served the requisite two years in the king's military service. Along with noble blood and a desire to serve, his ancestry had bequeathed him an aptitude for swordsmanship, a genius at managing men, and an innate ability to lead. Darius' sergeants and generals quickly recognized Mordechai's abilities in combat as well as in strategizing and moving men and materiel, and they decorated him, and advanced him above his peers. By the end of his time in the king's service, Mordechai had decided that while he possessed the skills to allow him to rise in military ranks, he preferred the planning and the thinking to the battlefield. Over the course of his two years of military service, he had made his reputation and, incidentally, many friends.

He had also crossed swords with and bested a fellow soldier, a man named Haman Memuchan, who, as a result, harbored deep personal resentments against Mordechai. Haman never forgot his humiliations at Mordechai's hand. This early rivalry between the two men would sow the seeds for deadly consequences two decades into the future, when Darius' son, Xerxes, ascended to the throne.

A brilliant and comely young man, Mordechai slipped easily and enthusiastically into court life, and at the age of twenty, fresh out of army service, he was among the minor advisors to Darius. A season of disease claimed his parents and many others, and during his mourning year the community elders thrust upon him the care of a newborn cousin. The disease had also claimed the baby's father, Mordechai's uncle Avichayil, before she was born, and her mother had died giving birth to her. Mordechai was the nearest male relative, and besides giving an orphaned cousin a much-needed home, the elders hoped that caring for her might assuage his own sadness.

But the orphaned baby Hadassah was not young Mordechai's prime interest. He took her in, as was his duty and to the delight of his housekeeper, Poupeh, giving the baby a home and all she required, but she was incidental to his main concern. Mordechai was a serious and ambitious courtier, spending long days at the king's outer court, listening to and participating in the discussions of the diplomats and satraps, making alliances, doing small favors, keeping as close as he could to the goings-on within the halls of power. This maneuvering and *knowing* were as essential to Mordechai as breathing. He became respected among Darius' courtiers as well as those of his son and successor, Xerxes, as a man who could be depended upon, who told the sometimes-painful truth, and who kept their confidences. Politics was Mordechai's first love.

Now, in the third year of Xerxes' reign, a thirty-five-year-old Mordechai found himself spending more and more time in the company of the men who were scions of the men of Jerusalem's Great Assembly. Besides court politics, organizing and running his secret network of men and women was another outlet for his keen mind and his passion for politics and planning, one that Mordechai excelled at. With these "brothers" he could be himself: sophisticated, worldly, yet at the same time connected to his ancestral One-God. They met monthly in the sheltered basement rooms and wine cellars of each others' homes in various locations around Susa and its outskirts. What began with five men — two elderly grandfathers and three younger men — had grown over the decades to a core of fifty. They discussed God, Persian politics, the dangers in the streets and marketplace, women, news from Judah, news of the world wars, prospects for their futures, and their enemies. Mordechai and the Sanhedrin brethren lived assimilated, Persian lives, but secretly kept on alert. They never forgot the fact that they were scattered exiles in a foreign kingdom, at the mercy of a foreign king.

By day these men of the Sanhedrin Brotherhood held positions that enabled them to see and hear all the news. One man, a silk merchant, drank endless cups of sweet *ghahveh*, Persian coffee, at dives near the Tigris, in the company of itinerant travelers and river barge sailors, or with those who had just returned from months sailing the Erythrean Sea. Another was a wine dealer, who spent time inside the palace and who counted among his friends members of the royal guard and the royal Cup Bearer. Still another was a translator of contracts and other legal documents whose associates were members of Persia's learned and legal families. The group even had as a member one property agent who knew every building, grotto and field in and within the surrounds of Susa, and who employed brokers for properties in the more remote regions of the Empire. One member was a scribe, one of hundreds who had been vetted to transcribe events or publicize laws or edicts for the palace and its multiple bureaus into the Empire's many languages and dialects. Another Brotherhood member was an expert equestrian, one of the king's stable of trusted messenger-horsemen. Slowly and judiciously, under Mordechai's careful stewardship, the group of men had become a tight and trusting unit.

With the Babylonian exile one hundred years before, the original Sanhedrin had ceased to function formally. Instead, the surviving and hereditary members as well as vetted recruits went "underground." Their leader and mastermind was a man known to the Brotherhood only by his code name: Raaz.

Old Daniel

When the Babylonians overran Jerusalem in 600 BCE and exiled the Judean nobles, there was among those captured a young man of about fifteen years old by the name of Daniel. He and his three boyhood friends, Hananya, Mishael and Azariya, were tall and handsome, whip-smart, politically astute and vigorously healthy. In short, they were exactly the kind of young men king Nebuchadnezzar of Babylonia wanted among his courtiers. So the king ordered that the boys be trained for a period of three years, during which time they mastered the Babylonian language, literature and customs. The boys were naturals. They absorbed and exceeded everything the king's tutors could teach them, and since they had been nobles in their homeland, they already were familiar with proper behavior at court. The symbolic last step before sending the boys into the king's service was to assign the boys Babylonian names. This signaled that their indoctrination was complete, and the young "Babylonians" joined Nebuchadnezzar's panel of counselors.

Daniel and his friends proved to be a gift to the king's court. They were adept at making alliances and smarter than the other courtiers, and the king elevated them accordingly. But a number of the king's seasoned advisors, and some of the younger aides as well, felt their status and positions were threatened by the Judeans, and they were skeptical of the newcomers. Though outwardly Daniel and his friends were quintessential Babylonian nobles, it was noted and resented among some courtiers that the four Judeans kept to their strange vegetarian diet, their odd customs, and that they did not carouse with the other young nobles in the evenings.

Daniel's tenure outlasted nearly every other courtier, stretching for more than eight decades. He served not only King Nebuchadnezzar and his two Babylonian successors, but also Cyrus and Darius, the Persian kings after them. Babylonian or Persian, in Daniel's mind the form of government remained virtually identical: at the epicenter was an all-powerful king whose word was law, and spinning around him was a constellation of courtiers, advisors, opportunists, sycophants, servants, queens and concubines, guards and soldiers, competitors and assassins. There were, predictably, betrayals and physical trials—ordeal by fire for Daniel's friends and the lions' den for Daniel—but Daniel and his friends had survived them all. Daniel's long-lived influence at the highest levels of power transcended world politics, and with great age he achieved near-invincible and almost mythic status.

Even when he grew too old to advise the Persian king, Daniel remained within the palace, a presence without a portfolio. It was not an unusual sight in Xerxes' palace to see the now-stooped, extremely thin and bald Persian noble dressed in elegant but simple robes, walking slowly through the marble corridors, his hands clasped behind his back. He had no acolytes, and was attended by only one servant, a fearsome giant of a man named Abbas. Abbas, of indeterminate age and nationality, was a mute who had attached himself to Daniel sometime after the episode in the lions' den and who dressed, fed and guarded his master.

It could sometimes be heard said in the palace, "Who is that old fellow?" pointing to the aged Daniel, who walked everywhere soft-footed and with impunity, and who sometimes appeared at the royal banquet table to eat in silence and then disappear. The response was either "Who knows?" or a variant of "Oh, that's Old Daniel, he served the king's father and grandfather. He's a pensioner now. Don't pay him any heed."

And so no one paid any heed to Old Daniel, the wisest man in all of Persia, the silent old man who knew a century of secrets.

Haman the Agagite — Beginnings

One thousand years before the birth of the Achaemenid Empire of Cyrus, Darius and Xerxes, the kingdom of Egypt—the richest and most powerful country in the ancient Near East—had been brought to its knees by the One-God of the Israelites. The overturning of the Egyptians by the God of the Israelite slaves sent shock-waves of awe and fear throughout the people of the known world. Yet mere weeks after the drowning of Egypt's formidable army of chariots in the Reed Sea, as the ragtag and exhausted Israelites walked through the Wilderness of Sin on their way to the holy mountain to worship their God, an army of Amalekites assaulted and massacred the Israelite stragglers.

In the rock-strewn valley of Refidim the Amalekite army violated all codes of war and nomadic life, attacking an unarmed and dehydrated Israelite multitude who posed no threat to anyone. They pounced on the tail-end of the moving sea of ex-slaves, attacking unsuspecting women, children, babes in arms, nursing mothers, the lame and the old. It was an act of cowardice and bloodthirsty barbarism. Only through the courage of a young Israelite warrior named Joshua and the supernatural intervention of the One-God were the Israelites able to rout the marauding Amalekites in a pitched and prolonged battle.

After burying gruesome thousands of their hacked and slain families, and from that day forward, the name "Amalek," whispered or spoken aloud, evoked a visceral hatred among the Israelites. Thenceforth the nation of Amalek occupied a unique spot in the annals of the Israelite people: they were a sworn enemy of the Israelites and their One-God forever.

Four centuries pass, and during that time the outnumbered Israelites suffer years of torment from their hostile Canaanite and Philistine neighbors, punctuated by some miraculous victories. Eventually, during this time, the Israelites choose their first king: a tall and handsome man named Saul, the son of Kish, a Benjaminite. Saul is a modest man and also—critical to the beleaguered Israelites—a fierce warrior. Saul leads the Israelites in conquering their surrounding enemies of Moav, Ammon and Edom; and in a particularly fierce battle they also defeat their old enemy, Amalek. Their One-God had commanded King Saul to destroy the Amalekites utterly—both on the battlefield and in their walled city—leaving no remnant alive to rise and wage war against the Israelites in future years. But King Saul, taking pity, perhaps, on a fellow monarch, spares the life of Agag, the Amalekite king, violating the Divine command. Instead of dying by Saul's sword, the captive King Agag, literally with the blood of Israelite women and children on his hands, is slain instead by Samuel, the fierce Israelite prophet, and Saul forfeits his kingship to another.

Fifteen generations of Israelites and Amalekites come and go, and the mutual enmity between the two peoples persists six hundred years later as real and as fresh as if the battles had been fought yesterday.

Thus it happens that in 483 BCE, in the third year of Xerxes's rule, a descendant of King Agag of Amalek by the name of Haman Memuchan, and a descendant of King Saul of Israel by the name of Mordechai Bilshan, meet in Susa.

Haman the Agagite has a seat among the king's advisors, and Mordechai—whose ancestry has been kept secret for more than a century—is a minor noble in the outer courts of the palace. As yet unknown to the two men, they are on a collision course.

The Magic of Daniel, Hananya, Mishael & Azariya
The Time is 600 to 550 BCE
In Exile in Babylon and Persia

The four exiled young men, raised as young Jewish nobles in a Jerusalem that was no more, sat talking urgently together in a stone room in a holding cell in the outer wall of King Belshazzar's palace fortress. The four, tall for their ages and darkly handsome, are under no illusions. Their world has narrowed to this room, one another and the king's demands. Right then they were under attack for refusing to eat the king's meat and drink the king's wine with the other young nobles who were in training for places in the king's court. They were being held in this windowless room until the king's advisors could convince the king that the boys' brilliance was not of value to the kingdom; that they were more trouble than they were worth; that the king should order them executed for their impertinence. The chances were slim that their lives would be spared.

As it happened, not only did the four Judeans survive the pressures to conform, but they excelled at the examinations pressed upon them by the king's tutors, impressing the king, who placed them in special training to enter the rank of *magi* or royal wise men.

But a new and dire crisis was now upon them. The king has had troubling dreams which he refused to divulge, and which, understandably, none of his *magi* or magicians are able to interpret. In anger and frustration the king has issued an order to destroy all the useless wise men of Babylon, which includes Daniel and his friends. In a stroke of good fortune, with the help of his One-God, Daniel is able to interpret the king's dreams, saving the lives of all the *magi*. The king promotes Daniel to a coveted position in the King's Gate, and Daniel brings along his three friends to serve as royal advisors in the greater province of Babylonia.

As time passes, the three friends — renamed Shadrach, Meshach and Abednego — are separated from Daniel and are tested by jealous court advisors of the new Babylonian king, Nebuchadnezzar. Everyone in the kingdom is required under the king's new law to fall down and worship the giant golden statue that the king has had erected in the plain of Dura. Because it is known that the three courtiers cannot violate their One-God's Second Commandment forbidding idol worship — ensuring that they will refuse to bow to the king's statue — the enemies of the Israelite nobles are sure that they have hit on a plan to eliminate their Judean rivals once and for all.

For the king has decreed that the penalty for failing to bow is death by fire.

Angered by the boys' defiance and valor, while secretly outraged that his own law will be used to deprive him of the company and counsel of men he has come to admire, the king perversely orders the furnace in the belly of the royal fortress to be made seven times as hot as usual, the quicker to be done with the gruesome punishment. The three Judeans are bound and led to the iron-clad stone furnace, whose blast-doors are pulled open with a fourteen-foot-long iron pole-hook. The heat is so intense that as the guards thrust the men into the flames the guards themselves are burned in an instant. Yet miraculously, while the young men's leather bindings are vaporized by the fire, Shadrach, Meshach and Abednego are not killed. Through a small window in the furnace wall they are seen walking about amidst the flames, fully clothed, and some witnesses even swear they see a fourth figure; an insubstantial but other-worldly shadow-man walking among them.

The king was so impressed by the men's miraculous salvation that he had the furnace shut down, and when the men walked out unharmed he not only restored them to their positions as his personal advisors, he also decreed that their One-God could never again be maligned in his kingdom.

What King Nebuchadnezzar was unaware of was that the three men did not emerge from the furnace unscathed. While not a hair on their heads was singed, nor was there even the slightest whiff of fire on their skin or clothing, the experience of hours in the furnace altered the young men forever. All three experienced the agony of the fire for an infinitesimal second, and as a result each man bore its mark.

They had been thrown into the fiery furnace as Babylonians; but when they were touched by the flames, the power of their Hebrew given names—consecrating them to the formidable One-God—had acted either as a conduit or as their shield. In the magical alchemy of the flames and the intercession of their shadow-angel, Shadrach, Meshach and Abednego became transformed into a mixture of the qualities inherent in each of their two names, the first Hebrew, and the second Babylonian. Each name, laden with the power of its respective history, transferred its essential qualities to the young men, so that no longer were they simply *magi* to the king. From that day forward they were secret Yah-Men, or as they were later called: Yeomen; men who were charged with the power and the responsibility to perform great and loyal service to their liege.

Abednego, whose name in Babylonian meant "servant of Ishtar," bore the Hebrew given name Azariya, meaning "God will help." Connected thus to his One-God, Abednego/Azariya emerged from the furnace with great spiritual strength. He was unshakable in his moral principles, and was now newly able to perceive, understand and combat Evil—the other side of moral uprightness—wherever it dwelled.

Meshach's name in Babylonian meant "shadow of the prince," while in Hebrew he was Mishael, or "He that is the strong God." Meshach/Mishael's time in the king's furnace infused him with new and extraordinary physical strength. He was thenceforth always a protector of royalty.

But it was Shadrach who bore the deepest and darkest scar. When the king's guards were leading him down into the stone bowels of the king's fortress Shadrach had been overcome with doubt. His mind veered from the Covenant of Certainty that the three companions had sworn to their One-God and to one another, and he was convinced that perhaps it was not worth suffering the fires of Hell to uphold one small Commandment. His name in Hebrew, Hananya, meant "grace of God," but his Babylonian name meant "servant of sin." Thus, within him was an incendiary mixture of the Godly and the Satanic.

And so, when Shadrach/Hananya was touched by the fire, the stab of agony made room for his doubting self to override his certainty. In that instant he experienced the tortures of Hell. Satan's touch destroyed Shadrach's ability to perceive things clearly. He emerged from the furnace with one eye a deep green, and the other his natural-born brown, an indelible emblem of his fall. While he now possessed the power to perceive Evil and Doubt in others, the great tragedy of the new Shadrach was that his love and comradeship with Daniel, Meshach and Abednego had morphed in that fiery instant into a hatred as deep as their trust had once been. He bore the deep, secret shame on account of his doubt, and he envied the others their certainty. The fiery touch had burned the truth from his soul, and the invincible foursome was no more. Shadrach had gone over to the Other Side.

As for Daniel, over time he had distinguished himself in service to the kings of both Babylon and Persia. It was while in the high service of Darius, Xerxes' father, that envious satraps, who resented being made answerable to Daniel as the king's governor, sought to undermine and do away with him. They came as a committee to Darius and convinced him, in the name of unity of the Persian and Median Empire, to issue a written and unalterable decree that anyone who worshipped any person or god other than Darius within the next thirty days would be considered treasonous. Punishment for treason was death in the lions' den. Predictably, Daniel was found praying in his chambers to the One-God, and Darius, though he had great affection and respect for Daniel, was cornered into enforcing his own edict.

Daniel, no longer a young man, was thrown into the lions' den and the mouth of the cave was sealed with a giant boulder. The king's whispered words sounded in his ear: "May your One-God, whom you serve loyally and unwaveringly, deliver you." Despite this, the king, in full view of the crowd of nobles and satraps, sealed the entrance to the lions' den with his signet ring. Daniel was a dead man. That night, the king was distraught, foregoing all food, entertainment and sleep. He was at the sealed cave entrance at first light, calling out to Daniel, "Daniel, servant of the One-God, has your God rescued you from the lions?"

The king dropped to his knees when he heard Daniel's clear voice answer him from behind the rock, "May the king live forever!" He ordered the boulder rolled away and there Daniel stood, tall and unscathed, the lions purring loudly and curving around his legs in feline figure-eights, licking his hands.

The overjoyed king ordered Daniel's false detractors to be thrown into the lions' den in his stead.

But unbeknownst to the king, Daniel had emerged from the lions' den subtly and strategically changed. The man whose names meant "inspiration of the sun" and "God is my judge" had been spared grisly death, but he was not unscathed. Upon entering the lions' den, in the instant before his God's protection had shielded him, one of the lions had pounced and bitten Daniel on his calf. It was only a nip, but the lion's teeth had felt like a thousand needles. Almost instantaneously the shield of protection had descended, the pain receded and the lions became tame. Strangely, instead of mauling him, the lion's bite had gifted Daniel with some of the creature's powers. Daniel acquired the great cat's super-sensory abilities to see in the dark; to run swiftly; to approach silently; to sense and sniff danger. He also gained the ability to understand the speech of the animals.

There was one additional consequence of this incident. One of King Darius' guards, a giant named Abbas, who had been the one to thrust Daniel into the den and who stood guard at the boulder through the night, was also transformed by the experience. He was so affected by his guilt at sending Daniel to his death that he was struck mute when Daniel walked out of the cave the next morning alive and whole. So Abbas, whose name in Pârsi meant "lion," left the king's service and attached himself to the magical Daniel, serving and protecting his new master with loyalty and awe.

Vashti — Beginnings
In the Palace of King Belshazzar

The palace was burning. The noise was deafening but blessedly still distant from her chambers. The girl Maheen could hear smashings, clashing of weapons, shouts of men, horses neighing, clangs of shod hooves over stone, and, over everything, women's screams. The smoke and smell of burning fabric, wood and flesh hung in a low cloud, even in this far corner of the women's palace in her secluded nursery. The girl cowered on her small bed and watched Razma, her aged handmaid, quickly and methodically pack two traveling sacks. Maheen's eyes were wide with terror. She was king Belshazzar's daughter, child-princess of Babylonia, and on this night she would become an orphan, a fugitive, and a prize.

The impossible had happened; the Persians had invaded Babylonia, and Cyrus the Persian would soon rule supreme over a kingdom that had never known Persian domination. Razma had heard whisperings of the rapine horrors of the Persian invaders, and so she did what she was born to do: she protected her royal charge with her life and planned their escape. The princess' eunuch, a pensioned warrior-guard, had handed Razma a sheathed dagger before running for the horses. "Use this if you must," he whispered to his old friend. "I will be back; listen for me under the window and be ready!" Then he was gone.

Razma finished her packing and dragged the two belted bags onto the balcony that faced a garden courtyard. She wrapped Maheen in a hooded traveling cloak and carried her to the balcony stairs to await the guard. Razma trembled; or was it Maheen? The two of them, child-princess and protector, waited in the smoky darkness watching the flames rising into the night sky above the king's palace in the near distance. Razma's straining ears heard shufflings below. The eunuch had come back for them. He rounded the corner leading two saddled horses, their hooves wrapped to muffle any sound, their heads and muzzles sheathed in burlap to prevent their panicking.

"Come! They are searching for her now!"

In a matter of moments the three were gone, the princess' small form blending into the shape of the travel sacks atop the horses. Young Maheen, tightly held by Razma, had been warned not to make a sound, and the obedient princess kept her eyes shut tight and her own screams inside her head.

The fugitives, led by the eunuch, an old hand at military campaigning, took advantage of the chaos in the palace and capital city of Babylon to evade Cyrus' search parties. In the way of victorious armies since the advent of war, the vanquished or dead king's daughter was universally sought either for display, abuse or ransom, or, if she was a beauty or could be of some use, to be wed to the victorious king as a token of goodwill. The eunuch and the princess's handmaid, prudently assuming the worst, were intent on spiriting the king's daughter to safety. For three days the eunuch drove the horses northwestward, in the general direction of Asur. His thought was to seek asylum with Belshazzar's royal allies in the vicinity of Assyria.

Unfortunately for Maheen, her days of freedom were to be short-lived. Cyrus, an energetic, clever and determined conqueror, hunted the fugitive princess himself, and, by thinking like the old eunuch, Cyrus soon picked up their trail. Things moved quickly after that. Once caught, the princess and her two guardians had drawn the Persian king's admiration; the eunuch and the handmaid had held their weapons in steady hands, and likewise their young charge stood unflinching before Cyrus and his soldiers. When Cyrus pushed the princess's hood onto her shoulders he could see that the terrified but silent girl held the promise of character and some beauty. In a magnanimous gesture he was never to regret, he spared the lives of the princess and her guardians and took the girl into his palace to groom as his future bride.

In this way princess Maheen of Babylonia grew to young womanhood and became Persian bride and queen to Cyrus the Great. Years later her own youngest daughter, Samar, married the king's prized general, and *her* daughter — granddaughter of Queen Maheen, wife of Cyrus the Great — was named Vashti.

Vashti
483 BCE
Year 3 in the Reign of King Xerxes

Queen Vashti was no longer young, but even at 30 years old most would say she was at the height of her physical beauty. Maintaining her figure, her dancing musculature, her hair and her skin took up most of her time. Plus, she had half a kingdom's riches at her disposal, and ostensibly everything she could desire: servants, jewels and clothing. Plus, she was consort to a virile king. What she pined for, however, was what had been denied her: she had no child. Vashti, whose name in Pârsi meant beauty and goodness, had come to her political marriage with reasonable expectations. She would become wife to Xerxes, joining their two peoples, Babylonians and Persians, and in time she would produce an heir to cement that union. She would age with beauty and respect, and would gracefully reign over the House of the Women as queen mother.

But she had not reckoned on Xerxes's appetites. The king, once he discovered that Vashti was a superb and graceful dancer with a matchless figure, took care to spill his seed on the ground whenever he called her to his royal bedchamber. He did not intend for his exquisitely shaped queen to become pregnant and fat, her breasts pendulous. The king used Vashti's body for release only, something he surely could have taken by availing himself of one of his harem, or one of his concubines. But he enjoyed watching his queen dance. It paradoxically relaxed and aroused him. She also was not an unresponsive bed mate, and he intended, for the time being, to keep the status quo. *There is time enough,* he thought, *to sire sons from the Queen.* He could always take another young wife, perhaps this time from the royal family of Egypt, thus achieving two aims: quieting the restive Egyptians, and producing royal heirs. Xerxes was utterly self-absorbed and more than a bit sadistic. He knew that Vashti wished for a child, but he laughed in her face and deliberately ignored her wants.

Vashti had come to Xerxes twelve years earlier with a dowry from her royal mother and grandmother. One of Razma's hastily packed travel bags that long-ago night had contained a queen's ransom, and Razma had added to it, hidden it, and had guarded it fiercely, so that with the passage of decades its value and weight had increased. Vashti's inherited handmaid, Razma's granddaughter, had prudently contrived to keep a fair share of the young Vashti's treasure back from Xerxes's eyes and hands, leaving her with a bride price sufficient to content the king and swell his treasury. Vashti's personal fortune—a treasure box of golden coins, a small case of jewels, her clothing, her royal maids, her personal eunuch and a beloved mare and stallion—were kept close, within the queen's wing of the women's compound. In a kingdom as splendidly rich as Persia, the queen's wealth, quietly held, was subsumed to the king's grand displays. It was easily overlooked and forgotten.

The other prize that Vashti had brought with her to Xerxes' palace was a knowledge and understanding of power. She had learned this from her father, Xerxes's prized general, just as she had learned from him how to ride like a Persian horseman. The general had been charmed by his athletic young daughter who, though not a beauty, was an elegant and natural rider, eager to learn, and even as a girl she moved as one with the horses. The young Vashti had shadowed her father whenever he was not campaigning with the king's troops. Some would say the lessons of power well-learned held more value than gold coins or sparkling jewels. And as the twin to true power was often loyalty, another of Vashti's father's gifts to her was the transferred loyalty of his personal aides.

The day was coming when Vashti's fortune would save her life.

Vashti came to crave time away from the House of the Women. The concubines snickered about her and some even turned their backs on her in silent derision. It was an open secret that Vashti yearned for a child, but that Xerxes had other uses for her. This devalued Vashti in the eyes of the other women. Added to this, after her father's recent death Vashti found herself missing his strong presence at her back; she found herself without a defender. She was utterly alone except for her longtime handmaids and her eunuch bodyguard. She felt as if she were suffocating, living out her days in a hostile cage. If only she had had a child to love, she would have been content. But as things stood, Vashti, queen of Persia, was guarded at every moment of every day. It may have been a "soft" guard, to be sure, but the House of the Women had decorated iron latices on its windows.

Vashti discovered her sole moments of freedom lay while riding her beloved horses, especially now that she was missing her father so. At sunup every day Vashti—accompanied by her eunuch guard—walked to the small stables within the women's compound. Her hour of riding on the rocky sand or through the royal orchards was her respite. Even then she was not quite alone, as Vafa, her trusted royal groom, accompanied her, riding a short distance away, respecting her station and her privacy.

But the Persians were great believers in Fate, and Fate set a foot into Vashti's world in the person of a stable groom.

One dawn Vashti arrived at the stables as usual, her palace guard by her side. As usual, her horse, Anoush, as well as the groom's horse, were saddled and ready, But her familiar groom was nowhere to be seen. Instead, both steeds' reins were held by a tall young man who appeared both uncomfortable and proud.

"Who is this?" Vashti asked her guard. "Where is Vafa?"

The eunuch guard, keeping his weapon hand free, approached the young man and interrogated him while Vashti watched. She was fascinated that the young man did not flinch at the inquisition nor did he appear servile or humble in her presence. His dark eyes swept over her from her black braided hair to her sand-colored split tunic, her small, belted waist, her riding pantaloons, to her soft, sueded riding boots. Vashti stood for his scrutiny. She was not a virgin to blush and look away. She was queen of Persia, she was a grown woman, and she was fascinated by this handsome, arrogant groom.

In turn, Vashti looked her fill, as well. The man held himself like a young prince. Starting at the top, as he had done, and all within a matter of no more than a few seconds' time, she took it all in: his blue-black hair; his broad and muscled shoulders not quite concealed by his loose, tan canvas blouse; the leather belt that rode low on his lean hips; the tan riding trousers encasing defined horseman's muscles, tucked into soiled and worn calf-high boots. And he stood, his proud head of-a-height with her horse's forelock notwithstanding her prize steed's measure was a legendary nearly eighteen hands. The new groom radiated youthful male vigor.

His name was Jamshid, and he was Old Vafa's 21-year-old nephew. Vafa was hoping the young man — who could ride anything on four legs — would slip into his spot as the Queen's groom when it soon came time for Vafa to bow to his age and content himself with tending vegetables in his wife's kitchen garden. Vafa had held Vashti's hand as she had ridden her first pony. He was proprietary about who would assume his duties. So his nephew was taking over two days per week as a trial.

Once the queen's guard had vetted him, Jamshid stood aside and in silent invitation held his tanned hand palm-up at the horse's stirrup, the gesture of courtesy belying the fierce look in his eyes. Vashti walked toward her horse, placed her hand on the saddle pummel, her booted toes in Jamshid's callused palm, and she vaulted gracefully up. After mounting his own horse, Jamshid respectfully held his steed a horse's length behind the queen's.

Vashti's eunuch guard signaled the groom to be off, first issuing his laconic warning: "Watch her!" Then the eunuch settled onto the bench at the shaded entrance to the royal stable block. It was time for his morning nap.

Looking back, what happened between the queen and the young groom was inevitable. At its most basic, it was a situation where a striking-looking older woman of a high social class was powerfully attracted to a strong, silent, younger man of lowly station. But of course this was no ordinary older woman; Vashti was queen of Persia. Perhaps Vashti deserved her few moments of freedom and ecstasy in Jamshid's arms. Perhaps they could have gotten away with cuckolding the king in his own palace. But two consequences followed, one predictable and the other a surprise: Vashti fell pregnant, and Jamshid fell in love with the queen.

The King's Banquets
483 BCE
Year 3 in the Reign of King Xerxes

Xerxes, settled now in Susa after years of prohibitively expensive military campaigns, finds himself king of the largest single empire in history. He is ruler over 127 provinces or minor kingdoms spread out over 7.5 million square kilometers and three continents. These numbers and distances are staggering, and from a practical standpoint, ungovernable. Most of his subjects are not native Persians; some of them might not even realize that they are part of the Persian Empire; and most speak languages the king cannot understand. The most pressing issue facing the king is that the royal treasury is dangerously low in funds. Apart from the financial worries, lurking in the back of Xerxes' mind is the terror that haunts all kings: the very real threat of coup and assassination, a haunting fear that walks in lock-step with xenophobia.

So Xerxes chooses to address the problem he can solve: he will put on a show with the aim of unifying his varied subjects behind a munificent monarch. He will speak a "language" every nation in the Empire can understand: he will dispense free food and drink on a grand and royal scale, and he will do so in a prolonged way, displaying an excess of royal splendor the likes of which none of the people of the civilized world have ever seen, nor will again.

His first banquet was one that the king intended would be spoken about in every corner of the known world. It lasted six months, and was aimed solely at the nobles of the 127 kingdoms he now ruled. The party was held in Susa, the capital that Xerxes had recently refurbished and augmented. His fortress had several banquet halls so grand that a servant at one end of the hall could neither see nor hear his counterpart at the other end. There were meeting rooms boasting arching ceilings, and inlaid floors of whitest alabaster, intricate marble mosaic inserts of gold, sapphire, emerald and ebony. Xerxes flaunted his wealth and the health of his monarchy in an unprecedented display of generosity that tipped over into profligacy. He opened the royal kitchens and wine spigot, providing Persia's nobles with free travel, lodging, feasting and drinking for a period of six months. The nobles were served their meals on silver platters, they dipped their fingers in scented water in individual mother-of-pearl bowls, and they drank wine from golden goblets poured from glass pitchers. The king's intent was to garner for himself hundreds of new high-

powered friends and good-will emissaries. He was bent on
turning skeptical and doubtless hostile, annexed peoples into, at
the least, submissive, or at best, supportive citizens. His gateway
to the people themselves was their noblemen: the princes, satraps,
and under-governors. He hoped to so impress the nobles that
upon their return to their provinces they would spread word of
their enthusiasm for their new, generous king, and would thereby
quell any discontented murmurs.

All because at his essence Xerxes was an insecure king. And as
coming events would show, his insecurity was not unfounded.

The first extended banquet was for the princes and nobles of
the entire Empire, including members at court, the king's cabinet
of advisers, and the legal officials in Susa. Also invited were the
king's army officers, and high-born free men of Persia and
Medea — known by the term *kara* — men who had been granted
tracts of land by the king.

The banquet was for males only. While there was no cultural
prohibition against women at Persian banquets, to suit their
purposes Persian kings often restricted their feasts to men only.
This made sense if the king's aim was primarily political and if his
Persian courtiers had their instructions to carry out: each shared
meal and refilled wine goblet was an opportunity to impress,
befriend and influence the newly conquered princes. The Persians
were noted for their love of wine, and their king was renowned
for his love of women. So the stag nature of the months-long
banquet was a deliberate move. There was great anticipation
among the princes, army officers, satraps and governors that the
king would not send them home to their wives without their
having enjoyed unparalleled food and wine and exotic female
entertainment, and their hopes did not go unfulfilled.

Once every week throughout the six-months of the banquet,
on a day chosen by the king, Persian dancers specially chosen
from the royal House of the Women were summoned. Wreathed
in diaphanous veils, the girls' sensuous and hypnotic hour-long
dance, performed barefoot with cymbals on their fingers and toes,

to the accompaniment of flute, lyre and drums, was an unqualified thrill for the drunken men.

It was the king's appetites and caprice that dictated the terms of the banquet and entertainment, and its very existence, nature and duration. The implication was that just as the king could and did order that all in attendance drink his fill, the king also could terminate his generosity or the entertainment on a whim. The extremes of the king's absolute and unpredictable power on the one hand, and his extravagant generosity on the other hand, were ever on display.

An After-Party for the Common Folk

After six months away from their homes and treated to excesses of those substances that even the nobles typically ingested with an eye to the purse and prudence, the king's visitors were replete with food, drink, and feelings of privilege. As their party wound down and they prepared reluctantly to leave Susa and return to their homes, the king announced yet another party: a seven-day after-party; this one open to all the *common* people in the capital city of Susa. The citizens of Susa had lived through six months of crowded revelry from which they had been excluded. When the drunken princes, officers, satraps and governors departed, the king would be left with his capital city in a shambles, its natives pressed into service to set it to rights. So the king hit upon a masterstroke. He ordered his palace gates to be opened wide; he invited *all* the citizens of Susa into the lushly planted courtyard gardens—the private outdoor oasis they had only ever heard about—where he had ordered long banquet tables set up. The king set about appeasing and rewarding the citizens of Susa with a weeklong, lavish taste of royalty.

There was no sand, or even dust, in the king's *bitan*, his colonnaded outdoor banquet garden. The very air seemed to be colored a young green; the scent a mix of floral and spice. Under the swaying branches of acacia and willow standing at intervals stretching for a quarter kilometer in four directions, and flanking a central reflecting pool, were oblong tables covered in purple damask. The tables groaned beneath silver chargers of sliced meats, hot and cold; pewter serving bowls laid with glossy eggplants and peppers, pickled or stuffed with cheese and currants; crystal pedestals overhung with the sweetest of plums, peaches, kumquats and grapes, sugared and candied. Ethiopian youths in red cylindrical caps, wearing broad-sleeved white tunics and saffron-colored trousers stood at attention day and night ready to serve, remove and refill. And of course the wine carafes were bottomless.

If Xerxes intended to win over the common people of Susa, then with this public weeklong reception — during which virtually the entire population of the capital city filed through the palace's courtyard gates to eat and drink and gawk its fill — it would seem he surely had succeeded.

Hatching a Plot

Unnoticed by the revelers, standing by the pillars and under the balustrades, were two advisors to the king — recognized faces who passed to and fro with ease — who watched with veiled distaste as the street hawkers, cloth merchants, fruit sellers and butchers, their wives and unruly children — up to ten thousand per day — swarmed through the garden courtyard of the king's palace. These men frowned on the king's show of strength and magnanimity, thinking it a waste of the royal treasury. But they realized his move was immensely popular. The two men were on the lookout for chinks in Xerxes' armor; their broad plan was to catalogue the king's security weaknesses and personal vul-nerabilities, report them to their *ban*, or secret commander, and await instructions.

Biktan, an average-looking man in court dress, caught the eye of Teresh, his fellow *saris* across the courtyard. Biktan tapped the corner of his eye and signaled, *Watch and wait*. Both men chafed at the inaction, but their *ban* — the man of shadows who was only a disembodied voice to them — paid handsomely for accurate information. The men had been in place in the King's Gate for two years now, and just lately their persistence had begun to pay off. Last month they had passed their *ban* a copy of the king's closely guarded daily schedule and guard rota, one day in advance. He had slipped them a pouch of coins as payment, and hinted that they were soon to be chosen for an important assignment.

So at the king's courtyard banquet Biktan and Teresh melted into the background and counted and memorized the king's bodyguards, their proximity and their weaponry.

The Tent of Xerxes was pitched over half the outdoor garden pavilion. It was constructed of silken draperies in royal blue and purple, hung on pillars of silver and gold fifteen feet high, and fastened with tasseled cords of linen. During the six-month-long party the elite of Persian society had rotated through the king's enormous indoor table and each person had feasted on at least one meal in the king's presence. In contrast, at this seven-day party there was no hierarchy or order to the guests; the king's table was always set and ready, and every citizen of Susa could and did vie to sit at least for a few minutes in the presence of their king. Even if the king was only glimpsed at the elevated dais a quarter-kilometer away.

There had been entertainments along with the food and royal display: roving jugglers and clowns; trained dogs dancing on their hind legs and dressed as couples; and tiny, hatted and nimble-fingered monkeys hopping from their royal handlers' shoulders onto the laps of delighted diners, grabbing a bite of food off their plates and eating it to the sound of the guests' laughter. There were minstrels singing love songs and plucking wordless tunes on their lyres, and roving flutists wandering among the crowded diners.

Mordechai and his Friends at the King's Banquet

Among the thousands of people attending the king's seven-day party were Mordechai and three of his friends from the Sanhedrin Brotherhood. As residents of Susa they all were officially invited; but Mordechai had special entrée to the festivities given his status as a minor courtier. So in addition to sitting together and enjoying the fruits and stuffed vegetables at the laden table, Mordechai had taken his friends on a tour around the perimeters of the garden. They walked through the tall stone colonnades, stood next to flowering vines as high as a man, glimpsed the off-limits chambers guarded by giant eunuchs, and strolled the outer walkways of inlaid marble mosaic. They were impressed.

"So, Mordechai, do you get to eat like this all the time?" joked Shimon.

While the men all had Persian names they used every day, amongst themselves they were known by their given names, the names they had grown up with inside their homes. But Mordechai had instilled in them a deep caution. None of them spoke the Hebrew language of their fathers except in whispers in windowless rooms amongst themselves, and then just for prayers and to keep up some facility. They spoke their native Pârsi in their everyday interactions, but conversed with each other in Dari, a Pârsi dialect. The dialect sounded very like Pârsi and used the same Persian alphabet, so when speaking it they aroused no suspicion. But Dari was unknown in cosmopolitan Susa; it was a mountain language spoken primarily by the tribal people of the Indus. Because Mordechai and his friends did not wish to risk being overheard, it was in Dari that they spoke now.

Like Mordechai, his friends dressed to reflect their station, and they fit in among their peers wearing linen tunics belted over silk trousers, with their hair curled and secured by small turbans or by bands around their foreheads, soft leather sandals strapped onto their feet. They looked like what they were: noble men of Susa aged in their mid-thirties; urbane, articulate and privileged. Mordechai, in his obsession for secrecy and privacy, had taught them well: *Remember always to blend in. Don't draw attention to yourselves. Speak softly; all walls have ears.*

Mordechai smiled, answering his friend. "Believe it or not, I eat better than this at my own table. Since most of the food here is forbidden to us as Jews, when I sit at the king's table with the other courtiers I take only from the fruits and vegetables and nuts, and try not to draw attention to what I eat and don't eat. I keep the focus on our conversations about politics or court matters."

"Or women," interrupted Shimon with an elbow jab at his friend.

"Often," Mordechai agreed. Then, more seriously, "I have kept the secret of my people and kindred, like my father did before me, and this practice has served me — and all of us — well. Our fellow Persians do business with us and befriend us because we grew up side by side with them and we *are* Persian. Adding our Jewish ancestry to the mix would confuse them and only spark centuries-old prejudices. You know the old saw: *How can you be a loyal and good Persian if you are also a Jew?* As if my Jewish ancestry makes me any less a loyal, native Persian than the next fellow who was born and raised here as I was. No, my friends, it is far better to keep our origins secret. As Persians we are accepted at court and are treated equally among the other nobles. There is no point in raising old specters of suspicion and hatred among our Persian countrymen. To all intents and purposes we are just like them."

"I wonder how long you can keep the secret, though, Mordechai, with Hadassah growing more beautiful and eligible by the day," injected Shimon. "She is how old now? Fifteen? If she hasn't already, soon she will be asking you to allow her to be out and about, at least to shop in the bazaar, and people will take notice, Mordechai. And then you will have a line of fathers of suitors knocking at your door. If you intend to keep her from a Persian suitor you must betroth her to another — to one of our own — and do it quickly."

"Speaking of which, has she chosen a Persian name yet?" asked Eliezer.

"No, not yet," Mordechai said, frowning in thought. "I had hoped to keep her at home for a few more months. But I think you are right, my friends. The time is coming, and very soon now, when Hadassah will leave my home and set up a life with another. I have, indeed, seen members of the Brotherhood looking at her when she serves us. Come to think of it, you are not innocent of this yourself, Shimon!"

"I would have to be blind not to appreciate Hadassah. We are single men, you and I, Mordechai, and I would have spoken up sooner, but I was afraid to poach in your territory. She is your uncle's daughter, and would be permitted to you. Do *you* think of her in that way?"

Only as close a friend as Shimon could have asked this question, and he deserved a candid answer. Mordechai had ignored his blooming romantic feelings for his ward for the past three years, since she had reached young womanhood. His feelings had blindsided him. He was an unemotional fellow whose *raison d'être*, he always thought, was his work. So he had concentrated on treating Hadassah in a neutral and brotherly fashion, and never, ever, had he given the girl any reason to suspect that he thought of her as a potential wife. As worldly as he was, underneath it all Mordechai was only a man with his heart in his throat for a girl who spoke to him as a ward to a guardian. Hadassah treated him as a niece would treat an uncle; with affection devoid of romance. So Mordechai hesitated.

"We are as close as brothers, Shimon, and giving Hadassah to you would have made me very happy, and, as well, would make us cousins. But because of this I will say to you what I have not admitted even to myself: I *do* feel about Hadassah as a man feels about a woman. And now that I have said this I am sick with dread. What do I do with my feelings? What if she doesn't feel that way about me?"

Shimon put his muscled arm around Mordechai's shoulders in the way good friends do. "Mordechai, we all of us knew this would happen even if you did not. My advice to you is to speak to Hadassah soon; let her hear how you feel, and get her thinking about this. Women are a breed apart, my friend, and Hadassah is more private than most, having no mother or sister to confide in. Who knows but that she is just waiting for you to make your move? In fact, why not speak to her tonight, while your courage is up?"

"I might do just that," Mordechai answered thoughtfully. The four friends sat and continued to talk of other things on this last day of the king's second party.

But Fate or Providence had other plans for Mordechai and Hadassah.

A Desperate Queen Vashti

By the evening of the last day of the king's weeklong party the anticipation among the revelers had reached its apex; surely the king would summon his royal dancers tonight.

The king's strong, bearded face was florid with drink. He surveyed the crowded scene through half-closed lids as he leaned back on a maroon-colored damask cushion. He was well satisfied that his show of excess and generosity had achieved its aim. From the murmurs and bows, the smiles and tributes, he was clearly popular not only with his nobles but also with the people of Susa. He gauged it the right time to spring his surprise to end the event.

Xerxes raised his finger, summoning Mehuman, his chief chamberlain, from his seat nearby. Mehuman bowed his head so he could hear the king's words.

"Go to Queen Vashti's chambers. She is entertaining the wives at a party of her own, but enough of that. Now is the time for her to be by my side. You are my spokesman, Mehuman. Bring her this message from her king: Tell the queen that I require her to appear before me now, tonight. She is to come alone, without a retinue, adorned only in her dancing veils and her dancing slippers. Tell her she must wear her jeweled crown and to let her hair flow free. She will dance before the company and will display her beauty to all. She will give them a treat they will remember every night in their dreams. Her dance will be a gift from their king. Wait for her, Mehuman. Take the other *sarisim* with you as escorts. Go now and bring Queen Vashti back with you."

So Mehuman tapped the shoulders of his cohorts, all trusted chamberlains to King Xerxes — Bizta, Harvona, Biktan, Abagta, Zetar and Carcas — and they accompanied him through the scented twilight, over the marble walkways to the women's compound. They had escorted the queen at the king's behest on other nights and to other parties, where she had performed the graceful and powerful Persian veil dance, her lush and forbidden beauty on display for only the one dance, after which she disappeared back into her royal quarters. The seven chamberlains were themselves looking forward to this night's performance, as the queen had not danced for the king since the great banquets had begun six months before.

A slightly drunk Mehuman rapped on the locked outer door at the southwest corner of the queen's gate.

"Let us in, Fatima, you old dragon! We have a message for your queen!"

Old Fatima, the guardian of the queen's chambers, stood in the doorway and blocked Mehuman's way with her draped bulk.

"You will tell me your message and I will relay it to the queen."

Mehuman smirked as he told her. Fatima longed to smack his face. "Wait here," she said.

She turned to the enormous guard, standing behind her with a spear as tall as he was. "Yousef, watch them. I will go to Her Majesty."

Fatima walked quickly to the queen's high-ceilinged dining and entertainment chamber, where the queen was hosting the nobles' wives at her own party. The women were reclining or sitting, smiling and laughing, displaying their bracelets and finery and telling each other lies about their husbands' prowess. Soft notes of lute music played in the background. At their center, on a slightly raised dais, was seated Queen Vashti, watching it all, regal but silent and unsmiling. Her handmaid, Razma's granddaughter, stood, as always, at her right hand. The women had heard the knocking and most of them appreciated that this signaled a summons. The room quieted.

Old Fatima, who had detected Vashti's intimate secret but had told no one that she knew except for the queen, now approached her mistress and bowed low, but did not speak.

Vashti had gone still at the loud knocking. A strong woman, these past few months she had been terrified, expecting and dreading a summons from the king to dance for him and his drunken guests. With the passage of time and the absence of a summons, Vashti had allowed herself to hope that she might be spared the necessity of a confrontation with Xerxes. But, a general's daughter at her core, she had heeded the words of her informant in the king's service that tonight would be the night, and she had prudently used the time to ready herself for the break. The sturdy belted travel bags — the same ones Razma's grandmother had packed two lifetimes ago while Babylon burned — were hidden and ready. One bag held her treasure and her mother's jewels; the other held her clothing and tiny embroidered swaddling clothes. Two months ago she had sent her trusted messenger to Aram, and she now possessed a royal warrant from the Assyrian king-in-exile guaranteeing her protection. Her handmaid had this afternoon prepared food parcels and skins of water. The stable was on alert and her lover, the groom Jamshid, was impatient to leave.

Now that the moment of her defiance was at hand, Vashti fought for calm. *Treat it just like another performance*, she thought.

Standing by, Old Fatima — Razma's granddaughter — noticed the protective placement of the queen's hand over her silken belly, which showed the subtle but unmistakable shape of a woman with child. Fortunately, because of the queen's superb muscle conditioning and loosely draped clothing, neither her courtiers nor the women at her table had any inkling. But the handmaid detected the subtle tremble of the queen's hand. As Vashti's confidant, she had tended her mistress through the emotional and physical rigors of these past three months. A loyal and trusted servant, she knew that Vashti's lovely spine was steel, and that if, as predicted, the king would demand tonight that she dance clad only in veils and crown, Vashti could not go. Thus, the handmaid was already putting her mistress' escape plan into play.

"Speak, dear Old Fatima," commanded Vashti.

"Your Majesty, please forgive the intrusion. Mehuman and the *sarisim* are waiting in the vestibule. They have been sent by King Xerxes to summon you to dance the veil dance clad in your jeweled crown with your hair flowing to your waist. They are standing by to escort you there now."

Vashti sat immobile, saying nothing, but thinking: *Xerxes does not bid me to come, as is proper. Instead, as is his wont, he demands that I appear, and he sends his flunkies to escort me, like a prisoner or like a parcel. It is just as well; I am nothing to him. These will be my last words to him, through his messengers.*

Vashti's face paled, and Fatima wondered if her mistress would faint.

"Your Majesty," Fatima prompted, "what shall I tell them?"

Vashti stood up, her black hair a shining curtain held in place by her hammered gold tiara.

"I will speak to them myself, Fatima." Vashti stepped off the dais and walked out of the salon. When she stood in the vestibule facing Mehuman and the *sarisim*, she looked at each man in turn. They stood by expectantly, assuming they would be escorting her back to the king's party. They were in for a shock.

In a clear voice Vashti said, "Mehuman, you may tell His Majesty King Xerxes that Queen Vashti refuses to dance for the king's drunken friends."

Mehuman sobered instantly. In all his years serving Xerxes he had never heard anyone refuse a royal summons. He also feared having to repeat the queen's words to Xerxes' face, as the king's hair-trigger temper was legendary. Mehuman knew the consequences to the queen would be dire. Who knew what an angry king would do to the messenger?

"But Your Majesty..." he began.

"You may go now. Return to the party and repeat to the king exactly what I have told you."

The seven speechless *sarisim* bowed out of the queen's palace and walked slowly back the way they had come. There was no trace of their drunken camaraderie now. Six of the *sarisim* were

intensely thankful that it fell to Mehuman to tell the king that
Vashti had refused to dance. They truly feared the king's reaction.

And they were right. Mehuman and the *sarisim* hesitated at
the arched entry to the palace garden nearest the king's dais.
Mehuman had thought to whisper Queen Vashti's refusal in the
king's ear, but the king had spotted his men and was too far gone
with drink to be circumspect. Mehuman braced himself.

"Ah, Mehuman!" Xerxes called out. "You have done as I told
you?" The king looked around at the assembled crowd in the
manner of a monarch about to bestow a surprise gift on his
subjects. "Well, is the Queen making herself ready? Is she come?"

Mehuman approached the king's table and hesitated. "Yes,
sire, I mean no, sire. I did relay your command to the queen
herself. But you see, Your Majesty, the queen is not coming." The
area around the king and the *sarisim* had quieted. Mehuman
pressed on, anxious to finish breaking the bad news. "The queen
bade me to tell you these words: 'Tell His Majesty King Xerxes
that Queen Vashti refuses to dance for the king's drunken
friends.'"

Mehuman's words fell into the silence, and only a communal
intake of breath was audible. Xerxes' face was immobile for a
fleeting moment, and then it turned as deep a red as his seat
cushion. He stood up, raised his muscled right arm above his
head, and struck his scythe-scepter onto the banquet table,
splintering the tabletop, smashing crystal, and scattering food,
wine and crockery onto his guests. The assembled multitude was
motionless with shock and terror. The music had stopped and
even the chittering animals ran for cover and were silent. The
king's rages were storied. The visitors in the palace garden as well
as the king's advisors were at once fearful and fascinated. What
would Xerxes do?

Xerxes clenched and unclenched his left fist. He was
unaccustomed to feeling helpless and humiliated. In fact he took
pains to assure that everyone in his royal coterie was agreeable in
the extreme. He had been prepared tonight to revel in the
peoples' gratitude; to watch their slavish appreciation of his
queen's beauty. And now, in an instant, and at the whim of a
mere woman, he was as nothing in their eyes. All his posturing
and generosity would be for naught now. A king who could not

even command his queen and be obeyed was nothing but a laughingstock. He was overcome with a desire to throttle and strangle Vashti, and would have done so on the spot if she had had the temerity to refuse him to his face.

Instead Xerxes lashed out at Mehuman. Breathing hard, the king turned to face his advisor and without a word he backhanded him with his muscled left hand. Mehuman staggered and fell to one knee, blood pouring from his split cheek, the bone protruding. The king stood over him and leaned down and hit Mehuman again on the downstroke before he could get up. Mehuman was down on all fours trying to see through the blood and the pain, the shame of being the brunt of the king's anger. The other six advisors backed away. They were all strong and armed with small weapons, but none would have sacrificed himself for Mehuman. When the king lost control there was no telling where he would stop.

Through a red haze Xerxes looked down at the heaving courtier and the pool of blood at his feet. He turned away and stared down the ruined table. He felt nothing for the bloodied messenger; the man got what he deserved. He should have dragged the queen here if need be. Let everyone stare and shake with fear. He was king of all Persia! He would not be humiliated by a woman. He would deal with her later, he thought. If he was to salvage his reputation he must assert his power *now*, and seize the initiative quickly and decisively. And he must do so publicly. So Xerxes turned to face his cabinet ministers, ranged down the table to his left.

"Carshena!" he thundered. "You are the wisest minister-of-the-law in my kingdom. Tell me — tell *all* of us! According to the law, what shall be done to Queen Vashti for refusing to obey a reasonable royal command by her king, as conveyed to her by my *sarisim*?" The king seated himself, awaiting Carshena's response.

Carshena was the most respected among the first-rank of the king's seven cabinet ministers. He and the king were of an age, and he had been the king's First Cabinet Minister for the past three years. In truth, he considered himself the brains of the monarchy. The king was a fearless warrior, but had a weakness for drink and for women, and was a hothead in all things political and domestic. This was not the first time the king had reacted in anger, expecting his First Minister to think of a way out. And Carshena was thinking fast. He knew every one of the king's thousands of laws that governed every aspect of Persian life. Indeed, it was Carshena who had written most of them. Some of these laws were predictable and necessary for keeping control over a wide-ranging empire. But others were capricious and oppressive, and were altered or added to daily depending on the king's fancy. For instance, there was the law that everyone was required to drink himself into a delirium at the king's banquet. And its partner law that enabled the king's soldiers to enforce this drinking-law at sword's point!

From the corner of his eye Carshena saw two servants helping Mehuman stagger from the banquet, and others who were bent low, silently mopping up the blood. Carshena swallowed, sweat dotting his upper lip and brow. He was in the hot seat. Finding the queen obviously and instantly guilty of insubordination, and then sentencing her, was the easy part. But that would solve only half the problem. It would still leave the king in the position of having been publicly humiliated—in effect emasculated—by his queen; an untenable situation. Carshena needed a bold and outrageous diversion to save the king's face. How to publicly assert the king's control over Vashti in a way that deflected or mitigated her insult to him? Carshena searched his mind for the solution, while the king glared at him.

It was Memuchan, the youngest and lowest in rank of the seven cabinet ministers, who piped up before Carshena could formulate a solution. He stood and faced the angry king.

"Your Majesty, if I may suggest a way." The king frowned— Xerxes could not remember the minister's name—but hearing no objection, Memuchan rushed on. All eyes were on him.

"Queen Vashti's refusal to obey the king's summons is an offense not only against Your Majesty the king; it also is an offense against *every* man in every corner of the Empire, whether of high or low station." The king was listening to him now. Everyone in earshot paid close attention. Warming to his idea, Memuchan continued.

"It is an offense against the Empire itself, because the queen is the symbol of ideal womanhood in Persia. By her insubordinate behavior this day, the queen has given license to *all* wives in every province of Persia and Media to follow her example to disobey — nay, to despise — their husbands. Word will travel speedily, and the situation will become unbearable."

Memuchan stopped for breath and watched the king's face to gauge his reaction so far. The king was still listening, so Memuchan prepared to continue. He had in mind the beginnings of a plan he was sure would appeal to the proud and insecure king. Memuchan's boldness surprised himself; he had not planned to take to the oratorical spotlight just yet, especially when the king's anger was so potent it could bubble over and scald anyone who was in the way. But Memuchan was impatient. He had sat silently for three years in the last chair of the king's advisors. He had listened to endless pandering by the more senior men to the king's wishes, and never once had he heard anyone utter an original idea. He, Memuchan, had plenty of them!

"Your Majesty, the first order of business is to punish Vashti swiftly. I respectfully suggest you issue a royal edict this very day — tonight! — which will become the irrevocable law of the land in every corner of the Empire. Your edict will banish Vashti forever from the king's presence. It will make it a punishable infraction even to speak her name. She will be a living ghost, confined to her quarters for the rest of her life, never to set foot outside her own gate. She will of course be forbidden to any other man. She will be humiliated every day of her life. This is a fitting punishment for a queen who flouted her husband's summons.

"Further, every wife in every province of the Empire will be required to treat her husband with respect. This will extend to each and every aspect of domestic life, even to the point of addressing her husband like a king in his own home, in his native tongue. It will be the law.

"And finally, Your Majesty's edict will announce that you will give Vashti's crown and position to another, more deserving young woman. Your Majesty will choose someone more compliant, more to his liking."

Memuchan had been energized during his speech. Now, in the silence following his monologue, unsure of its reception, he resumed his seat. Everyone awaited the king's reaction. Only Carshena knew for certain that the king would agree; he had no choice. Carshena also knew that his own days were numbered. He had been bested by the lowliest cabinet minister.

Xerxes sat up straighter now, his eyes still flashing, but not in anger this time; his impotent rage had turned to triumph. The king enjoyed a good fight, and this young minister had just handed him the perfect solution to the Vashti debacle: he would disclaim and divorce Vashti, and turn his personal humiliation into a national rallying cry! *All* the men in the kingdom, high-born or low, would henceforth wield unquestioned power in their houses. It was simple and brilliant.

"It is an excellent plan!" the king announced. "What say you, ministers? Do you agree?" At their quick verbal assent the king hammered the table with his scepter. "You, er," — the king's advisor on his right leaned over and whispered the young minister's name to the king — "Memuchan! You will draft the edict and will supervise its speedy release. The royal scribes will write the parchments and will translate the edict it into every language of the realm. Let the Royal Guards go at once to Vashti's palace and restrain her there. So be it!"

The relieved king raised his scepter and added magnanimously, "Now, let us all enjoy this last night of the king's banquet! Minstrels, play! You are all commanded to stay and eat and drink your fill before you return to your homes."

But the party was over. In a subdued but triumphant flourish the king had retained his dignity, and anyone who thought him a fool kept the thought to himself.

Unnoticed by anyone, a black-skinned servant boy in his uniform red cap and saffron trousers bent low and quickly made his way out of the palace garden. He skirted the kitchen tents and melted into the purple night. When he was out of range of the lighted torches he broke into a run and soundlessly and nimbly climbed the high wall surrounding the queen's compound. On the grass outside the queen's chambers he whistled a pre-arranged bird call. Razma's granddaughter came to the openwork window covered by an iron grille.

"Speak!" she said.

"They are coming for her now!" And the boy disappeared into the night, back to the party.

Inside the queen's chambers, all was in readiness. Unconsciously mimicking both grandmothers' escapes a half-century before, Vashti and her handmaid were caped and dressed in split tunics and trousers, and soft leather boots for speed and travel by horseback. Vashti's old eunuch hefted the belted travel bags. "Come!" he hissed. They let themselves out through the camouflaged secret door in the queen's bathing chamber, closing it behind them. Soundlessly they filed quickly behind the palace walls, skirting the gardens, where they surprised a peacock, ending up behind the stable block. Four horses were saddled, packed and ready, and Jamshid, looking like a warrior, held their reins. He clasped Vashti to him for an instant with his free arm, then boosted her onto Anoush, her familiar steed. "Have you got the king's letter of passage?" he asked. Vashti nodded and patted her underarm, where she carried a secret oilskin pouch. The old eunuch and the handmaiden, in surprisingly agile moves, also mounted their waiting horses, quickly securing the travel bags to the saddle pommels.

Only minutes had passed since the servant boy had whistled his warning. Jamshid took point and the four rode like the wind, heading by a pre-arranged route, northwest, toward Aram.

When the Royal Guards pounded on the queen's door, the house maid answered their knock. They pushed past her and their captain demanded, "Where is the queen?!"

"Why, she is asleep in her chambers. The women's party ended an hour ago. All is quiet now."

"Has anyone entered or left in the last half-hour?" he asked.

The maid, who knew nothing of Vashti's escape, answered candidly. "No one."

The guards, though brutish and arrogant, had not been given leave to harm anyone in the queen's house, especially not the queen herself. They were loath to roust the queen for no reason. After all, she was under house arrest and their job was to guard the doors and prevent anyone entering or leaving. Any questioning or re-ordering of the queen's household could wait until morning. They looked to their captain, who hesitated.

The housemaid, always eager to keep the peace with the king's officers, said, "Would the guards care for some refreshment? The kitchen staff are drinking tea and having some date cakes before we douse the torches. Join us."

The captain's decision to drink tea in the kitchen with the pretty housemaid rather than personally check on the queen's presence sealed his fate and bought time for Vashti.

When it was discovered the next day that the queen had escaped during the night, the guards mounted a search, but they were no match for the combined skill of Jamshid, who rode like a god; the wily old campaigner; and the general's daughter. Vashti and her treasure had simply vanished into the mountains of Mesopotamia. Eventually, she and Jamshid were wed, she had her baby—a boy who grew up to have spirit and grit—and they lived out their lives in anonymity and comfort in a distant, foreign kingdom.

And Vashti's name was never again spoken in Persia.

Mordechai and his sober friends watched the royal drama from their table off to the side of the royal dais. They were aghast, as was most of the multitude. But it was only Mordechai who grasped the gravity of what they had witnessed. He had just watched the precipitate end to the queen's reign. More than that, for the first time ever Mordechai had seen the king in action with his royal mask off. Circumstances had allowed Mordechai, a student of power and politics, to view, close-up, the behavior of a dangerous monarch. What Mordechai saw was an all-powerful man who, in a fit of pique, overlooked years of pleasure with his queen and instead took overt delight in causing her speedy destruction. All this was in punishment for a single infraction that he himself had provoked. One moment the queen was his cherished object to be displayed and admired; the next moment she was relegated to the damned. No thought had been given to alternative methods of dealing with her. She was instantly expendable.

Mordechai saw this as a lesson in how the king of Persia and Medea worked. A person who crossed this king would be given no second chance. The king took pains to appear benevolent, in-control and generous-spirited, but in reality he was insecure and coldly calculating, utterly absorbed by his own present interests: his power, his appetites, his longevity. In reality the king was that most dangerous of monarchs who demanded absolute obedience and fealty, admitting to no moral or circumstantial mitigation. Xerxes was a pitiless tyrant masquerading as a benevolent king.

This revelation had the potential to be world-changing, and a political creature like Mordechai already was thinking of the ramifications for himself and for his people. Little did he know how close to home and how tragically these rippling conse-quences would strike.

Old Daniel

Old Daniel, standing against a pillar, was watching, too. He had seen and heard the king's request, Vashti's refusal, the king's enraged reaction, and Memuchan's inspired plan. There was now an open spot in Persia for a queen, and from long experience Daniel knew that a hole in the totem of power would cry out to be filled. The key was to stay ahead of the other hungry players and have a hand in the filling of it. He moved away from the courtyard garden and whispered to Abbas, who nodded once and backed away.

Mordechai never did get to speak to Hadassah of his love that night of the queen's escape. Within hours of leaving the party — hours ahead of even the king's knowing — two informants — one from within the king's palace and another from the queen's house — had sent Mordechai coded messages telling of Vashti's disappearance.

Mordechai spent part of that night secreted in a hidden cellar room in a safe house not far from the palace in Susa as the crow flies; a house that was as different from the luxury of the palace as the surface of the moon. A hide tanner who was a member of the Sanhedrin Brotherhood owned a secluded stone shed set in a field at a distance from his residence. No one other than his two tanners ever approached the shed, and then only during the daytime. The toxic smell of the tanning acids was a natural repellent. It was in a room beneath the shed floor, accessed by a trap door and stone stairs, and lit with squat, smokeless candles, that Mordechai met with his Control.

The person Mordechai faced across the stone table was hooded and shadowed. He was known as the Raaz, Persian for Master of Secrets. His voice was a deep, scratchy hush that projected from the recesses of the hood. He had been Mordechai's mentor and intelligence master for fifteen years, instructing Mordechai in the painstaking arcana of setting up a network of trusted informants. Under his tutelage Mordechai had brought the Sanhedrin Brotherhood from defunct to vitally active, instituting a sophisticated and speedy intelligence web. More important even than his guidance in the mechanics of setting up a spycraft network was his unerring analysis of the politics of the Persian king and court.

It was the political opportunity that Vashti's disappearance had created this night that was the subject of their meeting. The Master was speaking, and Mordechai was listening. He knew the Master sometimes spoke in a monologue as if to himself, but all the while he would be educating Mordechai in the ways of statecraft and human behavior; in past sessions he had dissected each person on the king's cabinet and those in more lowly positions in the court, in the King's Gate, and in the House of the Women.

But tonight the Master had an urgent agenda. He began speaking without prelude.

"When the king discovers that Vashti has slipped through his guard his anger will be rekindled, and he will relive his public humiliation at her refusal to dance. Her disappearance will only add fuel to his wrath. But knowing Xerxes, he will threaten with slow death anyone who even whispers that the queen has escaped. Their instincts for self-preservation will keep the servants' and guards' mouths sealed shut. As far as the Persian people are concerned, they will be none the wiser, and will adhere to Memuchan's new edict. Vashti's name will never again be spoken in Persia.

"We then come to the problem of whom the king will turn to when he is ready to select a new queen. Xerxes will be in no rush. He has bedmates a-plenty and I predict it will take several years before he decides he misses a queen and seeks a replacement. But that will not stop the strivers and courtiers from jockeying and plotting. Each will be seeking to advance his own replacement.

"Because make no mistake, Mordechai: this is a rich opportunity for a skilled and clever Master to place an agent intimately close to highest level of power in the Empire. The person who can place and then control Xerxes' new queen will be in a position to rule the entire Persian Empire. The odds are long, but it would be a boon above any other if by some twist of fate and opportunity *we* could be the ones to control the new Queen of Persia."

Mordechai was as still as a statue. What his secret Master had just proposed was fantastic. Would such a thing even be possible?

"Master, what you suggest is impossible. Surely Xerxes will choose his new queen from among the daughters of familiar or rival royalty; from Egypt or even Greece. How could a courtier, much less we, in the Brotherhood, influence the choice of the next queen? We have no power in those distant realms. And even assuming we are somehow able to do this, how would we control her once she was installed as queen? She will have surrounded herself with her own trusted maids, guards and spies."

The hooded Master coughed or laughed; Mordechai could not tell which.

"Mordechai, have you learned nothing in all these years? It is the situations that seem most uncontrollable that most often contain within them a window of possibility. And I will tell you, Mordechai, that I have had a vision."

Mordechai must have raised an eyebrow or exhibited some small hint of surprise or curiosity. The hooded Master continued.

"Did I not foretell Vashti's disappearance months back? Did I not position my spies inside her palace for just this very day — to know of her movements before the king did? There is more to "knowing," Mordechai, than what you can actually see and hear. "Knowing" involves a practiced intuition and a quality of listening that is deeper than sound, more eternal than the present. I will need to pass this ability "to know" on to you, Mordechai, before much more time passes."

When Mordechai demurred, the hooded Master continued.

"I am very old. You are young and strong and you have the makings; but you aren't quite ready yet. You have steady nerves, a formidable memory, a keen ability to assess others, and a linguistic genius. And the men trust you. All these are essential qualities of a spymaster. But there is more. There is another ingredient that you have yet to acquire: you must listen to the wind."

With Mordechai's attention focused intently on his hooded face, the Master continued with a calm urgency.

"Hear me, my young friend. *I* have listened to the wind. The Evil is coming to Persia, and from opposing vectors. It will come from the familiar, and it will come from the unknown. For this reason our tools to combat it and to keep our people and our heritage alive must be honed *and expanded*. You have human tools already in training whom you can raise to an alert; and another human tool will be put into your hands very soon. We will step up our meetings, you and I. I will teach you to read the bird calls and to sense the ripples of the wind. You will hear and see *and know*, in present time, more than you thought possible. There is not much time, not much time."

The Secret Master pushed himself up from the cellar table. Mordechai thought he was done, but over his shoulder, as he mounted the stone steps, the Master added, "You must use this window of time, before the king decides to choose another queen, to ready the Brotherhood. They are your advance guard. And look to your own house, Mordechai."

With those cryptic words the Master pushed open the trap door and let himself out into the night. As soon as Mordechai had shifted the marking stone on the shelf so the tanner would know they had been and gone, the candles snuffed out simultaneously. Mordechai sighed. He was nearly accustomed to the touches of magic the Master employed to signify his power and his presence.

When Mordechai climbed the stairs the Master was nowhere to be seen. Faithful Abbas had been sitting on a rock at the edge of the field, watching. As if by magic the two men, Master and servant, had simply disappeared. Mordechai never got used to the abrupt appearance and disappearance of the Master.

This night, however, he spent no time wondering at the man's powers. He worried at his warning. In Mordechai's world danger was always present, though held at-bay by the work of men like the Brotherhood. If the Master was worried, Mordechai thought, it behooved him to warn the men and to make plans.

Could the Master position a woman of his choosing to fill the empty slot as Xerxes' queen? And what did the Master mean by his words "look to your own house?"

As he made his way back into Susa proper and along the streets to his house, his thoughts turned to Hadassah. She would be asleep when he returned. He sighed, thinking he would speak to her another day. Sleep for him was far off; his work was just beginning. He let himself into the quiet house and sat down to write his letters in disappearing ink made from his recipe of lemon juice and goat's milk.

From the shadows, and undetected by the usually vigilant Mordechai, a soft-footed man had followed at a distance on the deserted streets. How much had he seen and heard?

Hadassah

Still awake as the night moved into its second quarter, Hadassah's ears stretch, listening. From her sleeping chamber she hears Mordechai let himself into the sleeping house. From experience she knows his routine: he will sit and write or think in his small salon, perhaps for an hour, before making his way to his sleeping quarters.

Hadassah is troubled. She had loved her guardian forever, but also had been *in love* with him for as long as she could remember. She had secretly gifted Mordechai with the purest of romantic love fueled, initially, by her gratitude. She knew his every mood and expression, and understood his thoughts sometimes before he uttered them. Mordechai represented everything desirable and strong in her eyes.

But now, as a young woman, Hadassah is beset with doubts about her ability to change her status from ward to wife. Lately she has sensed Mordechai's withdrawal when they encounter one another about the large house or when they eat at table just the two of them, with Poupeh cooking and serving. Gone is the ease and friendliness they had shared as she grew up. She fears that Mordechai is about to betroth her to one of his Brotherhood. Esther was anxiously aware that Mordechai's friends, though scrupulously polite, looked at her differently now that she had become a woman. While most of the men had been familiar to her for years, and some of them were nice enough, she could not bear the thought of leaving her home and the man who had watched over her for the whole of her life. She fretted. What would Mordechai do?

The time had come for Mordechai to assign Hadassah a Persian name, as very soon now she would be permitted to go out alone, with a servant beside her, into the bazaar to shop for the household. She must become accustomed to her Persian name just as she was utterly Persian in all other ways, except, of course, in her inner heart. She was Persian, yes, but she was also a Jewess. Her great, great grandparents had been exiled from Jerusalem with Israelite King Yehoyakim and the other Israelite nobles, and they had settled first in Babylonia, and then, decades later under Persian kings Cyrus and Darius, her people had become Persians. In all ways her people were loyal to their tolerant Persian kings and at-one with their Persian neighbors. Over the past century her Jewish neighbors had married into Persian families, served in Persian army garrisons, and were treated as Persians in all business dealings, even serving as witnesses to contracts and licenses. Persian Jews testified in court on both sides of the legal issues, and their causes were adjudicated by judges blind to their race.

But notwithstanding the leniency of Persian laws and society, Hadassah knew that when the time came she would be promised in marriage to a Persian Jew because that was the tradition that had been handed down in an unbroken chain in the family of Kish of the Benjaminite line. Mordechai had drilled her in the catechism: *You must at all times conduct yourself as the native Persian you are, but never forget your people and your One-God.* She fervently hoped that he would propose *himself* as the man to wed her. She remained guardedly optimistic because as yet Mordechai had not taken a wife. Hadassah allowed herself to hope.

Hadassah already had privately settled on her Persian name; she secretly thought of herself as "Esther," meaning "star" in Pârsi. A star was distant but bright, keeping to its designated place in the heavens and glowing when all else was in darkness. She thought it a perfect fit; she was content not to draw attention to herself, but to shine in her own tiny sphere. The name Esther was also a version of the name of the Persian goddess Ishtar, embodying love and war, referring to the brightly glowing planet Venus in the night sky. Hadassah knew herself to be a quiet but effective fighter. Had she not fought for her very life from the moments of her first infant cry, and thrived—despite the absence of both father and mother? And her final reason for choosing the name Esther was that, in her penchant for languages, she delighted that in Hebrew, the secret language of her ancestors, her new name meant "hidden." Hadassah smiled at that; hadn't she kept her love hidden for most of her life? Wasn't everything she thought and felt hidden within her and unknown to anyone else? Yes, the Persian name Esther suited her perfectly. She only had to tell this to Mordechai. Perhaps she would broach the subject of her choice of Persian name tomorrow.

As it happened, Hadassah was unable to corner Mordechai about her name change or anything else. It took months for the turmoil in the palace to cool down after Vashti's banishment. Mordechai threw himself into days spent listening to his fellow courtiers jockeying for a place for their chosen queen-to-be, analyzing rumors and events, and he spent nights with his Master or with the Brotherhood.

One evening, Hadassah was preparing the evening meal, as Old Poupeh had been ailing all that day. Hadassah, concerned for her beloved housekeeper and friend, had put the woman to bed, a jug of cool, crushed lemon water at her bedside. Hadassah's mind was focused not on the pastry she was stuffing with meat and currants, nor on the two colorful plates she had set on the table, ready for herself and Mordechai. She was worried about Poupeh, about Mordechai, and about her own future. What was to become of her? Lately she had eaten her evening meal alone or in the company of Old Poupeh, keeping Mordechai's plate warm in the wall hearth beneath a brazier, against his late arrival. He did not appear even to notice her existence these days, so busy was he; gone at sunup and back when all were asleep. If she didn't know better she would have thought he was deliberately avoiding her.

As she mused, the door opened suddenly. Mordechai stood in the doorway and stared at Hadassah. She had been on his mind at that very moment and to see her standing in the kitchen room, so very beautiful, when he had not set eyes on her in days, was momentarily startling. Mordechai's heart was in his throat and he stared.

Hadassah's hair, tied back with a string as she cooked, was coming loose in tendrils around her unadorned face. She was wearing a long, tan homespun shift tied with a brown cord. Her arms were bare and dusted with pastry flour, her feet were in flat household slippers. She stood very still. Mordechai filled the doorway, his face in shadow, the setting sun limning his broad shoulders.

"Mordechai," she whispered.

He found his voice. "Why are you preparing dinner? Where is Poupeh?"

Will we speak of trivialities, and never of what is on our minds? she thought.

"She is overcome by the heat, and is not feeling well. I put her to bed. Preparing an evening meal for two is no effort at all." Then, in a spark of spirit she added, "Why, Mordechai? Would you have stayed away yet another night if you knew we would be eating the dinner meal alone?"

Mordechai calmly closed the half-door and leaned against the wall cupboard. "Are you unhappy about something, Hadassah? Please say what is on your mind."

Well, she thought, it appeared that this was to be the time and place for her to state her piece. In the kitchen, with flour on her nose and a fragrant soup on the grate. She wiped her hands on her cloth apron and stood straighter. She took a step toward Mordechai and spoke urgently about what was in her heart.

"Unhappy? Yes, Mordechai, I am unhappy. Why have you distanced yourself from me these past months? In years past we could talk about anything. You used to unburden your day to me, invite me to express my thoughts. I exulted in this. But lately you are a stranger. You have left me alone, but a mistress in your house, no longer a friend and confidant. Take a good look at me, Mordechai. I am no longer a child; I am a grown woman. You have taught me much. I speak several languages, I can calculate numbers in my head, I can cook and pluck and sing and weave. But I have no one with whom to share my dreams. I have no friends except for Poupeh, the daily maid, and the gardener. My world is within these four walls and my society consists of the men of the Brotherhood whom I have known since childhood. It is time for me to take my place in Persian society, time soon for me to be betrothed, time for me make a home and to have children. Are you planning all this without consulting me?"

Hadassah, watching Mordechai's inscrutable face, stood at the table side and waited for Mordechai to answer her outburst. Would he be angry? Would he remain silent, ignore her words and plea and go on as before?

Mordechai had watched her closely as she spoke, his mind in a turmoil, though his face showed no emotion. He came towards her and took her hand in his. *So small, but so competent. So beloved. How to tell her that she meant everything to him?* It seemed the time was now and the place was here, in this warm and redolent kitchen of the house in which he was born, that he must tell Hadassah of his love. He had planned it differently; in an arbor of the fragrant Temple Tree, heavy with blooms.

Hadassah couldn't move. All her nerve endings were concentrated in the hand that Mordechai held in his. Her eyes were fixed on Mordechai's thoughtful face, willing it to give up his secrets.

"Hadassah, I have borne responsibility for your welfare since your birth, and from the moment Poupeh carried you into my house in swaddling clothes you have brought me only happiness. I have been distant these past weeks because I am keenly aware that you are a woman, and I am sick with grief that you might soon leave my house to belong to another. Right now there is nothing in the world that I want more than to take you as a wife for myself. Do you think you could look at me, Hadassah, and see a lover and husband instead of a guardian?"

Hadassah gently tugged her hand from Mordechai's grasp and sat down at the table. Her relief was so great that she feared her legs would give way. She clasped her hands in her lap and looked up at the man she loved.

"I can look at you and see a lover and husband because this is how I have imagined you for years. To be your wife and to stay here in this beloved house and raise our children. This has been my dream."

And thus it was that Mordechai and Hadassah plighted their troths to each other in the kitchen of the house where they had lived their lives. Hadassah took the Persian name of Esther and their small community rejoiced at their betrothal. They agreed to wait until her eighteenth birthday to wed.

Year Seven in Xerxes' Reign — Virgin Roundup!

Xerxes is missing Vashti. Three years have passed since her disgrace, and though no one in his kingdom ever speaks her name, the king thinks of her every night. In the strange ways of longing and memory, he recalls and magnifies all of Vashti's grace and physical desirability, while the echo of his anger and humiliation at her insubordination fade and recede. He has consoled himself by making his way through the women of his harem, but none of the dancers has Vashti's grace, and none of the girls understands his wants and needs in bed.

Xerxes is pining. He remembers Vashti's beauty, her majesty; he remembers how she loved him in the early days of their marriage, he regrets that he sent her away, and he awakens sad and pensive every morning. Xerxes wants a queen. *Why did Vashti defy me?* he thinks. *If only she hadn't refused to dance that night everything would still be wonderful. It was all her fault for defying me, but still, if she were here I would figure out a way to take her back, law or no law.*

The king's servants attending him in his private chambers are concerned at the king's depression. The king in a miserable state boded no good. They whisper with the royal advisors about the king's black moods, wondering what is to be done; it is known in the king's court that the situation in the private wing of the palace is unstable. The advisors worry that in his present nostalgic and needy state the king might launch an all-out search for Vashti and try to bring her back. And of course to them, contravening the king's own edict banishing Vashti was anathema.

It is the crafty Memuchan, now known simply as Haman, who hits upon a plan to distract the king.

But Haman is wary of advancing his plan outright; he is sensitive to the fact that, as Memuchan, it had been *his* plan three years ago that had encouraged the king to punish the queen in the first place; something the king apparently is now regretting. So instead, Haman plants the idea in the ears of the king's personal advisors and allows *them* to float it past the king.

The plan is as far from a royal match-making scheme as it could be. Rather than advising that the king invite all eligible princesses from the exclusive ranks of the seven noble families of all Persia to visit Susa and "audition" for Xerxes, they propose just the opposite. Counter-intuitively, the servants suggest that the king's search should reach out to *all* the eligible virgins in the Empire, *regardless of pedigree*. In fact, royalty is pointedly *not* a prerequisite. The girls need only be beautiful, young, and untried.

One of the king's personal attendants, long-accustomed to speaking to the king in his bed chamber, his bath, or any time the king is not actively engaged in affairs of state, advances the unusual plan one afternoon when the king is holding court. He speaks on behalf of all the king's attendants.

"With Your Majesty's permission, we propose a plan. Let Your Majesty appoint special officers in every province of the Empire to find and gather all the beautiful young virgins from even the farthest corners of Persia and Media." Seeing he has captured the king's attention, the attendant continues.

"Command these officers to transport all these girls to your royal fortress here in Susa, to be held exclusively in the Royal Harem. Let Your Majesty further command Hegai, the Guardian of the Virgins, to supervise and manage these girls. They will be provided with cosmetics and beauty enhancements to their hearts' desire. And after Your Majesty has had an opportunity to compare and consider all the women, he will choose from among them the maiden who best pleases him. *She* will be your queen instead of Vashti!"

Xerxes is paying close attention as his young adviser lays out the broad idea of a "competition" or "beauty contest" for selecting his new queen. The king is smiling by the time the attendant gets to the part about his choosing as queen the maiden who best pleases him. This sounds exactly like what he has been missing; the opportunity to try out every beautiful young virgin in his Empire! And the girl need not be—in fact it is preferable that she *not* be—royal. He has had personal experience with a beautiful but independent-minded royal queen, and that did not end well for him. No, this time he wanted a girl who not only was untried, but also whose primary aim in life was to please him.

The king approved the plan.

The Plan to Find a New Queen

Stage-one of the plan to find a new queen of Persia is put into action almost immediately. Just as Memuchan's plan to punish Vashti had targeted "all" the husbands and "all" the wives in the Empire, so, too, this plan to find a replacement for Vashti targets "all" the beautiful virgins in the vast Persian Empire. No wonder the king approved the scheme; it pandered to his twin desires for access to virtually unlimited sexual adventures, and for complete control over the girls and the sexual encounters! A virgin in his bed was by definition unable to compare her experience with the king to that with any other man, so the king would at all times be unchallenged and primary in his bedroom. Too, the kingdom's virgins will have no opportunity to politely decline being taken to the king's harem and thence to his bed. The plan described a *mandatory* roundup of the kingdom's beautiful virgins.

The royal scribes were set to work immediately in their guarded palace room, translating the king's edict and which explained that the roundup of the kingdom's virgins would begin in five days' time. The royal messengers were readied, the royal messenger steeds brushed and watered. No one but the king's closest advisors — and the scribes, of course — knew the contents of the edict, but the royal messengers were not really curious; the king issued edicts almost weekly.

The captain of the Home Guard was one of those who, of necessity, knew what was brewing, and he set about calculating men and arms, horses and transport. He worked with maps to divide the kingdom and allocate men and materiel. He had a very few days to plan a kingdom-wide dragnet.

Haman, who, as Memuchan, had suggested the idea of an Empire-wide competition-of-the-virgins to Xerxes' advisors, was feeling smug. He couldn't help but feel superior; another of his ideas had won the day with the king. Of course, he had had to suggest it from behind the scenes, but he was confident that his star was on the rise. Important people were taking note of him; it was only a matter of time before the king would, too. Also, he had a plan of his own that he was ready to put into play. Didn't he have a virgin daughter of the perfect age to be selected queen? Didn't everyone say that his Zareen was a beauty? Already several prominent fathers had approached him, trying to push their sons forward as suitors and proper husbands. He had been holding them off, playing one against the other, holding out for the highest bride-price. But now Haman set his sights on a bigger prize. He was aiming for the throne. With his influence at court and his spies in the palace and in the House of the Women, who better than himself to promote Zareen above the other girls? And once Zareen was queen there was less need to prop up Xerxes. Anything could happen.

There was more than one path to power, he thought to himself.

Mordechai's House

Late that same afternoon there was insistent knocking on the kitchen door. Poupeh muttered and opened the top half of the tradesman's gate to see the butcher's lad standing there holding a parcel wrapped in burlap.

"But I have not ordered anything from your master, Hami. What is this?"

"Take it, mistress. My master says to be sure to clean the insides very well before dressing and roasting it." The boy Hami said shyly.

Poupeh understood. "Ah, foolish old me. I did place an order. Lucky for me your master has a good memory. Be sure to say Poupeh thanks him." She took the parcel and gave the boy a coin. Hami smiled shyly and took the coin, then backed away from the door and was gone.

Poupeh shut and fastened the top door of the kitchen, then spread the butcher parcel out on the table. She unwrapped the burlap and then peeled away the fresh leaves that covered the bird. But she was not interested in how many meals she could make from it. Her strong hands felt around the bird and under its feathers. Then her hand disappeared to the wrist as she gently probed the end cavity. She felt something inside. With her sharpest meat knife Poupeh slit the bird from gizzard to tip, and spread its skin. There, wrapped in oiled cloth was a small folded scroll. She carefully wiped it off, cleaned her hands and made her way to Mordechai's salon, where he sat with scrolls and a quill and ink, thinking and writing.

"Master Mordechai, a message has come for you, brought by the butcher's boy. It was hidden in the bird."

Mordechai stopped what he was writing, thanked his faithful housekeeper, and took the wrapped scroll. After she left the room, silently closing the door behind her, Mordechai unrolled the scroll carefully, and spread it out in a patch of sunlight shed by the high louvered window. He began to read.

One Thousand Years Earlier — About 1300 BCE

Sarah was moving along slowly. Her feet were dusty, she was bone-weary, the sun was baking her shoulders and arms, but she was content. At eighteen years of age she had lived her entire life under the brutal lash of the Egyptians, but she alone — of her grandparents and parents, two sisters and an older brother — had survived to see the downfall of the tyrant Pharaoh and the liberation of her people from four centuries of bondage. She wondered about that. Why had *she* been gifted with life and freedom above all the other members of her family? Surely her elders were more deserving, since they had labored and suffered longest. But there was no time for philosophical reflection. In the haste to leave Egypt—they were given only hours' notice to pick up and leave, to prepare to simply walk out into the vast desert— Sarah had buried her thoughts and focused on packing some foodstuffs, a skin of water, and some clothing.

They had been walking for two weeks, and she reveled in the simple act of breathing in and out as a free person. She was a girl whose tomorrow was a happy mystery. She had only to waken and to walk; her days and years in the limestone quarry as a tunnel-runner because of her slight frame were over. Now, the quicker members of the Israelite tribes were far ahead of her and the other stragglers from her home tribe of Benjamin. Sarah had appointed herself as helper to an old man named Yochanan, whose leg had been maimed by a vicious slicing of an Egyptian taskmaster's blade as he had labored thigh-deep in the lime pits. As a result, one leg was shorter than the other, and so he walked with a stick. In front of her creaked a makeshift cart pulled by a boy of thirteen, and in which rode his heavily pregnant young mother. Sarah could hear babies crying and happy conversations, all a cacophonous jumble of what she now knew was the sound of free people. She could see lizards sitting motionless under rocks, and here and there tufts of yellow desert flowers beside a low, twisted bush. She registered and catalogued sounds and smells, sensations and emotions she had never felt before. Here, towards the end of the crowded multitude that had sprawled down the main highway of the city of Ramses, out of the city they had built, and away from the people that had beaten them, walked the women with their nurslings; the young children; and the slow-moving old and lame. There was no one to rush them.

Sarah breathed in the daylight, the dust and the freedom.

She felt the ground tremble before she saw or heard the attack. Through her thin sandals she felt a shaking that grew in sound and strength. Her first thought was that it was an earthquake; she had heard stories of such things, as quarry workers were terrified of them. And after having seen with her own eyes the plagues of the One-God and the splitting of the Reed Sea, she had an appreciation for great natural and supernatural doings. But no, this was different. With one hand on Yochanan's arm she turned her head and, looking behind her, saw and heard an oncoming wall of chariots and armed men. There were flashing swords, a cloud of arrows, and wild, shouted war cries. Her mouth opened in a soundless scream. At the moment they were upon her, she closed her eyes as a descending battle axe half as long as a tent-pole flashed overhead. Before she could think, Sarah fell to the ground, pulling the old man out of the way, rolling over and over like a lopsided human spiral, down into a shallow ravine. She never let go of the old man's arm, shielding his body while pressing them both down into the dirt.

Sarah stayed in her crevice without moving for hours, her head down. She memorized the sounds and smells. This time, though, they were a living nightmare of war cries, horses' hooves, shouting men, agonized screams of women and babies, and the smells of blood and sweat and dirt. She was trembling with fear but she dared not move her head or arm or try to speak to Yochanan, though she would have liked to give him some room, and to see if he was injured.

Much later, Sarah sat by a makeshift fire, her clothing in stained and filthy tatters, half her body coated with dried blood. She sat without moving, seeing again and again the aftermath of the attack seared onto her eyeballs. She had eventually rolled off the old man when the attack had moved on. "Yochanan, are you all right?" she had asked, gently turning him over. But Yochanan's dead eyes had stared back at her. The arm she had gripped in an attempt to save him was the only one he had left; his other arm had been severed at the shoulder by the battle axe. He had not cried out, not made any sound. He had bled and died, and all the time that Sarah had covered him in the shallow ditch she had shielded a lifeless corpse.

The scene had been a carnage. The pregnant mother from the wagon ahead of her had lain on the ground, hacked to pieces; her thirteen-year-old son lay headless nearby. And on an on, a sea of blood and agony.

She later learned it had been the Amalekites, and not the Egyptians as some had feared, who had ambushed the Israelites as they lumbered their way through the Wilderness of Sin on their way to their Holy Mountain to pray to their God. Amalek had attacked at the rear of the spread-out column of people, targeting the stragglers; massacring tens of thousands of women, the very young and the very old. The Israelites had not thought to fortify themselves; in fact, though over 600,000 strong, they were at their essence a horde of ex-slaves and immigrants, and they lacked any real weaponry. The young and the strong Israelite men had walked at the heads of the tribal ranks and moved at the front of the multitude to keep the pace and to keep order. It was their women and children, their blind grandfathers and crippled grandmothers, the slow-moving and vulnerable stragglers whom Amalek had attacked.

When she walked into the Promised Land forty years later Sarah had wept for joy. But she had also wept for the mothers and grandmothers, the fathers and sons, and for old Yochanan, who never made it to Sinai, and who would never see a land flowing with milk and honey. Sarah died in her bed an old woman, but she relived that day of the Amalek attack every night in her dreams.

Everyone who has ever personally experienced trauma — it could be the extreme deprivations of war or famine, prolonged child abuse, or the death of a loved one in front of his eyes — knows that he or she is never really free of it. It is not so much the power of memory, though memory is a tremendous force. It is more the power of the trauma's being so fresh and immediate that it *is re-lived* by the victim or witness every day of his life. In her nightmares, the young rape victim suffers through that long-ago violation every night, even almost a century later, when she is into her 90's. Similarly, the man who was starved nearly to death during a famine early in his life may, even in times of plenty and for decades to come, fill his plate to overflowing every evening at dinner, ever preparing against that famine. This is because in his mind *he is sure* that the famine will be arriving tomorrow, and on all the tomorrows that follow. The boy who saw his parents and sister hacked to death by enemy soldiers will evermore witness those killings in his mind's eye — as fresh as if they had fallen to the ground in front of him a moment before—until the day of his death as an old man years later.

Such is the nature of the lasting memory of extreme trauma. Though ended, the trauma is never truly past. It is fresh and painful and occurring in the present tense.

Sarah relived the attack by Amalek every day of her life. She married a man who had survived it; she retold it to her children, and to their children, and so on until the day of her death. So, too, the thousands of other Israelites who had survived the attack and had suffered through the Amalek trauma as Sarah had, also relived and retold their stories. There were thousands of stories and tens of thousands of painful memories. Centuries later, great, great grandchildren told the story of the ambush by Amalek as if it had happened *to them*. Their inherited memory of the massacre was fresh and personal.

Thus, it was one of Sarah's descendants—Mordechai, son of Yair, son of Shimei, descended from the family of Kish of the tribe of Benjamin—who "remembered" the trauma of Amalek.

And Haman Memuchan, an advisor to king Xerxes in the palace at Susa, was a descendant of Agag, king of Amalek, and he also remembered.

Mordechai's House

A message hidden inside a bird came from only one source: from Mordechai's spy within the palace, a royal scribe and secret member of the Sanhedrin Brotherhood, who relied in turn on a resourceful kitchen maid to speed a message to the butcher for delivery. The kitchen maid had eight children and was very grateful for the small pouch of coins she found inside her cloak pocket whenever she secreted and passed on any message from the scribe. She had no inkling what the message said, and would have been unable to decipher it had she been curious about its message; she was not curious.

Mordechai read the message, handwritten in the Aramaic of his forefathers: "Of highest urgency. Plan is in place to kidnap virgin girls throughout Persia for king's selection of a Queen. No time to lose!"

Mordechai moved quickly. He went next door to his neighbor's stable and told the stable boy to spread the pre-arranged code for an immediate meeting in the event of an imminent threat. "Tell them Mordechai says 'Serah!'"

The code word "Serah" signaled that the Brotherhood were summoned to convene that night at ten o'clock beneath the tannery floor. The boy leapt onto a mare and was off. The practice drills Mordechai had insisted upon had prepared everyone to move automatically and with dispatch. They would all be there tonight.

Abednego was also at work. He had known of the plan to round up the virgins virtually at the same moment the king's personal servants had suggested it. True to his name, his mission was to protect one maiden in particular: the very beautiful Hadassah. His old friend Daniel had foreseen that the young and beautiful Hadassah would be of critical strategic importance to the Jews in Persia and had charged Abednego with shadowing her. Now, with the imminent edict announcing a roundup of beautiful virgins, it would seem that Daniel's prophecy might be coming true in the immediate present.

"Don't let her know you're watching, Azariya," Daniel instructed Abednego. He called his old friend by his given name, the name they grew up with as children in Jerusalem and that they used with each other in private. "Watch over her and keep her from harm. She is just out of girlhood and she has no inkling of the power that her beauty and sweet nature can wield. Her time is almost nigh, and she is absolutely vital to us. Remember your Persian name! You are the 'guardian of Ishtar.'"

So Abednego stationed himself outside Mordechai's house to watch over Hadassah, whose Persian namesake was Ishtar, goddess of love and war.

As a wizened beggar Abednego drew no one's eye.

Meeting of the Sanhedrin Brotherhood

The cellar room was full. Twelve members of the Brotherhood who lived in Susa and the nearby towns who were able to come on short notice crowded onto the benches around the stone table. The smokeless candles lined the surrounding stone ledge, so there was light as well as privacy.

"Mordechai," Shimon spoke first, with the ease of a close friend. "What has happened that required using the urgent 'Serah' code? You've got us good and worried."

The "Serah" code was named for the apocryphal granddaughter of the Patriarch Jacob, a woman who was said to have lived for hundreds of years. Serah had survived centuries of brutal slavery in Egypt, she heralded Moses as the Redeemer of the Israelites, she entered the Promised Land, and legend even had it that she may never have died at all! During times of crisis, even just recalling Serah's name brought hope to the beleaguered Israelites, signifying that the One-God's promises would be fulfilled, and that miracles could happen.

The Sanhedrin Brotherhood had long ago agreed to use the single "Serah" code-word to signal a crisis and as a call to meet in summit that same night, at a pre-arranged time and place. The word was just a meaningless sound to anyone other than those in the Brotherhood.

Mordechai surveyed the men around the table. Though he didn't see eye to eye with some of them, he trusted them all. There were Shimon and Eliezer, his good-natured brothers in all-but-blood: Shimon, whose father was a skilled tailor, known as a magician with cloth; and Eliezer, who was a third-generation wine-maker. These two were content to remain in Persia for the rest of their lives, but they worried about their enemies and about maintaining the status quo. They were always looking over their shoulders, never having gotten over the humiliation of the ancestral communal exiles of more than a century before. After all, what had happened then could happen again!

There was Gidon, a silk merchant like his father and grandfather, who heard all the news of wars and royal marriages from traders who berthed along the Tigris and Euphrates Rivers. Gidon's family shipped their goods overland in time-worn routes; they were familiar figures on the quai, and they were trusted utterly as reliable businessmen who were honest, who listened well but who said very little. There was Natan, the anxious wine dealer who was on a first-name-basis with the king's cup-bearer and who didn't want to rock the boat. And there was Levi, who translated all legal contracts into dozens of the dialects in the Empire and who had a burning desire to return to Judah, to live in a rebuilt Jerusalem.

There was Pinchas the property agent, who, together with his six enormous brothers, knew every home, field and grotto in Susa and its environs for fifty kilometers in any direction. The seven were hot-headed family men, known for using their fists first, and often thinking second. Pinchas and his brothers were respected and feared by the Persians as well as by their own people. In fact, the Jews living as Persians in Susa's nearby towns often called upon Pinchas and his brothers to "talk sense" into Persian bullies who bothered their old mothers, taunted their sisters, or muscled in to their businesses. Pinchas and his brothers were their champions and their enforcers.

And there were a half-dozen more; farmer, jewelry maker, teacher and carpenter. Diverse and different-charactered, all were living good lives as Jews in Persia.

"My brothers, I have news. Xerxes is preparing to choose a new queen."

"So why does this merit a Serah code? The king's sexual appetites are none of our business," interrupted Natan, who was impatient to be home; his wife was expecting a child any moment. Mordechai continued speaking.

"It is absolutely our business, Natan, as all of you will see. Beginning in five days the king's men will be fanning out throughout the Empire. They have been ordered by the king to round up all the beautiful virgins in the entire kingdom. No heed will be taken of religion or race; the only criteria are beauty and virginity. Xerxes wishes to have his pick of the Empire's finest maidens. Understand, Brothers, that the king will audition each girl! We around this table know exactly what that means. And at the end of the 'contest,' the girl who pleases Xerxes most will be crowned Queen of Persia."

The men were stunned silent.

"That means our sisters…" said Levi.

"…and our betrotheds!" added Shimon, staring straight at Mordechai, who had gripped the table edge.

"Not while I have breath!" said Pinchas, pounding the table to a grumbled assent by his brothers. Some of the others nodded their heads and looked fierce.

"We will not be given the choice," said Mordechai. "Think! What will you do, yes, even you, Pinchas, and your brothers and their friends? Will you stand up against the king's armed guards? They will crush you like bugs, and you will leave your wives widows and your children orphans. Your homes will be burned and your shops looted and shut down. No, we haven't the strength or the armaments to wage a war against Xerxes' guards. We must think of more clever ways to evade the dragnet. And we do have a little time; we know about the king's plans but they don't know we know. And they won't be coming for the girls for five days yet. They are busy making their own preparations."

So the men got down to the business of organizing secret, round-the-clock migrations. Market day was in two days' time, which was in their favor. Thousands of people passed in and out of the metropolis of Susa on market day. The Jewish girls would be disguised as old women or boys; some of the girls would be sporting "warts" on their noses or limps in their gait. They would be dressed as Phoenicians or as Indus mountain folk. No one would pay any heed to small groups of two or three people at a time coming into or heading out of Susa. No one would notice that there would be no virgin girls left among the Jews of Susa and few left in Persia for Xerxes' men to grab for his harem. Mordechai counted on the fact that there would be so many other lovely girls for the taking that the king's wagons would be full.

Hopefully the guards would not consult the census scrolls. But even so, it was an innocent possibility that the young girls might be visiting relatives in other lands.

And in truth there would be many Persian mothers, fathers and uncles — not to say girls themselves — who would welcome the chance to be taken to the king's harem. They would think it a grand adventure to be pampered and primed for the chance to charm the king. Many would harbor hopes that *their* sister or daughter would be the next queen of Persia. And why not? It had to be someone... And perhaps some Jewish girls would even wish to try their luck. Mordechai couldn't save them all; he could only try.

"We must get word to the outer provinces. Lev, you have the horses and riders. We have done this before, for lesser matters. Use the postal roads, it's faster. Take no scrolls with you in case you are stopped and searched. Take coins for bribes, take bolts of cloth so you appear to be merchant messengers. Dress like caravaners. Live the disguise. Pack up tonight and leave before first light. The message must be relayed and it must be precisely the same everywhere. Tell the riders to say this: 'Mordechai says get your virgin girls out of Persia and do it immediately. In five days the king's soldiers will round up Persia's virgins by force!'"

"Pinchas," Mordechai looked directly at his enormous friend. "You and your brothers must swear with all of us here tonight that you will not resist the king's soldiers head-on. Better yet if all of you happen to be out in the fields or in other villages on the day of the dragnet, to keep you away from temptation. Swear with all of us that you will spirit the girls out of harm's way but will not engage the king's troops. This is for all of our good as well as for your own survival."

Eventually, all the men of the Brotherhood swore to get the Jewish girls out of the reach of Xerxes' men, and not to fight them. "For Yahweh!" They said in unison and with muted intensity. Fire was in the men's eyes; purpose was in the speed of their steps as they left the cellar room one or two at a time and headed out into the night.

When it was just Mordechai, Shimon and Eliezer left, Shimon spoke. "Mordechai, you must tell Hadassah what is coming, and prepare her to leave tonight or tomorrow. She can travel with my eldest niece, Rachel. We have relatives in Syria, and the girls can get a berth on one of Gidon's ships up the Euphrates. They can return home in a few months when all this has blown over."

Mordechai grasped Shimon's shoulder. "Thank you, my friend. Hadassah is not going to like this. She has never left Susa in her life. And since we have been betrothed, and her eighteenth birthday approaches..." Mordechai looked bleak.

Shimon and Eliezer climbed the steps and left the cellar, heading home quickly to begin their preparations, leaving Mordechai alone. His handsome face was lined with exhaustion, his shoulders rigid with tension. He placed his palms on the stone table and leaned his weight on them, his head feeling too heavy for his neck. All at once the candle flames fluttered, though the trap door had not been opened.

"Mordechai." The scratchy voice of the Master brought Mordechai's head around to see the hooded man standing on the other side of the table. He spoke without preamble. "Mordechai, Hadassah will not be going away with Shimon's niece Rachel. She will insist on staying with you, and she will stay until Xerxes' men come for her. Mordechai, hear my words: You must let her be taken."

"What are you saying?! Let her be taken?!" Mordechai erupted.

"You must let her be taken," he repeated quietly, his hooded head inclining in a nod. "She has a purpose, Mordechai." The Master paused dramatically. "Hadassah will be chosen queen. You must let her be taken to the palace."

With that astonishing statement, the man disappeared. The candles fluttered once more and then went out. Mordechai was left alone in the pitch-dark. His world had just crashed down onto his head and his heart had been broken in the time it took the Master to speak and to disappear. Knowing his way blindfolded, Mordechai climbed slowly up the stone stairs in the darkness, feeling twice his age. What would he tell Hadassah? How would the two of them be able to bear this?

While Abednego watched Mordechai enter his house from his spot on the corner, another pair of eyes also noted Mordechai's comings and goings.

Telling Hadassah

Early the next morning Mordechai did not go as usual to the palace courtyard to hear the latest news of the court and to listen to the diplomats' gossip. He had no stomach this morning for leaning against a pillar and translating overheard conversations in his head, practicing his language skills and strategizing about mundane political doings. He had not slept, and though he was washed and dressed fastidiously as always, he was troubled and preoccupied.

If Poupeh was surprised that Mordechai was dressed and pacing his salon at dawn, she said nothing, and went about her morning duties. Yesterday Poupeh had delivered the scroll to Mordechai with the explosive message about the upcoming virgin roundup, but she had not read it. Even so, Poupeh could read the faces of those she loved, and she saw the lines around his eyes and knew Mordechai was in crisis. She began to prepare breakfast, believing that even when facing a crisis people still needed to eat.

Mordechai paced and thought, and waited for Hadassah to stir from her chamber. With preternatural hearing his head came up a second or two before Esther's soft indoor slippers could be heard on the tile floor. She saw Mordechai standing in the hallway and her face lit up. She approached him expectantly but stopped short as she searched his face. Her hand shot out to grip Mordechai's forearm.

"What has happened, Mordechai?"

His eyes never leaving her face, Mordechai put a hand over hers and led her into the salon.

"Hadassah, I have spent half my life planning other peoples' lives; predicting and orchestrating their next moves; trying to protect our people by planning for the unexpected; trying to be prepared. But nothing in my thirty-eight years has prepared me for what I must tell you now."

"Mordechai, you are frightening me. Come and sit." Mordechai would not sit, so Hadassah sat at the edge of the settee and gripped her hands in her lap as she turned to face the man she loved. Mordechai stood rigidly, as if bracing himself against the lash. "Now tell me what you must tell me." She sat very still and prepared to listen.

"I will say it straight out, Hadassah, as you will hear of it in whispers within the hour. Xerxes is searching for a new queen. He has decided he will choose her from among the most beautiful maidens in all of Persia. To do this, he will be sending special armed officers to every city and town in the 127 provinces in the Empire with orders to search out and take the best of these girls back to Susa. The girls will have no choice; they will be taken — forced — to stay in the House of the Women and be prepared to be auditioned by Xerxes."

"How do you know this?" Hadassah whispered.

Mordechai did not respond; he just watched Hadassah as she processed and absorbed what he had said.

"What am I saying? Of course you know, and of course you are sure. When?"

"In four days' time. Only we few know, and this is thanks to our informants on the inside; the scribe who was preparing the edict is one of ours."

When she sat silent Mordechai continued. "The Brotherhood met last night and already we are moving our girls out of Susa, on foot, in trader caravans, by boat, on horseback. Messengers have been dispatched everywhere discreetly alerting our people. When the king's men come looking they will not find many maiden Persian Jewesses. Shimon wants you to leave Susa tomorrow with his niece Rachel. He plans to disguise her as a boy and spirit her out in the tumult of market day, with some wine merchant friends of Eliezer's."

"And you expect me to go with her."

"I would like you to go, yes. Hadassah, you are exactly what the king's men will be looking for. You are young, you are very beautiful, and you are a maiden. You will be a prize for them to bring back to the harem. Hadassah, understand that this is serious business. Whoever is taken will never return. She will never be allowed to leave the king's fortress. She will never again see the sunrise except from the inside of the Women's compound."

What Mordechai did not say aloud was that if Hadassah were found and taken by the king's men the two of them would never be wed. He couldn't bring himself to say the words.

He also had not told her of the Master's prophecy. He had decided over the course of the short night that despite the hooded man's words he would encourage Hadassah to leave the city. He fervently hoped she would agree to leave with Rachel. At least then Hadassah had the chance to grow to womanhood outside the king's harem, and the possibility existed that they might have a future together.

But first he owed it to Hadassah to explain in the starkest terms what she or any maiden would be facing if she were taken in the upcoming dragnet. For it was a certainty that if she stayed she would be taken by the king's men. Hadassah was a prize.

Hadassah could not bear to look into Mordechai's eyes as he spoke; the lonely terror of the narrow choice open to her was reflected in his face.

"Hadassah, you must listen. You must know precisely the danger you are facing if you stay. Once a girl is taken by the king's men she will stay in the House of the Women for months, even years, until she is summoned to the king's bed. Look at me, Dassi." Mordechai rarely used his pet name for his beloved except in their most private moments. It was his use of this name that brought the sheen of tears to her eyes. She fought them back and looked up at Mordechai as he went on, relentlessly cataloguing the facts.

"After the king has done with a girl she is sent to the House of the Concubines. It is possible she will never be called by the king ever again; even so, she is forbidden to any other man for the rest of her life. Even a physician will not be able to attend to her face-to-face. He would be able to examine only her tongue, with the rest of her body hidden behind a veil.

"And that's if you are *not* chosen queen," he continued. "If a girl is chosen as queen she will live under even more restrictive royal lock and key, in virtual seclusion within the Women's Compound, and at the beck-and-call of the king."

"Mordechai, why are you telling me these details? Do you expect me to faint away? I am a maiden but I am aware of what goes on between a man and a woman. I have assisted at many births, I have heard the girls and grandmothers talking. I have waited for eighteen years and I have imagined how it would be *with you*, with us. I am not afraid."

"Well, you *should* be afraid!" For once, perennially calm Mordechai allowed his anger and misery to show. "The king will not be like a husband who is anxious to please his new bride. It will be up to the girl in Xerxes' bed to please *him*. It is not likely to be easy for her."

"I will tell you what frightens me, Mordechai. What frightens me is the possibility that we might never wed. You are telling me that if I go with Rachel there is the possibility that we can meet up again somehow and somewhere, when this search for a queen is ended. That with luck we might have a life together. But that if I stay here with you in Susa I will surely be rounded up and taken to the palace, and we will never again speak to one another or touch as lovers.

"If that were all that was facing us, then my choice would be clear: I must leave Susa tomorrow with Rachel.

"But there is something else. I can tell. You forget that I know you, Mordechai, as well as I know myself. Your distraught behavior is way out of proportion to the fact that I must leave Susa tomorrow with Rachel. Other girls have done this before me, and you have safely spirited people in and out of difficult situations for as long as I have lived here. This is something you excel at, and as you say, the Brotherhood are assuming that the separations are only temporary.

"So I must ask you: why have you taken pains to emphasize for me the rigors of the life of a virgin in the Women's compound? Why are you so afraid for me if I will be leaving Susa tomorrow with Rachel?

"There must be something more. Something else is eating at you. What have you *not* told me?"

Mordechai sighed with resignation and finally sat down on the settee next to Hadassah. They faced each other and he took her hands in his. She had read him easily. And what did he expect? He was not hiding his feelings. Plus, he had trained this girl, since she was old enough to walk and whisper, in the craft of observing people closely, cataloguing their facial expressions, listening to their words, and "hearing" what they left unsaid. She was as proficient at this as his best agents. She was of a sweet and compliant nature — an orphan almost had to be resilient and compliant in order to survive — but her compliant nature masked a granite will and a strategic mind. If he did not tell Hadassah the whole of it, not only might she not leave with Rachel; she would surely be taken by the king's men without knowing the extent and import of her mission; doubtless the most difficult mission of her life. So he told her.

"There *is* more. I had planned on letting you leave tomorrow with Rachel without telling you this. But, well, here it is: The Master appeared in the secret tannery room last night after everyone else had left." Mordechai paused, his next words almost impossible for him to speak. "He told me I must let you be taken by the king's men; that you would be chosen queen; that there was a vital purpose to your being positioned in Xerxes' palace."

Hadassah was silent and still as a statue, her hands like ice in Mordechai's. This was much, much worse than losing her parents. After all, she had never known their love. This was like a tearing; like an excruciating cracking feeling in her chest. Hadassah felt lightheaded and heavy at the same time.

"What are you saying, Mordechai?" she whispered. "That the Master wishes me to remain here and *allow myself* to be taken?" Agitated, Hadassah pulled her hands from Mordechai's and stood up, facing him. "Well, I won't! Mordechai, what about our marriage? Did you not tell the Master that we are to be wed in three months when I turn eighteen? Surely Xerxes can find another beautiful virgin among the thousands in all Persia."

Mordechai watched as Hadassah said everything he had been repeating to himself all through the night. "He knows all this, Dassi. But the Master doesn't have the same human feelings as you and I. The Master is all purpose and no emotion. He is saying that your beauty may be the key to placing one of our own people inside, closer to the king than anyone has ever been, even closer than Old Daniel himself, who has been the confidant of four kings. The girl who wins the spot as the next queen of Persia will hold a golden key to power. The Master thinks it can be you, Dassi."

"Mordechai, listen to yourself. Are you convinced that this is even possible—that I will be chosen above the thousands of other girls? Would you give up on our dream of a life together as husband and wife for this gamble? Will I forsake my family and allow mysefl to be a courtesan to Xerxes? I cannot believe you or the Master would sanction this! I will wrap myself as a boy and leave Susa tonight rather than agree. How can you sit there so calmly?" Hadassah turned away, her arms wrapped around herself as if to keep from flying apart. Mordechai got up and held her to him, his chin resting on her head, both of them facing the window looking into his courtyard garden. He spoke to her intensely.

"I had to give you the opportunity to weigh the choice for yourself, Dassi. You can and should leave Susa with Rachel tomorrow. One part of me hopes you will do this. Or—or," and here Mordechai turned Hadassah in his arms and spoke directly into her eyes. "Or, perhaps there is another way." Mordechai paused, catching a glimpse of hope in the girl's eyes.

"What if we were wed immediately? I've been thinking all night. Once we wed and you are no longer a virgin"—here Mordechai actually appeared slightly embarrassed—"then you will no longer fit the king's criteria and you will not be taken!"

Hadassah's eyes opened wide, but she was cautious. "It sounds too simple a solution. But surely it makes perfect sense. If I am not a virgin I am disqualified from the dragnet." Hadassah had spoken this last statement slowly, as if testing it for flaws, her hope growing. A corner of Mordechai's mind was impressed with the girl's calm. Hadassah continued, "Should you send a message to the Master and propose this in light of what he told you? Should we wait for his response, or marry without his approval?"

There were more questions than answers, but Mordechai was energized. As Hadassah watched, he strode to his desk and wrote quickly on a small parchment using his special disappearing ink. He blew on it to dry the message, and as the letters disappeared he rolled it up, speaking quickly, as if to himself. "We will plan to wed quietly, in this house, the day after tomorrow, at night on the day after market day, one day before the takings are scheduled to begin. This will give you a day to prepare, and for me to gather the holy man and the witnesses, and to have a scribe ink the marriage scroll. Surely the Master will have responded by then. Surely he will see the sense of this. We have two agents inside the House of the Women at the present time; that must suffice. *They will get close to the new queen." That will have to be enough*, he added to himself. "I will get word to Daniel."

Mordechai called for Poupeh. "Poupeh, take this to the palace kitchen gate and have your friend pass it to Abbas for Old Daniel. It is urgent! Go now, please." Wordlessly Poupeh took the small scroll and instantly it disappeared within the folds of her blouse. Poupeh left the house at a trot, belying her age, wrapping her head and half her face as she went.

Abednego, watching from his beggar's corner, saw her go and thought, *Something is amiss. I will warn Daniel. Mordechai will watch over the girl.* He had a moment of hesitancy, then in an instant he was gone.

Planning a Wedding

Things moved quickly after that. When Poupeh heard about the wedding she became like a general commanding her troops, consisting of Hadassah and the daily girl. The girl stripped Mordechai's serviceable bed linens and replaced them with fine embroidered sheets and netting fit for a bride. For his one remaining night as an unmarried man he could sleep on his daybed. Poupeh began cooking a small wedding feast. No matter that she had barely one full day and night to prepare; it was enough time and it would be done according to tradition.

Hadassah culled her clothing and prepared her trousseau. Over the past year she had assembled her bride's wardrobe, secreting her wedding dress in a strapped wooden trunk in her chamber. Now she removed it gently, held it up to the light and laid it out on her bedroom divan. She sighed as she ran her hand lightly over the exquisite heavy *atlas* and *abrisham*, the heavy gold satin and silk layered fabric from which her bridal dress and tunic and its matching slippers were made. She moved a fragrant pouch of dried jasmine over the folded soft underthings and night clothes before she closed the bridal trunk.

Poupeh had herself embroidered the long, white lace head-veil which now hung in Poupeh's own chamber awaiting tomorrow. The loving housekeeper also had spent countless private hours sewing Hadassah's unique wedding-day floor-spread; the luxurious *termeh*, the cashmere spread that would cover the floor of the salon where the wedding ceremony was to be held. The feet of the newly married couple would be embarking on a special journey together, and the rug beneath their feet on that day would both speed and bless their trip. It was traditional for a mother to pass her wedding spread down to her daughter, but as Hadassah had come to Mordechai's house a newborn orphan, Poupeh had taken on the duty of creating the wedding spread for the girl she loved like a daughter.

Two tall silver candelabra were polished and the candles laid. They would be placed, lit, flanking the salon mirror, their glow an augur of the brightness of the bride and groom's future life together. All was in readiness inside Mordechai's house.

The Master answered Mordechai's question with one word: "*Tabrik*," meaning *Congratulations!* in Pârsi. On its face it seemed Mordechai and Hadassah had the Master's approval of their marriage. Esther was content, but Mordechai was troubled. The hooded old man had told him clearly that Hadassah was to be selected queen of Persia. The man had never yet been wrong in the twenty years he had been his Control. So Mordechai worried at this about-face. *"Tabrik?" Perhaps the Master has seen that Hadassah's quisma has changed*, he thought. *Fate was a fickle thing, after all, and Hadassah was due this happiness.*

Abednego was back at his beggar's corner, this time armed with two daggers. One large dagger in a leather sheath tucked out of sight in his waistband at the small of his back, and a smaller one sheathed and strapped to his right ankle. Both weapons were honed and sharp enough to split a human hair. Daniel had instructed him to be ready for anything.

To an onlooker, all was as it always was on the streets that housed Susa's nobles. But behind closed doors there was a controlled excitement overlaid by anxiety. Excitement because over the past day and night news had traveled quickly within the Persian Jewish community about Mordechai's advanced wedding date, intended to insulate Hadassah from the king's dragnet. By design, only the holy man, the witnesses and the scribe would be present, and instead of an overflowing houseful of guests, only Shimon and Eliezer of the Brotherhood would stand up with Mordechai. No other members of the Brotherhood could be spared. Hadassah had only the indispensable Poupeh and the daily girl to attend her, but she was content, anxious to begin her life as Mordechai's wife.

There was also anxiety and sadness behind the closed doors by the morning following market day, because by then more than half the Jewish community's maidens had been spirited out of Susa; most of the others would be gone by midnight. Mothers and brothers, fathers, lovers and grandmothers were fearful, and their houses were quiet.

The Evening of Market Day
Watching Mordechai's House from the Shadows

Alerted by the busy activity and the uncustomary bustling to and from Mordechai's usually sedate house, the bored watcher perked up. His secret *ban* would pay in coin for an accurate list of the numbers of people moving in and out, and he would pay even more for names. So the watcher started counting. He already recognized the lord, named Mordechai; his old housekeeper; several of his friends and frequent visitors; and the tradesmen's delivery boys. He wished he could have seen more of the lord's ward, a choice girl who rarely set foot out of the compound unaccompanied, and even then she was careful to cover herself with a shawl from head to waist. But the watcher smiled to himself as he recalled the girl's lissome shape; she couldn't completely disguise that.

He had not seen her at all in the past two days; come to think of it, he had not seen *any* of the young girls out and about the shaded side streets. From his watching post over the past weeks he had discerned a pattern: they traveled in small chattering groups early in the morning and sometimes in the late afternoon, when they often neglected to cover their faces. Where were the girls now? He would note their absence and depending on the *ban's* mood he would mention it in his report. Perhaps it would be of interest.

The Same Evening – Outside the Palace Wall

The watcher leaned against a pillar in the rear of the outer palace wall, at his usual spot. It was his "confessional;" he faced sideways, his profile but inches away from a filigreed iron and stone window embrasure cut into the wall two hands-breadths higher than a standing man's head. It was one of hundreds of similar, small fenestrations cut into the fortress walls. Small messages and possibly arms or even foodstuffs could be passed through the openings if need be, but no one standing outside on the ground could see into the opening. The person inside had the advantage of the high ground and could see not only the person at the outer wall, but also for many meters in three directions.

The *ban's* voice addressed the watcher.

"What is so urgent that you have abandoned your post and come here on a day we have not prearranged? You are fortunate that one of my men saw you standing out here and alerted me. It had better be important to risk a meeting in the daylight. Speak!"

The watcher resented the *ban's* tone, but he *was* the *ban*, the secret governor, and he was paying well. Truth be told the watcher was a little afraid of him. The voice was cruel, and the watcher had heard rumors that the governor controlled at least twenty informants, though he had never met any of the others himself. He was quick to answer.

"Master, you have asked me to watch and to note the comings and goings at the house of Mordechai. As you know, I have done so for the past weeks, and other than the three who reside there and the maid and delivery boys, the place has been quiet. But over the past two days this has changed. There is much movement in and out, by strangers as well as tradesmen, and the pattern of the three who live there has also changed." The watcher paused, unsure how the *ban* was reacting. Should he tell him the rest or was all of this uninteresting to him?

"Go on! You have more?"

"Well, yes. It's nothing specific, just an absence of general street traffic. Over the past weeks of watching I have become familiar with the pattern of the neighborhood. Over the past two days there have been no young women coming and going. It's like they have disappeared."

There was silence from the window. Then, a small pouch of coins was dropped from the opening and clinked onto the ground at the watcher's feet.

"You have done well. Return to your post and continue to watch and report, at our usual times."

The watcher stooped and retrieved his coins, then hurried on his way.

Haman moved from the window and walked slowly along the palace corridor, thinking. His spy had been watching Mordechai's house for weeks, and had turned up so little other than the prosaic comings and goings of the household that he had been ready to pull him from the job and post him elsewhere. But this latest bit of information was of potential interest.

Haman was one of the few courtiers who knew of the coming dragnet of virgins. It was a closely held secret as yet unknown to the king's ministers. The sealed letters announcing the operation had been penned by the royal scribes in every language of the realm and at this very moment were on their way by horseback across Persia via the king's royal messengers. The roundup action was scheduled to begin at dawn on the morrow. The king and his advisors — Haman preened a bit, as he had conceived and orchestrated this latest scheme, albeit from the sidelines — had determined that the best strategy was to keep the matter a secret until the last moment. They did not wish the people to become excited or agitated at the coming quasi-military operation. Granted, the mission was to choose a queen for Xerxes — on its face a worthy and even romantic objective — but at its essence the operation would entail kidnapping thousands of girls who had not yet been let out of their mothers' sight. It would be difficult under the best of circumstances. This part of the roundup actually appealed to Haman's sadistic nature.

Haman thought that it was interesting that the watcher had noted a falling off of street traffic, and especially an absence of young girls. Could the news of the coming operation have leaked? Considering this tidbit from his agent, this now seemed likely. Wary of coincidences, Haman's nose told him word of the scheme must have gotten out. If the people already were guarding their virgins it would make it extra-difficult for the soldiers to make their quotas. This was not going to be a popular undertaking in the best of circumstances; but if the girls had to be rousted and dug out of hiding places, it would not only slow things down, it would alarm everyone. This whole virgin search could backfire into a civil conflict, which was absolutely to be avoided.

Haman resolved to immediately approach the royal advisor who commanded the captain of the soldiers, and propose moving the operation forward by twelve hours. At least then they could potentially catch the people of Susa off-guard; their information would not have the operation beginning until the next day. Haman was a great believer in planning, but he also appreciated the strategic benefit of surprise.

And he relished shaking up the arrogantly confident Mordechai. Didn't Mordechai have a young virgin ward?

The Same Evening – Mordechai's House

By nightfall of market day all was in readiness in Mordechai's house. The side table in the salon was covered in a linen cloth, concealing some of the wedding delicacies ready for the small wedding feast: a basket of apples and pomegranates signifying love and fertility, and drinking bowls for the bride and groom made entirely of crystallized ginger to sweeten their future life. The tea urn was poised over unlit coals, ready to brew the traditional black bridal tea; the poppy seeds, salt and frankincense were in their shallow bowls, ready to ward off unwelcome spirits. And delicate blue and white flowers of the nigella herb clustered in low vases sent off a subtle and pleasing fragrance.

Hadassah was the only calm person in the household. She was eager for the ceremony, eager for the night, and looked forward, too, to the dawn, to the first day of her new life.

Evening of the Same Day
Outside the Royal Barracks

The captain of the royal home soldiers was not particularly pleased. In the past hour his orders had been changed and

"Operation Virgins," as he privately called it, was moved up; it would begin tonight instead of tomorrow morning. He was a lifetime soldier as his father had been, so he subscribed to the dictum that his was not to question political tactics; his was but to carry out orders. So, though as a military man he loathed surprises and likewise thought it odious to have his soldiers corralling girls from their neighbors' homes, he duly mustered his troops. It was a small detachment of one hundred men, half of them on horseback, all of them wearing light arms including spears, but no armour. He did not deem it necessary; after all, his objective was to collect virgin girls. How much trouble could they be? They also had two horse-drawn lorries, each with a capacity for one hundred girls, and each driven by a similarly armed soldier.

The Same Evening – Mordechai's House

Hadassah stood still in the hallway just outside the salon as Poupeh, dressed in a black caftan trimmed in orange piping, reached up to drape the bridal veil over the girl's hair and face. She secured the lace with a braided diadem of gold and turquoise linen. Hadassah was a vision in shimmering gold *atlas* satin, her eyes kohled and luminous, her deep auburn hair cascading to her waist, rippling against the dress and reflecting the lights from the candelabra. She looked across the room at Mordechai. *Had he ever looked more handsome?* she thought.

He was dressed in a tunic of deep blue brocade with midnight-hued trousers. Around his waist was an ornate leather girdle secured by a silver buckle, his family coat of arms chased into its surface. A short woven turban sat on his raven-black head. He stood tall, with Shimon and Eliezer flanking him. The holy man was at the desk reviewing the marriage contract.

In a matter of minutes I will be a married woman, thought Hadassah. *I will be leaving one room of the house that is my life, and entering another.*

Mordechai thought, *I will rest easier once this is done and behind us.* He had a nagging sense of foreboding, unable to banish the memory of the words the Master had spoken to him in the secret tannery room. He was not listening to the words of his two friends, who were making light sport of their boyhood friend about to wed at last. He looked over at the doorway and saw Hadassah, a column of gold and lace, her serene eyes trained on him. *Had she ever looked so beautiful?* he thought. *She is calm enough for us both.* Then he thought of nothing but her.

The Dragnet – Twelve Hours Early

As is the case with many cataclysmic events, they happen with such speed and confusion it is only much later that a person can replay it in his or her mind's eye putting the events in sequence. So it was, on the night that was to have been Hadassah's wedding to Mordechai.

Abednego, crouching in his beggar's corner, felt the ground tremble. In a blink he was standing straight, his disguise abandoned, his unsheathed dagger ready in his palm. He was poised to jump, but which way?

Haman's watcher, surprised out of a doze, moved back into shadowed safety in a side street. He would try to see what was happening, but he had no intention of getting caught up in any danger.

Abednego, about to cross the road to be closer to Hadassah's house, was cut off as dozens of running as well as mounted soldiers rounded the corner and swept into the street. A wall of horseflesh and a fence of spears and torches was set up at each end of the street, an armed soldier at the front and back doors of each house. Abednego willed himself to disappear, his body light as air as it flew above the street and reappeared — still invisible — inside Mordechai's salon, and he positioned himself, undetected, next to Hadassah.

All eyes in the salon turned to the door as the pounding began. The door exploded inward, armed soldiers spilling into the salon. Simultaneously Mordechai, Shimon and Eliezer reached for their hidden weapons, but of course they came up empty, as they had not thought to strap on sheath knives or even sling shots when they had dressed for the wedding. They were caught defenseless. Their instincts were to rush forward at the intruders; only the small room and the bride's presence had them hesitating. Mordechai instinctively grabbed Hadassah and pushed her down onto the floor behind him, out of harm's way and presenting a smaller target. The soldiers teemed into the house, leading with their spears crossed, scattering lamps and tables, crystal and foodstuffs. One candelabrum tipped over and as it hit the floor a flying candle ignited the cashmere bridal spread on the floor. Poupeh, terrified and outraged, threw herself onto the small flames. The holy man stood where he was, as if turned to stone.

Mordechai stepped up to the soldier in charge. A tall man, Mordechai nevertheless was a head shorter than the armed captain. "What is the meaning of this? We are engaged in a wedding ceremony! You and your men have no place here!"

The captain's instructions were clear: collect the virgins and leave everyone else alone. Do as little collateral damage as possible. Gather the virgins and move on.

"Stand down, sir. It's not you we want, it's the girl there." Abednego had lifted Hadassah up from the floor and he stood in front of her, an invisible shield. Amazingly, Hadassah leaned forward and whispered urgently to Abednego as if she could see him clearly:

"Are you sent from the Master? What would he have me do? If I resist they will drag me. If they take me by force, Mordechai will kill them to save me, and they will slay him where he stands and burn down the house with everyone in it. Does the Master want me to let myself be taken?"

Abednego turned to Hadassah, not wondering how it was that *she* could see him when no one else could. He knew there were some who were born to special powers, and others who rose to extraordinary levels of power and perception when faced with grave danger, called to step beyond themselves. Hadassah was clearly one of those who rose to meet the power.

"Yes, my lady, it is your *quisma*, your fate. I will guard you; they cannot see me."

"But Mordechai!..." Hadassah began, then she shook her head in misery and stepped out to stand before the captain. Her bridal dress was soiled, but incongruously, her lace veil was still pristine. Its delicacy highlighted rather than concealed her beauty, and the captain, with the shaft of his spear pressed up against Mordechai's throat, signaled to his men to "hold." This girl was surely a prize.

Hadassah, deliberately keeping her eyes from Mordechai, addressed the captain in a calm, clear voice, "I will go with you peaceably. There is no need to harm anyone here." She bent to lift Poupeh from the smoldering floor spread, and she kissed the old woman's cheek. Then her shining eyes turned to stare into Mordechai's raging ones.

Mordechai pushed futilely against the spear with all his might, his hands held fast behind his back by a soldier. Then, in a surge, balancing on one leg he kicked out backwards with the other and toppled the guard behind him. In an instant three honed spear tips were pointed at his heart and neck, drawing blood. He was a dead man before Hadassah's eyes. At the same moment, Shimon and Eliezer shouted a war cry and jumped onto the backs of two guards, holding on as the soldiers spun in the small room. The scene was a bedlam.

The captain had had enough of this softly approach and Hadassah saw that he was ready to signal the torch bearer to set fire to the house, the typical means of dealing with resistance to the crown. She felt Abednego's sturdy form at her side giving her courage. She saw the dagger in his hand. Gathering every bit of steel within her, she held herself back from throwing herself at Mordechai's chest. She would not cry; she would not allow the last image Mordechai would have of her be that of a red-eyed, sobbing woman.

"Shall we leave, Captain?" And with that, Hadassah turned and strode from the room with her head high, through the smashed door, away from the only home she had ever known, away from the only people she had ever loved, and from her girlhood dreams.

The night that was to be Hadassah's wedding night had become her fiery furnace; her lions' den. She had not been slain this night; and with help of the One-God, Mordechai would survive, as well. But she had been touched by the flame, she had been bitten by the lion. And as a result she was not the same girl walking out of the house as she had been that morning. That morning she had been a girl with a wedding to plan and a lover to please. Tonight, though she had not been a bride, she was no longer a girl. She was an agent, a honed tool.

From the moment the king's guards had pounded on the door to the moment Hadassah walked out with the captain, not even ten minutes had elapsed. In those ten minutes Hadassah had disappeared. In her place walked Esther.

In the end it was not terribly difficult to put the dragnet plan into action across the Empire on short notice, because already in place was a vast Empire-wide bureaucracy of satraps and administrators in all 127 provinces who took their orders from Susa. In the same manner that the king's men went house-to-house or farm-to-farm collecting quarterly taxes they could commandeer a contingent of — this time — "virgin-seekers" to spread out, find and corral the choicest girls in the Empire.

So, within five days of the plan's having been suggested, the kingdom's young women — most just out of girlhood — were rounded up, put on royal transports and trucked from their homes to the fortress that was the king's palace compound in Susa. Perhaps it seemed like an adventure to some of the girls; but to most it was a forced kidnapping; an involuntary plucking of the girls from their families and their sweethearts.

The cry went out in village and town across the Empire. The word spread that the king's soldiers were looking for virgins. The speed and relative secrecy of the abduction plan had worked in the king's favor. At first nobody believed the girls would be taken against their will. But when they witnessed their neighbors and cousins being dragged from their homes and their mothers' and lovers' arms, the citizens of Persia got the message. Mothers hid their young daughters in root cellars; some girls were bundled up, monies were exchanged, and the girls were hastily sent with a brother or servant on passing trade caravans to a different country; others strapped their breasts and hid their hair under workmen's caps to look like boys.

But Xerxes' men were relentless. Armed with census records they went house-to-house calling the girls by name. If she was not to be found they flogged brothers and fathers in the town square to compel them to disclose the girl's whereabouts. Those who fought back—father, brothers, and betrothed young men—were beaten or taken away in chains. The king's men had to steel themselves when they came to their own home towns. No exceptions were permitted. The king's edict specified *"every beautiful young virgin"* was to be taken and brought to the harem.

Before the week was out, in this country where a beautiful girl was worth her weight in silver, it was considered a blessing to be ugly.

This is because the king's virgin roundup meant an end to the maidens' dreams of hearth and family and it was correctly perceived as a tragedy. A maiden who entered the king's harem never left the House of the Women alive. Following her sexual initiation the girl was taken across the courtyard to the House of the Concubines, where—unless she had the great and unlikely good fortune to be chosen queen—she remained, not a virgin but also not a wife, until the end of her days. She was completely isolated and lost to her family. Some of the concubines fell pregnant and became mothers of lesser heirs to the royal line. But it was understood that an ordinary life was abruptly ended for these very young women. The king's dragnet essentially sentenced them to a lifetime behind "velvet" bars.

There was only one girl who would win the great prize of Queen of Persia and who would bear Xerxes' heir. But the chance of being chosen queen over literally thousands of other beautiful candidates was ten thousand to one.

On the Transport

The captain walked beside Esther down the street toward the waiting horses and wagons. He had seen the strength in the girl when she had kissed her maid, and when she had turned resolutely away from her would-be groom, her heart in her eyes. *Speaking of eyes,* he thought, *that fellow was a man with murder in his eyes if ever I saw one! Well, who could blame him? This girl was a beauty.* The captain had been a judge of men for thirty years, and could take the measure of a man—or a woman, come to that—speedily. He was not unmoved at having to break up the wedding of those two.

It was an odd parade: army captain, captive girl dressed in bridal finery, and a complement of soldiers trailing behind; an obscene mockery of a wedding procession. The girl stood straight as a tree, her dark eyes pools of sadness as she walked. Even though the girl did not need his physical support, the captain felt as if he should offer her his arm; as if he were her vassal and not she his prisoner. Her veil was still in place, and in the gloomy darkness, lit at intervals by the soldiers' torches, the top half of her form glowed as she walked toward the waiting wagon.

Much later that night, as the soldiers prepared to bed down in the barracks after rounding up and unloading two hundred girls in their first night's work, they recalled the first maiden they had taken. In half-jest some said she had looked like a spirit; others thought she had looked like a goddess. All thought she was the loveliest girl they had ever seen.

Though Esther's world had shrunk in the past hour to encompass only herself and her misery, as she stood in the waiting transport wagon she gradually became aware of the sounds of the surrounding night. She knew by heart the peaceful sounds in and around Mordechai's house and those of her neighbors. What assaulted her thawing senses as she waited was terrifyingly different. She heard pounding on wooden doors, male shouts of protest, women's sobs, girls' screams, sounds of scuffling, intermittent sounds of clanging weapons, young male voices swearing; threats, promises and pleas.

As the wagon filled, Esther stood in one corner as most girls jostled for wooden plank seats and others just sat on the floor. She heard, close-up, loud wailing and quiet crying, smelled the fear of the girls as they huddled nearby. There was even some giggling, and she sensed here and there a subdued nervous excitement. To most, this night of abduction was a wrenching personal tragedy; to others, it was an escape from an abusive father or uncle; an adventure. To still others, this was an opportunity, a chance at a one-in-ten-thousand shot from poverty and obscurity to royalty.

One frightened girl, not a day over fourteen, crushed close to Esther as the wagon jolted. "Aren't you afraid?" she asked.

Esther put her arm around the trembling girl, feeling much older and a little maternal. "No, I am not afraid, my sister. What are you called?"

"I am Elizeh. What's *your* name?"

Unhesitatingly, Esther voiced her Persian name for the first time. "I am called Esther."

Much later, in the final hours of the long night, Esther lay in a bed in a room with fifty other girls. Her young friend, Elizeh, who would not be parted from her, was sleeping curled up like a baby in the next bed. Only one or two other girls were still awake in the cavernous room, crying quietly into their pillows, or staring up at the dark ceiling. She wondered if her guardian soldier was still here with her, in the House of the Women. She sensed his invisible presence hovering, but it was more distant now. Still, it comforted her; she was not alone.

Her soiled wedding clothes lay neatly folded at the foot of her bed; she was clad in pale peach-colored nightclothes, exactly the same as all the other girls. This was the first night of her life that she was not sleeping in her own bed in Mordechai's house. She shook her head and refused to think of Mordechai. That way led to madness. If she thought of his face, of his arms around her, of his voice calling her Dassi, she would cry and cry and never stop. Instead she thought, *What would Mordechai do? What would he want me to do?* She thought of his instructions. She remembered clearly that he always told his agents to keep their true identities a secret. "Never disclose your people or your kindred," Mordechai instructed. "Never hand the other side any leverage. What they don't know can't hurt you or us. Practice responding to your new name until you *become* this new person."

Esther kept her eyes on the high window and from her prone position on the narrow bed she watched as the darkness faded first to grey and then to a yellow-blue. She resolved to keep to Mordechai's precepts. It actually made her feel closer to him. And she would live one day at a time. Who knew what was in store for her here, if she indeed had a mission? This place seemed to be her *quisma*, her fate.

As morning broke and before she dozed, Esther reflected that all through the chaos of the night's roundup she had not heard anyone saying "goodbye." It was just too final to contemplate.

Old Daniel

Daniel knew the moment Esther set foot within the palace grounds. Abednego would be her "angel," seeing that no harm came to her, and Abbas would be a physical presence around the House of the Women, not only watching the comings and goings, but also befriending Hegai, the Keeper of the Women. It was Hegai who held the keys to Xerxes' bedroom. If Esther could win over Hegai, she would have a smoother path to pleasing the king. But though Old Daniel could teach Esther a thing or two about pleasing a monarch *politically*, he could not coach her on how to please a sophisticated and sexually active potentate. Daniel feared that nothing in Hadassah's young life or in her imagination could have prepared her for this. He especially feared for the innocent girl who must somehow intuit, entice and charm a jaded lothario.

Daniel wondered how much of Mordechai's training Esther had absorbed. Could this unsophisticated, sheltered girl summon the discipline to distance herself from her personal trauma and live the role of a courtesan? This would depend entirely on Esther's innate character. How strong and how smart was she? *Time would tell*, he thought. And Heaven alone knew that in days to come their people would need to have a strong and smart agent as close to the vortex of Persian power as possible. Perhaps Esther could be that person.

The Watcher

The watcher ran all the way back to his palace rendezvous spot and paced impatiently until the *ban* appeared.

"Speak!" said the disembodied voice from the window above his head.

"Master, I watched from a side street and saw the king's soldiers enter Mordechai's house and come out with a tall maiden. She was wearing a wedding veil. The soldiers' gear was torn and they were bloodied. It looked like the people inside had put up a fight. Two guards remained at the front and back doors of the house with their spears drawn."

"What about the girl? Did you see where they took her?"

"They loaded her onto a waiting wagon, driven and flanked by more soldiers. While they were loading her up, other soldiers went in threes from house to house bringing out girls. There was lots of screaming and some struggling. That's all I could see from my hiding spot. When they had gone to every house on the street the soldiers and wagons left, but the guards remained at Mordechai's doors. No one else left or entered for about half an hour, so I came right away to tell you."

"Get back to your watch and report to me tomorrow; or immediately if there is any movement in or out of the house. I especially want to know where Mordechai goes."

The watcher waited for the pouch of coins, but none came. He hesitated.

"Get moving! This information was not worth any coins. I've already paid you more than you are worth. Bring me names and numbers. Go!"

The angry watcher pushed away from the wall and made his way back through the dark streets. He hoped the day would come soon when he would be in the position to do some damage to the *ban*, whoever he was. The man was evil. Perhaps he could send out some feelers of his own and discover his identity. He would keep his watch, for now, but he would also bide his time. He had some friends inside the palace. Someone would know.

Old Vendettas and Keeping the Secret

About five-and-a-half centuries had passed since King Saul's Israelite army had vanquished the armies of Amalek. That war had been sanctioned by the One-God of the Israelites, with instructions for the mighty Israelite king to take no prisoners. But King Saul had disobeyed his One-God, and he had taken pity on Agag, the Amalekite King. Saul spared Agag's life, and by this act of disobedience he had doomed his own kingship. It was Samuel, the fierce and powerful Israelite seer, who took it upon himself to publicly slay King Agag, slicing the captive Amalekite king in half with one blow of Saul's honed broadsword. With this act Samuel effectively ended two monarchies: that of Saul of Israel, and of Agag of Amalek.

The reason the Israelites had been instructed to wipe out Amalek's army and to show no mercy to their warrior king was the infamous massacre by Amalek half a millennium before, when the Amalekites had ambushed and indiscriminately murdered the unarmed and exhausted Israelite stragglers as they left the bondage of Egypt. The Israelites held that blood-soaked day in the very front of their collective memory and never forgot, forgave or trusted the nation or people of Amalek.

And Amalek, who had scorned the One-God of the Israelites and had lain in wait for them with murder on their mind, carried a burning hatred and desire for revenge in their hearts against the Israelites who had slain their king.

Over the ensuing centuries enemies came and went, kings and empires rose and fell, and the people of Israel and Amalek scattered and inhabited various lands of the ancient Near East. By the time of Xerxes' reign, the Israelites, descendants of that long-ago King Saul, had been in exile from their land and capital city for over a century, living as Persians in virtually every corner of the Empire. They were farmers and tradesmen and also advisors to kings. Likewise, the distant descendants of King Agag had risen to positions of influence and power in Persia.

In Susa, in the seventh year of the rule of Xerxes, Mordechai, a descendant of King Saul and a rising noble in Xerxes' court, was walking a path perilously close to that of Haman the Agagite, a courtier and advisor to Xerxes and a descendant of King Agag of Amalek. So far the two men had crossed paths briefly — when they both had been in military service under Darius, Xerxes' father; and now, two decades later in the court of Xerxes — sufficient so that each gave the other wide berth, both men feeling a dislike and suspicion of the other leavened by a manly rivalry. But this was not out of the ordinary; it was Haman's nature to be suspicious of everyone, especially of other nobles. Haman of Amalek was an advisor in the king's first circle, and he guarded his spot jealously. Similarly, Mordechai, one of the many young nobles at the outer circle of the court, and a secret Jew, was himself wary of Haman.

Unbeknownst to either Haman or Mordechai, seared ancestral memories and smoldering hatreds were on a personal collision course in the court at Susa.

A Spymaster Trains his Successor

Mordechai's secrecy about his origins was not unique to him. Many Jews living in Persia had no wish to readily be identified as Jews. Historically they had suffered sorely at the hands of indigenous people while living in countries not their own. Often the Jews were treated as potentially disloyal strangers, notwithstanding their having lived in the country for many decades, fought alongside their adopted countrymen in their wars, married their daughters, and advised their kings. So if they kept their customs at all, they did so in secret, within their homes or their hearts. Outwardly and in all important daily behaviors and interactions with the Persians, the Empire's ethnic Jews — as was the case with other conquered or exiled ethnicities and nationalities — considered themselves and conducted themselves as Persians.

So it was that Mordechai and Esther, Shimon, Eliezer, Pinchas and his brothers, and many like them, kept their ethnic identity secret, not disclosing to anyone their people or their kindred. They wished to conduct business and be treated in the streets and at court just as other people were in the vast melting pot that was the Persian Empire. Mordechai and others harbored a healthy distrust of foreign governments, having experienced either personally or historically their penchant for turning their back on the Jews living in their midst if it suited them. At its essence, Mordechai and his ilk felt the insecurity of living in Persian society. Even multifarious Persia was not free of a deep-seated fear of strangers coming into their society and taking jobs, resources and honors that they felt rightly belonged only to native Persians. Lurking just beneath the surface were resentments and ethnic stereotyping that only needed the smallest bit of license to come out into the open and do some damage.

It was this practical and psychological tightrope that Mordechai and his Brotherhood walked. They were Persian but "other." Secure, but watchful. Successful, but insecure. Nobility, but still and always immigrants and strangers.

It was Old Daniel—who had survived the lions' den to serve four kings at cabinet level—who recognized this insecurity and channeled it into productive behavior. Daniel had recruited Mordechai when he was a tall, precocious lad of fifteen. No doubt Mordechai reminded Daniel of himself and his three comrades a lifetime ago at that same age. Daniel believed that while monarchies change—he himself had served kings Nebuchadnezzar, Belshazzar, Cyrus, Darius and now Xerxes—the existential insecurity experienced by the Jewish exiles remained. To this end, Daniel knew he had to expand and train the next generation of agents and spies, watchers and informants. He needed someone who could take over from him when the inevitable day arrived and he could no longer run the network alone.

A stray conversation with the old man had piqued young Mordechai's interest, and that first conversation had grown into a deep and trusting friendship; so that before Mordechai knew it, Daniel had himself an operative. With the passage of years Mordechai's exceptional skills with languages and his photographic memory, coupled with his courage, his strategic mind, and a fearless dedication to protecting and preserving his people, made him—by Daniel's reckoning—the perfect person to succeed him. And Daniel was proved right as Mordechai became, first, an expert operative himself, and now, was himself almost a master of the secret art of running agents and acquiring and processing quantities of information.

And it was none too soon for Daniel's peace of mind. Time was running out.

Weeks before the king's dragnet of the virgins and Hadassah's abduction, there already was an urgency propelling him. Old Daniel had begun having premonitions of darkness and a coming danger. During the daytime, his vision would sometimes become covered with a red haze, and would remain so for some moments. Daniel was wise enough to respect these signs. He was afraid. And after a century of living alongside power, Daniel translated his fear into action.

Daniel wasn't sure at first whether his premonitions were flickers of the future, or if—in the way of the very old—they were personal or historical flashbacks. Only when his palace spy had told him of the king's imminent decree to kidnap the kingdom's beautiful virgins had he been certain of two things: a red terror was coming to the Jews of Persia, and Hadassah would be taken. Daniel connected the two and resolved to see to it that, as Esther, Hadassah would be in a position close to the power when the time came.

The Sons of Haman and the Amalek Baradari

Xerxes' Persia literally sat atop untold riches. Its vast area contained underground rock deposits hundreds of kilometers long heavily veined with pure silver. There was turquoise ore so close to the surface in caves near the trade routes that it needed only a small person to fit into cave openings wielding a hammer to set it free. Chunks of stone the size of hens' eggs in colors from brilliant blue to pale green were there, ready to be mined. And there were rubies, too, lying beneath the mountains of the Indus. There was also salt in enormous quantities underground, near the Caspian Sea.

Xerxes was quick to exploit these riches. He appointed his own satraps to travel to and live in the provinces where the minerals and gems had been found, in order to control the local governors and catalogue the output. The vast bulk of raw stones was sent to the king's treasure houses for storage, to be cut and set by master craftsmen as needed. Some stones were traded at exorbitantly high profit across the known world, including Greece.

Such labor-intensive industry required nearly an unending supply of strong men, adult males of slight stature, or small children or women. The work was backbreaking and conducted nearly totally under ground or in caves. It was also extremely perilous; the mines often had insufficient struts shoring up the earth as the ore was dug out of the mountains; there were frequent cave-ins, and of course, caves and mine tunnels were particularly susceptible even to gentle earthquakes or tremors. Plus, the candles and oil-soaked wicks used to light the tunnels gave off a toxic vapor asphyxiating the mine workers if the tunnels were not sufficiently ventilated. And finally, the possibility of fire underground was a constant fear. The multiple thousands of struts shoring up the tunnels, and the carts used to transport the ore were made of wood, and the necessary lighted torches and candles were inevitably knocked over in the course of the digging. The mine workers were terrified of a fire underground, knowing it meant a certain and grisly death.

As might be expected, the royal appointments as governors of the various mines were coveted positions even though they were often located in far-flung parts of the Empire. The opportunity for graft and for the skimming of gem dust or salt crystals was limitless, so that the governors of the mines and the satraps of the provinces where the mines were located became extremely wealthy. These royal appointments were recommended to the king by his court advisors, and if it pleased the king he might even appoint one of his own ministers to the titular post of "Governor of the Mine." The cabinet minister, uninterested in giving up the good life at court and traveling to the mountainous regions of the Indus, for instance, or even Greece, would himself appoint a local mine manager to run the enterprise in his stead. At all levels of the mining industry bribery, payoff and deceit oiled the bureaucracy of production.

Another prime area for corruption and abuse was in procuring a constant supply of slave labor for work in the mines. Local mine governors and satraps employed labor bosses whose job it was to supply the mines with a constant stream of human workers. Steep penalties were extracted if the boss' labor quota was unmet; labor shortfall meant slower production, which translated into lower profits. The labor boss was a critical linchpin in the process, and neither the satraps nor the mine governors paid any attention to how the labor was supplied, as long as there were bodies to do the work.

Haman Memuchan, the clever advisor whose suggestion for punishing Vashti after her insubordination had pleased the king, had been rewarded with a royal appointment as governor of a large silver mine in an area of Greece controlled by Persia. Because of the mine's distant location, rather than appoint a local mine manager Haman chose to keep the control, the profit and the bribery income close to home. He designated his two eldest sons to travel to Greece to live, so that they could manage the massive silver and lead deposits in the mountainous Laurion mine.

Haman's ten sons, aged in their late teens and early twenties, were copies of their father in terms of their lack of scruples and their ambition for amassing riches any way they could. But they were less clever, politic and patient than their father. Their solution to most problems was to exert brute force. In Susa they were known and feared as conscienceless thugs. Haman knew of their methods but neither expressed disapproval nor reined them in, as they achieved results.

Haman charged four of his eight sons who remained in Susa with the task of abducting young boys to work in the mines. Once a month Haman's sons would scour the streets of Susa; if they saw a stray beggar boy or an unaccompanied young boy out on an errand, they scooped him up, drugged him, and held him under guard in an empty building for several days until they had collected fifty boys. They would bind, drug and gag the captive boys and send them first, overland, and then via ship to work in their father's silver mine. They followed the same abduction procedure when the call came for strong hammer wielders. But because grown men put up more of a fight, Haman's sons tended to leave that end of the recruiting to the brothers at the distant mine site, letting their older brothers find their hammer-boys from among the local people.

After some months of this, the people of Susa had their guard up, and mothers and grandfathers held small boys close, especially if the word was out that the sons of Haman were on the prowl. There were more than a few households that had had a young son or brother go missing, and in a metropolis like Susa there was always someone on the street who had witnessed what happened. Rumors were rife that the Haman brothers had done the kidnapping, but no one would come forward for fear of violent reprisals. One father who had had the courage to confront one of the brothers and accuse him straight-out of abducting his young son, had been found the next day lying in his own blood in an alley with his right hand cut off. There had been no more public accusations. The missing boys' families mourned in private and kept their other children close.

Haman's sons recruited their friends to join them in whatever shady enterprise they had going. Over the course of three years the Haman brothers grew in number to a gang of about fifty young bullies, who called themselves the "Amalek Baradari." Amalek for their common ancestry, and Baradari meaning "brotherhood" in Tajik. But they were known in the streets of Susa as the Sons of Haman. Their main enterprise, apart from supplying boys for the mines, was to staff the local brothels.

The brothel portion of their "black" enterprise was run by Haman's remaining four sons. To supply women for their brothels Haman's sons employed thugs to troll the waterfronts and even distant marketplaces looking for lone street girls. They also relied on an anonymous Control inside the women's compound of the palace, and whose identity was unknown even to Haman. For years this Control had told them whenever one of the king's minor concubines was pregnant. This mysterious Control bribed a certain midwife to lie and say that one out of every three girl babies she attended to had been a still-birth. The compromised midwife would spirit the "dead" baby girl to waiting hands outside the wall, and the baby would be raised to young girlhood, orphanage-style, in a secret house along with other captive girls. The new mothers were practically girls themselves and were unsuspecting, especially since infant mortality was ordinarily high. Further, these young concubines wielded no power and had no protector even if they had suspected that something was amiss. This secret house, run by the Amalek Baradari, was a main supplier of innocent girls to Susa's brothels. The Sons of Haman had their fist in the till of all the houses of prostitution in the capital city, and they controlled its attendant drug traffic. They were fabulously wealthy and utterly corrupt.

At the time of the king's dragnet of the virgins, Haman's sons were poised to expand their brothel-baby enterprise tenfold. The House of the Women would be filled to capacity and the rota of virgins into and out of the king's bedroom would yield an overfull House of the Concubines, as well.

The fearsome Amalek Baradari, captained by the unchecked and amoral Sons of Haman, had thus spread their tentacles beyond Susa's streets and underworld into the women's quarter of the palace. Combined with their father's growing influence at court they were fast becoming an unstoppable political force in Susa. All this was going on under Xerxes' nose, either unsuspected or tolerated by the king.

It was into this cloistered, corrupt and dangerous world that an innocent Esther was thrust.

Shadrach

All this was observed from the shadow-world by Daniel's old friend-turned-nemesis, Hananya. Hananya had retreated from his blood brothers — Daniel, Mishael and Azariya — decades ago, bitter and morally bent after his experience in the fiery furnace in Babylon. He had spent the years since honing his dark, supernatural skills, and feeding his newly-discovered blood-lust, but had stayed mostly on the sidelines. Inwardly he sneered at Daniel's piety and upright service to successive kings. He ignored his former comrades' devotion to Daniel, to serving the One-God and to the mission of protecting their people. He had long ago rejected rectitude, morality and God, knowing his power was beyond such petty restraints.

Uninhibited evil exerted its welcome pull on Hananya/ Shadrach, which was why the Sons of Haman and the Amalek Baradari fascinated him. And because he enjoyed it, he used his power to manipulate events and cause disruption wherever possible. It was Shadrach who was the anonymous Control inside the women's compound who tipped the Baradari about the purloined baby girls!

Xerxes' Harem

The king's royal harem was a multi-building complex within the palace grounds, housed across the garden courtyard from the palace proper. It comprised a series of buildings of golden stone and white and jewel-toned marble and arched porticoes, echoing the construction of the palace but on a smaller scale, surrounded by a thick wall taller than the height of a man. Every window of the harem, whether facing the inner courtyard or built into the outer wall, was grated with intricate but sturdy metal filigree. Obsessive privacy, protection and exclusivity were the buildings' raison d'être.

Inside the harem there were multiple large and lofty columned gathering and lounging spaces with stone ledges on the perimeters, lined and covered in plump velvet and damask cushions stuffed with the softest feathers. The focal point of each of the main salons was a rectangular pool, in the center of which gurgled a stonework fountain, the main spigot fashioned either as a marble fish or a half-draped female figure. There were numerous rooms and apartments arrowing off the main lounging spaces, used for privacy or for storage. Beyond the storage rooms was a covered pathway leading to a vast building that housed the servants who worked in the royal harem, with separate quarters for women and eunuchs. The queen and lesser wives had living quarters connected by marble mosaic corridors and footpaths to the main salons of the harem.

But only the queen had private corridor access from her quarters directly to the quarters of the king.

Despite its airiness and luxury, the House of the Women was a fortress. There were only four doors providing access to the harem, two of which allowed access from the outside world. The harem's main door was in the southwest corner of the outer wall and it was through this relatively small door that the newest virgins entered the harem, and that most business was conducted. A second door that opened from the street wall directly into the kitchen quarters was for tradesmen and food deliveries, and was located a quarter kilometer from the main entrance and farthest from the king's quarters. A third door was in the corner of the wall closest to the king's wing of the palace, and was absolutely forbidden to anyone except the woman who was called to the king's bed on any given night. The fourth door connected the royal harem to the private quarters of the royal Guardian of the Virgins.

The harem, then, was an enclosed world populated by hundreds of essentially dependent women with time on their hands; and despite some outlets or occupations, all the women vied for the sexual attentions of only one man: the king. While this suited the king, it created a highly competitive and oftentimes toxic atmosphere within the cloister.

Within the harem at all times there was a jostling contention for *more*; more personal attendants, more exclusive cosmetics, more luxurious clothing, more personal space, more fawning by the youngest women, and more privileges. Because so few of the women actually were called to attend the king with any frequency, with time a cloistered girl's purpose narrowed to the goal of surviving as best she could within this women's world. Every action of every girl became focused on attaining ever higher levels within the harem's strict social framework.

Within the harem the moods and rivalries, tempers and insecurities, the granting and withholding of material privileges and favors by the persons in charge, all converged to create an unstable and fraught atmosphere. Imagined and concocted plots and intrigues occupied the minds of many of the harem's women. For a girl to survive in this cloistered women's world it was necessary to perfect the ability to tiptoe between the many schemes and personalities, and to curry favor. Ironically, the improbable goal of achieving favor with the king faded to secondary importance next to the prime goal: surviving within the House of the Women.

It is into this complex, foreign and often hostile women's world that Esther was foisted. For a girl like Esther, who has lived all her life in a home where she had every privilege, was a prime focus and was of genuine value—she was, in essence, a princess in Mordechai's home—waking up in the harem would be akin to being cast as an exile into a hostile and foreign country where everyone spoke and understood a language unknown to her. As a clever girl she would likely survive, but achieving the ultimate success—winning the king's heart—was a virtual impossibility. Her extreme beauty was in fact a hindrance, as it set her up as a rival to every other woman and girl in the harem. She was a neophyte, with no knowledge of either the protocol or the players. She also was a girl with a broken heart, which made her vulnerable. Without friend or champion, Esther was doomed to obscurity and a cushioned, living death.

Hegai

Guarding the House of the Women and the honor of the virgins was Hegai, a formidable bald giant sporting gold piercings in his ears and nostril and with prominent muscles. His eyes and intellect were sharp, and the maids and servants attending within the king's harem responded quickly even to his most subtle eyebrow lift with nods and scurries. Hegai had been in military service under Xerxes' father, Darius, and had served his king faithfully through hundreds of campaigns. Though barely fifty, Hegai had been considered too old for the battlefield, and so had been passed from Darius to Xerxes as Keeper of the

Women, which, next to the Royal Cup Bearer, was one of the closest and most trusted positions in the king's service.

Hegai controlled entrée to the king's bedroom. He controlled access to sex and, thus, to succession.

Though Hegai himself was not a eunuch, as Keeper of the Women he supervised a staff of several hundred persons including eunuchs, pre-pubescent boys, and female servants ranging in age from twelve years to over sixty. Hegai's wife of thirty years had died when he was away on his last military campaign, and the two had been childless. As service to the king was the center of his life, he was contentedly well-situated living alone in his modest quarters adjacent to the Women's residence. He was utterly devoted to his job.

All Hegai's staff were personally trained by him with quasi-military precision. Especially now, as they prepared to open the royal harem to one thousand new girls, there was much to do: beds to prepare, clothing to sew and launder, oils and perfumes to stock, food to order, cook and serve, translators to house. Hegai was a master at organization and he coordinated his quartermastering with Shaashgaz, a eunuch himself and Keeper of the Concubines, in charge of the parallel house across the royal courtyard. Shaashgaz's house had the extra function of running a small nursery for the youngest children of the king's secondary wives. From nurslings to age five the children of the concubines lived within the walls of the women's compound.

Hegai presented a fierce appearance, and truly he suffered fools not at all, ruling the House of the Women like a despot of a tiny country. But he had a well-guarded soft heart and he was a master at evaluating people. The instincts that had saved him, his men and his king countless times on the battlefield served him well as Keeper of the Women. He was well familiar with Xerxes' personality and volatile moods, and after years of presenting the king with women, he prided himself on knowing which girl would suit his master, and when.

His objective this time was unique, however. Hegai had never before had a hand in choosing a queen. He was looking forward to the challenge.

Esther in the King's Harem

Esther was heartbroken. When she awoke in her bed in the *khaabgaah*, the dormitory of the virgins, on those first few mornings, there was a blissful instant when she thought she was still in Mordechai's house, hopeful and betrothed. Then the awful reality pressed into her awareness like a glass splinter, causing excruciatingly sharp pain impossible to evade. The reality was that she was captive inside the royal harem and she would never again see her girlhood home or her beloved.

She had spent her first week in a miasma of misery, passively going through the motions of being processed by Hegai's servants. She stood on lines and went along without putting up any resistance. She was assigned a bed and was measured for clothing. She was issued two changes of daytime tunics and trousers and two night dresses. She was asked her food preferences and if she had any requirements for her beauty regime. At first she was numb to her situation; she was but one of the hundreds of kidnapped virgins held in the king's harem for his pleasure. But by the second and third weeks she roused herself, coming to terms with the reality that no rescue was possible or forthcoming. Once reconciled to this—that her identity as Hadassah the Jewess had once and truly ended—she literally squared her shoulders and *became* Esther, the Persian.

Perhaps it was Heaven-sent that Elizeh, her young friend from the transport, clung to her. Watching Elizeh mourn and withdraw and refuse to speak or eat, Esther saw that the girl was not only making herself sick; she was causing difficulty for the servants and had become a concern to Hegai. So Esther mothered the girl, holding her and speaking softly to her. She coaxed her to bathe, dress and eat, and in the process Esther began to see her own path to survival. She resolved to lock the door to her past and focus only on the present and her future. The platitudes she was whispering to the child Elizeh every night with some result, were slowly working their bit of magic on her, too. Esther, no stranger to tragedy, knew the formula for survival. After all, she had survived the death of her parents; she had become a cherished daughter-of-the-house to an at-first-indifferent Mordechai; she had eventually won his heart and that of everyone who had come into her small orbit. She would survive in the Harem, too. The key, she reminded herself, was to make no waves, become no one's enemy, and, if possible, find a protector.

Hegai

Hegai, keeper of the House of the Virgins with undisputed authority over his domain, was not unaware of Esther's ministrations to the distraught girl Elizeh. Esther had caught his experienced eye on the night she was brought in with the first transport. He recognized her even then — tattered and nearly catatonic with grief — as an exceptional beauty. He thought she could be on the short list of girls who might have a chance at becoming queen. But Hegai was a wise old campaigner and he did not rush his fences. He was looking for a particular alchemy of physical beauty and personal — *something*. He knew that part of his job was to scout out the virgins in his charge and put forward the few he thought could best fulfill the king's image of Queen of Persia. In this he intended to take his time in order to be sure. He had twelve months to observe and take the girl's measure.

Yet so quickly, he thought, this girl Esther was proving herself not only lovely to look at but also possessed of a kind soul and a compassion for others. She was singularly unlike the other girls who, once they got over the shock of being taken, took to the regime of unguents and oils and perfumes with avid and obsessive relish. This girl Esther was refreshingly aloof from the scramble for beauty treatments and servants. Hegai took note.

Esther had made the work of his servants easier by taking on the care of the girl Elizeh. She was clearly suffering great sadness herself; he had heard it from the captain of the Home Guard that Esther had been abducted moments before becoming a bride. That must surely be weighing on her, yet she exerted such discipline on her comportment and her emotions that her face and posture showed none of her misery. In fact, with each day that passed Hegai became more certain that she was the finest maiden in the harem.

This despite the bit of pressure he was feeling from one member of the king's court who had brought his daughter to the harem door the first day of the virgin dragnet. The courtier Haman thought a lot of himself; he had made it clear to Hegai's face that he expected the Guardian of the Virgins—whom he treated like just another of the king's innumerable servants—to accord his daughter special privileges and even to push forward her candidacy with the king. Hegai was above taking umbrage at the man's superciliousness, but he absolutely took his duties seriously and would resist with every fiber of his being a pressure to promote one girl over another. Duty was everything to Hegai, and he intended to make up his own mind in this, as in everything else he did for his king.

And the courtier's daughter, Zareen, was a nice-looking girl. She lived up to her name, and was in truth a golden vision. Yellow hair and bluest eyes, and a nice shape to her, if a bit too round on bottom. She also was not very tall. The blessing was that the girl seemed not to have inherited her father's pushy ways. She was respectful, if chatty. And she had a bed near Esther's. It would be interesting to see how they would get along. Hegai ran a tight operation and tried to keep the necessary jealousies and territorial battles in check. He allowed nothing to interfere with his objective.

Esther

Esther was worried for Elizeh. She had noticed several other inconsolable girls brought in with the first dragnet, and they had been tolerated or ignored for the first week after their arrival in the harem. Esther had a soft spot for the displaced and inconsolable, so she kept an informal tab on where the girls slept, listening to their soft sobs in the night. But abruptly after the first week, these night sounds were no more. Neither could Esther find the girls' tear-stained faces at meal times or in the bath house. She was careful not to draw attention to herself by asking questions, but she had sharp hearing and, as well, she understood several languages and dialects. She folded and refolded her Turkish bath sheet as she stood nearby to three girls whispering as they chose their perfumed oils.

"They took that girl from the Indus. They just came and got her during the night. In the morning another girl was folding her own clothing on the girl's bed," said one.

The second girl leaned closer. "I overheard one of the maids saying it was about time; that this was no place for cry-babies. We won't be seeing *her* again."

"Well, that's one less girl for us to worry about, anyway. Less competition," quipped the third. The other two girls giggled and all three moved on.

Esther's stomach lurched, though her face remained composed as always. She wished she knew what had become of the crying girls. But she strongly suspected it couldn't be good. She had been taught well, and she craved information. She wished she could ask someone. But she was wise enough to know that her best course was to keep her ears open and her sad young friend in as compliant a mood as possible. She had no desire to have Elizeh "dealt with" by the king's strong men. *Oh, where is my guardian angel when I need him?* she thought.

Abednego

Abednego was nearby, an invisible presence not far from wherever Esther happened to be. He waited until she had left the morning meal and was walking alone back to the virgins' *khaabgaah*, and, still invisible, he walked by her side. He waited for her to come out of her own thoughts and sense his presence.

"Oh! You are here!" Esther did not even break stride on the marble walkway. She took a peek to be sure she was still alone. "I yearn to know of Mordechai and Poupeh." She paused momentarily, listening to her instincts, then continued walking. "But of course, that is not why you are here. You have heard my thoughts and have information for me about the absent girls. What has become of them?"

Abednego took pity on the girl, all-duty on the outside, but yearning and sad within her pure heart. "Mordechai lives, but he rages inside himself, and paces every day, back and forth before the harem courtyard gates. He craves bits of news of you and bribes his kitchen spy. But time will cool both of your blood. As for Poupeh, she is always sad, pining for you, but she does her duty, and cares for Mordechai.

"Now about the missing girls. The ones who have not become reconciled to the harem and who pose a threat to the morale of the rest of the girls are taken out silently. They are drugged and brought to the brothels, where they will remain slaves for as long as they are serviceable. The Baradari brothers pay a high fee for these girls, for they are choice virgins. These girls will never be heard from again."

Esther gasped and stopped short. Her tender heart was wrung. "Is there no hope for them?"

"None. Not while the Amalek Baradari have control. If you value your young friend you must shake her out of her misery and instruct her to make the most of her new life in the House of the Women. This is the best fate open to her now."

Esther understood what her invisible guardian left unsaid: that his advice was equally applicable to herself; that the harem was her fate, and that she must deploy all her faculties in order to thrive and succeed here. She possessed the significant gifts of a strategic brain and an exquisite beauty. They were also her tools. She must use them.

Coming out of her reverie Esther sensed that her guardian had gone. She continued walking alone, her mind busy.

Hegai

Over the course of the six weeks since the first dragnet of the virgins, Hegai collected reports from his harem spies and he watched the girls himself. This was a serious business. By now the girls had begun being subjected to various facial and physical enhancements. Some who showed promise were permitted lessons in musical instruments, exotic dance, voice and song, even weaving. The very motivated ones were tutored in posture and the most able in languages. And some aristocratic girls were trained in archery and horsemanship. All this was with the view to producing young women who would hold the king's interest.

All Hegai's informants placed the girl Esther at the head of her classes. Of course Esther had had the advantage of having been tutored, in effect, for her entire life, by Poupeh, in the art of being both a lady and a hostess, and by Mordechai in the diplomatic and intellectual pursuits. Aside from her facility with languages, she was literate — she could read and write — as well as artistic, and had an unfailingly pleasing demeanor. But Hegai did not know or even care about Esther's provenance; all he saw was a ready-made queen.

One morning, two months after she had been taken to the harem, as the girls were dispersing to their rooms and occupations, an old, dignified woman appeared at Esther's side. Esther recognized her as Farah, the woman in charge of the harem servant girls.

"Will you follow me." It was a gentle statement, not a request, and Esther recognized it as a summons. She followed the graceful old woman. They walked through an archway that she had never passed through before; indeed, the girls had been warned never to trespass in that direction. The marble floor was a fine white with black mosaic borders. The walls were lined with tall veils of pale yellow. The woman stopped at a black door studded with star-shaped nails. She did not knock. There was a small opening at the top of the door that was covered and controlled from the inside. Esther heard the soft rasp of metal on wood as it slid open and closed. The door swung open noiselessly into a large apartment. The old woman bowed away leaving Esther standing in the doorway.

"Come in, Esther." Hegai was standing at a large window covered in filigreed ironwork and infiltrated by a live vine with yellow flowers. Esther took one step into the room, then another as Hegai motioned her to come near. She stood before him, not docile — she was not a servant — but attentive. Esther heard Abednego's instruction in her ear: *This is your fate, Esther. Make it your world. Succeed beyond anyone's expectations. Hegai is a key.* Esther lowered her eyes to her toes as befitted a girl being addressed by a "governor." Hegai smiled to himself.

"Esther, you have pleased me. You have excelled in all areas. I am told by Farah that the servants tell her that you aid them in their work in subtle ways, folding your clothing and bath sheets and those of the girl Elizeh. I am also aware that it is due entirely to your ministrations that Elizeh is at last acclimating to life here in the House of the Women. Farah says the girl has a sweet nature and is skilled at needlework. She can be of use here. Thank you." Hegai paused, and Esther, utterly surprised at the word of thanks, looked up and into Hegai's face.

"I am pleased to be of service, Master Hegai," Esther said.

Hegai was watching her intently, and what he saw confirmed his instinctive liking. Aside from beauty, this girl — not yet out of her teens — possessed compassion and understanding, and, importantly, an attitude of dignity and respect beyond her years. There was an aura of acceptance about her; there was no underlying tension or ambition that he could detect. She had a calming way about her and it radiated out to others; to him. He was momentarily stunned to feel this; at his age he had thought himself jaded and immune.

Hegai continued. "But Farah also reports that you have made no special requests for cosmetics, enhancements and treatments. Why have you not done so? Do you not enjoy being pampered?"

Esther did not respond immediately. She *had* been resistant to using the complicated cosmetics and beauty treatments that so obsessed the other girls. She had been accustomed while in Mordechai's house to using only scented bath oils and moisturizing creams, and some kohl around her eyes for special occasions. But since her aborted wedding night she had had an aversion to using even those. Of course she washed her glorious hair, but afterwards she coiled and pinned it at her nape rather than letting it loose or plaiting it with golden threads. She had twisted her hair in a knot in silent protest, unintentionally highlighting her graceful neck and her doe-eyes.

But standing before Hegai, she knew this to be a moment of truth; she must today—now—take the giant step from girlhood to womanhood. By trusting herself to Hegai she would be assenting to be a willing candidate for Queen of Persia. By so doing she would commit herself to making the effort to win the prize. She was sufficiently intuitive to know that this was the reason Hegai had called her before him. He wanted a sign from her that she would submit to being primed for candidacy. The paradox was that by submitting she knew she would thrive here in the world of the king's harem, where she had no wish to be. She had no choice but to plight her troth to Hegai; to put her future into his hands. She began by mending fences.

"I meant no insult, Master Hegai. It is that I have no experience with cosmetics and enhancements. I would welcome your guidance and Farah's instruction."

This was the perfect answer. Hegai nodded. "And that is exactly what we will do. From this moment you will conscientiously follow my precise instructions and those of Farah. I will appoint seven handmaids to attend to your dress, your hair, your skin, your diet and your athletic activity. You will be assigned special rations and an enhanced menu geared to bringing forth your best appearance and performance. Farah herself will attend to your instruction in the bedroom arts. You will be moved from the *khaabgaah* today, and will no longer associate with the other girls."

"I am grateful, Master Hegai." Esther hesitated; Hegai waited. Master Hegai, may I inquire what is to become of Elizeh?"

And Hegai, pleased at her interest, responded, "It is to your credit that you care for the girl. To put your mind at ease I will assure you that no harm will come to her. She is not fit for general harem duties; I will find her a place in the textile house, where she can have an easier time of it among the older seamstresses and needle-women. They will tutor her in embroidery skills and in lace-making, and she will have an opportunity to prove herself to them. If she does well she has the potential to become a valuable member of the palace staff."

Esther bowed her head in silent thanks. Hegai was going to great lengths to please her. She promised herself that she would repay him in kind by meticulously following his and Farah's tutelage. She also made a mental note to get word to Elizeh so the girl would apply herself to her needlework and not fret.

Hegai clapped his hands and instantly Farah appeared to hear his instructions. In no time at all the wheels were in motion. Esther was moved from the general dormitory into a private, three-room suite nearby to Hegai's quarters. The apartment had its own bath as well as a private walled patio with a sunken pool. Everywhere were flowering plants and lush greenery, indoors as well as on the patio and climbing its high perimeter walls. Farah took charge of Esther's beauty regime, following Hegai's blueprint.

Esther had no way of knowing whether she was Hegai's single, chosen candidate, or if there were several others also so favored, making her but a "finalist" in the great competition. But she lived up to her promise to him and applied herself to her preparations.

Esther

The special maids newly assigned to Esther were experienced at attending to royalty. Three of them had attended to Queen Vashti in lowly capacities and were sweet-tempered, possessed of valuable knowledge of the king's likes and dislikes, and eager to be of service to this new and favored lady. Once it became known among the harem's maids and servants that Esther had Hegai's imprimatur, they were eager to be of service, and Esther began cautiously to welcome their unobtrusive but solicitous company.

Though she missed her friendship with the girl Elizeh, her new elite status and its resultant segregation from the general harem population was a boon to Esther for a reason other than being fast-tracked to the palace. The competition to become queen of Persia was taken very seriously by most of the virgins, and some girls took their competitive zeal to extremes. While in the *khaabgaah* Esther's standout beauty had singled her out as a common target by several factions of girls. She became the object of much envy, petty and outrageous invasions of privacy, and, at first, small nuisance tricks and indignities. Both she and Elizeh had been followed into the private bath areas and spied upon by other girls, anxious to see if she was truly beautiful all over, if she covered up her imperfections with tunics and trousers, or if she had private beauty rituals they could copy for themselves. Other girls slid underneath Esther's bed at night to eavesdrop on any secret incantations she might make, or if she talked in her sleep. Still others copied her diet, watching her intently and counting the number of green grapes she ate, or how many drops of clover honey she put into her morning tea.

One time Esther had stepped into her slippers and was stung and bloodied by nettles that had been secreted in the toes. Another day she had found sand in her hair brush and in her body cream. But recently the attacks had escalated beyond petty to actually threatening. Just last week she surprised a live scorpion on her scented bed sheet when she turned down her covers; only her quick reflexes saved her from a deadly bite. And a day or two later she had became violently ill after taking just one spoonful of her usual afternoon meal of *fesenjen*, a pomegranate and walnut stew. The chef, outraged and fearful lest anyone think his cuisine had made one of the girls ill, took small tastes off Esther's plate when Elizeh brought it back into the kitchen; he detected a trace of poison on her spoon and reported the incident to Hegai.

None of these escalating sabotage behaviors sat well with the Governor of the Virgins. He questioned girls and staff alike, and because Esther's quiet ways had won her friends and supporters in the harem, within a day of the attempted poisoning the girls responsible were informed upon. They confessed and were quickly removed from the harem, their beds given to others. But following her narrow escape Esther had remained cautious of eating anything at all until Farah had sat her next to her and they had shared a plate. Esther would not be pleasing to the king if she were too thin.

So it was propitious that Hegai plucked Esther out of the harem's general population. Indeed, Esther was not only relieved be rid of the harem's intrusions; she also was aware that Hegai might well have saved her life.

Mordechai

For the week following Esther's abduction in the virgin roundup Mordechai's house and street were patrolled by two of the royal home guards. The captain had no hard feelings about the resistance by Mordechai and his two friends; indeed, he rather admired their behavior of that night. They had acted like men and, even without weapons, had tried to protect the young bride-to-be. But the captain could brook no serious opposition to his operation, and so he took the precaution of mounting a guard. The reality of the situation was clear to the people of Susa: the crown would not tolerate any interference with its edict to collect the kingdom's beautiful virgins for the king's harem.

But no law prevented Mordechai from suffering in private. He could barely sleep or eat, and his spies inside the palace and harem were useless to him. Apparently there was a crackdown and a moratorium within the palace compound, creating a virtual drought of any smuggled information. The need to know was eating at Mordechai. One night in the second week after Esther had been taken Mordechai paced his salon, Shimon standing at the window and Eliezer seated in the desk chair. The three were trying to reconstruct the early advent of the virgin dragnet. The shoe was on the other foot; Mordechai, long the cool spymaster, had become the distraught operative and his two "brothers" played the role of cool-headed, rational Control.

Shimon was reporting. "Mordechai, we have paid bribes, we have pressured the kitchen staff, and we are sure you yourself have left feelers for Abbas. Nobody's talking. Not Old Daniel, not the cook, not the scribe, and not the wine steward." Shimon sent a pleading glance to Eliezer.

"The way we see it," continued Eliezer, "this virgin roundup was so secret and unprecedented that the king probably put the word out that anyone passing stray information from the palace or the women's compound would be put to death. Nobody wanted to risk that."

"Also, the decision to move the operation forward by twelve hours was apparently last-minute," Shimon added. "I overheard the guard at the head of the street saying that they were not even told in advance that they would not be going home that night; this breached their usual protocol.

"For the hundredth time, Mordechai, it is not your fault that you had no advance knowledge that the dragnet had been moved up a day! The place was on an information lockdown. *Nobody knew.*"

"But 'knowing' is my business, Shimon. I'm responsible for her. I should have insisted she leave with your sister's daughter Rachel. I'm haunted by what Hadassah must be going through. My God! She's never been farther from this house than the bazaar, and that with Poupeh holding her arm tightly." Mordechai closed his eyes, torturing himself. Shimon and Eliezer looked at each other, sharing their friend's misery.

Abruptly, Mordechai tapped his fist on the wall next to the door. He straightened and seemed to gather himself. He approached Shimon and put his arm around his boyhood friend. Facing Eliezer and including him in his glance, he sounded almost like the old familiar Mordechai. "Thank you, my friends, for standing sentry on me this week. I suspect the truth is close to what you are both saying, but still, I am filled with regret that I didn't know earlier. That I couldn't hide her. That I didn't send her away, or marry her sooner." He shook his head. "I should have married her sooner." Mordechai paused, then seemed to gather himself. "But I will bury these useless thoughts. They are an indulgence we cannot afford. Starting now I will take it on *myself* to keep tabs on Hadassah. I have a limited access, and I have friends. I will walk the outer courtyard of the House of the Women, make my presence known, and when an opportunity presents itself I will find out how she is doing. This is *my* mission now: to watch over her." Mordechai flexed his shoulders. "Anyway, it's time I was back in the field."

It felt good to have even the skeleton of a plan.

"Well, in that case you'd better start thinking of Hadassah as Esther," cautioned Shimon. "Remember, you told her not to reveal her people or her kindred. She's a smart girl, Mordechai. She won't tell. She has been trained by the best. She will be all right. She's a survivor. Have confidence in her. She left here as "Esther" and that's who she is: a Persian girl from an aristocratic family, more beautiful and valuable than even she knows."

"And once things have quieted down a bit we can start to get messages to her so she knows we're watching," finished Eliezer.

The three friends embraced and Shimon and Eliezer left for their homes and their beds.

Mordechai stood alone in his salon, staring unseeingly down at his hands braced on his desk. *What can these hands do to help Hadassah? I fear we all are caught in a powerful whirlpool. Can one man – or one girl – make any difference? I will go tomorrow to patrol the courtyard of the House of the Women, and somehow I will get a message to Hadassah…to Esther, and one to Abbas. Old Daniel must see me!*

"Mordechai." At the sound of the familiar rasping voice behind him, Mordechai turned slowly. He stared daggers at the familiar hooded form of his spymaster. By force of will he held himself back from going to the man who had been his teacher and his Control for over half his life, shaking him and demanding why he had not kept the king's men from taking Hadassah, or at least warned him of the change of plan. He wanted to force him to promise to keep her safe and, however irrationally, to bring her back to him. But Mordechai only clenched and unclenched his fists and peered into the hooded and shaded face, allowing the Master to read all that was in his heart.

The hooded man spoke. "Esther is the one, Mordechai. She is the *only* one who can save us from the coming Terrors. This isn't about you, a foiled groom, and it isn't about one ruined Jewish virgin. It's about the life and death of *all* of us. She will need you to be strong, Mordechai. She must know absolutely that her life as Hadassah is no more, and that you are irretrievably lost to her. She cannot hold out any hope of a rescue. She became a sleeper agent as of the moment she was taken into the harem. Making a success of herself there, *as Esther,* is her only option. She must turn her back on one life and embrace another. And you must help her to see this. Otherwise we are all doomed."

It was a long speech by the Master's standards. Much rode on his impressing Mordechai with the gravity of Esther's mission. Mordechai absorbed the message, and kept silent. When he next blinked, the hooded man was gone, and he was alone in the salon.

Thereafter Mordechai single-mindedly arranged his time so that he could spend as much of his day as possible patrolling the courtyard of the House of the Women. As the weeks passed, Mordechai became a familiar and recognizable figure to the various courtiers, servants and guards in the busy outer courtyard. An affable fellow, he presented a dignified and concerned appearance, so that eventually the palace staff cautiously befriended him. Over time, they even sought his advice on various personal or palace matters. Mordechai's opinions were always measured and helpful, and, as was his intention, the staff at the outer courtyard came to expect to see him at his "post," and missed him if he was busy elsewhere. He let it be known that he had a familial interest in one of the girls who had been taken into the harem, but that was not unusual, as nearly everyone in Susa had been touched by the virgin dragnet. Nearly every courtier had a friend or cousin or cousin's cousin to whom they passed messages from home.

By night, Mordechai stayed in touch with his kingdom-wide network of agents. He read, wrote, strategized and responded to "flying" letters: scrolls and messages that were written in disappearing ink, cipher or code. Or the letters had been penned in the ancient language of Jerusalem's Temple priests, a script and language unknown and indecipherable to anyone who had not been taught its secrets by a master. The letters were sent via the fleetest horses, carried by sworn and proven messengers, and ridden over Darius's postal roads mostly overnight to all corners of the Empire.

Zareen

Haman had covered many palms with coins, bribing anyone susceptible, to hear how his only daughter, Zareen, fared in the House of the Women. Even so, it was only because a distant cousin of his mistress happened to be a lowly harem attendant that he discovered quite by accident that there was an elite category of girls being singled out by master Hegai for special treatment. Haman intended that Zareen would be one of those girls. He pressured his mistress's cousin and made promises he had no intention of keeping; he left small pouches of coins for his kitchen contact, and he left messages to be delivered to Zareen, telling her to ready herself with care, saying that she would be tapped to move out of the harem very soon.

Hegai was not susceptible to bribes, but neither was he naïve. He knew of the pressures being exerted by various courtiers to advance their daughter or cousin in the ranks of candidates for queen. But it also happened that Hegai was clever, and he knew the ways of his master, Xerxes. While Hegai privately placed his "bet" on the girl Esther, he was sufficiently experienced to know that his king might not see it his way. So Hegai hedged his bet, and — heedless of Haman's jockeying and bribes — he decided to advance Zareen — as different physically and temperamentally from Esther as she could be — to the finalist level. The girl was plump and curvy, blonde and blue-eyed, loquacious and experienced. Who knew what type of girl the king would want when the time came to for him to choose a queen? Hegai did not want to be left bereft of girls in the elite pipeline if Xerxes rejected Esther.

So Zareen, too, was taken out of the larger harem population and along with three other girls and Esther, she was primed for her special night of audition before the king.

When Haman heard of this he was extremely pleased. His star was ascending and everything was going according to plan.

Abbas

Abbas was kept busy as an elusive intermediary between Daniel and Mordechai. He had two tasks: The first was to keep an eye on Mordechai, and to let his master know if the man behaved in any way that could potentially draw the attention of the king's officers to him. Mordechai had spiraled into deep sadness after Hadassah had been taken, on the very night their wedding was to have taken place. So until Mordechai stabilized, his master insisted on knowing Mordechai's whereabouts at all times. He didn't put it past the man to infiltrate the harem to try to extricate the girl. Mordechai had powerful heroic instincts as well as a need to control people and events. Daniel had charged Abbas with watching and, if necessary, interceding to prevent Mordechai from doing damage to Daniel's own secret and incipient plan.

Abbas's second task was to watch over Old Daniel himself. Until Daniel officially passed the mantle of spymaster, he alone was the seer, the possessor of all secrets, the one who carried the complex and delicate master plan in his head.

In the House of the Women
Preparing for a Night with the King

As the weeks became months, the girls acclimated to Hegai's regime in the House of the Women as if they had been born to it. The period of quarantine and preparation was a total of twelve months, counted from the day each girl was plucked from her home and deposited into the harem, and ending on the night, one year later, when she would be called to audition for Xerxes.

Hegai's task, during these months of sequestration, was, first of all, to ascertain that none of the "virgins" was pregnant. Next, he allowed each girl the cosmetics and enhancements to bring to perfection her own special beauty. Hegai had no intention or desire to alter their individual personalities; indeed, the very variety of girls was staggering and no doubt would prove exciting to the king. There were shy country girls who had never been outside their village, sly city girls who were eager to try their skills, and every possible variety of inexperienced maid besides. All of them were readied, in turn, to vie for the greatest prize a woman in Persia could dream of: the one-in-ten-thousand chance of being chosen Queen of Persia.

For six months the girls were cleansed, rubbed and exfoliated, before being soothed and wrapped in sheets infused with oil of myrrh. Every trace of their past lives on skin, scalp and nails was erased; their girlhood was banished to a distant memory as the rigors of the harem took on their own rhythm. Most of the girls, accustomed to the dry, arid climate of their homes, were treated to anti-wrinkle and moisturizing treatments they never dreamed existed, and which turned back the clock, plumping their skin and making even the youngest of them appear childlike. Hegai's unguents were antiseptic as well as antifungal, and any skin conditions the girls had were treated and cured. Hegai charged his corps of expert harem women to inspect every crevice of every girl to ensure, as much as possible, tactile and visual perfection before they were sent to the king.

For the second six months the girls' skin was softened and perfumed with creams and fragrant emollients. Shepherd girls from the Indus mountains and servant girls from the great homes of Persepolis were massaged by expert masseuses on scores of tables laid out side by side in one of the great halls in the House of the Women. Soothing teas were brewed, steeped, cooled and sipped. At this final stage of their beautification, even the hidden spaces between the girls' toes were softened and tended. Oils infused with jasmine were rubbed into their hair, and the girls learned to walk erect from bath house to luncheon salon wrapped in heavy, heated cloth turbans.

Myrrh in particular was a wonder-oil, as it repelled insects, prevented sunburn, and promoted wound healing. It also was used in the incense candles that burned night and day in the House of the Women. The special blended oils of cassis, olive, and myrrh, and the potions of honey and wildflowers had the additional special property of uplifting the spirits and banishing feminine cramps and joint pain. There were no long faces in the harem by the end of the year of beautification.

Each girl was encouraged to use her native region's natural cosmetics, and once these concoctions were approved for use, the harem women were allowed to engage in cross-cultural cosmetic exchanges. The Egyptian girls were expert at lining their eyes with kohl. Persian girls demonstrated the benefits of henna on their thick black hair. And Greek girls used pomegranate juice to bring a blush to their cheeks and red to their lips. The girls watched each other closely, and they borrowed and hoarded cosmetics as it suited them.

The girls also used the twelve months to learn the Persian language and special Susan dialect if they did not already know it. The king required the girls to be versed in sufficient Persian to — if not converse — then to follow his commands.

Esther and the four other girls who had been culled from the harem were treated to a more exclusive and personalized treatment regimen that echoed but surpassed the schedule in use in the House of the Women. And while the general harem girls had the benefit and also the various drawbacks of feminine companionship, the five "finalists" did not. Because Hegai had advanced them over the other girls in the harem, they were individually sequestered in separate quarters within the palace fortress in a kind of luxurious solitary confinement. They were visited only by their maids and attendants, and their beauty regimens were secretly their own. It was noted by Farah and recounted to Hegai that while the other finalists demanded special and often rare creams, oils and enhancements, Esther made no demands; she had placed herself into Hegai's expert hands, relying entirely on his and Farah's beautifying suggestions.

Esther

Heeding Abednego's veiled instruction, and calling up reserves of inner strength she had not know she possessed, Esther walled up her sadness and threw herself into the role of short-list candidate for queen of Persia. She created a new world for herself in her cloister-within-the-cloister. It was as if the veil of misery had fallen away and Esther's natural optimism, resilience, curiosity and empathy returned in force. Esther began to take an eager interest in her new "home." She inquired about the lives and interests of her seven personal maids. While some of the servants were only a little older than she, most others were mothers and even grandmothers. Esther inquired about their families, and ensured that they had enough to eat and daily rest periods, so that over time the servants grew devoted to her.

Esther had the special touch of creating calm and pleasantness wherever she dwelt. In Esther's quarters one could hear the maids humming softly, going happily about their duties. The veteran palace maids, who, in their time, had served harem girls and queens alike, could distinguish a fine lady when they saw one. Esther spoke softly and courteously to the servant women in their own dialects, and she never spoke in anger. She was authentic queenly material in their eyes. There would have been nothing Esther could have asked of her maids and servants that they would not have acceded to happily and with alacrity. And in the way of servants, the maids whispered words of praise of "their" Esther to the other servants, so that word filtered up to Farah, the matron in charge, and thence to Hegai. Hegai smiled to himself, pleased that his initial judgment of Esther had proved correct. With every passing day He became even more convinced that Esther was possessed of the qualities of royalty. What remained was to have Farah tutor her in bedroom arts. Hegai sighed.

Mordechai

Mordechai spent at least three hours every day patrolling the outer courtyard of the House of the Women. The courtyard was a vast area where much informal court business was conducted, especially so since the virgin dragnet months before. The population of the House of the Women had swelled enormously, and there was a concomitant increase in the number of nonessential daily workers entering and leaving the compound. These new people were a fertile source of seemingly trivial information that, when combined with the information from Mordechai's reliable sources, provided an accurate picture of Esther's life inside.

Mordechai mingled with the other courtiers, listening and talking with them as he always had done. But since Esther's abduction he increased the pressure on his palace operatives and expected them to report directly to him on a regular basis. Additionally, it was known among the guards and harem workers that there was a courtier who would pay for accurate information about the girl Esther. If there was one thing Mordechai knew, it was to vary his sources of information and to analyze the data himself. It was the best way to know what he needed to know.

Thus it was that Mordechai knew that Esther had found favor with the Hegai, the keeper of the virgins. And he knew almost to the hour when Esther had been short-listed for seclusion and special treatment.

But even as he painstakingly established a presence and gathered information, throughout all the intervening months Mordechai made no attempt to contact Esther. The spymaster had instructed him that Esther's survival as well as the success of her mission hinged on her being able to close the door on her life in Mordechai's house, immerse herself utterly in the harem, master its complex social rules, and achieve recognition with the keeper of the gateway to Xerxes' bed. While the knowledge of Esther's ultimate destination—sharing the king's bed—caused Mordechai repugnance, agony and nightmares, he figured that in a macabre fashion these nightmares were something he and Hadassah—now Esther—shared. And if the Master expected Esther to rise above her personal tragedy, how could Mordechai do any less?

Esther

As the months passed, Esther's preparation time was rapidly drawing to a close. If possible, she was even more beautiful now than she had been on her failed wedding night nearly a year ago. She had been smoothed and scented, pampered and primed, and the tutelage, when added to her natural elegance, poise and culture, yielded a breathtaking beauty worthy of the crown. Even Farah's frank lectures to her about pleasing the king were taken in the girl's stride. The older woman was wise in the ways of men and women, and also had much experience teaching inexperienced girls about the bedroom arts. Esther absorbed it all, her doe-eyes wide and intelligent, her manner accepting. Esther was an excellent student; Farah presented her subject in an unemotional and calculated fashion, and counted on the girl's high intelligence, youth and quiet determination to win the day.

What worried Esther was not her ability to attract the king. She accepted that she was considered very beautiful; people had been telling her this all her life, though she had little or no conceit. Nor did she dwell on the mechanics of her night alone with the king, though that did cause her a secret anxiety—she was a virgin, after all. Rather, Esther's greatest challenge, as she saw it, was winning. She spent hours of private time considering how she could become the one woman the king could not live without. Sex, even creative and inventive sex, was plentiful and readily available to Xerxes via his harem. An unsophisticated sexual novice, Esther knew she was unlikely to provide the king with the most memorable night of his life. Instead, she sought to discover the "hook;" that special angle or emotion that Xerxes—the man *and* the king—most desired and needed. Once she discovered it, Esther was determined to be the girl to satisfy that need. So she set her formidable brain to analyzing what she knew of Xerxes, in hopes of coming to an understanding of the man. If she could do this, her plan was to make herself irreplaceable.

Haman

As a member of the king's advisory staff Haman had access to the gatekeeper who was in charge of admitting the daily servants who worked in the women's compound. Through this underground mechanism, greased with *bakhshesh*, or bribes, Haman had been exchanging letters with his daughter Zareen since her elevation to one of the five girls on Hegai's short list. He was obsessively curious about Zareen's competition, and had asked his daughter about the other four girls who had been singled out for special treatment. He stood in a palace corridor reading her response.

"Father, I do not know if I can answer your queries with precision. You see, we do not get any time to socialize with the other girls here in the palace, and certainly not with the girls back in the harem. But I was told the names of the other four girls, and one of them is familiar to me from our brief time in the House of the Women. Her name is Esther, and if it is the same girl, she is exceptionally beautiful. She was brought to the harem around the time that you brought me to Hegai. As I recall, she has hair the color of mahogany, and is tall and elegant, quite different from me. Oh, I know what you will tell me: we don't know what the king will prefer this time around. And of course I am hopeful of my chances and am making the most of myself. But really, father, all the girls think *she* may be the one. And you may even know her. She is some relation to a lowly courtier by the name of Mordechai, who hangs about in the courtyard hoping to hear any news of her. Well, it is time for a cosmetics lesson. I will give this scroll to the boy who cleans our *dastsuyi*, our toilets, with instructions to give it to your guard. Your daughter, Zareen."

Haman read the letter twice and fisted it into a ball. *Mordechai again!* he thought. He had vied with the man twenty years before when they had served in the same regiment, but since then he had ignored and surpassed the man, advancing to the inner court while Mordechai hung about as a lower courtier. He had not seriously considered the man as a threat for a long time. *What was Mordechai's connection to the girl called Esther?* Thinking back, Haman recalled that he had seen the girl once, about three years ago, waiting at the gate of Mordechai's house. A contingent of courtiers had been walking home together from the palace one evening. Passing by the various courtiers' houses in turn, when they passed by Mordechai's house Haman had glimpsed a girl as she swung open the gated door to welcome Mordechai home. She had been quite young. A man with an eye for choice female flesh, Haman had taken note of the girl's unusual color hair and her lissome figure, and had felt a stirring of excitement. Her face had lit up as Mordechai approached his house, and Haman had been struck by her loveliness. But the image had faded in the course of his busy schedule and as the years passed. Recalling all this now, Haman remembered his informants had told him that the man had a ward. *Why, the girl Esther must be Mordechai's ward!*

Now he spent a few moments thinking. Mordechai was a nobody; he was in the outer circle of striving nobles, a useful small-time power broker who helped out in diplomatic circles because of his facility with the many languages of the Empire. That this nothing of a man should have as a relation a girl who was beautiful enough to rival his Zareen for the prize of queen of Persia was enraging. It was anathema to Haman that this man's candidate might potentially win the title of queen. Haman could not bear the possibility that Mordechai might then be elevated within the court, and might even stand in a position of power greater than Haman's own! This was not to be borne. There must be a way he could get to this girl Esther, and eliminate her quietly. A pressure point during a massage; a poisoned hair pin stuck into her scalp. He would see to it tonight. The first order of business was to find a chink in Hegai's obsessive security.

Hegai's Strategy

Twelve months to the day after the first virgin roundup, Hegai began sending the virgins, one per night, to Xerxes' bed. Each girl was escorted from the harem to the king's royal apartment, flanked by Farah on one side, and a spear-wielding member of the king's Home Guard on the other. While most of the girls were eager and ready by the evening of their turn, the presence of Farah and the guard was not merely ceremonial; it served to bolster the confidence of the shyer girls if they needed it. Several of the girls had actually fainted dead away while being escorted to the king's chamber, and had been carried off to the House of the Concubines, their turn given to another. There were no second chances in this competition.

On their night of audition for the king the girls were permitted to bring anything they wished along with them, if they could convince Hegai that it was calculated to increase the king's pleasure. Some girls, most often from aristocratic families, knowing that the king enjoyed music, practiced endlessly on the *dotar*, a kind of long-necked lute carved from mulberry wood, and Hegai permitted them to bring the instrument with them on their audition night. It calmed the girls and no doubt also entertained the king. Other girls from the mountainous regions brought along the smaller *dozaleh*, a small wind instrument held in the palm and played by mouth, producing hauntingly plaintive melodies. Some few harem girls from the outer provinces had brought along their *dammam*, the small bowl-shaped goatskin drum that they hung from straps around their necks. The skilled drummer could practically entrance her audience with the nuanced, sensual percussions, and this, too, Hegai encouraged. Some girls performed veil dances, others strip-teases, and still others — girls of a different ilk — memorized poetry or performed small plays. The possibilities were as varied as the girls themselves.

The harem slowly emptied. Each girl spent her one night in the king's chambers, and then in the morning Farah and the Home Guard escorted the girl across the compound to the larger House of the Concubines, run by Shaashgaz, chamberlain to the king and keeper of the lesser wives. The auditioned girls found that their clothing and personal effects had, overnight, been moved to their new home, where they would spend the rest of their days.

It was exceedingly rare for a woman to be recalled by name to return to the king's bed after her one night with him. Many young women lived in hope; most learned quickly to find other pursuits and to adjust to their new, female-centered world. The most these "used" girls could hope for after their night with the king was that they would fall pregnant. In such an eventuality they would achieve a slightly higher status, and would have the duty of raising the young prince or princess in the House of the Concubines until he or she was five years old. There was also the very occasional opportunity of foreign travel with the king's entourage, when the king would select several of his concubines and their young children, and, along with hundreds of servants and soldiers, camels, cooks, tents and gifts, embark on a months-long diplomatic trip. The luckiest of the concubines experienced this, too. After that, well, there was always needlepoint and the endless beauty treatments and wifely gossip.

Hegai calculated that though the king reveled in having rounded up thousands of the kingdom's choicest virgins and having a swelling harem, he would lose patience with the game after about a year. So Hegai judiciously salted the harem girls with his chosen finalists, sending them in to the king at intervals of one elite finalist to every few hundred harem girls.

But Hegai strategically held Esther back from going to the king's bed early in the competition. He did not want her special qualities to be lost in the king's almost adolescent delight at being the focus of so much new, willing, virgin flesh. Hegai's plan was to bide his time, and to gauge precisely when the king had hit the moment when he was feeling a surfeit of sex, and was ready to select a queen. Hegai would monitor the king's mood closely and wait for that night. Only then would he send Esther to the king's bed.

There was only one palace girl left of the finalists besides Esther, and that was Zareen, the yellow-haired girl with ample curves. Hegai would be sending her in next. Hegai had weighed the odds of her charming Xerxes, against his plan to save Esther for last. It was a calculated risk that the king might choose the golden-haired Zareen after his night with her, and that Hegai would lose out on the chance to send Esther for her chance; but Hegai trusted his instinct, and gambled that the king would not be so decisive. Hegai intended to allow the parade of girls to wear down the king's appetite for the new and the eager, and in his calculation the time was almost ripe. He was banking on his king's curiosity about the next night's girl. And Hegai grudgingly credited the king's previous choice of queen; in Vashti, the daughter of a military man, the young Xerxes had selected a girl of quality, choosing her over princesses who had been thrust at him. She had had physical beauty as well as depth. And she had pleased the king for over a decade. Hegai mused that the king was missing Vashti now. Hegai was counting on the king's attraction to Esther's unusual and sensual beauty, and also on his appreciation of her majestic qualities to win the day.

Soon, he thought.

Esther

Esther's seven attendants had spent their lives inside the palace servicing the queen and the concubines. Even the youngest among them were experienced in strategic application of cosmetics, in massage and body treatments, in hairdressing and in wardrobe selection. But Esther's attendants were valuable to her for other reasons, as well. They were a trove of information about the king.

While submitting to their ministrations — prescribed exactingly by Farah and Hegai — Esther encouraged them to talk and reminisce. Esther, a skilled listener, was trolling for any and all scraps of information and clues about Xerxes' character and personality; the way he treated underlings, harem girls, concubines, even the former queen. She paid close attention as the servants eagerly told her of having personally witnessed the king's behavior and speech to his equals, his betters, his children, or his trusted advisors; his fabled rages, and, less frequently, his kindness. Esther, who understood several languages and dialects, eavesdropped shamelessly as the maids spoke softly amongst themselves in her presence, in their peculiar argot, as they cleaned her rooms or prepared her clothing, gossiping happily, remembering other preparations, other girls, other queens.

Bit by bit, Esther was constructing a three-dimensional emotional profile of the king. How did he behave, speak, react? What had the *other* girls told their maids the mornings after? What did the maids see for themselves in the event the girl had remained silent? Was she humming with happiness, or was she bruised? Was she fearful of being called to return to Xerxes' bed, or was she eager for the chance?

And what did the servants see or overhear about the king's behavior at court?

There was much information to be gleaned from servants. Royals most often paid no attention to them, even speaking personal or political confidences in their presence. Also, many of the palace "walls" and room dividers were of insubstantial fabrics, allowing sounds to travel easily. The illusion of privacy encouraged royals to speak their minds, heedless that their conversations were likely overheard. Some of Esther's maids were married to these palace servants, and husbands told wives about the king's and courtiers' business and behaviors.

Raised in the house of a spymaster and trained to observe, catalogue and unobtrusively extract information practically since she could walk and talk, Esther amassed much data. Painstakingly, she analyzed what she knew and formulated a strategy.

Very early one morning, after spending a sleepless night making columns of notes in coded Aramaic, the ancient language of her ancestors, Esther sat back on her divan, her tablet on the low table. Finally, she had before her the picture of the man Xerxes. And none too soon. She knew that Hegai had been holding off sending her to the king until he had worn himself out with the sameness of the other girls. She also knew that she had, at most, a few weeks before her turn would be called. She closed her eyes, relishing the pre-dawn quiet. No servants stirred; even the birds had not yet awakened.

Who is Xerxes? she thought. *He is a man in the prime of his life, with a voracious sexual appetite. No news there. He had enjoyed the strong and beautiful Vashti both in and out of bed. All the maids attested to that. He enjoyed speaking to her, walking with her, toying with her, sleeping with her, watching her dance. He was proud of her, and of his ability to have tamed and mastered her. This was a key.* Esther tapped her finger on the low table, continuing her unspoken analysis. *Xerxes missed Vashti terribly, even now, years after his angry blunder banished the queen and woman who had fascinated him. Even the many girls from his harem had not touched Xerxes' yearning for Vashti. This, too, was a key.*

Esther pondered Xerxes' complexities. She saw a man who craved, not submissiveness, but obedience. An obedient, strong, beautiful, and, yes, intelligent woman would be more of a prize to Xerxes than a passive mannequin, she reasoned. Anyone could easily dominate a vapid vessel; the mere presence of his crown would do the trick, intimidating any ordinary girl. But it took a powerful and fascinating man to win the attentions and obedience of a prize.

Esther saw, in a flash of clarity, that while her beauty was necessary to *attract* the man Xerxes, it was not sufficient to fascinate and to keep him. For that, she must employ and display in turns her intelligence and spirit, her reassuring strength, her pleasing personality and her undemanding but steadfast character. She would bestow all of these on the king; she would offer him not only her body, but the gift of control over a strong and alluring woman.

And overlaying all this was Esther's air of mystery. She must at all cost keep secret from the king her origins and her people. She must appear to Xerxes as if she had been fashioned especially for him. She would be a mystery woman with no past; a cultured and poised woman with a focused willingness to subsume herself in obedience to him. Her past would remain shrouded, but her present and future she would bestow on the king alone. *She* would be the prize he did not know he was seeking.

Esther spent days puzzling out the king's desires and motivations. She desperately needed to understand Xerxes the man, if she intended to win the queen's crown. What did Xerxes most want?

She kept returning to one glaring chink in the process to select the new queen. Everyone assumed that Xerxes wanted his queen to be a virgin, untried by any man but himself. She reasoned that presumably that was in order for Xerxes at all times to feel superior to his bride, powerful and in control. He could be certain of dominating her only if he "stacked the deck," being at all times more sexually experienced than the girl in his bed. But Esther perceived a fatal flaw in this reasoning. It did not allow for a possibility that the king wished for *more* than simply virginity in a mate. Esther was certain the king wished for more than that; virginity was a necessary threshold requirement, but it was not sufficient to retain the king's fascination. This was where all the virgins' plots and plans to win the king failed utterly, from their inception.

Esther reasoned that if what the king most desired was a virgin in his bed, then this contest was doomed to fail, as each girl had a built-in obsolescence after her first night! There was no chance a non-virgin would ever be called by the king for a second night with him, because of course by the end of her first night she was no longer the virgin he required!

There had to be *another key* to Xerxes. Esther was certain that her key to the king lay in tapping this hidden desire.

So Esther listened intently when Farah instructed her in the bedroom arts, but she also paid strict heed to Farah's descriptions of the elements of seduction. Esther intended to excel in the first key element, but then so did the hundreds of other girls. Almost more essential, she reasoned, was to excel in the additional elements of enchanting the man; fascinating him; stimulating his curiosity. In her, Xerxes must have and possess *all* women: the virgin for the excitement he craved, and also the experienced courtesan who surprises and entrances. She needed to be *all* women in order to keep Xerxes returning to her night after night. To this end, Esther learned from Farah when to submit, when to appear to resist, when to initiate, and when to hold back. She prepared a mental list of subjects she would discuss with Xerxes, and of legends she would tell him.

She would master the elements of sex, but more than that, she would seduce and fascinate the man.

Esther resolved to be different in all ways from the other virgins.

Her next stratagem grew out of overhearing the girls giggle about what they would ask from the king. It was known within the harem that the king sometimes bestowed a small gift on girls that pleased him, or he fulfilled a small request. Esther reasoned that because the king's days were consumed with fielding requests for favors—from other nations, from courtiers, from family—Esther resolved *never* to ask a favor of Xerxes, or to ask questions about matters of state and politics. She would confound him. She would stay away from initiating discussion of politics and real-life court intrigue. Once he trusted her there would be plenty of time for her to encourage him to voluntarily talk to her of these matters. But for her audition night she would be disinterested in his *crown*; she would focus instead on the *man*. In preparation, Esther scrupulously conceived and rehearsed involved stories and tales in which a noble and powerful monarch—modeled on Xerxes himself—fought and won battles, loved and won beautiful women, and was ruler of all the eye could see, from horizon to horizon.

Esther groomed herself not only to seduce the king, but also to fire his imagination. A night lasted for only twelve hours; she intended to prepare a varied menu for Xerxes to sample, and to use every minute of her night to her own end.

Haman

Before putting a black marker out on the girl Esther, Haman wanted just one good look at her. If possible, he wanted to observe her without her knowledge. But he had no luck trying to gain a foothold into the wing of the palace that housed the apartments of the harem finalists. All palace walkways were guarded. The public spaces were literally cut off from the private ones and were heavily patrolled. That the palace servants recognized him was a boon as well as a bane; this allowed him to move about relatively freely in the public areas, but it prevented him from gaining entrance into the women's corridors. Hegai's guards did cut him some leniency, though, assuming he was hovering nearby in order to send or receive word from his own daughter, Zareen, who was one of the favored finalists.

So Haman took himself outside, and walked the perimeter of the palace courtyard adjacent to the walled-off women's apartments. He had no specific plan, just an idea that perhaps the guards were less watchful in the courtyard, where the walls were high and thick. He was unsure which of the walled gardens belonged to which girls' apartments, so he patrolled the opposite end of the quadrangle from the cloister walls, keeping them in his sights from a distance.

As it happened, luck was with him. A small wooden door in one of the walls opened and a young woman stepped out. She had something in her hands and bent down to place it gently on the sandy soil outside the wall. He focused for an instant on her hands, and saw that she released a dove into a tree bed. Perhaps it had flown into the cloister and hurt itself, or had fallen from a tree branch. He knew girls placed great store on caring for injured birds and small animals, though he himself enjoyed torturing the creatures.

It was when the girl stood up and took a deep breath before turning to re-enter her walled garden that Haman stood motionless. In that instant the sun shone on her face and hair, setting her aglow. Her tall, slim silhouette stirred his loins. He had never in his life even thought of the word "enchantment," but that is what possessed him. The next instant the girl was gone, called inside by an old servant, the thick door in the courtyard wall shut and locked. His pulse beat a tattoo in his throat and he, a married man with ten children, two mistresses and an evil heart, felt infatuation and a strong surge of lust.

So this was Esther, he thought. On the spot Haman abandoned his inchoate plan to do away with the girl. He had an instant vision of the girl with hair like a flame wearing the crown of Persia, and intuitively knew that his ambitions of planting his own daughter in Vashti's place would come to nothing faced with this girl as competition. Strangely, the looming loss of an opportunity to plant his puppet—his daughter—within the king's innermost circle, paled. His overweening ambition was sidelined by a suffusion of anger mixed with a powerful surge of possession and jealousy when he contemplated Xerxes taking *this* virgin girl to his bed. He clenched his fists. That the girl was somehow connected to the upstart courtier, Mordechai, only strengthened Haman's twin feelings of desire and destruction.

There is more than one way to power, he assured himself. He intended to have the girl for himself, one way or another.

Shadrach

Unbeknownst to Haman, he was being observed and studied. Shadrach, master of evil, had been watching and waiting for decades for just such an opportunity with a man like Haman. When Daniel, Shadrach's ex-friend and nemesis, had waxed great and gone on to serve four successive kings over the past eight decades, Shadrach had kept in the shadows. He had banked his anger and the desire to destroy, and had practiced his black art of mind control on lesser beings to sharpen his skills. But now, with Daniel aged and ignored, Shadrach saw his chance. Before his eyes stood the perfect vehicle for bringing down Daniel and his plans for succession and survival of his precious people. At the same time he could feed his own sexual depravity; destroy what was pure; and advance a murderous foe of the One-God to a position of high power. The enormity of evil he could unleash just by planting some ideas in a man's mind almost made him giddy.

Haman was the perfect instrument for Shadrach because he already embodied, in human microcosm, the same intentional evil as a supernatural Shadrach. Haman would be his agent.

Haman

The thought flew into Haman's head as if by magic. If he could have the girl Esther *before* her turn came to go to the king's bed, then he could kill two birds with one stone: by slaking his lust with Esther he would disqualify the girl from auditioning for the king, leaving his own Zareen with a clear path to becoming queen. And in the same stroke he would deal the upstart Mordechai a humiliating and fatal blow. Putting forward a girl as a virgin for the king's harem, when in fact she was nothing of the sort, was a hanging offense.

Mordechai

Mordechai made his way home when the day was cooling into evening. He was walking on the far side of the palace wall, beyond which lay kilometers of sand dunes. The sere landscape afforded protection at the northern borders of the king's fortress; it was possible to see enemies coming hours before they could come close enough to do harm. In the solitude of the waning day, Mordechai reflected on what had become his life. He was now all-duty; any thoughts and plans of romance and love had been burned out of him the night Hadassah was stolen from him. He figured he had made good use of the past twelve months, befriending the palace guards and chamberlains, listening and memorizing, always watching, cataloguing information, and planning his moves. All with the objective of keeping tabs—to the extent possible—on Hadassah. While at the same time, for the good of his people, and to keep himself from going mad, he worked hard to cauterize his heart so as not to bleed for the loss of the girl who was his heart's desire. But though he presented a resigned face, Mordechai still dreamed of his Hadassah every night.

His spymaster, Old Daniel, had admonished him roundly. That part of his life was over. Hadassah was dead and Esther stood in her place, their secret weapon. The Terror was coming, and if his people were to survive, they would need a friend very close to the power. The Master was certain that Esther was that tool and that weapon. Her beauty would be the key to the king's bed chamber and, with luck, to the crown and proximity to power.

"Mordechai." The familiar rasp, projected from the hooded figure by his side, stopped Mordechai cold and had him turning to face the shadowed Master.

"Master," Mordechai acknowledged him. He gave his report: "The agents are poised, ears sharpened to hear any and all rumbles of trouble. The runners, the riders and the scribes—all have been primed. They go about their normal activities, but they are on active reserve." Mordechai paused. When the Master remained silent, Mordechai understood the man had not come to hear his report. He had come to tell Mordechai some news. So Mordechai waited.

"Esther's turn is very soon." The Master paused to see if Mordechai would flinch; the man did not move a muscle. "She has not been alone. Abbas has been keeping ears and eyes on her, and Azariya has been her guardian angel since the night she was taken. She is a girl to be proud of, Mordechai. The quiet ones often are," he muttered *sotto voce*. "She remembers all your lessons. She has kept the secret, not revealing her people or her kindred, though this has not been a simple matter. I have come to tell you that in three days she will be called, and thereafter she will either be sent to the House of the Concubines or, in the best of worlds— but let's not tempt the fates—she will remain in the palace."

Mordechai had tensed at the mention of three days. At Daniel's behest, once Esther had entered the harem Mordechai had had no direct communication with her. Both he and Hadassah had been instructed to make the break cleanly. He wondered now if she ever thought of him. But then, catching himself, he hoped she did not. A true agent-in-place would not survive for long unless she immersed herself completely in her new identity. Slipping into nostalgia or regret, or allowing her old self to intrude even momentarily, could prove fatal. While Mordechai-the-man would have wished for a different scenario, as an objective spymaster he fervently hoped Esther's training and character had girded her for what lay ahead. She would need strength and focus.

But the Master was not yet done.

"Azariya tells me that he has felt and perceived much dark activity. It is diffuse during the day, but at night he senses it clearly. This means that Hananya has grown bold and strong. He is not even bothering to mask his activity, except from me." The Master paused, allowing Mordechai to intuit the implication of what he had said.

"You are saying that Esther can be in danger." Mordechai knew the story of the long-ago transformation of Hananya into the depraved and wicked Shadrach. He did not doubt Shadrach's powerful need to destroy, and his blood turned cold at the possibility of Esther being in his sadistic crosshairs.

"Yes," replied the Master, "and not just Esther. If Hananya is audacious and unshielded with his thoughts, then it is almost certain he has found a human vehicle through whom he will act. And it is logical that he will attack at our weakest point, which right now is probably Esther. He assumes she is alone and unprotected, but of course she is not. Abbas, Azariya and I will be shielding her at every moment. What concerns me is that she will be unprotected once she enters the king's bed chamber. She will be on her own there, though we will be close."

"Do you mean to say that *Esther* could be Shadrach's human vehicle?" Mordechai, instantly terrified and incredulous, actually grabbed the Master's robed arms. He dropped them immediately, taking small pacing steps in his agitation.

"Not his vehicle, but his *victim*, Mordechai," the Master responded. "He can only choose as his human vehicle someone who is already primed for evil. His thoughts would have no chance to take hold of Esther. We must figure out who his chosen vehicle is, and block him or her in time to save Esther."

The Master, there one moment, was gone the next. Mordechai was left standing alone on the desert side of the fortress, his mind already clicking into warrior mode.

Esther's Turn

It was time. Farah told her she would be called to go to the king's bed tomorrow night at sunset.

For over a year Esther had buried her secret heart and had submitted to Hegai and Farah's ministrations. And she had bloomed beyond expectation, becoming Hegai's masterpiece. Unbeknownst to anyone she had bent her prodigious mind to deciphering the puzzle of Xerxes the man, and had developed a plan and a *modus operandi*. She was oiled, primed, honed and ready, as any proper tool or weapon should be. She had one purpose: to entrance the king and win the crown.

She did not feel the ripples of evil that were battering the protective shield that Abednego had thrown up around her. She sensed Abednego's invisible presence, as she did whenever he was near, but he did not speak with her. In her mind she referred to him as her guardian angel, with the emphasis on "guardian." She was comforted by just the thought of him, and she recalled that nightmare night of one year ago, when, though he was invisible to everyone else, she had seen his bulk standing at her side, his hand on the hilt of his dagger. Every princess had need of a champion.

Haman

He was driven by a compulsion. For the past two days and nights Haman had pulled in favors, worked his palace informers, offered bribes, and resorted to threats. He intended to snatch Esther from the cloister, out from under the very nose of Hegai. His plan was to drug and silence her, wrap her in a cape, and spirit her to one of the secret houses he had readied. He had banished all his servants for three days, and had told his wife Zeresh not to expect him.

It was his experience that no one was kidnap-proof, just as no one was assassination-proof.

His plan did not extend past having the girl in his sole control and at his disposal. He intended to bind and disorient her, the better to bend her to his will. If necessary he even had the means to keep her lightly drugged and passive for a week. After he had finished with her he would either put her under and drop her at one of his sons' brothels, or he would do away with her. It depended how much of a struggle she put up and how much physical force he would have to use to subdue her. If she was too battered by the end of his time with her she would be of no use in the brothel and would have to be eliminated. Just the thought excited him.

What also excited him was, first, the prospect of foiling Hegai, who had snubbed him once too often. And second, the delicious irony of stealing the king's march, exerting the king's right to the Empire's prize virgin. Haman would best them all.

The problem was that the security in the cloister was proving extraordinarily tight. Over the past two days, and to no avail, he had tried substituting one of his own dark slaves for one of the harem's waiters. He tried bribing the gardener to absent himself for just ten minutes from his appointed place tending the cloister's vines. He had even tried to have his own man — a small and deadly Ethiopian — secret himself inside the women's laundry. It was fortunate that the man had been able to escape when Hegai's guards had accidentally discovered the security breach. But there were no medals given for effort. The bottom line was that he had made no headway, and now time was running out. It was unfortunate that he had had to leave it to others to try to get close enough to the girl to drug her. He could not risk everything by getting caught in the cloister himself. As it was, he imagined one part of his mind looking down at himself from a great distance, marveling at his audacity even to attempt this scheme. The other part of him was driven by an uncontrollable urge to have the girl.

Desperation made him bold. He had one last chance, and his man, anxious to redeem himself in Haman's eyes, had suggested the way. It was Farah's habit to pay a visit to the girl Esther every night before bedtime. Though Haman could not know that this was the girl's last night before she was to be called, he relied on the old woman's nightly regimen. The plan was for his man to lay in wait for old Farah, knock her out, bind and gag her and stuff her in one of the cloister's hundreds of storage closets. Then he would quickly dress himself in her clothing. The old servant wrapped herself in so much cloth that the chances of detection were slim. Dressed as Farah, his man would not be stopped or questioned. He would gain entrance to Esther's apartment, and the rest would be child's play.

Esther

Esther was looking forward to her nightly visit with Farah. The old woman had been a mentor, mother-figure, and confidant to her these past twelve months, and tonight she could use a friend. She had creamed and perfumed her skin and had slipped into her favorite night dress, a soft, sleeveless cotton shift that covered her from neck to ankles.

But Farah was late. Esther was always on alert; this had become her nature since arriving in the harem and by now it was second-nature living in the palace cloister. She fretted. Was the old woman ill? Her knees had been plaguing her for months now, though she hid this from Hegai. But if it had only been her knees, Esther knew the old woman would have come. Where was she?

Farah

The old woman had prepared a small package for Esther, her favorite of all the girls she had ever tutored. Her gift contained two items that were so costly and unavailable that they had acquired legendary or mythic status, and it was unlikely that any other harem girl possessed them. Farah had secreted them and planned to present them to Esther tonight, the girl's last night as a virgin. She intended for her star pupil to win the queen's crown, and had planned this gift for weeks.

The first item was a small embroidered lace pouch containing hand-picked, still-fresh blossoms from the yasmin vine. These blossoms—plucked by Farah herself during the nighttime, when they were at their most fragrant and potent—had aphrodisiacal, sedative, and also antiseptic properties. The tiny sachet was worth its weight in pearls, so effective was it at calming first-night nerves, stimulating the sex drive, and soothing and healing small irritations and scratches.

The second item was a miniature vial containing a potion she herself had mixed, containing the rare essence of the saffron blossom. The saffron essence was a proven aphrodisiac for both men and women, and Farah planned to instruct Esther in its use tonight. It always paid to have a secret weapon up one's sleeve.

Farah planned to harvest the yasmin blossoms tonight, before visiting Esther, so that the blooms would be at their peak of freshness and fragrance. The old woman had cultivated her own wild yasmin plant, twining it with an ordinary olive bush to help disguise and protect the rare plant from human and animal foragers. The hybrid and unattractive bush grew in a walled cul-de-sac behind the harem kitchen garden and was accessible either through the kitchen, or by using a little-known gardener's path, little more than a shallow, sandy drainage ditch that hugged the outer palace wall.

Farah's choice to harvest the blossoms herself, and her decision to take the outside shortcut that night, saved her life and that of the girl Esther.

Haman's Deadly Weapon

He was small for a man, little taller than a boy. But he was an experienced assassin, devoid of emotion; a man who enjoyed his work. He had failed in his attempt to infiltrate the harem laundry the night before, sliding out of the room undetected when the armed guard had made an unscheduled check of the great holding baskets. He intended to make up for that failure tonight, disable the old woman watchdog, and kidnap the girl Esther for his master. He had studied the nightly route of Old Farah, matron of the harem, and had secreted himself in a corner, hidden by a tall curtain-wall, along the route she would take to Esther's rooms in the palace cloister.

The old woman was late. The Ethiopian worried, so he followed his instinct and as the corridor was deserted at this time of night, he risked leaving his hiding place and made his way silently down the marble walkway to Farah's private door. With a small tool produced from a pocket in his sleeve, he silently slipped the lock and let himself into the woman's chambers. In an instant he knew the room was empty. *But where had she gone?* He would have seen her if she had followed her usual route. He across the chamber and tried the door to the walled garden. It slid open easily. *So this is how she left,* he thought.

All the private chambers had small gardens with thick walls higher than a man's reach. And a very few of those had small wooden doors recessed into the thick walls. The doors were mostly used for secret assignations, but could also be used, as in Farah's case, for quick access to the girls' rooms or the kitchen garden. The Ethiopian tried the wooden door, leery of creaks, which he knew were deliberately left un-oiled to warn of an intruder. He opened it slowly, just enough to fit through sideways. He stepped out onto the sand and onto a sand spike.

The Ethiopian knew he had stepped into a deadly trap a second before the metal snapped shut on his ankle. Too late, he had felt it through the soft sole of his shoe. The curved blade sliced halfway through his ankle and the man saw stars, shoving his fist into his mouth to keep from crying out. He had only seconds before he passed out from loss of blood. He tore off his shirt and wrapped it tightly around his ankle, and, using the outer walls for support, he held his trapped right foot in one hand, sand spike and all. He was soaked in sweat and was already in shock, but, desperate to escape, he hobbled his way, circumnavigating the palace perimeter until he reached the unused queen's stable. The place was unguarded and, one-handed, the Ethiopian picked the lock on the outer door. He was dripping blood and breathing in shallow wheezes, but he heard only the voice in his head urging him to find a mount and escape. An experienced thief and bareback rider since childhood, the man entered the small stable, quieted the startled stallion, and pulled himself awkwardly onto its back. The horse protested the unfamiliar weight and the smell of blood, and whinnied loudly.

"Shhh, you donkey! Out we go," he rasped.

And more slowly than he would have liked, the Ethiopian walked the horse out of the stables door and, dripping blood, disappeared into the desert night.

Abednego

An invisible Abednego watched the Ethiopian ride away and grunted to himself. Alerted by the conversations and screams projected onto his dreams by Shadrach's black powers, he and Daniel had taken precautions and had prepared for stealth attacks against Esther. Guarding Esther had meant guarding Farah, too, so earlier in the night he had planted sand spikes outside several strategic doorways leading to and from the two women's quarters.

"A good job tonight, Azariya," the familiar rasp was accompanied by a bony arm on his shoulder. Old Daniel, hooded as always, spoke to his childhood friend. "We stopped this attack in time, my old friend, but where will the danger come from next?

One valuable piece of intelligence we now have is that we know who Hananya's vehicle is. It is the Ethiopian's master, the man Haman. And Esther is his target." The spymaster paused, thoughtful.

"I will be close, Daniel. Abbas is hovering, too. And the girl herself is very smart and very cautious. We must trust that if we stay on watch on the outside, she will do her part on the inside. We have no choice. Remember that when she enters the king's private quarters she is on her own. Even I cannot go there. It is shielded."

"And don't you dare worry her, Azariya, by letting her know Haman has her in his sights. She has enough on her mind right now. Our job now is to watch over her and also to keep eyes and ears on Haman every possible moment. I don't want him as much as going to the bath house without one of us — visible or not — watching him. Mordechai will be of help there, as he crosses paths with the man daily. I will put Mordechai in the picture. Though when he hears that Haman tried to have Esther drugged and kidnapped, our emotionless junior spymaster will turn into a wild man." Old Daniel sighed. "Watch them, Azariya."

Old Daniel disappeared, the door to the small stable yard left ajar, the only sound the night wind coming off the dunes.

Esther

It was late. Her room was in shadows, lit only by two small oil lamps. Esther's ears stretched, listening intently for Farah's soft knock. When it came she flew to the door and whispered, "Who?" Only when she heard the old woman answer her did she throw the bolt and open the door just enough for Farah to enter. She bolted the door behind her, and the women embraced briefly.

"I thought perhaps you were not coming," said Esther, speaking softly and smiling at her friend.

"I took the time to bring you a special gift." Farah drew Esther over to a divan and they sat together. She brought the small package out of the folds of her capacious tunic, placing it in Esther's hands. "Open it, my dear."

Esther was overcome. An orphan, she had only ever experienced Poupeh's motherly love, and felt blessed to have found another open heart in this alien and, yes, hostile place.

"Thank you, dear Farah, but I do not require any gifts. Your friendship and guidance are gifts enough." But Farah gently pushed Esther's hands, and so the girl pulled the string and unfolded the cloth. She saw the small sachet and the tiny vial, cushioned in batting. She touched them reverently, then searched the old woman's face in silent query.

"The yasmin sachet is for you to brush over the sheets and pillows, scenting them before the king joins you in his bed. I have tonight harvested the freshest blossoms and tied the sachet with my own hands, so it is at its most potent. As for the vial, it contains saffron essence, and is powerful magic. You will take both of these with you when you go to the king's bed chamber. They will stimulate and arouse, and also soothe, as I have instructed you. The first you will use in preparation, and the second you will use in your own judgement, as the night progresses."

"Thank you, dear Farah. I will take them with me and will do as you say." Esther paused. "I know that the time is ripe and that I am ready to be tested; to find my destiny, but I am sorry to leave you."

"Not a permanent leave-taking, my dear. It is a graduation. And my guidance and deep affection for you go with you tomorrow night. You will not be alone, Esther."

The old woman rose to leave and Esther hugged her hard, the old woman's head not quite reaching Esther's shoulder. At the door Farah whispered, "Think of your namesake, Esther. Ishtar was the goddess of love, and also the goddess of war." And she was gone. Esther bolted the door and stood for a moment, lost in thought, holding Farah's gifts. Then she moved purposefully to her small cloth satchel that she had prepared to take with her when she went to the king. She re-wrapped the sachet and the vial carefully, and buckled the bag closed, tucking it into her wardrobe ready for tomorrow.

Esther went to the divan and lay back, pulling a light cover over herself. She would sleep lightly and keep watch. She had felt a crowding of dark shadows when she had opened the door to let Farah out, and she knew there were strong forces in the air that would try to block her. In her right hand, under the coverlet but at-the-ready, Esther held a small, double-sided dagger. She had found it in its fitted sheath beneath her pillow just that morning, and had recognized it immediately. It was the same dagger that had been in the palm of her guardian angel the night she was taken from Mordechai's house. She had secreted it in her tunic pocket, and had felt its comforting weight all day. She would keep it with her tonight and every moment until she went to the king.

"Thank you," she whispered aloud.

Abednego, invisible and watchful outside Esther's garden wall, heard her and smiled to himself. Every princess needed a champion.

Mordechai

"Haman," repeated Mordechai. He was standing in his salon that same night. Old Daniel, hooded and still as a statue, told him about Abednego's threatening, true dreams foreshadowing Shadrach's encroaching evil, of his need of a human vehicle, and of his choice of Haman as the instrument of his destruction. What the old spymaster had held back was that Haman had already made two attempts to kidnap Esther. Ever the master puppeteer, he waited to see how far Mordechai, his chosen heir, would take the implication of these new developments. Would the man's emotional attachment slow down or cloud his analysis?

Old Daniel watched as Mordechai paced; he could almost hear his protégé's thoughts.

Shadrach's show of power is the sharp tip of the knife, testing the "tenderness" of his chosen prey. Projecting dark battles, red hazes and screaming women and children onto Abednego's mind and thoughts is only the first step. Shadrach will be compelled to act out his long-banked sadistic plans. But to do so he needs a medium, a human instrument to carry his sword. The mind of his chosen "instrument" would need to be open and subject to Shadrach's compulsions and direction, but that person also would be acting of his own volition. Such a man would willingly feed his own as well as Shadrach's dark compulsions. Shadrach could only send his human instrument in a direction the man himself had a will to go.

If Haman were that instrument, where might Haman – controlled by Shadrach – try out his power first? What did Shadrach desire and Haman perhaps covet? Shadrach had a mad desire to foil Daniel, his old comrade; to destroy his people; and to dishonor his One-God.

And Haman, thought Mordechai, *what did Haman want above all?* And instantly Mordechai knew the answer, at the very moment the question surfaced in his mind. *Why, above all else, Haman would desire to be king! And to undermine Xerxes, Haman would first attack or subvert the king's weakest link, to best test the strength of his dark powers against the monarch.*

Mordechai stopped pacing and faced his mentor. Daniel thought that this was a Mordechai who had aged ten years in the past twelve months. This new Mordechai appeared more dangerous than circumspect. The spymaster faced his pupil, watching as stillness became understanding; and understanding became, first, cold anger, and finally an intractable hatred.

"Haman," he repeated. "Haman will go after Esther, the virgin with the best chance of being chosen queen," said Mordechai, speaking his dawning thoughts aloud. "And *we* will go after *him.*"

Old Daniel nodded. "Haman has already tried," he agreed. At Mordechai's look, Old Daniel quickly told him what had happened, and added, "We stopped him, Mordechai. Abbas and Abednego and I. Esther is safe, she is guarded and she is armed."

Then Mordechai surprised even his old mentor. He moved into strategic mode with speed and purpose. He wasted no visible emotion on a Hadassah who was no longer.

"With respect, sir, but a mute giant, an invisible guardian angel, and an ancient spymaster are not sufficient army to do battle against a force of evil a century in the making. We need something stronger." Mordechai was pacing and speaking

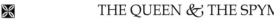

deliberately, his strong hands gesticulating for emphasis. "We need a *true* army of our own. Because for sure Haman is not in this alone. To combat Haman we will need men to watch and monitor his sons, the Amalek brotherhood. The Baradari are not just bullies, thugs and passive whoremasters. They are active merchants of human flesh; they control the traffic in soiled virgins. If Esther is in Haman's sights, we can be sure his sons will figure into this, too. Haman will need a method of disposal, and you can bet he will use a route that has been used before. What better route than through his sons' whorehouses?"

Old Daniel remained silent, watching as his pupil came into his own, and a plan took shape.

"I will set watchers on the Baradari brothels as well as on each of their homes. We will monitor Haman and the comings and goings of his wife and household. He will have an invisible shadow. I have the manpower to do this, and it will be done by this time tomorrow.

"Next." And here, Mordechai stopped his pacing and turned to address Old Daniel head-on. "My Master, while my men can and will surveil other men—and if needs be, engage them in combat—we do not possess the requisite power to monitor and counteract the inhuman force that is Shadrach. His power far exceeds anything we can muster. We cannot even see him! Though we can, unfortunately, experience the strength of his dark forces once he unleashes them, it does us no good only to perceive the wake of his destruction. We need intelligence. We need a weapon that can meet Shadrach on an equal playing field." Mordechai peered into Daniel's hooded and shadowed eyes. "We need Meshach."

The spymaster heard Mordechai out. It was at the mention of his lifelong comrade's name that the old master turned away. He had known this moment would come, and in one part of his mind he was proud that Mordechai had called him out. But he had no sure way of calling up his boyhood friend. Meshach—whom he had grown up with and served with for over four decades, always privately calling him Mishael, his boyhood name—had changed radically that long-ago night in the King Nebuchadnezzar's furnace, and he had gone underground.

Daniel's mind brought up the memory of Mishael from so long ago. As clear in his mind's-eye as if it were yesterday, Daniel remembered.

Daniel, Mishael, Azariya and Hananya

Banned from the furnace room, all through that terrible night half a century ago, Daniel had been on his knees on the stone floor of his chamber. He had been deep in meditation, communing with and supplicating his One-God on behalf of his three "brothers." At dawn he had run from his palace quarters, flying down the dungeon stairs into the bowels of the vast furnace chamber of the palace fortress, edict or no edict. He had stopped breathing as the guard had used the long iron hook to open the furnace door. When Mishael, Azariya and Hananya had walked out, Daniel had almost wept with disbelief and wonder, and, rooted where he stood, they had huddled in a wordless embrace, heads bent. Daniel's arms had gone around Mishael and Azariya, but strangely, Hananya had held back, excluding himself from the circle of brotherhood. At the time Daniel had paid Hananya's behavior no heed.

Only later, after the four had bathed and eaten, and before the three would be returned to their own quarters, had they compared "wounds" they had sustained while in the king's furnace. Each man had been touched and enhanced by the superhot flames.

Daniel remembered being speechlessly thankful that Mishael, his special friend, had been returned to life. He remembered Mishael standing in front of the others. On the outside, Mishael had appeared to be the same fellow he had always been: tall, built to walk with kings, with an engaging smile, a sense of humor and a keen analytical mind. It appeared that only his voice, which had always been a statesman's voice, at once compelling and comforting, had been altered. The heat of the furnace had seared his vocal chords, so that he now spoke in a hoarse whisper. Just days later, despite his vocal handicap, Mishael was absorbed back into the king's service as a trusted advisor. But though he had otherwise *appeared* much the same, Mishael had been profoundly changed. After his night in the furnace Mishael had come to have the strength of ten men, the endurance of ten bull oxen, and the acute hearing of ten wolves. But even as he had grown new and supernatural powers, Mishael's heart had stayed true.

At about the same time, Daniel had been promoted to Royal Cup Bearer, and was moved to chambers adjacent to the king's. His comrades had been split up, sent at the king's behest to represent the crown in the courts of other lands. The four had met together one last time. Daniel was remembering their meeting and Mishael's wonderment.

In a changed voice, Mishael had addressed the others, saying, "I am much the same, my friends, but also very different." Mishael had picked up the oversized fireplace poker, a meter long and five centimeters thick, and, poker in hand, he had given the stone fireplace floor a solid *thwack* to demonstrate the poker's solidity. With three pairs of eyes on his hands and the echo of iron on stone still ringing in the room, Mishael theatrically gripped the fire prod with both hands, and, holding it horizontally, with his eyes on Daniel's, he slowly and dramatically bent the tempered iron as if it were a river reed. He handed the U-shaped iron to Daniel, who hefted it and handed it to Azariya, who tested it and in turn handed it to Hananya.

"Impressive," said Hananya, holding the U-shaped bar in his own two hands, trying to straighten it; it wouldn't budge.

"Can you bend it back, or will we need a new fire-prod?" quipped Azariya in his friendly way.

Mishael had retrieved the poker from Hananya and effortlessly bent it back.

"Are you changed in other ways, too, Misha?" asked Daniel, using his close friend's nickname.

"Yes, along the same lines, but nothing as dramatic as what you've just seen." For some reason Mishael had held back from disclosing to the others the extent of his strength and newly sharpened sensory acuity. He revealed it to Daniel later that same night, in private and for his ears only.

Mishael couldn't articulate what instinct had kept him from telling all to the others, but Daniel had had his own suspicions. Daniel had felt even then that Hananya had been changed the most by the furnace, in a vague but shadowed way. Since the moment they had walked out of the furnace door Hananya had been distancing himself from the others. And if he, Daniel, had intuited that Hananya was somehow no longer aligned with the others, he did not doubt that Mishael had felt this, too, perhaps even more keenly now that his senses had become enhanced.

When Daniel and Mishael had embraced at parting and wished each other good health and success, Daniel had whispered in his ear, "Watch yourself, Misha. I sense that Hananya is hovering on a precipice. He may be welcoming the dark forces instead of repelling them."

Mishael whispered back, "I will watch, Daniel. But I worry about you. Hananya was always closest to you. He might turn on you first."

Back in the present, Old Daniel shook his head, clearing his memories.

"Yes, it might be time to summon Mishael. Set up your surveillance, Mordechai. Do not underestimate either Haman or Hananya." And the next moment he was gone, the flickering candle flames the only sign that the air in the salon had been disturbed by a coming and going.

Mordechai sat at his desk and began to assemble the ingredients for his invisible ink. He would send out his letters tonight, calling ten of his best agents into active service. He already had one agent inside the harem, and for the past year she had been keeping an eye on Esther and keeping him apprised of the girl's welfare and the goings-on.

Esther

In the end, the ordeal went more smoothly than she had dared hope.

Twenty-four hours after having gone to the king's bed, Esther lay, wide awake, in a luxurious bed in special chambers adjacent to the king's. Just that morning, after their night together, the king had walked with her to his door. As she was about to leave, and at the last moment, Xerxes had put out his hand to stay her from walking back the way she had come the night before. He had dismissed the two waiting guards, who, every morning for the past year, had escorted a deflowered virgin from the king's chambers to the House of the Concubines. The night guards had never yet escorted the same girl twice, nor had the daytime guards ever been sent away empty-handed. It was unprecedented that the king had chosen to keep a girl after her time was up. The day shift guards appreciated what this meant, and though they kept their professional demeanor and silence while on duty at the king's private chamber door, they were impatient to go home and tell their wives that they were the first to know that the king had chosen his queen.

Esther had been stunned. She had expected to be escorted to her new home in the House of the Concubines. But her luck and instinct—and Mordechai's training, Farah's lessons and potions, and her own thick mahogany-hued hair—had apparently won the day. Because she was an honest girl and subject to self-analysis, Esther gave a good deal of credit to her preparation and tactics.

First of all, she mused, *I am a mystery to Xerxes.* When the king had asked her some questions to put her at her ease, as he did with every virgin, Esther had smiled and demurred. *Sire, is it not a good game to play, pretending that I have come to you from the gods? I have no past; only a present, here with you tonight. Does this not appeal to you?*

And the second principle she followed was one she had intuited on her own: *I will treat the king as if he were an ordinary man, and the man as if he were a king.*

Xerxes

Xerxes was enchanted. Throughout the night Esther met and parried each of his personal inquiries with mystery and riddle. Xerxes was intrigued and pleased. All the other virgins had chattered away endlessly in the way nervous girls do. He didn't blame them, and had tolerated it for the sex, but it was one of his least favorite aspects of the parade of virgins in his bed. But this new girl—this Esther—was different. She had been utterly lovely, good-natured, and preternaturally quiet. Xerxes found it simultaneously calming and provocative.

As for the sexual game, the king had been excited and expectant. After an hour of conversation and even some laughter, he had been on a knife-edge of attraction. And she did not disappoint. Esther was in all ways compliant to his wishes, while still managing to offer the unexpected: she was virginal, of course, and he had anticipated and enjoyed this. But additionally, and a pleasant surprise for the jaded Xerxes, the girl had been alternately playful and alluring, reticent and enigmatic. In effect, she was several fascinating women in one beautiful package.

Not only that, but to the king's delight, in between bites of delicate foods and sexual play Esther had told him stories and woven fascinating adventure tales. He had been on guard for the girl to ask him about court protocols or to ask a favor; all the others had done so, once they had grown a little comfortable in his presence. But in this, too, the girl Esther confounded his expectations. She expressed no curiosity or interest in court matters or politics. She was focused entirely on *him.*

Treat the king as if he were an ordinary man.

Esther's tactic was wildly successful. For the first time in years Xerxes felt like the most important and powerful man alive, and not because of the literal and figurative crown he wore. With Esther, Xerxes the *man* was the sole object of her focus and attention; the "king" was left in his throne room. It was exhilarating.

Xerxes thought that not since Vashti had the night passed so quickly. When morning came and it was time for Esther to leave him, he had accompanied the girl to the door of his enormous suite. He walked a bit behind her, which was not the protocol. But he had enjoyed watching her walk. *She is a tall, cool number,* he thought. *As lovely walking away as she is from the front.* On impulse, he had put out his hand and touched her hair, one long stroke from crown to ends. It was an unusually tender and winsome gesture for a man such as Xerxes. But this girl Esther brought out the yearning in him. He was overcome with dual feelings: a fear of abandonment and also a possessive longing. The prospect of letting her walk out of his sight, even for a day, was not to be borne. Xerxes had become so accustomed to one-night-women that it came as a surprise to him as he stroked Esther's hair that this pleasure he felt in her presence did not have to end; that he could ask her back for another night. That if she pleased him so intensely it was within his power to make her his queen and have her with him always. She could sit at his side at court and he would be envied. He would have her to himself day and night. The thought tantalized him.

Eventually, Xerxes let Esther leave him later that morning. But even hours later, surrounded by sycophantic courtiers and demanding diplomats, thoughts of her and flashbacks of their night together crowded out thoughts of matters of state. By that same afternoon he had summoned Hegai, Keeper of the Virgins.

"Tell me about Esther," the king had asked Hegai, without preamble.

Hegai, secretly inordinately pleased that his instinct about Esther had been correct, retained his objective military demeanor.

He had served the king and his father before him for more than half his life, and he sensed success.

"My king, I am delighted that the girl Esther pleases you. I cannot tell you much more than what you yourself must have observed. Recall that Your Majesty instructed me not to inquire about the girls' backgrounds; only to gather them into the House of the Women, and to ensure their virginity and their loveliness. Your instructions were clear: *Neither are you to inquire as to their provenance. It is the king's province to do so if he so desires.*"

The king stared hard at Hegai, and raised one imperious eyebrow. Xerxes knew that Hegai had his spies.

Hegai smiled at the king, with the courtly familiarity of a longtime advisor. "But I have had Esther under observation from the moment she entered the harem twelve months ago. My people have watched her closely, literally day and night. That she is a rare beauty among beauties is obvious. She also is confident and unfailingly kind; she has never raised her voice at the other girls — and as Your Majesty can imagine, there has been provocation — or at the menials. She does not gossip or spend her time on nonsense. My people tell me that everyone — from Farah, the mistress of the harem, to the lowliest bath attendant — is her willing servant. It is obvious from her speech and deportment that she is from an aristocratic family, and as well, she needed no tutoring in matters of manners or court behavior. But Sire, she never speaks of her people or her kindred. That remains her secret."

Xerxes was thoughtful. Over the years he had relied on Hegai in matters that literally involved life and death, and the man had never once disappointed him. Xerxes was nobody's fool and when it suited him he was a shrewd judge of men. He knew that Hegai had hand-picked Esther for him, and he smiled. The man's instincts in battle and in the harem were still sharp, still as reliable as the sunrise.

"She is quite perfect, as you say, Hegai my old friend. She pleases me inordinately. Have Esther sent to me tonight, as well. I will have no other maidens in my bed until further notice."

So Hegai and Farah prepared Esther for an unprecedented second night with the king. Farah eased the girl's well-hidden nerves, and she herself attended to her, bathing, perfuming and creaming her. She spread soothing oils on her skin and rinsed her thick russet-toned hair with henna. She had the seamstress speedily sew a new gown and a new nightdress from rare bolts of gossamer silk kept in Farah's locked fabric room. Farah knew she was grooming the next queen.

Xerxes

And so it was. The second night with the girl Esther was even more intriguing and exciting for Xerxes than the first had been. This time Xerxes attended closely to Esther's nuanced speech and behavior, unaware that the girl was in turn observing him, and cataloguing his reactions, which of course caused her to be both anticipatory and exquisitely responsive to him. She was precisely right for him in every way. Xerxes surprised himself when he realized the excited desire, longing and protectiveness he felt towards Esther was what he had been searching for since losing Vashti. With the objectivity born of the passage of time, Xerxes admitted to himself that both he and Vashti had acted impetuously that night of his banquet five years ago, and since that night he had had cause to regret it. Now Xerxes longed for a special woman who was dedicated to him and to whom he could return whenever it pleased him. She would smile and welcome him, and be agreeable in all things. He had promised himself that for his next queen he would seek the least impetuous and most placid of girls, one who would never provoke his temper and who would accede to his every request. But he also wished for something more... He wished for a true queen, someone not unlike his own Queen Mother, Atossa.

He thought that, in Esther, he had at long last found that treasure. The girl was a beauty, and she seemed to have no sharp edges. She was as compliant and deliciously pleasing to him as his most secret dream. For the first time in nearly a year he had been able to drift off to sleep in another's presence. This was extraordinary! He trusted very few people, and was suspicious of all the palace guards. His hand-picked intimates were vetted and reliable, but the trusted circle kept narrowing. The more vast his empire, the wider the net of secrecy and distrust he had to cast.

Yet with Esther Xerxes had relaxed. Her calming voice as she told her stories acted like a hypnotic anodyne. On their third night together she sat in his bed chamber, and, stroking his head, she whispered him to sleep. *Sleep, Xerxes. I will keep watch. Fear not.* He had not had to disclose his fears to her; she just seemed *to know.* And in fact, he had drifted off to sleep, waking refreshed, into a room filled with morning sunlight. The first thing he saw was Esther, sitting on the divan at his feet, her doe-eyes wide, watching him. His heart had turned over in gratitude and, surprisingly, with stirrings of love. He trusted Hegai, he trusted his own warrior's instinct, and now, it seemed, he trusted Esther. Xerxes laughed mirthlessly at himself. He had considered himself to be above infatuation, but here he was, an experienced campaigner, willingly placing himself under the undemanding but thrilling spell that Esther wove.

Xerxes resolved to keep the girl Esther close; he would crown her queen.

Esther is Chosen

Xerxes' summons had come as a surprise to Esther. She had been with him every night for a week, and was exhausted. She had assumed that on this, the seventh night since she had first gone to the king's bed, she would be accorded the time and privacy to rest and bathe. But this was not to be. Farah unobtrusively entered Esther's chamber, washed and dressed the girl, and coaxed and cooed to her, while feeding her energizing bits of dates and apricots, and a diluted wine flavored with peach juice.

"Come now, Esther, you must build up your strength for your night with the king. My instinct tells me that tonight he will give you the royal diadem encrusted with rubies set in rose gold. This tiara will be his betrothal gift, and from that moment you will be his designated queen. This is what you have worked for. You are meant to be queen. Come."

Esther was loath to worry Farah or to vex Hegai, who waited outside her door to guard and escort her himself on her walk to Xerxes' chamber. She had no appetite and dearly wished for twelve uninterrupted hours of rest. But to please them and for her own good she nibbled and sipped and in no time at all she stood, flanked by Farah and Hegai, outside the king's quarters.

The great, twelve-foot high wooden door, studded with iron and built to withstand a siege, swung open. Esther walked in alone, past the familiar bowing Nubian servant. He smiled as he gestured her inside, toward the king's receiving chambers. He liked this tall girl with the soft voice and calm eyes, so unlike the other girls who came to the king's bed.

Esther stood unmoving in the next doorway, and Xerxes looked his fill. Esther was a tall vision in pale turquoise shot with gold threads. The diaphanous tunic was belted at her impossibly small waist, a deep blue silken sash with tiny golden tassels almost brushing her ankles, and her harem pants of a fluid silk in the same deep blue. The king's eyes, looking their fill, were drawn to Esther's magnificent hair. One night early in the week he had told her he preferred it unbound, and, ever since, she had worn it loose to please him. Now it hung to her waist, a curtain of fluid mahogany, framing her shoulders, her white skin, her glistening eyes, and her perfect shape. With the light from the anteroom behind her, her form was limned in soft gold, and he perceived her as if haloed.

Xerxes approached Esther, one powerful arm outstretched. She responded by walking toward him, meeting him in the center of the marble-floored receiving room, in front of a solid circular table of polished acacia wood. On the table, atop a deep purple cushion, sat a circlet of gold, studded with colored stones. His eyes on hers, Xerxes reached with his free hand and picked up the circlet. Facing her, he placed the diadem onto her head. Esther broke eye contact, her thick lashes shadowing her pale cheeks as she looked down at her own feet.

"Esther, you are now betrothed to me. In a week's time you will be Queen of Persia."

Esther was speechless with a combination of exhaustion and exultation. She also felt waves of relief and gratitude. After all this, to have been sent to wait out her days in the House of the Concubines would have been, for her, a living death. She raised her head.

"Thank you, My King. I will do my best to please you always." At that, Esther swayed on her feet, the tension and physical exhaustion of the past week having taken their toll. And the surprised king, acting quickly, caught her to him and carried her to a divan. Misinterpreting, he assumed Esther was overcome with the surprise and thrill of being chosen queen.

"Boy! Boy!" He called out. "Bring wine and smelling spices for Esther, and be quick!" He did not want anything untoward to happen to this special girl now that he had found her.

Esther revived within minutes and blushed hotly, embarrassed that she had fainted — for the first time in her life — at the king's feet. She was not to know that Xerxes was charmed and touched that this most composed, lovely creature apparently needed his protection.

A New Queen of Persia

Once the king made his choice, events moved quickly.

By the first of the next week the king authorized the palace to announce to his kingdom what he had known in his heart after that first night. The royal scribes were summoned, and the message went out via runners and couriers on horseback, in every language and to every corner of the Empire. "His Royal Majesty Xerxes I, King of Kings, King of all Persia and the Indus, and Pharaoh of Egypt, has chosen a Queen. Her name is henceforth Esther, Persian Star, Queen of the Persian Achaemenid Empire."

The palace was abuzz. Overnight, Susa was festooned with flags of purple and gold; colors representing the reigning king and his chosen queen, respectively.

The actual marriage ceremony was to be held in one month's time, following a truncated protocol. Because the bride-to-be was an orphan, and the bridegroom was the king, the typical sequence of, first, two *khastegari*, or family meetings, followed by *baleh boran*, public announcements of dual intention and exchange of gifts from one family to another, and third, the *namzadi*, the family engagement party, were all dispensed with. There was a festive *hana bandan*, the henna night, at the House of the Women, a bitter-sweet ceremonial party for the harem girls, who of course had lost out to Esther in their quest to be queen.

Esther

Later on the night following the henna ceremony Esther sat in her chamber, examining her hennaed hands, feet, and hair in the gilt-framed mirror. She looked foreign to her own eyes. *Who is this girl?* she thought. Paradoxically, she thought it fitting that she could detect no trace, in this hennaed creature reflected back at her, of the old Hadassah, the girl she had been. There was no trace of Hadassah for the reason that Esther had replaced her. This new girl "Esther" was in all ways a Persian bride. Together with Farah and her seven maids, Esther schooled herself to celebrate the night of her transformation.

For more than a year Esther had not permitted herself to recall her first wedding night. Just the memory of her home, of Poupeh and of Mordechai still sent a shaft of pain through her heart so real and deep she thought she would surely pass out from it. By dint of sheer will-power she had kept her memories locked away. Instead, she had thought of herself as a soldier in an exclusive and secret army, with a critical assignment. Her mission was to win the heart of the king, and thence to capture the crown of Queen of Persia. Once in place, she had been assured by her invisible guardian angel, she would be in a unique position from which to orchestrate a future rescue of her people during a period of coming Terror. And Esther had applied herself, body and mind, to achieving this prize. That it was about to be handed to her in this royal wedding ceremony was at once astonishing and utterly final. As she submitted to the ministrations of her maids, the fussings of Farah and avuncular instructions of Hegai, Esther privately vowed that from this day forward she would never again revisit her prior life in her memory or her yearnings.

Xerxes Weds Esther

The marriage ceremony itself was relatively small in scale. It was held in the king's throne room, which was crammed with king, queen, elite courtiers, favored diplomats, guards, and of course Hegai and Farah, who hovered at the periphery under the archway, wearing private, jubilant smiles.

On the very outskirts of the arched corridor adjacent to the throne room, next to a pillar, stood Old Daniel, unmoving and unnoticed, his eyes intent on Esther. Nearby stood the faithful Abbas, his eyes roving through the crowd, always returning to keep watch over the column of white that was Esther, his master's creation and his hope for the future.

In the thick of the small crowd of well-wishers inside the throne room stood Haman, advisor at court. He could not help but stare at Esther. Her hair, her face and eyes, her slim but full-breasted figure. He was perspiring. He alternately clenched and unclenched his left fist, while his other hand fingered his *khanjar*, the thin and deadly dagger that he kept in a hidden pocket in his right sleeve.

Watching Haman, but invisible, was Abednego. He had given his dagger to Esther, but had replaced it with a slightly heavier and even sharper model. He silently dared Haman to try something. The fearless guardian itched to do damage to the man who had had Esther in his evil sights.

Outside, in the courtyard of the House of the Women, Mordechai paced and brooded. He was not important enough in court hierarchy to merit an invitation to the wedding ceremony, and for this he was profoundly grateful. He thought his heart had broken weeks ago, on the night of Esther's audition with the king. In truth, it was on *this* day, the afternoon of the king's wedding to his lost love, that his broken heart was turned to stone.

Xerxes and Esther stood together before the throne and the Zoroastrian priest. It was a public elevation of commoner to royal, and was achieved in a stately manner, relatively quickly. On a dais two steps above the floor and canopied in deep violet brocade stood Xerxes and Esther, flanked by unmoving giants bearing spears taller than they were. They were the king's personal guards.

Xerxes was dressed for the occasion, wearing his ceremonial fluted golden *kulah* or royal crown. He wore a tight-fitting blue and purple tunic, the royal robe atop his broad shoulders adorned with golden rosettes and long ribbons trailing behind. The cloth of state, worn only for special occasions, was draped over his left shoulder, clipped in place by a golden eagle pin. His thick black hair and beard were curled, braided and oiled. His flowing trousers were tucked into his soft sueded ankle boots, and his short dagger was, as ever, in a belt at his waist, despite his finery. The king was never unarmed.

Esther, standing tall and ethereal at Xerxes' side, was clothed in shades of white and gold, a double-tunic of semi-sheer silk shot with gold and silver threads, layered over opaque silk of palest rose, piped in turquoise. Her harem trousers were of palest gold brocade, and her soft boots were fashioned of the same gold silk. Her exquisite hair was plaited and hung in a thick rope over her left shoulder, braided with the thinnest gold and rose threads and bound with a tiny golden tassel. Her long veil, of white gossamer silk and held in place by a golden bandeau circling her head and worn above her eyebrows, trailed past her knees. When the sunlight shone through the throne room skylight it struck Esther's radiant hair, and people who had attended the brief crowning ceremony spoke about it for weeks afterward. When the king had placed the ruby-studded golden diadem onto Esther's head, people swore that sparks had shot skyward, giving truth to the meaning of her name: "star." It also signified, to the superstitious Persians, that this royal marriage was blessed by Ishtar, the goddess of love. The Empire had a new queen.

Esther's Coronation Banquet

Xerxes, never loath to drink and make merry or to display his imperial wealth to his courtiers, foreign diplomats, and his subjects, held an exclusive week-long party to celebrate the coronation of his new queen. The banquet began immediately after the wedding ceremony, and was held in one of the gilt and marble colonnaded banquet halls of the palace. Only court officials and trusted military elite and their bejeweled wives or sweethearts were invited, and summoned courtiers from even the farthest reaches of the Empire made sure to attend. They came to pay homage to Xerxes, of course, but in large part also to see for themselves the vaunted beauty of the new queen.

"Esther's Banquet," as the party became known, echoed in lavishness the king's Empire-wide parties of earlier years. Long tables draped in purple held bottomless platters of cured and thinly sliced meats, bowls of golden peaches and ruby pomegranates, pillows of honeyed dates and cascades of sugared grapes. There were crystal towers and pedestal compotes filled to overflowing with pistachios and almonds, raisins and apricots. The wine, too, flowed as at past banquets, freely and endlessly. Servants were vigilant and attended to the king's guests almost before their goblets had been emptied.

The main difference at this banquet was that the new queen was on display not as a veil dancer, but as a regal and exquisite figurehead. Everyone in Persia was intensely curious about the girl who had won out against all the other beauties in the vast Persian Empire. Was she as beautiful as rumored?

Esther did not disappoint. With Hegai orchestrating her every move; with Farah softly commanding the royal seamstresses; and with her seven maids hovering, bathing, combing, creaming and feeding her, the new queen was at her peak of youthful elegance and radiance. On each of seven days Esther appeared in a different gown, and depending on the fashion statement desired, her hair was either coiled and pinned at her nape, or plaited with golden threads, or curled and left to cascade to her waist. Imperial privilege and the Empire's wealth were on display, and regardless of her costume, Esther wore the royal diadem as well as various magnificent pieces of crown jewelry. She did not appear in the same finery twice. On one night she wore a ruby teardrop the size of Xerxes' thumb around her neck, suspended from a rose-gold "rope" and cradled in her clavicle. Another night she wore a double-strand necklace of pearls the size of hail stones, hanging gracefully from neck to waist. And so on, culminating, on the last night of the week-long banquet, in her wearing the king's special wedding gift, a hammered gold collar set with cabochon emeralds.

The unanimous consensus of the high courtiers and officials was that this new queen was everything they could have expected and more. Esther was a success. Her natural charm, and her ability to briefly respond to diplomats and satraps from far-flung corners of the Empire in their own languages, surprised and captivated everyone at court. The king preened at Esther's triumph. He was actually seen smiling, and remained at Esther's side all night. The king, at least for the time being, was beguiled by his new queen.

So much so that Xerxes used the occasion to bestow coveted royal land grants on a number of nobles and satraps whose provinces lay in strategic geographical spots of the Empire. In this way the king secured loyalty to the crown among the faraway governors upon whose military support he needed to rely, but whose distance from the court left them less susceptible to his influence and oversight. The king had learned, at the knee of his father, Darius the Great, how to manipulate and wield his political power.

Further, in an impulsive but brilliant move that confounded his treasurer and purser but endeared Xerxes to his subjects, the king announced a twelve-month remission of taxes in celebration of the new queen. He also instructed his royal quartermaster to commission caravans, and to load them down with foodstuffs from the royal storehouses. They were to travel to each and every province in the Empire, distributing gifts of food and wine to Persia's common folk, celebrating Persia's new queen. No member of the Empire would soon forget Xerxes' wedding day.

Mordechai

One month after the royal wedding, Mordechai, at his usual post in the courtyard of the House of the Women, was approached by a liveried messenger who bowed at the waist and presented Mordechai with a small scroll. It bore the king's seal, and was tied with a purple tassel. Mordechai broke the seal and unrolled the scroll. He stood very still. For a fleeting second he thought perhaps it was a message from the queen. It was, instead, a letter of appointment addressed to Mordechai Bilshan, nobleman and courtier to the king in the courtyard of the House of the Women.

Mordechai Bilshan was hereby advanced in service to the king, to a post at the King's Gate.

Mordechai allowed himself the hint of a smile. The king's messenger had aroused the curiosity of other courtiers, but consistent with his studied reticence, Mordechai considered it unseemly to emote publicly. His promotion would be known at court soon enough. Right then, though, Mordechai knew with a clear certainty that his promotion to the King's Gate was Esther's hidden hand at work. *Daniel was right*, he thought. *Esther as Xerxes' queen is our secret weapon.* Mordechai's presence in the outer courtyard of the House of the Women had allowed him to keep his eye out for Esther; in a fitting *quid pro quo*, now that Esther had risen to royal, she was watching out for him. By engineering Mordechai's promotion to a minister at the King's Gate, Esther was keeping her Control as close as possible without arousing undue notice.

A Second Virgin Roundup

Haman's evil mind was hard at work. Even after Esther's marriage to the king Haman was not yet ready to give up on his daughter, Zareen. His deep disappointment that she had been passed over for queen fueled a new scheme. One morning, about one month after Esther's banquet, Haman approached Xerxes as he sat on his throne during a pause in the morning's affairs of state. Haman thought the king looked a bit haggard; as if he had not been sleeping well, or was bedeviled by pressing matters. Haman gauged that it was a good time to press his plan.

"My king, if I may inquire, what is to be done with the entire apparatus that has been built up to gather the Empire's virgins now that your majesty has found a queen? Attendance in both the House of the Women and the House of the Concubines stands at about three hundred, and, with all due respect, costs the king's treasury many thousands of *darics* to maintain."

Haman watched as the king's distracted look sharpened. Having strategically raised the dual topics of money and women he had the king's attention, so he pressed on.

"Now, if my king derives pleasure from the virgins, and the concubines, and intends to continue to call upon them even now that you have found a new queen, then why not allow the Home Guards to do one more virgin roundup before the practice is discontinued? In this way your majesty will have a deep supply of virgins for a good long time."

Haman's intention was to remind the newlywed king of the fund of virgins and concubines at his disposal. His suggestion verged on the overly-familiar, and was therefore a risk, but Haman felt a compulsion to press the issue. Haman's spies had told him that Xerxes had not called for *any* girls from either the House of the Women or the House of the Concubines to come to his bed for several months, ever since the night that Esther had first gone to him. Because exclusivity to one woman was never an ideal the Persian monarch aspired to, Haman sought to stimulate Xerxes' interest in other bed partners. Once the king's ardor for Esther had cooled and he resumed his practice of calling for a new virgin or for one of his concubines, Haman intended to press his own daughter, Zareen, forward. It was not necessary for her to be queen in order to have the king's ear. Royal mistresses or concubines were privy to much pillow talk, and could exert subtle pressure when necessary. Haman intended for Zareen to be a regular in Xerxes' bed.

There is more than one path to power, Haman thought.

The king appeared to think about it. He was not presently availing himself of the pleasures of the women in his harem, but the future prospect of having a fresh and deep fund of virgins and concubines at his disposal pleased him. And as a newlywed king still besotted with his new queen, he also thought that perhaps a few of the newest girls could be helpful to his Esther in some way. She could train them as her personal maids. Women placed great store in surrounding themselves with other women. So he nodded at Haman.

"This is a good idea. Have the Home Guard conduct one more small roundup of the Empire's maidens."

Haman murmured and bowed out of the king's presence, and made straight for the station of the Captain of the Home Guard. He felt certain that now that he had planted the idea of varied and exciting bed partners in the king's mind, Xerxes would soon tire of the exclusivity of his young queen, and would issue his call to Shaashgaz in the House of the Concubines. When that happened, Zareen would be ready to fill Xerxes' needs very well indeed. Haman had no intention of leaving the matter of the king's choice of bed partner to chance. He would alert Zareen to stay primed and ready. He would plant a pouch of gold *darics* in the right palm.

Mordechai – Minister at the King's Gate

At his new post at the King's Gate, Mordechai was now a full-fledged member of the king's court, and so was in a position to function as a set of eyes and ears on behalf of Xerxes — and Esther. He was no longer a roving under-cabinet functionary, patrolling and lobbying in the outer courtyard of the House of the Women, striving and straining to pick up any tidbit of news or to trade a favor for information.

With Esther's elevation to Queen of Persia Mordechai was promoted to the inside track of court life. Not only did he now have access to the throne room on days the king held court; as minister at the King's Gate Mordechai now also merited a small office inside the imposing gateway to the royal court chambers. The King's Gate was actually a vestibule annex to the palace, housing the administrative arm of the day-to-day political workings of the monarchy. The royal scribes had their rooms within the King's Gate. It housed the royal record rooms as well as storage rooms for supplies of quills, ink, parchment scrolls, sealing wax, candles and candelabra. All vetted members of the king's court had their chambers within its unglamorous walls. On days when the king held court, the King's Gate was a hive of activity, abuzz with conversations in dozens of dialects, the halls ringing with shouted calls for royal pages bidden to ferry orders, messages and newly-scribed directives and laws to and fro. Because of their proximity to power, chambers in the King's Gate were a highly coveted privilege.

Mordechai's room within the King's Gate soon became a destination. Petitioners and other courtiers now sought *him* out, asked his advice, gathering round his desk at all hours discussing and dissecting the day's talk of taxes, trade imbalances, preferences to friendly princes, and court intrigue. His office in the King's Gate signaled to all that its occupant was a man to be trusted, a man of importance, and a man with access either to the king himself or to those who themselves had the access. It was an information way-station.

As secret heir-apparent and disciple to Old Daniel, and a man to whom information was his life's-blood, Mordechai was in his element, and — aside from his buried personal tragedy — he was precisely where he wanted to be. He was positioned at the information crossroads of Persia's imperial power.

While there were many ministers with small offices in the building formally known as the King's Gate, the official designation of "Member of the King's Gate" included a special subset of a few trusted ministers to the king. Even longtime members of the general court were unaware which Members were ordinary courtiers, and which possessed the insider's clearance bestowed only by the king himself. From the king's standpoint, he was best served if none of the ministers and courtiers knew for certain who among them was watching and listening. This kept them on edge. In reality there were fewer than twenty such elite Members of the King's Gate, known in whispered conversations only as *gausaka*, meaning "the hearers." Independent of any political or geographical interest group, their brief was to be on the alert for anything treasonous or potentially disloyal to the crown. The *gausaka* reported directly to the king or queen, through a vetted intermediary.

A Member of the King's Gate was, effectively, the king's eyes and ears; a royal listener and informer. Mordechai's experience over the past fifteen years under the tutelage of the secret spymaster; his photographic memory; and his facility with language and dialect, made him uniquely qualified for this post. He was loyal to Xerxes for the reason that so far, under Xerxes—as under his father Darius before him and Cyrus before that—Persian Jews were accepted at most levels of Persian society. They were by and large treated well, and ethnic abuse was the exception, not the norm. Daniel's position as Royal Cup Bearer and his and his friends' positions as royal confidants to four kings had long given the Jews a measure of status and trustworthiness. As a group they pledged fealty to Xerxes and contributed more than their population share to the royal fisc. So Mordechai unhesitatingly pledged his loyalty to Xerxes—the reigning monarch. Xerxes' continued good health and good offices meant that Mordechai and his people would continue to thrive, enjoying the open Persian society and the status quo. As a Member of the King's Gate Mordechai was perfectly positioned close to the power of Persia, to keep watch for the king, the queen, and, incidentally, to lend an influential hand to his people if it came to that.

The Puzzle of the Second Virgin Dragnet

Almost at once Mordechai heard of the advent of a second virgin dragnet. It was to take place this very week, and he was surprised as well as troubled. *Why did the king need more virgins?* Mordechai worried the puzzle. Though in a secret part of his heart the thought curdled his blood, facts were facts. Xerxes already had found his perfect queen, and the word in the courtyard of the House of the Women was that since Esther's first night in his bed Xerxes had spent every night with her. *So why stockpile more virgins? The only reason was that the king was*

anticipating a time when he would tire of his new queen. Did this mean that Esther's position was in jeopardy?

This last thought was like a bucket of cold water in Mordechai's face. Esther's position as queen promised some measure of direct access to Xerxes, but with the second influx of virgins to the harem it was more than possible that her influence would become diluted. The king already had a dozen sons and daughters from his concubines, so he did not need Esther for breeding just yet. He would probably take his pleasure with her until his blood cooled, perhaps before allowing her to become with child. The king was not only in no hurry; he also was an inveterate lothario. That he had been satisfied with only Esther for the past month was an aberration. Mordechai came to appreciate first-hand the fleeting nature of political security. Such a will-o'-the-wisp did not exist. Expedience, yes. Security, absolutely not.

But other than Mordechai, no one at the cabinet level seemed even remotely concerned about the second virgin roundup. Their king was not monogamous, and it was not expected that he should be so. Mordechai consoled himself that Esther was still in the closest possible proximity to the king. Assuming no one succeeded in planting another girl in Xerxes' bed with countervailing interests to Esther's and whom the king heeded, Mordechai felt he could bide his time, watch and wait. Let Esther work her sweet magic on Xerxes, exclusive bed partner or not.

Of course, Mordechai was not aware that Haman was working overtime to undermine Esther's position with the king. But Old Daniel was aware. He met with Mordechai that very night, in Mordechai's chamber in the King's Gate, and advised him to stay vigilant, work his informants, consolidate his power, and be ready to move men or information. Mordechai's mission was gradually and relentlessly to strengthen his influence in the corridors of power against the day when his power would be needed by his people.

Old Daniel was positioning Mordechai to be one-half of his secret weapon against the day, hopefully distant, when the Terrors would come. Esther was the other half; but Daniel had not yet called her into action. For now, Daniel set Abbas to watch and listen in the palace hallways, kitchen, banquet halls, and stables. No one paid the mute giant any heed. Daniel also set Abednego to protect Esther, which he did by hovering out of sight. Old Daniel was their puppeteer; their Control. Daniel still had daily visions of blood, and Abednego heard the voices of Shadrach. The two of them were pushing back against the coming wave of evil with whatever tools they could muster.

The Assassination Plot

That same night, Biktan and Teresh slunk away from the outer window in the wall of the palace at Susa. It was past midnight, they were angry, and they wanted their beds. They had had a dissatisfying secret meeting with their *ban*, the man who gave them their orders and, sometimes, pouches of gold coins. They had gone as usual to the appointed outer window where they waited to hear the harsh voice speak from behind the grille above their heads. Tonight the disembodied voice admonished and threatened them:

"It has been over a month since you have provided me with any useful advance information about the king's movements. At this rate we will all be bent over and walking with sticks before we can mount a successful operation against our target. The time is right! The king is distracted by the new *jendeh*, his new whore, in his bed. His guard is down, he is vulnerable. Get me the schedule of his movements and I can lay an ambush. You have one day to do this. Otherwise you are useless to me and will be replaced. Now get out of my sight."

No pouch of coins was tossed from the window this time. Walking away in the dark, the two gatekeepers were torn. They had agreed two years before to become paid informants to a highly-placed cabinet minister who never showed his face; they knew him only as a voice. They fed him information, and in return he paid them handsomely, but he was also mercurial, paying only if it suited him. The important, added incentive for the two gatekeepers was that the voice had promised them elevation to ministers at the King's Gate if their information led to the king's assassination. And they had agreed for the reason that without his patronage they would have remained mid-level gatekeepers for the rest of their lives, watching other, less-clever men advance in position and status. Their only hope of advancing themselves was to gamble on this unseen minister. They had counted on his unscrupulous ambition carrying them to the King's Gate.

But right now, they were not so sure. The *ban* was hungry for information and he was mean; he treated them like dogs. They muttered to each other of their mutual antipathy for him.

"This *ban* is a snake and a sadist. You notice *he* doesn't risk his neck to find out the king's schedule. He whips *us*, and complains when we have nothing to give him. *He* should try sneaking around behind the backs of the king's bodyguards. The king's movements are more closely guarded than the virginity of a princess," complained Biktan.

"And he is never alone!" added Teresh.

"If *we* can't find out his daily schedule in advance, no one can. We know every one of the king's guards, and every secret hiding place and shortcut. Problem is, no one is talking." Biktan was thoughtful. "And another thing, Teresh. What makes you think this *ban* will even honor his promise to reward us once we have done his dirty work?"

"You are right, of course. We will need to uncover his identity and soon. That will be our life insurance." The two conspirators laughed nervously as they made their way through the deserted courtyards.

As they walked through the now-deserted Susan Gate, a shortcut to their homes, Teresh had an idea. "Who says we need to report to the *ban*, anyway? Why can't we shadow the quarry and assassinate him on our own? Then we would get all the credit. The *ban* would owe us big-time if we "sold" the assassination to *him*. He would pay handsomely to be able to claim that *he* had penetrated the king's guard and killed him in his own palace. He would be a hero among a certain faction. To keep us happy and on his side all he has to do is elevate us to the

King's Gate. The two of us would be a formidable team if we could pull this off."

Biktan agreed. "And why not! We can do the deed on our own. How difficult can it be? Everyone in the palace is floating on a happy haze since the Banquet of Esther; their guard is down. This would be the perfect time to strike."

Warming to the idea of a large reward, elevation to the King's Gate, and besting the odious *ban*, Teresh embellished on his friend's idea, ticking off their advantageous position. "We are perfectly placed at the gate between the king's private quarters and his public chambers. We are old familiar faces here; everyone knows Biktan and Teresh, and the Home Guards are our friends. No one will even look at us twice, let alone suspect us. And afterwards, we can resume our posts as if nothing had happened. We could even misdirect the search! All we have to do is find out the king's daily schedule and shadow him. There will be an opportunity. He must be alone *some*time. What about catching him at the 'pot?'"

"And we don't even have to plan a disposal as we did with the others, added Biktan. "With the king, discovery of his dead body will be key. Chaos will follow, and our *ban* will move in."

The two conspirators walked through the dark and empty alleyways, lit only by small oil lamps hanging from brackets at strategic corners. And they talked, laying their grisly plans, proposing alternative means. A cloth reeking with medicinal *kapur* held over the king's nose and mouth to render him sedated and silent; a vial of poison tipped into his wine cup; a dagger between the ribs tilted upwards into the heart; perhaps a quick broken neck; or a strangulation from behind with a sharpened bowstring. They rejected the latter as too messy.

Mordechai Overhears

Unseen by Biktan and Teresh, there was one other person still awake and about. Mordechai had just doused his lamp in his chamber in the King's Gate after Old Daniel, his spymaster, had wordlessly disappeared. Mordechai's chamber door was slightly ajar; he had been on the verge of shutting and locking it and making his way home. His room, on the second floor of the King's Gate annex, opened onto a tiny inner landing adjacent to one of the stone archways buttressing the fortress walls. When he heard the voices below him, he stood stock-still and listened.

Mordechai's chamber in the King's Gate was actually perfectly positioned to capture sound from the stone rotunda beneath it. It was an undetected phenomenon that the Gate's surrounding vaulted stone arches, curving fifty feet above the stone floor, created pinpoint echoes at certain strategic places within the structure, so that a person speaking softly on the floor might be overheard with perfect clarity from a distance high above. From his years of listening to conversations in the gateways and courtyards of the palace, Mordechai had identified one of those sound-sensitive listening spots. So when he was elevated to minister at the King's Gate Mordechai requested a particular small room above the busy Susan entryway. The chamber was windowless, little bigger than a storage closet, and was not in use or demand. But because of the unique acoustics of the cloister housing it, while standing in its narrow doorway Mordechai was able to clearly hear a whispered conversation far below him.

In this way the low voices of the two men directly beneath his perch carried distinctly in the now-empty archway. Natives of Turkey, at Persia's northwest border, for privacy and out of longstanding habit Biktan and Teresh spoke to one another in their own dialect of *Kaba,* a raw Turkish. They had not reckoned on being overheard at that hour, or of anyone in or around the palace and of the noble classes being familiar with their rural idiom. But Mordechai Bilshan, whose name meant "warrior and master of many tongues," understood *Kaba* perfectly; it was a cousin language to Pârsi and Arabic, and besides, he had run numerous agents in Turkey, and so was fluent in its dialects.

Fate is sometimes a smiling imp. And that night Fate teamed up with Coincidence, allowing Mordechai to clearly overhear

Biktan and Teresh's plot to assassinate the King of Persia. Mordechai automatically committed every word to memory, including the speakers' names as they addressed and congratulated each other.

As the two unsuspecting conspirators walked out of the great Susan Gate and into darkened Susa City and home, Mordechai was still standing—motionless out of habit and training—on his tiny landing. But his mind was racing. This was the stroke of luck he was waiting for but could not have predicted. Fate had just handed him a perfect opportunity to ingratiate himself with the king by exposing and foiling an assassination plot against him. Speed and secrecy were essential.

But how best to proceed?

In a flash Mordechai saw how simultaneously to secure Esther in Xerxes' graces and also to seal his own loyalty in the king's eyes. He would pass the information this night, in code via trusted messenger, to Esther the Queen, and he would instruct her to divulge it personally, and only to the king himself. She would be handing the king both his life and the power to dispose of the lives of his would-be assassins. The king, a seasoned tactician and general, would see that the two plotters were apprehended and punished. It would be up to the king whether to keep the whole thing a secret, or to make the thwarted plot public and the two captured conspirators a gruesome public spectacle.

It unfolded just as Mordechai expected.

Mordechai had hurried home from the King's Gate, and in invisible ink had written one word on a tiny piece of parchment: the word was "Serah," the top-secret code signifying immediacy. He attached it to the foot of one of the pet doves he kept in a dovecote on his roof, and sent the trusty bird on its way. Within the hour the homing-dove had returned, with a cryptic message containing three numbers only. It was the coordinates of the window in the thick palace wall where Mordechai would wait. In the deserted night he had moved like a spirit, and dressed all in black, he was undetectable. As he crouched under the high grilled window, he heard a soft rustling. It was Hatach, trusted personal messenger to the queen.

"Speak, Master Mordechai. The queen begs you to tell me of the emergency."

The voice was vaguely familiar to Mordechai, and in a corner of his mind he registered satisfaction that even inside the palace Esther was being watched over by someone from the Sanhedrin Brotherhood. He told Hatach of the plot and the conspirators, and instructed Esther under no circumstances to tell anyone but the king, and then only in private.

All had been accomplished before dawn, and back at his home, Mordechai lay awake watching the sunrise through his grilled window and wondering what the day would bring.

The Plot is Foiled

Hatach roused Farah, and Farah, with Hatach at her heels, waited on a tufted bench in Esther's outer vestibule for the queen to return from the king's bedroom. Half an hour passed before they heard Esther's soft steps approaching. A surprised Esther encountered her two impatient and serious-miened aides.

"Dear Farah!" whispered a worried Esther. "What brings you here at this hour?"

"Life and death, mistress," she told the exhausted queen.

"And Hatach," added Esther, acknowledging the loyal messenger. "It must be something dire to rouse you both from your beds. Please come in and tell me."

Once inside the queen's apartment, the door locked behind them, Hatach told her.

Esther allowed Farah to bathe and dress her hastily, in garments fit to wear when waking the king. Esther walked back the way she had come just an hour before, the king's guards nodding at her in familiar obeisance as they passed her through to

Xerxes' chamber. She waited at the closed door, solemn and respectful, for the king to bid her enter.

A smiling, smug and tolerant Xerxes greeted her.

"Back so soon, Esther?"

Ignoring the innuendo, Esther told Xerxes what she knew, and the name of her source. It was part of Mordechai's plan that the king should know that while it was Esther's guardian who had detected and disclosed the assassination plot, it was Esther's lips that had warned her king.

Biktan and Teresh were arrested that very morning, and three days later, after being held and tortured in separate cells in the palace dungeon, the men confessed. Punishment for plotting to assassinate the king — base treason — was death. The king chose to make public only the fact that the two men had committed a treasonous act. He did not care to advertise the fact that there were men within the palace with assassination on their minds. This attempt on his life had come too close for comfort. The king wanted Biktan and Teresh to die painful and slow public deaths. The two were flayed alive and their barely-breathing bodies impaled on stakes in the public square. They lasted two days before breathing their last.

The city of Susa, jubilant just weeks earlier at Esther's coronation banquet, was brought low at the gruesome public evidence that all was not a bed of roses within the corridors of the palace.

And as for the matter of the assassination attempt, Mordechai's loyalty and quick thinking in tipping off the queen and thus saving the king's life was duly recorded in the king's Book of Days at the king's behest.

Haman, the king's close advisor and for his own protection, had urged the king to make Biktan and Teresh a public spectacle and execute them as soon as possible. Xerxes had done so, seeing the power and satisfaction in swift justice. But only later, as the two men had lingered in the miserable twilight of pain-beyond-bearing and not-yet-death, did the king have second thoughts. It might have been better to try to bleed the two for information about a possible ring of conspirators. Were the two working alone? Now he would never know.

The king had not been told of the two men's screams under torture, swearing to existence of a *ban*, a secret manipulator, the mover, instigator and banker behind the assassination plot. The royal butchers had spoken amongst themselves of the two prisoners' consistent screams, which had signified some measure of truth, as both men had confessed the same story separately, while under extreme torture. The captain of the prison brigade sought out Haman, the king's advisor who had been giving them their orders, and told him of his suspicions of the existence of a ringleader still at-large.

"Pay the prisoners no heed. They are raving and will try anything to save themselves, the lying curs."

"But Master Haman, the same exact story from each of them…" the captain had tried once more.

"Enough! Are you an old woman? Do as you are told and finish the job. Take them to within an inch of their lives and then impale them on the stakes. And I will hear no more nonsense about a *ban* or your own life will be forfeit."

So the king, normally not a fool, but extremely shaken by this close call and eager to restore order and safety to his life, chose to consider this assassination attempt an isolated plot fortuitously foiled. Haman breathed a secret sigh of relief, and vowed that the next time he would either do the deed himself or have one of his sons — perhaps Dalphon, the clever and silent one — act as his proxy.

One prime effect of the failed assassination attempt was that Xerxes closed ranks. No longer did he hold daily open-court meetings with fourteen of his advisors sitting in the semicircle as cabinet ministers. No longer did the king ask — first the younger, lower-level seven, and then the longer-sitting, seven higher ministers — for advice and opinions before issuing a law or granting a favor. While he kept his daily court meetings for show and protocol, he now held tight to the political reins, narrowing his trust from fourteen ministers to only one.

Xerxes, shaken by the Biktan and Teresh affair, elevated Haman, son of Hamdata the Agagite, to be his second-to-the-king, in charge of all state security, and he placed all the day-to-day decisions of governing into Haman's hands. The king chose Haman deliberately; he badly needed a viceroy who was ambitious and unscrupulous. The king intended for Haman to act as his proxy, as a royal enforcer with strict instructions to grind any incipient rebellion or perceived disloyalty under his heel. Haman's prime duty was to restore and enforce order in the kingdom. Xerxes reckoned, incorrectly, as it turned out, that it would be easier to exert control over just one man than over a full cabinet. Xerxes' error was in his choice of viceroy.

Shadrach was jubilant, his fist pumping the air.

Old Daniel felt a thunderclap and he shuddered.

Abednego heard maniacal laughter in his nightmares that waxed so loud he could not sleep.

And Mordechai, a momentary hero who had saved the king's life, was quickly forgotten.

Xerxes Closes Ranks at Court

The king, realistically fearful now of coup and assassination, elevated Haman Memuchan from his place in the seventh chair of the second group of seven ministers, to pre-eminence over all the cabinet ministers, scores of courtiers, and every political leader in the Empire. Haman's is now the only voice the king hears on all matters political and diplomatic.

There is no containing Haman's euphoria. His arrogance and ego know no bounds. He has leapfrogged over all his peers and betters, and now stands as de facto viceroy and chief-of-staff to the most powerful man in the world. With Xerxes' sons still children, Haman is, as the saying goes, but one heartbeat away from the throne.

Haman saw his dream coming true before his eyes, and so easily! He even thought that an assassination might not even be necessary. He was so close to the exercise of imperial power that for practical purposes he could control the empire while ostensibly acting at Xerxes' behest. And there was one great advantage to being second-to-the-king: any would-be assassins sent by others would target the king, and would not have *him* in their sights! This lucky promotion could be his secure steppingstone. All the while that he was carrying out the king's wishes and plying whispered suggestions in the king's ear, he also could be consolidating his own power; placing his sons and hand-picked cousins in strategic ministerial positions. He would edge out the ministers loyal to Xerxes, and pack the king's court with men whose paid fealty was *to him*.

Haman would be positioning himself to supplant the king at a future time of his choosing.

And in the back of his mind, but looming larger with his every thought, was the possibility that Fate might have given the beautiful Esther into his hands, after all. As Queen of Persia she was no more than the bedmate of the king. As second to the king, and with frequent proximity to the inner chambers of the palace, who knew if *he* would be the next man to attract her attentions. *All women were jendeh*, he thought, whether for power or for riches, and he, Haman, his power ascendant, might even be her next objective. How sweet would it be to have her dancing to *his* song! He grew excited just thinking of the possibilities.

The ministers and courtiers were taken by surprise by the king's hasty, leapfrogging appointment of Haman, an appointment which disregarded traditional rules of protocol, seniority and patronage.

Though they grumbled amongst themselves, insulted and wary of what Haman's surprise appointment augured for them, they backed away from confrontation with this arrogant and newly powerful vizier. They had no experience with a malevolent dictator; their tenures had been under the pluralistic autocracy that was Xerxes' kingdom, and Darius' before him, where the king sought advice of ministers, possibly even to excess. Never had they served a king who had allowed but a single minister to arrogate to himself so much unchecked power. They were leery and cautious.

They whispered among themselves what they were quick to observe: this newly dominant Haman, clever and manipulative in the ways of politics, was also a frightening bully. The slightest perceived offense would set off his hair-trigger temper. Already two longtime courtiers — who had dared to question Haman's authority in open court right after he had been elevated to top minister — had gone missing. The unspoken suspicion was that Haman had ordered their "disappearance." His sons, the corrupt and fearsome Amalek Baradari, no doubt had been commissioned to handle the disposal. One or two brave governors privately ventured the opinion that the man was even slightly mad.

All members of the king's court were justifiably fearful and wary. Because Xerxes already had given the new vizier a free hand, there was no appealing Haman's abuse of station. The ministers and courtiers, satraps and princes, thus stripped of any influence or proximity to power, kept a low and unthreatening profile at court, taking care to avert their faces and to bow low when in Haman's presence.

Haman thrived on the power he wielded and on the fear he generated. With Xerxes' tacit approval he introduced and enforced a new Empire-wide rule of proskynesis: an Edict of Public Prostration requiring that all citizens bow down low before a god, the ruler, or his proxy. In Haman's mind, bowing low *to him* — just as bowing to the king demonstrated veneration of station and respect — was not only his due; it was now, fittingly, the law.

Xerxes

In the wake of the Biktan and Teresh affair, the king became suspicious of everyone: ministers, princes, courtiers, servants, the palace cook, even the harem girls. Fearless on the battlefield, Xerxes now felt exposed and besieged in his own palace and in his kingdom-at-large. He would not drink a drop without his Royal Cup Bearer's approval; he would eat nothing that had not been vetted in his presence by his royal tasters. Also, he was having trouble sleeping; he imagined a silent assassin behind every drapery fold. Xerxes was afraid to close his eyes.

The only woman he wanted in his bed at night was his new queen. He trusted and desired her, and — extraordinary but true — with Esther by his side he could relax his constant vigil and let sleep take him. Several times since the failed coup she had told him, "Sleep, Xerxes, and I will keep watch. Rest now." And surprisingly, he had done just that, fallen asleep with his head resting on her shoulder. The first time this happened, he had awakened refreshed hours later, to find Esther sitting in an upright chair by his bedside, fully dressed, having kept a solitary watch during the night. At first Xerxes had smiled at the image of his queen as his unlikely bodyguard, but when he approached her he saw her hand resting on the hilt of an unusual dagger on her lap.

"Do you know how to use that?" Xerxes had asked, nodding at the weapon. He had leaned down and touched the dagger's tip. His eyebrows shot up when he saw it was deadly sharp.

"Good morning, My King. I know enough to surprise anyone who makes the mistake of getting too close to you." Esther smiled and slid the dagger into its case and then into the folds of her tunic.

The king had been delighted with Esther's response, and the nightly arrangement seemed to suit him. No one but Esther and Xerxes knew that the fear of coup and assassination kept the king awake nights. It was their tacit secret.

Mordechai

Mordechai was laboring under powerful needs and emotions, all pulling at him from several directions.

First, Mordechai had a strong need for political power, information, and control. As an essentially political creature, Mordechai was aware that he was better positioned now than at any time in his life to be in actual proximity to the seat of power. With Esther as queen, and with his position as Minister at the King's Gate, he theoretically had a direct line to the most powerful king in the world. He was certain he could effect change if he were judicious and lucky. And he was poised to intervene for his people in the event Daniel's premonitions of the coming Terrors came true.

But while his political star was beginning to ascend, Mordechai's heart was weighted down by a countervailing pull on his emotions: His one true love had been torn from him and was now queen, bedded and wedded to the king he was sworn to protect. The emotional discipline and inner strength required to keep Mordechai's rational and emotional selves separate was prodigious. The brilliant and restrained Mordechai was able to do so, but at great cost to his emotional self. His operatives noted that he was colder than he had been in past years; that he no longer made allowances for their slight variations in plans; that he seemed harsher on himself and with them; and that he was more willing to take risks than he had been. And all—including his lifelong housekeeper Poupeh—noted that his temper, hitherto leashed and rarely seen, was closer to the surface.

Mordechai, who had lost his parents early in his life, and whose only "siblings" were his friends in the Sanhedrin Brotherhood and the agents he controlled, was emotionally well suited to his chosen work. He was tightly focused with no emotional ties. With his betrothal to Hadassah, however, all that had changed; for three years he had flourished and luxuriated in the unaccustomed happiness he had felt at her requited love.

After Hadassah had been literally wrested from him as they stood together waiting to exchange vows, however, Mordechai had changed. He had more than reverted to the single-minded man he had been before losing Hadassah. Restrained at knife-point by the king's Home Guard as he watched her being led away from the marriage canopy, and then holding himself back from attacking her captors and rescuing her from the harem—a suicidal mission at best that would likely have killed them both as well as Poupeh and all those inside his house—were the most difficult things Mordechai had ever experienced. Yielding to his spymaster's explanations, premonitions and reasoning, Mordechai had allowed himself to knowingly forfeit, irretrievably and on pain of death, his one chance at personal happiness.

Giving up Hadassah for the greater good of saving his people from an unformed and as-yet purely speculative future "Terror" was Mordechai's personal test; it was his "fiery furnace," his personal "lions' den." And, as would be expected, he did not emerge from it unscarred.

And finally, once Mordechai learned that Haman, a rival from his past, now one of the king's closest ministers and his political superior, had had personal designs on "his" Esther and had meant to do her harm, the ordinarily rational and cool spymaster saw red whenever the man's name was mentioned.

Which was why Mordechai absented himself from the King's Gate for two days after it was announced that Haman had been advanced to the highest advisory seat in the royal court. He did not trust himself not to jump the man and choke the life out of him.

Mordechai was torn and tormented. To further Old Daniel's master plan to position secret Jews close to the seat of power — people loyal to Xerxes and essential to palace governance, but remaining always in the background — Mordechai had to tamp down every emotion and political instinct he possessed.

Haman, who had attempted to kidnap, rape and destroy Esther, remained untouched and at-large, and loomed as an even more powerful threat now that he had been advanced to viceroy. Mordechai's antennae about the man, and whispers he had picked up at the King's Gate and through his informants, left Mordechai virtually certain that Haman had been the brains behind the Biktan and Teresh assassination attempt.

But Mordechai had no proof. And with Haman's clever manipulation of Xerxes' fear of coup, he was in a much stronger position than Mordechai to influence events. The political situation was precarious.

Old Daniel sent Abbas with a coded message warning Mordechai to take care *not* to provoke Haman; in fact, to lay low and stay out of his way. Haman, always on the lookout for a scapegoat — someone upon whom to lay blame for the king's security lapses; for the shortfall in the royal treasury; for any slights to his own enormous ego — was now in a position to do great damage. At a whim he could demote Mordechai, undermine Esther, and potentially endanger the status quo of the nearly three million Persian Jews in the Empire. Daniel feared that in a rash move Mordechai might potentially blow the entire secret operation and years of undercover work out into the open.

Mordechai read the spymaster's message, then held it to a candle flame and watched it burn. Deep in thought, Mordechai waited until the flame touched his fingers before releasing the burned scroll fragment.

Persians and Zorastrianism

Given the vast size of the Persian Empire — spanning nearly eight million square kilometers, stretching across India, Asia, Africa and Europe and containing 50 million people — its diverse populations held scores of ethnicities and religions.

But Xerxes, the royal family, the Persian elite, and a plurality of ethnic Persians throughout the Empire subscribed to the religion of Zoroastrianism. It was a polytheistic religion that emphasized the dualistic struggle of light against dark and good against evil. Its prophet was Zoroaster, who had mythic ties to Cyrus the Great, and its priests were called *magi*, who sacrificed animals on fire altars to multiple male and female deities, notably to Mithra and Ishtar. The *magi* priests were closely linked to the Persian monarchy, and they answered to the Persian kings. They were the chief transmitters of Persian myths and traditions both religious and secular, and — significantly — the *magi* were respected interpreters of dreams and omens. It was these latter functions that gave the *magi* enormous influence in matters of state. Cyrus and particularly his grandson Xerxes were known to consult the *magi* on matters of royal succession, interpretation of ominous royal dreams, the warding off of evil omens, and whether and when to wage war.

Understandably, given the power the *magi* wielded, there was a problem with charlatan *magi* who professed to foretell the future, and who, eventually known as *magicians*, skillfully tricked nobles with sleight-of-hand maneuvers in order to curry favor, manipulate events, and advance and enrich themselves. Many charlatan *magi*, sensitive to what the king wished to hear, or more ominously, responding to private interests of those who had bribed them, would tailor their tricks and predictions accordingly.

For all these reasons Persian kings were reliant on selected trusted advisors to help them sort the "real" omens or interpretations from the sham.

Throughout the centuries of the Achaemenid Dynasty, given the multi-national peoples conquered and annexed by Persian kings, while there was a clear preference for Zoroastrians among the influential court elite and the state leaders, other ethnic religious practices were generally tolerated. There was no state-sponsored compulsion to worship Zoroastrianism. There were, of course — given human nature and cultural and tribal differences — pockets of intolerance and abuse in parts of the Empire. At the many large and small borders local blood was shed over land rights and in grazing wars. At the coastlines there was intense competition for lucrative entitlements to shipping privileges on the Erythrean, Caspian or Black Seas. And there was always local violence between worshippers of the religions of Zeus and Marduk; of the Mother-Goddess and Ishtar; of Baal and Yahweh. Even the sophisticated cosmopolitan city of Susa was not immune to religious and economic chauvinism.

During times of prosperity and stability, the varied ethnic Persian peoples lived side-by-side more or less peacefully. But an unwelcome consequence of political disorder at the highest levels was a trickle-down tendency to assign blame and incite hatred toward different or vulnerable "others." It was just such potentially lethal scapegoating behavior on a mass scale that Old Daniel, Mordechai and the Sanhedrin Brotherhood feared would erupt against the Persian Jews under an evil and volatile viceroy such as Haman. These fears manifested themselves in Daniel's visions of blood; in Abednego's screaming nightmares; and in Mordechai's and the Sanhedrin Brotherhood's hyper-vigilance.

Haman's Promotion

Political fortunes rose and fell quickly after the investigation and subsequent public deaths of Biktan and Teresh. Haman's profile as second-to-the king was dramatically publicized at court when a single seat was placed for him only two steps below and to the right of Xerxes' throne, and a step above the other courtiers' and diplomats' chairs. In fact, even before his seat was ceremoniously put in place, Haman had already begun lording it above the ministers who had, until recently, been closer to the king and more revered than he.

After the attempted assassination, the king no longer trusted his team of ministers.

With Haman's dramatic promotion, the fourteen named ministers were effectively deposed, relegated to an outer vestibule whenever any serious state business was conducted. They no longer conferred with the king, and only retained their titles and salary and remained at court to keep up appearances. But the damage was done; their honor and station had been sullied. And courtiers both high and low now chafed under their demotions, suffering under Haman's heavy hand. They watched, powerless now, as Haman issued edicts both petty and large, and prepared to install his brutish sons, his corrupt cousins and his mistress' lascivious brothers at court. The composition and tenor of Xerxes' court was altered almost overnight. The man Haman was flexing his muscles, heedlessly and sadistically glorying in the power of his new position.

Even Mordechai, whose fortunes had seemed to be rocketing upwards after he uncovered the assassination plot, in a matter of days also had been closed out, ironically by the very king whose life he had saved. Mordechai's political career came to a full stop.

The only voice Xerxes heeded in the throne room was Haman's.

It did not take long for Haman to become universally resented, hated and feared within the palace, though not a man would risk openly opposing him.

Mordechai Collides with Haman

Until one day, when Haman strode imperiously through the colonnaded archways of the King's Gate.

Out of deference to Daniel's cautionary messages and his years-long habit of secrecy, Mordechai had thus far managed to stay out of Haman's way. Since the day, a week previously, that Haman's Edict of Public Prostration had been issued, Mordechai had kept out of the public eye. He remained closeted in his chamber at the King's Gate running his team of operatives, or in the other high ministers' rooms, conducting what business they could, and exchanging information and speculating about their precarious political fortunes in this new political reality. Mordechai recalled the young Haman from their military days two decades earlier; even then he had been petty, envious and vengeful, with a hair-trigger temper. So Mordechai studiously avoided crossing paths with the new second-to-the-king, not wishing to confront or provoke the man whose delusions of grandeur had been realized, and who viewed himself as quasi-royalty.

On this day, one week after promulgating the Edict of Public Prostration, Haman intended to flex his political muscles. He deliberately entered the colonnaded area of the King's Gate, where—pre-Biktan and Teresh—the king's most trusted ministers had gathered daily to conduct the king's business with the Empire's satrap governors, foreign diplomats, and high-level personages who controlled the various enterprises vital to the crown. On this day Haman intended to put to the test the ministers who, just weeks before, had snubbed or disregarded him. He derived a childish pleasure in watching Xerxes' subjects, servants and ministers — essentially everyone he encountered within the walls of the fortress of Susa — scurrying to bend, bow low and prostrate themselves like reeds in a gale whenever he passed. But he had yet to walk through the busy hub of the King's Gate before the noontime break. He was looking forward to it, expecting the rush of almost sexual pleasure he derived from everyone's fear and reluctant obeisance.

Mordechai conferred with Old Daniel, with his Brotherhood friends, and with his closest confidants, Shimon and Eliezer. He spent sleepless nights analyzing the problem of Haman's rise to vizier, and his having eclipsed and sidelined the king's more senior ministers and advisors. Mordechai, along with every thinking Persian Jew, had seen or lived this precise fact-scenario before: a relatively benevolent monarch is turned, overnight, into a paranoid despot, followed inevitably by the quick rise of an opportunistic, ruthless second-in-command. This same situation playing out in Xerxes' Persia boded no good not only to the Jews throughout the Empire, but also to any Persian citizen voicing an opinion not held by a fearful ruler and his tyrannical viceroy.

The prime question on Mordechai's mind is whether to knuckle under to Haman or to resist him.

Mordechai's first concern, given his unproven but strong suspicions that Haman had been the prime mover behind the Biktan and Teresh affair, is that Haman appeared to be moving to craftily sideline — if not eventually to replace — Xerxes, by pandering to the king's fears of coup and assassination. "Let *me* handle this, My King. Do not concern yourself with that," are phrases that Mordechai and his spies have heard Haman speak to the king time and again in past days.

Mordechai could discern, if no one else could, Haman's game plan: Haman intended gradually and systematically to usurp Xerxes' power until he, Haman, controlled not only the court, but also the crown. Haman was unobtrusively boxing the king into a situation where the king comfortably *thought* he wielded power, but where, in reality, he was only a figurehead. Over time and unnoticed by Xerxes, the political tables will have been turned; ministers and concubines, bodyguards and generals, will have been replaced by people loyal *to Haman* and not to Xerxes. At that point Haman's *coup d'état* would be fact, except for the ensuing blood bath.

Once Haman controlled the military, dominated the court, and intimidated the harem and the queen, all that would be left before seizing the crown of Persia would be to kill off not only Xerxes, but also his children.

Haman as Empire-Idol[†]

Mordechai instinctively knew that in the event of such a coup, Haman as king would be intolerable. Haman was evil, sadistic, utterly corrupt, and devoid of compassion. Xerxes, even at his most imperious, had been a relatively tolerant monarch and a formidable general. He, like his father Darius and his grandfather Cyrus, understood that his own greatness and the continued health of the Empire depended, at its roots, on the well-being of his subjects. This understanding contributed to making Xerxes a "reasonable ruler" in the experienced eyes of Old Daniel, Mordechai, and Persia's Jewish citizens.

Another essential characteristic of a "reasonable ruler" that Xerxes had embodied until the recent assassination scare was that he had sought out and promoted men of differing talents and opinions as advisors to the crown. In this way the king was able to hear and consider all sides, develop an informed grasp of

---

[†]The term "Empire Idol" was coined by Yoram Hazony in his book, *The Dawn: Political Teachings of the Book of Esther*, Shalem Press, Jerusalem, 1995, to describe kings or viziers who make themselves objects of worship.

events, so as to be in the best position to govern well. Listening to multiple advisory voices can temper a monarch's ego, and in this way most evil impulses are kept in reasonable check.

But Xerxes became the very opposite of a "reasonable ruler" when he made Haman's voice the single one he sought for advice. By advising and deciding on all matters in private—instead of in open court—absent any consultation with others, the king was led inexorably in Haman's single, unbalanced direction, giving Haman's twisted, amoral and self-centered nature full flower. The king heard only Haman's voice; only *his* opinion. No voice dared opposed his. Haman played on Xerxes' newly-kindled paranoia and fear of coup and assassination, creating a monarchy whose decisions were all fear-driven.

As a viceroy Haman was poison. As a successor monarch, he would be a disaster.

Haman was setting himself up to be Persia's Empire-Idol, the unquestioned single, god-like voice ruling the largest single Empire in the known world.

Mordechai, lifetime political observer and student of Daniel—who had served four monarchs—knew all this, and trembled. Xerxes—before elevation of Haman—was an imperfect ruler, but at least he had listened to multiple advisory voices. Xerxes *now*, under the poisonous influence of delusional and power-hungry Haman, was shaping up to be calamitous.

Stability and peace for the Persian Empire and for Persia's numerous ethnic populations—including Persia's Jews—were dependent on Xerxes' continued tenure—but *without* Haman. The question persisted in Mordechai's mind: How could he help rid Persia of Haman? Was the solution to submit and silently genuflect, or was the solution to resist and confront, provoking a crisis?

Side-by-side with the very real and perilous political reasons for Mordechai's distrust and hatred of Haman, were the potentially explosive personal ones.

First, Haman was the living descendant of King Agag of Amalek, the sworn enemy of the Jews, and Mordechai was a living descendant of King Saul of Israel. The mutual enmity between their peoples stretched back one thousand years and was still alive and potent. Of course, Haman was yet not aware of Mordechai's ancestry, but the two had struck rivalrous sparks against each other two decades earlier as youths. Mordechai knew that if Haman were to discover not only that he was a Jew, but also a descendant of the royal line that had gone head-to-head with his own royal ancestor, all gloves would be off and the vizier's destructive power would be even more focused and vicious.

And then there was the matter of Haman's having targeted Esther. Mordechai could tolerate, even navigate with some relish, a purely political struggle with Haman. But when Haman had set his perverse and lethal sights on the queen, he had unknowingly made the coming struggle a personal one, turning Mordechai into Haman's worst nightmare. Fortunately, thanks to Old Daniel and Abednego, Esther was safe. But Mordechai knew that an added impetus for Haman in his quest to undermine and dethrone Xerxes would be to possess Xerxes' queen.

Esther was temporarily safe from immediate murder only because of her childlessness. Without an heir she posed no overt threat to a usurper. Historically, men who deposed a seated monarch were quick to rape, imprison, otherwise subjugate or even kill the seated monarch's queen, both in order to humiliate her and to quash any thoughts of resistance, and also to demonstrate to the populace that a new entity now dominated *everything* that had belonged to the former king. But if the queen happened to be beautiful or wealthy or powerful in her own right, the usurper oftentimes kept her alive—and his prisoner—for his own purposes.

Noontime at the King's Gate

It was noontime, one week after the Edict of Public Prostration was passed into law, making it mandatory for everyone in the

King's Gate to bend and bow down low to the king and to Haman. The ministers at the Gate, mostly free of obligations now that the king had stopped holding a plenary court session, out of habit milled about the vaulted atrium, talking to one another, exchanging worried opinions about their uncertain futures. Even Mordechai, who of late had taken to remaining within his small second-level chamber or in the nearby rooms of other ministers specifically to avoid the necessity of genuflecting to Haman, on this day was on the floor of the atrium, off to the side, leaning on a pillar, watching and listening.

At noon precisely Haman the Agagite, second-in-command to Xerxes, strode into the colonnaded atrium that was the King's Gate.

The Significance of Bowing

Bowing from the waist or neck as a gesture of honor and respect was an almost universally recognized and accepted, cross-cultural custom. It was a simple and eloquent display accessible to all, even to the very old. In the ancient Near East this simple bow from the waist was a practiced greeting among tribesmen; between brothers after a long absence; between grown children and aged parents, uncles or grandparents. It was certainly practiced between slave and master and was accepted protocol between commoner and king.

Jews as well as other ethnic peoples bowed from the waist or neck routinely. There was nothing in their culture or religion that forbade such a simple display of respect.

But the simple waist-bow, used frequently in daily commercial as well as personal interactions, was a world apart from the *religious* bow. The religious bow was a more complicated and effortful movement, and was reserved for use in devotional service in a temple, or to demonstrate obeisance to a deity. The religious bow involved three movements: first, one bent at the knees; next came the waist-bow, with one's head and eyes facing the ground; and finally, one sank to the ground onto his knees and continued to bow his head until his forehead rested on the floor. In some cultures this last position—body folded into thirds· and forehead resting on the ground—was held for hours during worship or religious meditation. Rising from the religious bow was done at the conclusion of the prayer.

Haman's Edict of Public Prostration was significant for the reason that—in a dramatic departure from protocol—it mandated a *religious* bow—not a simple waist-bow—whenever a minister, citizen or servant was in the presence of either King Xerxes or Haman. Haman had managed to convince the king—genuinely fearful of coup and assassination—that requiring a religious bow, or prostration—recognized by all as a demonstration of fealty reserved for prayer or cult worship—was a reliable show of loyalty to the crown.

The Edict of Public Prostration was in force in the public sphere closest to the king and crown: within the King's Gate, where ministers, diplomats, satraps, courtiers, pages and servants gathered. Biktan and Teresh had been lowly gatekeepers, yet they had had access to knowledge of the king's whereabouts and were therefore a chink in the king's ring of security. Haman effortlessly manipulated the king's fear after the recent close call, convincing him that *everyone* in the King's Gate was a potential traitor, and requiring *all* to jump to attention, genuflect, bend and bow low to the ground in the presence of the king or his vizier, bearer of the king's ring.

The religious bow was acceptable to some peoples, and unacceptable to others. Spartan ministers to Persia, for instance, refused to prostrate themselves to Xerxes, claiming that free ethnic Greeks did not prostrate themselves before another human being. Of course, there was no love lost between Xerxes and the Greeks. But for most citizens of Persia, the religious bow, when applied in a non-religious context, was at worst an inconvenience. To Jewish Persians, following a more theological imperative than the Spartan ministers, affecting a religious bow to anyone or anything other than to their One-God was an outright violation of their religion. The Second of Ten Commandments governing Jewish religious life prohibited Jews from worshipping anyone other than the One-God, their invisible deity. In practice, only during devotional prayer or meditation were Jews permitted to bend, bow and prostrate themselves. Performing a religious bow *to a living person* or to an idol or graven image was considered idol-worship, and was an extremely serious religious transgression punishable by death.

Mordechai was particularly aware of the Jewish prohibition against affecting a religious bow in vain. It was ethnic lore that his mentor, Old Daniel, and Daniel's three friends, Mishael, Hananya and Azariya, had been subjected to similar loyalty tests in Babylonia and Persia half a century or more ago. In a brutal test of their obedience to the king, Daniel's three Jewish friends had been accused of disobeying the Babylonian king's command that everyone bend, bow low and genuflect before a giant golden statue of himself. In fact, as Jews they were patently prohibited from affecting religious bows to a graven "god" who was not their invisible One-God. It was not a matter of loyalty to the king, which they avowed, but of religious imperative. But under the rigid royal edict they were sentenced to death in the fiery furnace by the king for hewing to their religion and disobeying the king's law.

In the end the three men had been miraculously saved from death, and the story of their resistance, and of their adherence to the Commandment forbidding acts of worship to men or other gods, became mythic among Babylonians and Jewish exiles alike.

Mordechai's Dilemma

For his thirty-eight years Mordechai had kept his Jewish origins a secret. His exiled people had learned, by painful experience, that in order to live in peace and achieve any measure of success in their adoptive countries they were better off blending into the country and citizenry, and not revealing their origins. And as a spymaster working toward the safety and security of his people and his country, maintaining a strictly Persian persona was key. But the expedient, public Mordechai did not reflect the private person and his closely held moral scruples. Mordechai was acutely aware that if he came up against Haman's Edict of Public Prostration—one he was forbidden to obey—his secret might be forfeit.

Mordechai was experiencing an eerily familiar existential dilemma: Should he *submit* to the law of the land and genuflect and bow to the ground in religious obeisance to Haman— thereby transgressing his religious Commandments and possibly forfeiting his eternal soul? Or should he *resist* religiously bowing to Haman, Persia's new "Empire-Idol," thereby drawing attention to himself, running the risk of being condemned as treasonous?

Time was running out.

Mordechai met with his mentor on the third night.

"Master, how much longer shall I and my men remain silent in the face of this Haman? He moves quickly to establish himself as Xerxes' voice. Today the new law is that all in the King's Gate must genuflect and bow low to him as to a god. Who knows what will come next?"

The Master nodded once, and spoke from his hooded cloak. "The danger is real. If Haman is successful in sidelining all the king's ministers and speaking for Xerxes, *all* the citizens of Persia will have cause to mourn. And none more so than our people, who have been stateless newcomers, first in Babylonia and now in Persia. If Haman secures his spot as Xerxes' voice, it would not even be necessary for him to risk assassinating the king. The king would have handed the power to him—bloodlessly."

"Which is all the more reason for us to act *now*," interjected Mordechai, "*before* Haman has time to insert his sons and cousins into the ministers' chairs. Once he has secured his position and has insulated himself from any dissent, the king will be a goner.

Haman will effectively rule Persia, and there will be no ousting him." Mordechai slapped his palm against the surface of his writing table to punctuate his statement.

"You are not wrong, Mordechai," responded Old Daniel, thoughtfully. "Politically, the absolute best—and oftentimes the only—time to move against a foe is when he is unstable, before he has become entrenched, surrounded by supporters and sycophants. And as regards Haman, you're right; he is still a loner in Xerxes' 'house.' All the other ministers, to a man, detest him. My spies have heard their talk."

"It's as I said!"

The hooded Master held up his hand, signaling to Mordechai that he heard him, but had not yet finished. "But—it's a long way from disagreement and private dislike of a king's second-in-command to open confrontation. All that you have done so far is stand off to the side and avoid bowing down. Fortunately for you, Haman has taken no notice. But know, Mordechai, that in the present political atmosphere an open confrontation or disagreement with Haman might be construed as rebellion, or— God forbid—treason. *Then* where would you be? Remember, Mordechai, right now Xerxes is accessible to only one minister. You would have no recourse if Haman were to accuse you of treason."

"But if we wait, Master, even one more week, Haman will in the meantime appoint a cousin or a son or any number of like-minded weasels as ministers. Before we turn around the King's Gate will be populated with nothing but sycophants and Haman's bully-boys. Delay is our enemy, Master. Speed is Haman's tool."

"What would you propose, Mordechai? At this point no one but the courtiers and ministers at the King's Gate are subject to the odious edict requiring bending and bowing nose to the ground whenever Haman passes. No one else in Persia is even aware of such a law, or even that there is such a man named Haman who is second-to-the-king!

"If you were to push back, Mordechai, what would you do, and what would you hope to achieve? Rule-One is never to take an action without an objective in mind and a reasonable chance of achieving it."

Mordechai had thought about this precise question for the past week, since the order to genuflect down low in Haman's presence became law. He had the outline of a kidnap plan at his fingertips. "My objective is to rid the Empire of this man. Just say the word, Master, and I will have Haman 'disappear.' I have the manpower on stand-by to mount a clandestine grab, and the resources to stow him in an underground safe house or to ship him overland to a redoubt in the Indus Mountains. What we do with him after that is another matter entirely. But getting him out of the palace with no one the wiser—that's as good as done, if you give the okay."

The spymaster turned away, his hooded silhouette in the candle-lit room casting an enormous shadow over wall and ceiling. He reviewed the possibilities silently, in his methodical way. Mordechai could have acted on his own, without his old mentor's imprimatur, but Daniel had lived a long and perilous life, had controlled hundreds of informants, conducted countless snatches and interrogations, and ordered untold enemies' "disappearances." Daniel's experience in four royal courts, each one rife with plots and counterplots, was valuable, and Mordechai knew and respected this. Still, they were small-time compared to what Mordechai was proposing. This one operation had the potential to blow the monarchy apart. Kidnapping the king's vizier could backfire, forcing the king to retaliate and making him even more paranoid and remote. There was always the possibility that Xerxes would replace the "missing" Haman with another of similar or even more tyrannical stripe.

Or—the operation could potentially fail, in which case Mordechai and the Brotherhood might be exposed, and Haman would be strengthened.

And—a strengthened Haman could convince the king to take revenge against not only Mordechai but also against Esther, who had been Mordechai's ward. Perhaps she was in league with her guardian? Daniel thought that the possibility of endangering Esther had to be avoided at all costs.

Currently, Esther was safe, Daniel thought, because she was a smart girl, and had heeded Mordechai's advice, keeping her people and her kindred a secret. While some of her servants knew she had a connection to a courtier named Mordechai, no one knew she was related to him by blood. That single fact kept Daniel calm.

In the end it was his daytime visions of blood covering everything in sight that pushed Daniel to okay the plan to kidnap Haman. The possibility of ridding Persia of a man who had attempted to rape and destroy Esther; who almost certainly had been behind the plot to assassinate Xerxes; and who, as wearer of the king's ring was even now poised to speak in the king's name as a first step in a grab for the crown, was worth the personal risks.

"Do it," he told Mordechai. "And do it soon, before the man does serious damage."

And the spymaster disappeared, leaving a guttering candle and a thoughtful Mordechai in his wake.

Mordechai spent what was left of the night making a plan, involving four of his most seasoned agents. His idea was to involve as few people as possible in this risky enterprise, ensuring speed and secrecy. Two operatives to effect the grab, and two others to assist in the body transfer. It would take place in three days' time, while the new vizier was still cock-sure, and before Haman became suspicious or watchful. He sent messages written in code on tiny parchment scrolls in his special invisible ink, hidden inside butcher's parcels; and others on prosaic egg shells delivered to agents' kitchen doors. He activated Benjamin and Yehudah, Pinchas and Hulda. All four had worked together successfully on past sensitive undercover operations. Hulda was a thirty-year-old beauty who knew how to lure a man, or at least to distract him just long enough for her partner to hold a drugged handkerchief over the quarry's nose and mouth. And she was deceptively strong. She could "help" lead the disabled man away.

Mordechai scheduled a meeting of the four operatives, the only time they would be together, so that he could issue his detailed instructions to the four of them at one time, answer any questions, and so that the four would recognize one another.

With luck and timing the snatch would work.

But unfortunately for Mordechai, his kidnap operation was fated never to take place.

Mordechai Does Not Bow Down

Mordechai had avoided bowing down low to the ground twice in the past week, when Haman had stridden into the King's Gate and had walked diagonally across the colonnaded atrium. Mordechai had stood unmoving behind a side pillar and watched the vizier strut unheeding through the clusters of ministers, who hurriedly bent low, throwing themselves down onto their knees, their foreheads on the stone floor. The atrium had grown suddenly and unnaturally silent a moment before, and remained so until Haman, alone and aloof, had disappeared through a far archway.

Once conversation buzzed into life again, several of Mordechai's minister-colleagues had approached him. They spoke frankly and discreetly, men who were at ease in conversation with one another.

"Mordechai, why do you disobey the king's law and stand when Haman passes? Don't you know that under the new law all of us here in the King's Gate are required to bow down low to Haman and the king when they pass?" asked one man.

Mordechai had listened respectfully as another seasoned minister interjected, "Of course, the law is really all about licking the boots of this new viceroy. The king *never* shows his face out here anymore, not since Biktan and Teresh scared the stuffing out of him."

"It's all about paying homage to that sadist-fellow, Haman. Mark my words, the man has designs on the throne," said the first man.

"But seriously, Mordechai, why do you court punishment? Why don't you just bow down low like we all do, odious as it is, and be done with it?"

Mordechai had clapped his hand on the nearest man's shoulder in a gesture of camaraderie, and had walked away without answering them. The ministers, all old timers, had shaken their heads and whispered among themselves that this smart young minister was not long for his post if he kept up this brinksmanship. Which was too bad, they thought. Mordechai was a pleasant fellow with a sharp mind and a grasp for political subtlety. A good colleague to have in ordinary times. But the situation at the King's Gate had turned from collegial to dangerous literally overnight, and other ministers and lowly pages and servants had doubtless also noticed Mordechai's silent insurrection.

In truth, at the time, Mordechai had not yet decided to take a stand against Haman. He had half hoped to sit-out the Edict of Public Prostration by avoiding the King's Gate when Haman was expected. But he had been curious to see the viceroy up close, to watch his quarry's posture and facial expressions as he passed through the Gate. He believed in knowing his enemy. And Fate—and Shadrach—laughed at Mordechai.

No Course but to Resist

Mordechai was playing for time. He knew—as Daniel knew, having himself resisted prostrating himself to King Darius decades earlier, ending up in the lions' den—that when pressed to treat a tyrant as a god, the principled, heroic Israelite could not submit. His minister comrades were right; his refusing to bow low to Haman was dangerous brinksmanship. Haman would not be able to tolerate even a single incidence of disobedience. For a tyrant, for a man who had set himself up as an Empire-Idol as Haman had, he must begin as he would go on: he must squash even the smallest expression of resistance to his rule of law.

So it was a certainty, once Mordechai stood tall behind that pillar as Haman passed through the King's Gate, that he was on a collision course with Haman; it was just a matter of time.

Mordechai's mentor, Daniel, had resisted the tyranny of the Empire-Idol, and so had his ancestral heroes: Abraham against King Nimrod, and Moses against the Pharaoh.

To Mordechai, religious obeisance to a human Empire-Idol was as anathema as worshipping a physical statue-idol. Prohibition against submitting to a human Empire-Idol was not just a distant Commandment. To Mordechai, adhering to its stricture was as necessary as breathing. To the Jew of the ancient Near East, idolatry represented the negation of the sacredness of human life; it represented submission to child sacrifice and the death of independent thought; it squashed all "other" voices. Daniel knew this existentially, and Mordechai sensed it: submission to Haman would mean the beginning of the end of Persian Jewry.

The Jews of the ancient Near East were known by several descriptive names. They were the Children of Israel, which described their ancestral provenance. They were Judeans, connecting them to their homeland of Judah. And they were Hebrews, which described their independent mode of thought and worship. This last name — Hebrew — was key to understanding this people that had resisted Empire-Idols for 1,500 years. The precise definition of "Hebrew" meant "person from the *other side*." Someone whose beliefs were strange, "other," or contrary.

A deeply principled Jew simply could not allow himself to worship a physical idol, or likewise to "worship" at the feet of a human presenting himself as a god.

For this reason, as surely as a Jew would resist religious bowing to a tyrannical Empire-Idol, that same Empire-Idol would just as surely move speedily to quash or destroy the resister. The Hebrew or Jew presented a contradictory voice, and so was an inherent threat to the Empire-Idol's absolute power. The principled Jew would go along with the Empire-Idol as *political* figurehead. But he would refuse to pay *religious* obeisance to him. When, as now, the Empire-Idol conflated politics and worship, he placed the Jew in opposition to law. And thus, to the Empire-Idol, a steadfast Jew inherently embodied treason.

For Mordechai, who for all of his life had been a strong and principled man with a sense of responsibility both to his native Persia and for his ethnic people, the Commandment to resist the human idol was a private imperative, a *modus vivendi*, a way of living with his One-God and with his own conscience. Up to now, he and his parents and grandparents had served the King of Persia with unquestioned loyalty and proven fealty; he and his father before him had served with valor in the king's army; there had never been a need to stand up and proclaim his Jewishness or his independence of thought and worship. Under Xerxes — *pre*-Biktan and Teresh — his life as a Persian had included and implicitly *allowed* his Jewishness. That he and his Brotherhood chose to keep their Jewishness a secret was a measure of their caution, born of national memory of centuries of ethnic persecutions and exile. He had dedicated his life to service to the crown, *and* to the continued well-being of his people. Up to now the two missions had not been incompatible.

With Haman's new law, Mordechai and others who believed in the One-God and were forbidden to genuflect except to their God were automatically outlaws.

By planning Haman's kidnap, Mordechai's strategy was to eliminate the Empire-Idol before he caught wind of Mordechai's resistance. Unfortunately, Mordechai's timing was off.

Haman had enjoyed his surprise walk through the King's Gate, watching the snooty ministers scurry to drop to their knees and press their foreheads to the stone floor. He thought he would do it again; no point in letting the men at the King's Gate grow secure. Their days were numbered anyway, did they but know it. Very soon not one of them would remain. He had plans to replace them one-at-a-time with his own flunkies, men who knew how to show their gratitude; men who would rubber-stamp and enforce any edict he proposed, or would look the other way if he ordered an elimination.

On the second day, Mordechai again stood, unobtrusive and behind a pillar, when Haman strode across the atrium of the King's Gate. Again all the other ministers bowed low, and again Mordechai's fellow-lawmakers asked him—on this day and on the next day, as well—why he disobeyed the king's law by not bowing down to Haman.

On the third day Mordechai explained why. "My friends, I am a Jew. I am forbidden by our Commandments to genuflect and prostrate myself to any man or flesh-and-blood king. I can so bow *only* to our One-God, whom we call Yahweh."

The ministers were surprised into silence. As Persians they were aware of the literally hundreds of different ethnicities and peoples who comprised the Empire. Most had no predisposition for or against Jews, but they were aware that Jews were in some important ways different from them.

"But Mordechai, you dress like us; you look like us; you speak as we do; you have lived among us forever. We never knew you as a Jew. We know you as a Persian, same as all of us," said one of his fellow ministers, unbelieving. The others nodded.

"Does your Jewishness require that you forfeit everything you have worked for?" asked another. The surrounding ministers murmured their agreement, and looked to Mordechai.

Mordechai placed his hand on the minister's shoulder, responding to him and to all his fellow ministers. "Majid, my friend, your question is serious, and deserves a serious answer. Simply stated, it is forbidden to me, as a Jew, to set human glory above the glory of the One-God. Prostrating myself to Haman in the way I prostrate myself only to my One-God, and obeying the letter of the king's law, would be a most serious sin. It would endanger my eternal soul to do this, as it would be a tacit refutation of the basic tenet of my faith: that there is only *One* God. My refusal to bow to Haman is not a political or even a personal act; it is a religious one. As a Jew I am forbidden to do it. I am forbidden to treat Haman like a god."

"Even if it means prison for you, or worse?" asked Majid.

"It has never been a jailing or hanging offense in Persia to worship a different God. Let us hope it won't come to that," answered Mordechai.

The ministers dispersed, muttering and whispering among themselves. They were worried for Mordechai.

Haman is Told:
"Mordechai the Jew Will Not Bow Down!"

On the fringe of the small circle of ministers conferring with Mordechai was a small, dark man, dressed as everyone else in belted tunic, trousers, and soft boots. He was one of the last-appointed of Xerxes' ministers, and so had not yet been vetted and assigned a room at the King's Gate. Nor had he, as yet, been accepted as one of the trusted circle; the older ministers barely noticed him, which rankled the new man, who was impatient to advance. Just lately he had become one of Haman's paid informants, agreeing, for a pouch of gold coins and the promise of a coveted chamber in the King's Gate, to keep his ears open and to convey to Haman anything of potential interest that he happened to overhear spoken among the other ministers.

The man thought that Haman would pay handsomely to hear not only that Minister Mordechai would not bow down to him, but also that the reason advanced for his disobedience was that he was a Jew.

So the informant told Haman, and also let the incident be known among the other ministers. He knew that the ministers' political competitiveness, their dislike of Haman, and their basic curiosity would prompt them to quickly spread word of Mordechai's insurrection beyond his trusted circle.

The new man's instinctively foresaw an epic political joust absent drawn swords. It was a battle of the ministers, and all those within the King's Gate were anxious to see who would be left standing. Would Mordechai's conviction forbidding religious bowing to Haman win out against the viceroy's monumental ego and the force of the king's law? What would become of Mordechai the Jew if Haman won the day?

Haman Reacts

Haman decided to see for himself. The very next day he strode, unannounced, through the atrium of the King's Gate, and homed right in on the colonnaded pillar where he was told Mordechai would be standing. Sure enough, Mordechai was standing there, unbowed. The two men locked eyes. Haman, standing in the midst of a veritable crowd of bent and prostrated ministers, felt something snap within him when he saw Mordechai standing tall and alone. He literally saw red, and began to tremble with the force of his anger. If the two men had been alone, Haman would have attacked Mordechai with his dagger, such was his almost uncontrollable reaction.

Shadrach

Daniel's turned boyhood comrade had sent his savage thoughts out to Haman, with the view to inciting the viceroy into an excessive reaction to Mordechai's refusal to bow down. Shadrach was delighted thus far with Haman as his "vehicle." The man was proving a fertile, almost perfect conduit. Haman's own brutal thoughts and intentions were already in place; Shadrach merely projected his own bloodthirsty designs onto Haman's sadistic thought-channels. Haman's own fiendish inclination lapped up his thought-suggestions and built upon them. It couldn't have been easier.

Don't they ever learn? Shadrach mused angrily to himself, thinking about his former countrymen. *We've been through all this before! First Daniel, and then Mishael, Azariya and myself. Principled*

Jews, to a man, we stood up to Nebuchadnezzar and then to Darius, refusing to bow down to the king or to an idol or image of the king. And what did it get us? Fires ten times hotter than the flames of Hell, and the teeth of a pride of lions tearing into our flesh. What a monumental waste! Well, this time Mordechai and Daniel have provoked the wrong man. Haman is conscienceless. He is more brutish than Nebuchadnezzar, less relenting than Darius.

This time, Haman's red wrath will not only tear into Mordechai, but also into all the Jews. I have read Haman's thoughts, and he will have his revenge. The man takes Mordechai's refusal to bow very personally, and he will not sit still for personal insult. Blood will flow like a river in the streets of Susa. Let's see how much pain Daniel and Mordechai can take. I'll enjoy watching Daniel and his protégé and their people meet their violent end. Perhaps then I'll have some peace.

Haman

Haman was aflame, anger and humiliation mixing and percolating within him. *Mordechai!* he thought. *The rival of my youth has come back to plague me! And so now it turns out, by his own admission, that the man is a Jew?!* Haman turned on his heel and marched, eyes forward, out of the atrium. Angry as he was, Haman knew the value of holding back and striking from a position of strength. Still, walking away from the gauntlet that his former rival had thrown down was against his basic nature. He itched to retaliate, and quickly. As he walked to his quarters, his mind raced.

How dare he defy me, the king's vizier? He is the only minister in the King's Gate who refuses to bow down! I am flouted in public, and by a Jew, no less! He is a nothing. He is less than nothing. He is a dead man. But no — dying is too quick, and too easy a punishment for him. I need to make a deeper cut. I must think of something bigger...

Haman pondered his retaliatory move all day, proposing and then discarding ideas. At home that evening, he sat in the salon and his wife Zeresh listened as he poured out the story of the

Edict of Prostration and of the events in the King's Gate: the defiant arrogance of one man, Mordechai—a Jew—who refused to bow down to him.

Zeresh

Zeresh had been a beauty in her youth, twenty years ago. Dark eyes, ebony hair, and lush curves. More, she was the eldest daughter of a spice merchant in Susa, a wealthy man with no sons. She had set her eyes on the arrogant and handsome young Haman, son of Hamdata the Agagite, and had prevailed on her father to approach Hamdata to suggest marriage terms. Though Zeresh's father could refuse his daughter nothing, he harbored reservations about the match. His sharp eyes perceived that the young man Haman was "hungry" for everything: advancement, women, power, riches. And though he came from an ancient and noble family, Haman himself was virtually penniless. Zeresh's father sensed that Haman could be trouble down the long road of life. His daughter would bring her fortune to the marriage, but this mercenary young man would control it. It galled Zeresh's father that her hard-earned dowry might be squandered by this man. He worried that his beautiful and clever daughter might be making a bad bargain. But Zeresh insisted, and in the end she had her way and was wed to Haman.

Her father had been right. Haman had proved to be a faithless husband and a tyrannical and brutal father. During the first three years of marriage and after siring two baby sons, Haman, never a tender lover even when they were newlyweds, showed his true colors. The first time he struck his young wife across her face was over a perceived slight when she was still nursing their second son. He had stormed out of the house, leaving a weeping and bruised Zeresh, a terrified toddler and a screaming infant. Needing constant adoration Haman began spending his nights in the beds of mistresses, leaving his wife alone, with the babies, a housekeeper, and her shame.

Zeresh had fled to her father's house after that first time, but after listening to her tale and grudgingly allowing his wife to minister to their daughter's swollen face, Zeresh's father had sent her back to her husband, following the custom of the time and place.

After that, Zeresh never again fled to her parents' house. She endured her husband's infidelities and rages, bore him six more sons and one daughter, and ignored his mistresses and their two bastard sons.

Until one night. After a savage beating where Haman had used his open hands and also his balled fists on her, and after he had raped her, Zeresh—dutiful and submissive Persian daughter and wife—decided she had had enough. She vowed to herself that that was the last time Haman would touch her, ever again. She had remained silent throughout the beating, biting her cheek to keep herself from crying out, as her cries would have excited and enraged Haman even more. Her husband enjoyed inflicting pain and hearing her plead for mercy, so she denied him that satisfaction.

Zeresh had a plan.

That same night, after Haman had gone to sleep, she left their bed and took his *khanjar*, his razor-sharp dagger, from the secret pocket in his tunic hanging in his wardrobe. Zeresh, her cheek split and oozing and one eye purpled and closed, and nursing a cracked rib, sat in a straight-backed chair by the bed, her husband's dagger in her right hand. Some instinct woke Haman, and he sat up, startled to see his wife sitting up in the dead of night. He opened his mouth to berate her, but then, by the moonlight showing through the curtain, he caught a glimmer of the knife blade. Instantly he changed his tack, pretending he had not seen the *khanjar*.

"Zeresh, what are you doing sitting up in the cold of night? Come to bed before you catch a night spirit. I will warm you."

But Zeresh was no fool, and she had had all night to think. She raised the *khanjar* deliberately, and let it catch the moonlight. She wanted Haman to see it and to be afraid. She held the dagger expertly, using her fingertips on its hilt instead of grasping it like an amateur. She twisted the knife slowly, in a seemingly casual manner, as she spoke. She watched Haman watching the blade. She had his attention now.

"Listen to me, husband. When I was seven years old my uncle, my mother's brother, came to me in the night and tried to make me perform sex acts with him. I cried out and my mother heard, rushing in just in time to save me. She told her brother that if he ever so much as looked at me, or came close enough to me to breathe the same air as I did, she would castrate him. You see, my mother was a butcher's daughter, and she knew the ways of the knife better than most men. My uncle never bothered me again. And the very next day my mother taught me to wield the *khanjar*." She paused, allowing Haman to absorb the implication of her words.

"You are a brute and a sadist, Haman, but believe me when I say I am no longer afraid of you. In fact, because I crave power as much as you do, I am prepared to come to an accommodation with you. With my father's money, your ambition, and my assistance, you can make your way to the top of the king's cabinet. But—touch me again without my permission, and I swear to you—on the eyes of my children—you will end up with less than nothing; you will end up a eunuch, bleeding in a gutter."

Ever since that night, Zeresh slept in a separate, locked bed chamber in her own small house. And Haman never again raised his hand to her, instead venting his sadism on his mistresses and on the whores in his sons' brothels.

As the years passed, secure in the knowledge that behind closed doors she held the upper hand in her household, Zeresh was more or less content to serve as her husband's advisor. She had a quick understanding of strategy and an instinct for politics, and Haman, appreciating the value of her counsel, consulted her more frequently now, after two decades of marriage, than he ever had when they were young.

For now, Zeresh thought, *it was enough*.

Zeresh's Idea

That night, Haman unburdened to Zeresh the entire matter of Mordechai's refusal to bow.

"Mordechai's offense cannot go unpunished! His refusal to bow is a challenge to my control, and is a humiliation. I will cut him down for his open defiance, but I want the punishment to be something slow, painful and public. And I want to move quickly, making a show of strength, sending a clear message to others who might also get it into their heads to challenge me. I need a plan."

Zeresh had listened carefully, and, sitting across from her husband, she held up her hand. "Husband, you miss the point. Punishing or even killing Mordechai would rid you only of the one Jew. But there will surely be another of his tribe to take his place. They are everywhere, they are clever, and they know how to manipulate kings. Come to think of it, isn't that silent old stick—that ancient minister at court who is followed around by a deaf mute—isn't he a Jew, too? He was an advisor to Xerxes' father, and he is *still* hanging around, probably whispering into the ears of other ministers and even the king himself. *He's* got to go, too.

"No, husband, the way I see it, you would be a fool to dispose of only Mordechai the Jew. The better plan—the only plan—is to take advantage of his infraction and devise a scheme that will strike at *all* the Jews of Persia. Eliminate *all* of them and you will not forever be looking over your shoulder, wondering if yet another Jew, a member of Mordechai's rebellious people, will arise to defy you. Be done with them all in one fell swoop, striking fear into the hearts of *all* Persians, and spread your power and influence beyond the palace and Susa. Such a broad scheme will project you onto a larger stage, and will make you a force not only within the King's Gate, but throughout the Empire."

Haman was silent. Zeresh had hit a bull's-eye once again. It was an evilly brilliant idea. He would figure out the details, but the broad plan was perfect. But he expressed only mild appreciation to Zeresh. He needed the woman, that was for sure, but no good would come of giving her a swelled head from excessive praise. She was, after all, only a woman.

"Thank you, wife. I will consider your advice."

Devising a Killing Scheme

Early the next morning, walking quickly through Susa's empty streets on his way to the palace, Haman parsed the details. The first order of business was to work his way around Xerxes, to get him to agree to an Empire-wide killing scheme. In Haman's lifetime there had never been an ethnic "cleansing," a sanctioned killing off of a single population within the vast and varied Persian Empire. But it was not unprecedented. Just fifty years previously there had been a mass killing of *magi* under King Darius; and fifty years before that there had been a massacre of Scythians.

To get the king's permission and imprimatur this time, he knew he would have to appeal to at least one of the king's key interests: his own safety; the state of his treasury; the readiness of the military; his queen, or his harem. Haman thought he had hit on the perfect combination of paranoia and avarice, but before presenting the plan to Xerxes he needed to be assured of the plan's success. He moved through the morning-quiet palace corridors directly to his private palace chamber.

His first order of business would be to consult the Oracle.

The Oracle

In the Ancient Near East, at the time of Mordechai, Haman and Xerxes, and as far back as nearly two millennia before their births, men had practiced cleromancy—a casting of lots or rolling of dice, the consulting of an Oracle or other means of random prediction—to reveal the will of the gods or the fates. Kings asked the Oracle whether and when to wage war. Priests asked the Oracle to differentiate the holy from the profane. Judges asked the Oracle to distinguish between the innocent and the guilty. Generals asked the Oracle to reveal the secret hiding places of their enemies. Ordinary men consulted the Oracle about whether to undertake a perilous journey. Women consulted the Oracle about whether they should marry, and on the issue of fertility and childbearing.

Predictably, since reliance on the Oracle was pan-cultural, depending on the region or country, the Oracle was known by different names to different peoples.

Pre-Islam, the Arabs consulted the *Kaaba*, arrow shafts shorn of arrow heads or feathers, etched with either of two words: "command" or "prohibition." The *Kaaba* were stored in a protected container in the city of Mecca, watched over and deciphered by men known as Guardians of the *Kaaba*.

The ancient Israelites consulted the *Urim and Thummim,* a singular and unique golden breastplate with inlaid colored stones—some say the earliest *Urim and Thummim* were of wood or bone—worn by their High Priest, and used to communicate directly with their God, Yahweh. Because early *Urim and Thummim* were used to determine guilt or innocence, use and guardianship of the *Urim and Thummim* was restricted to the High Priest, the impartial authority figure.

Later on, as use of *Urim and Thummim* widened in scope, the High Priest consulted it in order to pose almost any direct question to the Deity. In answer, the *Urim and Thummim* would glow, the stones either spelling out primitive or coded words, or indicating a simple "yes" or "no." Another legend says that the *Urim and Thummim* were two "speaking stones," one black and the other white. Either way, the constant was that while the ordinary Israelite could pose the question, it was only the High Priest who, through use of the *Urim and Thummim*, engaged in direct communication with the Deity and so could decipher the response.

The meaning of the words *Urim and Thummim* was "light" and "perfection," or, perhaps, "light" and its opposite: absence of light.

It is likely that the various descriptions of the *Urim and Thummim* were all at least partly authentic; any variations in their oracular use depended on location and epoch—on where and when it was used.

Whether through the *Kaaba* or the *Urim and Thummim*, or through oracular sticks and stones, priests or magi across the ancient Near East sought to speak directly to a higher force.

Over time, however, in the various cultures of the ancient Near East, as populations spread out and travel became more arduous, it became burdensome for people to journey to the main city to pose their questions to either a Guardian or a High Priest. So it devolved to local wise men, known as shamans, or to oracular illuminators, to function as the stand-in human vehicles for interpreting the word of the Oracle, thus rendering advice on a smaller, more intimate scale.

But of all the oracles in use at the time, the perceived power and magic of the *Urim and Thummim* remained most deeply rooted in the minds of the ancient Israelites and their Mesopotamian neighbors. It is not surprising that decisions to wage war, victories won, or fortunes amassed—allegedly based on the divinations of the *Urim and Thummim*—made possessing the priestly breastplate into a legendary and coveted quest, not unlike the later myths of the elusive Golden Fleece. Men who craved power dreamed of owning it. Successive invading kings directed their generals to capture the Israelite Temple in Jerusalem precisely in order to seize for themselves the Temple's riches, which they hoped would include the priestly and magical *Urim and Thummim*. Kings fantasized about the untold power they could wield if only they could harness a medium that allowed them to speak directly to a god or to a fate!

Still, regardless of its form or mythic desirability, and its wide use in the ancient Near East, by any name the Oracle was a flawed instrument that was subject to error. Its first flaw was inherent to the Oracle itself: nearly all Oracles were by their nature "binary," meaning they indicated a simple basic choice: yes or no, go or stay, guilty or innocent. Its decisions were devoid of any subtle valuations or shadings. The second flaw was that the Oracle was administered by humans, meaning the question posed to it might have been inexpertly worded or ambiguous, thus yielding an inconclusive result.

Or—and this was a common outcome—the Oracle's response was incorrectly understood or interpreted, depending on the bias of the person analyzing the response. A related, serious flaw in the Oracle was the possibility that the person interpreting it was subject to bribery and corruption. In either of theses two instances—the first inadvertent, the second deliberate—the "reading" of the Oracle would either be faulty or distorted.

The Theft of the *Urim and Thummim*

When the Babylonians conquered Judah, more than a century before Xerxes ruled Persia, King Nebuchadnezzar followed his basic conqueror's pattern: he ordered that Jerusalem, Judah's capital city, be burned to the ground; he exiled the Israelite noble class; and he had their Holy Temple sacked and burned. But before he did so, King Nebuchadnezzar, in a private conversation with his most trusted general, swore the man to secrecy and told him about the *Urim and Thummim.*

"I charge you to search for this priestly breastplate, my trusted friend and warrior. It is likely housed somewhere within the Jews' Holy Temple in Jerusalem, and if it is not hidden, it will surely be well guarded. Do whatever is necessary to find and secure it. You and only you are to have possession of it until you return to Babylonia. Do not speak of your quest, or tell anyone of the breastplate's powers. Let your men think you want it for your king because of its precious gold and rare stones. Bring the *Urim and Thummim* directly to me. Swear an oath that you will do this."

And Nebuchadnezzar's general had sworn to his king.

But the Israelite priests, seeing that Jerusalem was lost and the Temple was about to come under the torch, were determined to prevent the powerful *Urim and Thummim* from falling into enemy hands. They had taken precautions.

Alone and by candlelight on the night the Babylonian invaders had entered Jerusalem, the Temple's High Priest had wrapped the holy breastplate in linen and sheepskin and buried it beneath the stone floor of the Temple's eastern wall, in a waterproofed box lined with oiled parchment. The High Priest had worn the *Urim and Thummim* for fifty years, and had faithfully interpreted its oracular magic. Parting with it was like losing one of his five senses. So as an added safeguard, before sealing the box, the High Priest had laid his gnarled hands on the wrapped bundle and had pronounced a protective incantation. Muttering in ancient Aramaic, the High Priest, knowing nothing human could lessen or *erase* the Oracle's powers, had instead jumbled them. The *Urim and Thummim* would henceforth speak accurately only when in worthy hands. In other hands, it would speak a flawed "truth." And finally, the High Priest had devised an incantation that consigned to a fiery Hell anyone who purloined or abused the *Urim and Thummim.* Then he buried the box, secreting it beneath a heavy Temple paving stone.

Unseen and undetected, a young menial within the Temple, a paid informant of the Babylonian general, had shadowed the High Priest, noting and reporting the breastplate's hiding spot.

Thus it happened that King Nebuchadnezzar of Babylonia came to capture and possess the *Urim and Thummim*, the powerful Oracle of the Jews. But unbeknownst to anyone, the Jews' Oracle now bore a protective charm as well as a curse.

It is not known whether the *Urim and Thummim* ever were consulted by Nebuchadnezzar, or by Belshazzar after him. What *is* known is that in a historic turnabout, the hitherto-unconquerable Babylonians were defeated by the Persian army, and among the captured treasures was the box containing the *Urim and Thummim*. Persian King Cyrus, and Darius after him, showed commendable insight into the potential magical powers of the captured *Urim and Thummim* — and a healthy superstition and respect for it — by appointing Daniel, the exiled Jewish noble and trusted advisor to kings, as its custodian.

It was Xerxes who, in the wake of the recent Biktan and Teresh affair, transferred safekeeping and stewardship of the Jews' Oracle to Haman. Abbas, the mute giant, and Mishael and Azariya — known as Meshach and Abednego — had watched the iron key to the room housing the *Urim and Thummim* pass from Daniel's key ring to Xerxes, and thence to Haman. Daniel and his comrades shuddered. The evil Hananya-turned-Shadrach laughed. And Haman secretly rejoiced.

There is more than one path to power, he thought.

Mordechai

It is the twelfth year of Xerxes' reign; five years since the king selected Esther to succeed Vashti; two months since Biktan and Teresh had been hanged for treason in the public square at Susa; and mere weeks since the king elevated Haman and sidelined the rest of his cabinet. Mordechai's loyal heroism in discovering and reporting the assassination plot against the king has been recorded but forgotten. Haman has engineered a royal edict requiring all those in the King's Gate to execute a deep and prostrating religious bow whenever he or the king passes by. And ironically, instead of reward or adulation for his proven loyalty to Xerxes, Mordechai has acquired notoriety for refusing to bow down to Haman. His explanation—that as a Jew he is forbidden to prostrate himself to any idols, whether they be human or man-made—has had no effect on Haman's red rage. Haman sees only that he has been defied and publicly humiliated by a Jew, and especially one who has been an irritation to him since their youth.

Mordechai is now the object of curiosity, pity, and even schadenfreude, as all within the King's Gate wait to see how Mordechai's principles of faith will stand up when pitted against a powerful Haman's vengeful ire.

On the day he refused to bow down to Haman, Mordechai deliberately remained on the atrium floor at the King's Gate afterwards, rather than returning to his small chamber. He knew the other ministers would want to hear, again and again from his own mouth, the explanation for *why* he refused to bow down. The ministers, some of whom had been his close political allies, had crowded round him, firing comments in their anxiety or excitement.

"Now you've really done it, Mordechai. This fellow Haman will come down on you with his weapons drawn," said one older minister.

"I still don't see the point of all this. Why did you defy him and disobey the king's law for such a simple thing as a bow?" said another.

"Why couldn't you just have bowed down and been done with it?" was the overriding question and genuine amazement for these most practical of politicians. In their minds, there was no point in taking a stand against the king's viceroy if there was nothing concrete to be gained, and worse, if it brought a guarantee of grave repercussions.

So Mordechai tried once more to articulate for them how deeply the religious bow cut against his fundamental principles. But to an extent, Mordechai's hands were tied. How could he tell theses mostly decent men that their acquiescence to bow to

Haman, a human Empire-Idol, was, in its way, also promoting evil? That knuckling under to a man who saw himself as a god was the first slippery step away from freedom and toward enslaving themselves? That compliance to the law requiring "worshipping" Haman was, in a very real way, the beginning of their own demise and the death of their tolerant and melting-pot way of life? They simply did not see it that way, and would turn in anger against *him* for calling them complicit or cowardly. And the irony of it was, that by executing the religious bow—over in a matter of minutes, really—they would have bought life for themselves, albeit temporarily and at the whim of the Empire-Idol.

Still, Mordechai tried to explain.

"My friends, I am a Persian, as are all of you. I was born right here in Susa as my parents were before me. I grew up playing in the same streets as some of you. My political allegiance is to our king and our Empire. I have dedicated my life to the same work as you all have done: furthering the prosperity and welfare of our country. And recently, fortune smiled on me, allowing me to uncover the murderous treachery of Biktan and Teresh right under our noses, in the process saving Xerxes' life.

"But I am also a Jew. To be a Jew is my religion, as yours is Zoroastrianism. One of the fundamental Commandments governing a Jew is the prohibition against bowing down in a religious bow—genuflecting and prostrating ourselves on the ground—either to an idol or to another man, even if he is a king. Such a *religious* bow is a man's personal prerogative. Never before in Xerxes' Persia have we been required to demonstrate our loyalty to the crown by violating our religious beliefs. The fact that I saved the king's life within past weeks speaks most articulately to my proven loyalty and fealty to Xerxes. Requiring a religious bow is a mute and unnecessary pantomime of a loyalty test, unworthy of us as free Persians.

"And there is the added fact that this man, Haman the Agagite, is the direct descendant of a people who have been ancestral enemies of my own people, the Jews, for a thousand years.

"My friends, it is no simple thing to try to explain deeply held feelings or a deeply held principle. Try to understand that while I can accord the king's vizier simple courtly respect" — and here Mordechai mimed inclining his head, as everyone at court was wont to do daily and often — "I *cannot* — on my religious soul and personal integrity — prostrate myself to Haman the Agagite *as if he were a god*. This is absolutely forbidden to me as a Jew; it is one of our Ten Commandments, the words we live by. And as a Jew I am prepared to — actually, I am required to — die, if need be, upholding this Commandment."

The small crowd of ministers had formed a semicircle as Mordechai began to speak. Now they were momentarily silent, not a one of them willing to break the spell of his words. However slender the thread of his argument, Mordechai's rationale made sense. Persia was comprised of so many people, religions and ethnicities that the crown gave wide berth to one another's different beliefs. Tolerant heed was generally paid to reasonable religious practices within the vast Empire. So while it took courage and not a little recklessness to stand against the new, volatile vizier, both Mordechai and the ministers had a credible expectation that his reason for disobeying the edict would be found acceptable.

And as Persians, they could certainly understand and respect a thousand-year ancestral enmity.

Even so, some ministers instinctively feared that Persia's tolerant ways were a thing of the past under Haman. Having witnessed up-close the man's temper and megalomania, given the choice they would have refrained from going up against him. Others secretly thought, *While principles are fine things, what good are your religious principles if you are thrown into the king's dungeon for the rest of your life, or if you are burned in a furnace or hanged for treason?* Some of the older ministers, who had acquired some knowledge of the exercise and abuse of power, suspected that Mordechai would face serious sanctions instead of benign sufferance.

The gap between Mordechai and the other ministers effectively became a gulf the moment Mordechai was willing to risk everything for a principle, and they were not. These men were politicians, not heroes, and certainly not martyrs. Mordechai's refusal to bow down — however rational it may have been to him — meant political and perhaps even actual suicide, which was a far greater anathema to the other ministers than was bowing down to a vainglorious and sadistic autocrat.

As he made his solitary way home that night, Mordechai felt tired. Setting aside his personal disappointments, he had one abiding regret as he faced what was sure to be serious punishment. Having painstakingly acquired a proximity to power over the past three decades, he thought now — with real sadness — that he would never get the chance to use this influence to benefit his own people.

But even Mordechai, a master tactician, underestimated the new vizier. Haman blindsided everyone. What neither Mordechai nor any of the ministers at the King's Gate appreciated was the depth of Haman's humiliation. None of them could have predicted the nature and scope of the punishment Haman would devise.

Only Daniel had seen the red haze. Only Abednego had heard the maniacal voice of Shadrach. The Terror was almost upon them.

Haman Consults the *Pur*

At sun-up on the morning following his consultation with Zeresh, Haman strode through the deserted palace walkways. He made his way past sleepy palace guards who jumped to attention, mentally noting that he would replace them all with his own men soon enough. He did not slacken his pace until he reached a side corridor of the palace nearby to the apartments where state business was conducted. He walked directly to an unmarked wooden door, thick and studded with iron. Sorting through the laden key ring chained to his leather waist girdle, he found the heavy iron key and slid it home, turning the lock.

The small, windowless chamber was dark. Silently, Haman's personal eunuch, a diminutive Ethiopian, appeared at the doorway holding a small torch.

"Allow me, Master." He preceded Haman into the chamber and lit the lantern sconces on either side of the door, casting a soft light inside. The room contained only two round tables, both of acacia wood. On one lay an engraved wooden ark. Within it was housed the *Urim and Thummim*, the stolen Jews' Oracle that had passed via conquerors' right into Persian hands. The other table was empty.

"Is there anything else I can do to serve you, Master Haman?"

"Summon the royal magi! Roust them from their beds and say the royal vizier commands their immediate presence. Bring them here to me!"

"At once, Master." The Ethiopian bowed out of the chamber as silently as he had appeared, pulling the heavy door closed behind him.

Haman's plan was to have the royal conjurers activate and consult the powerful *Urim and Thummim*, asking for a precise, propitious date—month and day—for his planned Empire-wide genocide of Mordechai and his people. Haman wanted all the signs to be aligned in his favor before his audience with Xerxes later in the day, when he would present his scheme and seek the royal imprimatur. Haman knew that if he tried to enact an Edict of Persecution on his own initiative, the king—always sensitive to overreaching, but even more so now—might balk at his aggressiveness. Whereas if the Jews' destruction were cannily presented, and the king's paranoia and vulnerability subtly exploited, the king might okay the killing scheme outright. It was a calculated risk to consult the *Urim and Thummim* on his own beforehand, but Haman was impatient to begin and he relied on his coming presentation—with the blessing of the Jews' Oracle in hand—to convince the king and win the day.

Haman paced. Within minutes the two magi were standing at attention, one of the men still adjusting his sash, the other visibly perspiring. Even in the few weeks since Haman's elevation to second-to-the-king, his reputation had become known. This vizier issued rapid-fire commands and doled out punishment for even a moment's hesitation. So the two magi hurried to respond to the early morning summons, suspecting it boded no good. However privileged they were, living in the fortress of Susa, the magi were still servants of the king. If this Haman wore the King's Ring and wielded the king's authority, then however irrational or surprising his command, they were prepared to try their best to fulfill it. They wanted to keep their jobs and their heads.

"Close the door and wait outside," Haman ordered the eunuch. "No one is to enter without my say-so."

The servant backed out of the chamber and the door clicked shut.

Without preamble, Haman addressed the magi. He had thought out how much he would tell them. The matter needed to be sufficiently urgent to have summoned them so precipitately. But would they activate the Oracle just on his command? He decided to tread cautiously to start.

"I have before me an extremely pressing matter of state. Tell me, when you are asked to determine a date to wage war, which Oracle do you consult?"

The taller and calmer of the two magi answered the vizier.

"We cast the lot, Master, the *pur*. The king and his general will ask us the questions, such as whether to wage a war, or whether or not to attack, also what month and day. We pose the questions one at a time, throwing the *pur* for each inquiry. The Oracle will answer us through the *pur*."

"Have you ever consulted the *Urim and Thummim*? asked Haman.

"I have, Master," answered the fat, perspiring magus. "Years ago, when we fought the Greeks."

"Hmm. As I recall, that was not one of the *pur's* great moments." Haman was referring to the Battle of Marathon. Haman pinned the perspiring conjurer with his gaze. The man murmured in agreement, clearly uncomfortable, recalling that the magi and the Oracle had failed to predict Darius' ignominious defeat at the hands of the Greeks in that decisive battle. After a pause, Haman continued.

"I have a matter of paramount national importance to ask the Oracle. It concerns a battle date, and entails the safety of the

Empire. I will need my choice of date to be absolutely correct before I assure the king later today that all signs are favorably in accord. I would like you to ask both the *pur* and the *Urim and Thummim* for a month and day on which to wage this battle. Can you do this?"

The tall magus spoke up. "You would have us pose the questions twice? First using the *pur*, and afterwards asking the *Urim and Thummim* for confirmation?"

"Yes. Can you do this?" countered Haman. He was taking no chances.

The two magi turned to each other and came to a tacit decision.

"Technically, it is possible, Master. But we will need the king's authority before activating the *Urim and Thummim*. It could mean our heads otherwise," said the fat one.

Haman wanted to throttle the spineless coward, but he held onto his temper. He also wanted the Oracle's date confirmation like he wanted his next breath. He was determined to go before the king with the month and day of the proposed annihilation, and to treat the matter as a simple ethnic cleansing, one that would be beneficial to the wellbeing of the crown and Empire, and that would be accomplished all in a single day. Having taken the measure of the magi, Haman decided to try a bluff; to intimidate rather than cajole.

"Do you dare to doubt me?" Haman allowed his anger at Mordechai and the entire situation to boil over. "Xerxes has made me vizier, second only to him. He has entrusted me with the key to this room! I am empowered to consult the Oracles at my discretion. You will act at my command and activate the Oracles! And you will ask them now, in front of me!"

Haman's anger was genuine, and the magi saw this. Haman was red-faced, vibrating with emotion. Again the magi looked at each other in silent understanding and communication. *Survival, at all costs.* The tall one spoke.

"Of course, Vizier. We will treat your word as a command from the king."

So Haman signaled the magi to get to it. He stepped off to the side and watched them at work. First the two men stood facing what would have been the room's eastern wall. They stood erect, arms upraised, palms turned inward, their faces turned upwards, their eyes shut and their lips moving. Haman became aware of a low hum. The magi were chanting, preparing to activate the Oracle.

Minutes passed. In unison the two magi stopped their chant and lowered their arms. They continued facing the wall, and the tall one approached it, touching the wall gently. Haman heard a soft *snick*, and a small, nearly invisible panel door opened outward. The tall magus reached into the wall cavity and removed a deep-blue velvet pouch and a folded velvet cloth of gold and purple. He spread the cloth on the surface of the second round table, and, cradling the pouch reverently in his palm, he upended it and shook out two ivory dice onto the cloth, each die the approximate size of a hen's egg. The dice were hexagonal in shape, heavily inscribed with black and red letters and pictograms. The magi began chanting again, the tall magus simultaneously rolling one die in his hands as if to warm it. With the smaller magus still chanting, the tall one raised his voice in a kind of supplication, rubbing the die all the while, then, in a sudden silence, he cast the die onto the cloth. His face fell as he peered closely at the upper face of the die.

"Well? What does it say?" demanded Haman.

"The *pur* does not assent to the first month of the year. We must throw it again," answered the fat magus.

Eleven more times the conjurer cast the lot until finally, reading the die after the twelfth roll, his face registered satisfaction.

"The die has settled on the month of Adar, the twelfth calendar month, eleven months from now."

Haman grunted, and the magus replaced the first die and picked up the second one, hypnotically repeating the chanting, rubbing and throwing ritual as with the first die, the other magus humming a chant all the while. Eventually the taller magus turned and addressed Haman.

"The *pur* designates the thirteenth day of the twelfth month, Master Haman."

Haman nodded, and tilting his head subtly, he indicated the second table with his chin. "And now, for our confirmation."

The first magus carefully returned the dice to their pouch. He folded up the table cloth and returned it all to the wall cavity, pressing the spring-door flush with the wall panel. Meanwhile, the second conjurer approached the table where the carved ark lay. His companion stood off to the side as the smaller man opened the ark and removed a bundle wrapped in aged sheepskin. He lay the bundle on the table beside the carved box and unwrapped it slowly.

There was no earthly reason the small chamber should momentarily glow with a flash of light, but a bolt of white radiance shot from the uncovered breastplate and ricocheted around the room, extinguishing itself mere seconds later back on the exposed breastplate. The magus stepped back from the table. This time there was no chanting. The conjuror crossed his forearms over his chest, bowed his head, and stood in respectful silence for a full minute, his lips moving silently. He appeared to be uttering an incantation, but in reality he was sending up a prayer to the Jews' One-God, Yahweh, asking forgiveness for arrogating to himself what had been the singular right of the Temple High Priest a century ago. And requesting a response to questions he was about to pose.

Haman shifted his feet with impatience.

Eventually the magus held up the *Urim and Thummim* breastplate and affixed it with a strap around his shoulders and chest. From the bulge of his muscles as he lifted it, it was clear that the breastplate was heavy. It was also magnificent. Its rose-gold backing seemed to glow in the room's torchlight. Inlaid into the breastplate's front face were twelve enormous colored gemstones, each bearing strange black or gold engravings, lettering or etched pictures of animals. Haman thought he heard a humming, but he must have imagined it because the two conjurers were silent.

The moment the breastplate lay against his heart the magus murmured his request, first in Pârsi and then in a language Haman did not recognize. Haman was about to challenge the man but thought better of it. He held himself in check by force of will; Haman was not accustomed to relinquishing control, and he hated that these magi — admittedly, only temporarily — had a power over him, wielding a special knowledge he did not posses.

It rankled that he needed them. His hands were tied when it came to speaking to the Oracles. Only the magi possessed that ability.

The faint humming resumed, so that Haman actually felt a buzzing inside his head. He held one hand over his eyes and placed the other palm against the wall for balance. He felt dizzy, as if the floor had shifted. *Was it an earthquake?*

The feeling passed and the humming stopped, and the magus opened his eyes and addressed the vizier.

"Master, I have your answer. The *Urim and Thummim* confirm the *pur*. The date for your proposed military action is the 13th day of the 12th month of Adar, eleven months from now.

"This is as I expected," said Haman, perspiring. "Put the Jews' Oracle back in its box. When we leave this room the two of you will speak of what we did here today *to no one*. Is that absolutely clear? Say it!"

And the two men said in unison, "We will speak of this to no one."

"Violation of this promise will mean your deaths!"

The magi stood at attention, absorbing the sincerity of this vizier's threat. They would keep their promise.

When all within the chamber was as it had been an hour before, Haman opened the hallway door and the three men exited. When the Ethiopian eunuch stepped inside to douse the sconces, it seemed to him that the carved ark on the table gave off a glow that became weaker by the second. He quickly backed out and pulled the door shut. Haman locked it, dismissed the magi, and ignored the Ethiopian. He strode quickly toward his private room.

He had to plan a meeting with the king.

Alone in the corridor, the Ethiopian thought about the glowing box. He thought he heard maniacal laughter just at that moment, and he shuddered.

Abbas

Because he slept on a pallet just inside the door to Old Daniel's palace bedchamber, and had developed extra-sensitive hearing to compensate for his lack of speech, Abbas knew the moment Haman entered the side corridor to stand before the door to the Oracle chamber. The vizier had not modulated his voice as he barked his orders, and the sound traveled clearly in the pre-dawn quiet. Abbas slipped soundlessly out of Daniel's room, his hand instinctively hovering above his dagger. He would slip closer and listen.

So Abbas heard and saw enough to know that Haman had activated both the *pur* and the *Urim and Thummim*, and had been given an answer to whatever questions he had posed. Abbas grew cold, a feeling of foreboding engulfing him, and he went to rouse his master.

Meshach

Hovering invisibly just out of sensory range of Haman, Meshach, Daniel's other faithful boyhood friend, knew that Haman had entered the chamber of the Oracles and that he had gotten the answer he sought; he also knew that both the *pur* and the *Urim and Thummim* had disclosed to the magi a month and day. But Meshach did not know the particulars. Meshach appeared at Daniel's bedside moments before Abbas and Abednego.

Abednego

Abednego's violent and roaring dreams had awakened him. He immediately concentrated his mind on Esther, and sensing that she was safe and asleep, he transferred his thoughts to Daniel. Sensing serious agitation there, Abednego willed himself to Daniel's side. He became visible just as Abbas was explaining to Daniel what he had seen and heard, and he saw his old friend Mishael leaning against a wall.

Daniel

"You did well, Abbas, my old friend. It is fortunate for us that you have no need of sleep." Daniel held his hand momentarily on Abbas' shoulder. "I was dreaming of the red haze just now. And if I am reading Azariya's and Mishael's appearance here correctly, you both felt it, too." Daniel had called his friends—known now as Abednego and Meshach—by their Israelite names. The other men nodded, and Daniel continued.

"Haman has taken an unprecedented step by having the *Urim and Thummim* activated on his own initiative. He is getting bolder. Putting our dreams and intuitions together, and factoring in what Mishael has seen, plus the fact that this has happened immediately on the heels of Mordechai's refusal to bow down, it is a certainty that Haman is planning retribution."

The three men silently agreed.

"This is what we have been expecting and fearing. There is blood on the way. The Terrors are very nearly upon us. We cannot foresee the precise details, but we need to brace ourselves for something unprecedentedly evil. I am a very old man and I don't fear much, but I am afraid of what Haman will do with Shadrach behind him."

"Perhaps he asked the Oracles for a date for Mordechai's execution," offered Mishael.

"Haman would not need to consult both Oracles for that. Something bigger and worse is on his agenda; I feel it in my bones. Mishael, stay close to Haman. I want to know the moment Haman tells the king whatever he is plotting. Azariya, guard Esther. Abbas, with me. I'll warn Mordechai myself this morning. This is bad." Old Daniel, hooded and gaunt, shook his head.

A moment later the room was empty.

Haman Petitions Xerxes

Haman waited outside the throne room for his audience with the king. In the "old" days, pre-Biktan and Teresh, the enormous doors to the king's reception rooms had stood open at all times. The king had relished striking awe into the hearts of all those who came before him, seeking to appease him with gifts or to appeal to him for a boon. The open doorways allowed a visitor or courtier to view a portion of the palace's magnificence: an expanse of rooms richly clad in white and gold marble, and to see the inlaid onyx and lapis floors stretching off into a vast inner distance. Xerxes had spent lavishly on his fortress palace, with the intent to impress and intimidate. But now, fearing conspiracies and assuming that listening ears were everywhere, the king often kept the doors to his throne room closed and guarded when discussing matters of state.

As Haman waited impatiently — to be kept waiting like an ordinary satrap was intolerable! — he reviewed his strategy.

Speed was essential. Haman did not want Xerxes to get even a whiff of yesterday's incident at the King's Gate. If the king thought that in suggesting this killing scheme Haman was motivated by personal pique and a desire for revenge, it was unlikely he would approve it.

Also, Haman intended to paint a picture to the king of a race of people living off the fat of Persia who followed their own laws, disrespected the king, and even posed a serious threat to his sovereignty. In his present paranoid state of mind Xerxes would hopefully agree with a plan to neutralize such a threat. Haman thought he would not be surprised if a grateful Xerxes were to reward him for being zealously vigilant on his behalf.

"The king will see you now, Master Haman." The giant of a guard opened the tall studded door and Haman approached the throne. The king was nearly alone in his throne room. His bodyguard was standing on the dais to the king's left, spear and dagger at the ready; and the royal scribe sat at a small table the base of the stairs. Haman ignored them and approached the king's dais. He inclined his head in an honorific bow, and stood before Xerxes awaiting permission to speak.

Xerxes' throne was on a dais two steps above the floor of the throne room. By design, all suppliants were required to look up to the king. Likewise, the king, from his elevated seat, looked down onto courtiers and petitioners. This protocol was a thorn in Haman's side. He was biding his time until *he* would be the one seated above everyone else. But for the time being he expertly played the part of the king's obedient servant.

"What urgent business brings you here, Haman? I am told this couldn't wait until our regular meeting tomorrow."

Haman knew he had to catch the king's attention straightaway. To this end his plan was to paint a quick picture of his discovery of a threatening menace.

"Your Majesty, I come to alert the king about an important matter of state security, and also to present you with an infallible solution to insure your safety."

"Speak, Haman." The king leaned back in his throne, prepared to listen to his second-in-command and head of security.

"My king, there is a certain group of people who are widespread and scattered throughout your kingdom, so numerous that they inhabit every province of the Empire. These people are a different breed, unlike any others in the realm. They have their own laws, their own language, their own way of writing, and their own god. They have their own governing societies, they adjudicate their own monetary and property disputes, and they marry their own. Their laws and everyday practices differ not only from ours, but also from those of the rest of the people in all the 127 provinces of your Empire. These people function almost like a state within a state.

"What makes these people dangerous, my king, is that they blatantly flout the king's decrees, at their discretion perversely ignoring or disobeying the laws that keep the order and govern everyone in the Empire."

Haman paused here, strategically allowing Xerxes to absorb the implication that his Empire was harboring a fifth column within its breast. Haman was banking on the fact that the king would make the connection to his recent scare, a too-close-for-comfort assassination plot by vetted persons from *within the palace*. He intended that his "revelation" about a strange and separate people spread out across the Empire and infiltrated within every aspect of life within the kingdom would present a truly terrifying threat to Xerxes. Especially the part about their comprising many of the Persian army's trusted soldiers. Haman wanted the king to worry that such a threat could come at him, literally, from any quarter!

When the king remained thoughtful and silent, Haman pressed his point, skillfully going beyond exaggeration to outright fabrication. He watched the king closely to gauge his reaction.

"Majesty, these people number nearly three million strong, and not only do they hold themselves apart from and above the king's law, but they still enjoy the financial benefits of living in Persian society, including the king's generous grain allotments, property grants and tax remissions. These people are a burden to the Empire and a potential source of defiance and destabilization.

"There is no value at all in Your Majesty's continued largesse towards them. Better to be rid of them now, *before* they conspire to do harm to the Crown."

Xerxes was listening intently. "And you have a plan?"

Haman had decided *not* to explain to the king that his goal was to murder all the Persian Jews on the one appointed day. Instead, he proposed to choose his words carefully so as to give the king the impression that the Jews would merely be rounded up and enslaved. The appointed day would signify the day of the "roundup," but this would be doublespeak, as the day of the round-up would in fact be the day of the mass slaughter.

A mass round-up was not a foreign concept to Xerxes, having recently given the order for a second forced gathering of the kingdom's virgins. And a slave round-up was much more palatable than a genocide. There was always a need for slave labor somewhere in the Empire: in the king's fleet, as galley slaves; in the silver or ruby mines; in the stone quarries, as stone cutters and "mules;" and in the king's army, as conscripted soldiers. Haman would hand Xerxes a ready-made solution to the manpower problem.

Haman held his breath, hoping that the king would be too distracted to ask him the identity of this dispersed and menacing people in their midst. Neither Xerxes nor Darius nor Cyrus before him had held any animus toward the Jews. In fact, Cyrus and Darius had had Jewish scribes and Cup Bearers, the most trusted posts in the king's entourage. At present there were numerous Jews in Xerxes' royal service, and the king placed great store in them. Haman worried that if the king asked the name of these people before issuing the edict, he would not agree to it.

So Haman hastened to answer the king.

"If it please Your Majesty, my plan is to issue an edict curtailing this people's freedoms, and inscribing their enslavement."

Haman cleverly and deliberately misled the king, using the Pârsi word for "enslavement," *kurdas*, when his true intention was "destruction," *kardan*. Haman relied on the similar sound of the words, on the king's anxiety, and on his own oratory skill in urging the need for haste, to cause Xerxes to miss the subtle difference. And Haman's strategy worked. The king never did ask the identity of the people whom he had targeted. It was sufficient that Haman had identified a treasonous threat and that he proposed a means to eliminate it.

Haman saw that Xerxes was on the verge of acceding to his petition, but that something held him back. Haman, ever practical and fiendishly determined, had come prepared. He knew that Xerxes, like any king, was unlikely to grant a request without receiving something in return. Granting a request was an exercise of power, and for those in power, most transactions were reduced to the basic exchange of a *quid pro quo*.

So Haman played his ace, sweetening his request with a monumental financial incentive. He wanted it to be impossible for the king to turn him down.

"Majesty, let the edict be written as I request, and I will pay ten thousand talents of silver into the hands of the royal pursers to enrich the king's treasury."

Haman allowed the enormous amount of his offer to resonate in the room and in the king's mind. Ten thousand talents of silver was an outrageously large sum. And Haman well knew that an infusion of silver of this scope was particularly timely. The royal fisc was dangerously low in the wake of the king's military campaigns, his lavish banquets, and his twelve-month remission of taxes after Esther had been elevated to queen.

Ten thousand talents of silver was fully two-thirds of the annual royal budget. It also was enough money to finance and sustain a fighting force of twenty-thousand armed men for one year. It was definitely enough to turn a king's head. Xerxes' response was not long in coming.

In silent assent, his eyes still on Haman, the king slowly and dramatically twisted off the gold signet ring that he wore on his right index finger. The heavy ring was engraved with the royal seal of Persia—a profiled, crowned monarch in warrior stance braced to shoot his royal bow. Possession of the king's signet ring was the *sine qua non*—the indispensable prerequisite—to acting in the king's name, with full royal authority.

The king held out the ring, and Haman reached up to take it. Unnoticed by the two men, when the king had twisted the heavy ring off his own finger it had glowed purple for a long moment, and was warm for the instant it remained in the king's hand. Once in the vizier's palm, however, the ring was cold as ice. Haman noted to himself that the ring had better be worth its weight in delegated royal power and prestige; it certainly would be burdensome to wear. As he pushed the heavy signet ring onto his own left index finger—only the king wore it on his right hand—it glowed blackly for a blink of time. It could have been mistaken for a shadow.

The Power of the King's Signet Ring

For a thousand years the kings of Persia had sealed and authenticated their royal warrants, decrees, diplomatic pouches and missives by dripping molten sealing wax — colored crimson, deep purple or gold — onto the parchment or cloth opening, then quickly pressing a heavy, hand-held stamp to the warm wax, sealing the document shut as the wax cooled and hardened. Sometimes strips of royal cloth were criss-crossed in a complex, identifying knot and stamped and sealed into the hardening wax.

Historically, the royal stamp, or seal, was an intricately engraved relief, either circular or rectangular, bearing a miniature and distinctive royal image. The seal could have depicted the profile of the particular ruler, with distinctive crown, hair, arched nose, lips and chin, an earring in his ear, his fist holding a drawn spear or armed bow, his full name and royal bonafides engraved around the perimeter, similar to a struck coin. Or it could have depicted an eagle-god, its wings spread in flight, arrows gripped in its talons, etched mountains beneath, ringed by a royal fortress and bearing a trilingual inscription in Persian, Elamite, and Babylonian. Or the seal's design could have been of a rampant lion facing a likeness of the charioted king, the royal armor bearer at his side, arms akimbo holding a loaded bow, royal palm trees flanking the scene, a Persian inscription surrounding. Depending on the monarch's preferences, the royal seal might even have borne an engraving of a royal lion hunt, the king's muscled arms holding the reins of the speeding chariot, a slain animal beneath its wheels, the royal fortress in the background.

The seal's design usually remained the same and recognizable throughout the monarch's reign, with certain small but distinctive details — known as "tells" — etched into the stamp and changed randomly by the royal treasurer specifically to thwart forgers. Because of the stamp's importance and imposing size and weight, and the need for its reliable authenticity, it was entrusted to a vetted, close advisor known at court as the Bearer of the King's

Seal. This trusted chamberlain was at the king's side at all times when he sat at court, when he met with foreign diplomats, and in the field during wartime campaigns. When not in use, the royal seal was safely stowed in its thick velvet pouch lined in silk, its intrinsic drawstring ropes tied securely around the chamberlain's wrist. Behind closed doors of the palace it was quipped in whispers that the chamberlain even slept with the precious seal.

But over the centuries it became more convenient, secure and portable for the king simply to wear his seal, so it was reduced in size to fit onto an imposing gold signet ring. The king or his trusted vizier would wield the signet ring in much the same way as their precursors had done with the larger seal, stamping it into sealing wax to authentically signify royal mandate. As before, the various monarchs altered the image on the signet ring to fit their preferences.

When the Babylonians conquered Judah in 586 BCE and looted its holy Temple, among the riches plundered were twelve huge, twenty-karat gemstones from the vestment cache of the Israelite priests. The twelve colored stones, set into the front of the high priest's *choshen* breastplate, were only part of the priceless Temple treasure the victorious Babylonian king kept for himself. Decades later, when Cambyses I—who briefly succeeded Cyrus I, Xerxes' great-grandfather—conquered Babylonia, the Temple's treasure found a new home in the Persian kings' treasure houses. Persians appreciated and respected god-magic, and it was no secret that the One-God of the Israelites had performed extraordinary—some would say supernatural—feats of military might on behalf of the Israelites, even to vanquishing the virtually unconquerable armies of Egypt and Assyria. The Temple High Priest, while wearing the stunning and potent *choshen* breast plate embedded with the twelve priceless gemstones, had called on their One-God to intervene on behalf of the Israelites. Witnesses told of the priest's incantations, the rumbles of thunder from a clear sky, and the answering glow of the various gemstones. Only the High Priest possessed the code to decipher the seemingly random, speaking glow of the stones, and by following the message of the gemstones the Israelites either waged war against their enemies or held back. Sometimes the Israelite generals disregarded the message of the stones, to their detriment. The *choshen* was always right; their One-God spoke through the stones.

Another "treasure" appropriated from Babylonia by the victorious Persian kings was the brilliant, young exiled Israelite noble named Daniel. In addition to his clear vision and unwavering honesty, Daniel seemed to possess the ability to channel communication with his powerful One-God. Thus, over time Daniel became close advisor to Cyrus the Great and to Darius the Great after him, serving Xerxes' father and grandfather for an extraordinary term of fifty years. Cyrus and Darius were canny and practical kings, and their long tenures testify to their skill at judging men, waging wars and administering peace. They benefited politically as well as militarily from Daniel's prescient advice, and in deference to Daniel's One-God, rather than looting the individual breastplate stones, these kings left the breastplate intact, appropriating only one or two small gemstones from the Temple cache and fixed them into their signet rings. Each king hoped thereby to channel not only the power of the stones themselves, but also any residual magic of Daniel's God.

Xerxes' signet ring was thus very similar to the one he had inherited from his father, Darius the Great. Xerxes' royal goldsmiths had re-set the small Temple gemstone — a rare and clear light-blue amethyst, the color of the Persian sky — alongside the relief of the rampant lion facing off against the profile of a muscular king braced to shoot his loaded hunting bow.

What neither Cyrus, Darius nor as yet Xerxes knew, was that as long as Daniel lived in the royal palace his presence ensured that the royal signet ring — bearing the smallest of the Temple stones — retained the power to reflect and enhance the intentions of its wearer. The ring's power enhanced the wisdom and judgement of Darius the Great and Cyrus before him; it enhanced the military might of their son Xerxes, and unfortunately, now in the possession of Haman, son of Hamdata, it would enhance his ability to counsel and promulgate evil. Such was the power of the Temple stone.

And while Old Daniel could watch these events play out, he was powerless to alter the will of Xerxes, who of his own volition had handed over his signet ring to the evil vizier. Daniel hoped his God would grant him the good fortune to outlive this villain, and to see the signet ring placed into the hands of a better man than Haman. But considering his advanced age that was asking a lot, and Old Daniel was having recurring dreams drenched in a blood-red haze.

It was the small gemstone on Xerxes' ring that had glowed warm when in Xerxes' hands, but that had grown heavy and cold and shadowed in black when in Haman's palm. Daniel had seen that shadow and understood that it represented violence and death, and he feared for his people.

The moment was indescribably sweet to Haman. All his life he had craved power, or at the very least, immediate proximity to real power. Yet true power had eluded him, and he had remained an unknown and unrecognized functionary in the king's service, watching other men of lesser ability supersede him. Here, in this one unexpected and eloquent gesture, the king was literally handing Haman his heart's desire: the power to act as king.

Haman, son of Hamdata the Agagite, sadistic, power-mad schemer and obsessive enemy of Mordechai and the Jews, slipped the King's Ring onto his left index finger, and became, in that instant, an extension of Xerxes.

The king had the last word: "I have granted you the power to do as you see fit with these people you have described, who pose a threat to me."

And in an imperial move, the king reciprocated Haman's extravagant offer of the ten thousand talents of silver with one of his own.

"After you enslave these people, by royal warrant I hereby grant that all their possessions are yours—to keep, or sell, or to distribute to your mercenaries, as you see fit."

Haman, overcome momentarily with the gifts of power and the promise of the uncounted riches belonging to the Empire's three million Jews, inclined his head in thanks to Xerxes.

"Majesty, I beg your leave to attend to this matter before the day is out," and Xerxes waved him on his way. Haman strode from the throne room, his speed and posture bepeaking arrogance and purpose. Nothing and no one would stand in his way now.

Shadrach's laugh was a roll of thunder, though the sky remained cloudless. Later, some people swore that when the thunder rolled they had felt the ground tremble.

The Death Decree is Signed and Sealed

Haman stalked into a nearby room, high-ceilinged and flooded with daylight. The royal scribes sat in two long rows at their specially constructed tilted desks, ready to take dictation in any of the languages of the realm. He stood at the top of a short staircase overlooking the scribes, and began:

"Attention! You are to stop all other work immediately, and prepare to take down what I am about to dictate to you. Write it down carefully, word for word. My words are spoken with the full power and authority of His Majesty, King Xerxes."

Haman held up his left hand, and displayed the King's Ring. It glinted in the light, and the meaning was clear to all. Haman was to be obeyed without delay.

He began to dictate:

~~~~~

EDICT of the KING
On This 23rd day of the Third Month of Sivan
in the Twelfth Year in the Reign of Xerxes

~~~~~

By the ORDER of Xerxes
Supreme King of All Persia, from the Indus to the Elephantine
and all the World

~~~~~

NOTICE
Is hereby given to All Satraps, Governors and Officials
In every Town and City
In all One-Hundred-and-Twenty-Seven Provinces in the Empire
In the language and script of every People of the Realm
And
EDICTS Are to be dispatched with haste on
This Day via Royal Couriers
To Every Province in the Realm
So that All may Know and Obey this, the King's Edict.
These Orders are Hereby issued in the name of King Xerxes
And are Sealed with the King's Signet Ring
And are This Day hereby enacted into
IMPERIAL LAW:
1.
To Destroy,
To Massacre
And
To Exterminate
All the Jews in Persia,
Young and Old, Children and Women,
On a Single Day, exactly Eleven Months from Today,
That is, on the Thirteenth Day of the Twelfth Month
which is the Month of Adar.
And
2.
To Plunder All the Jews' Possessions.

~~~~~

Bi'anjam.
So Be It.

~~~~~

When Haman finished pacing the small landing and dictating, the room was silent as a tomb. Two of the royal scribes were Jews themselves, and their hands froze on their quills. Their faces blanched and their hearts trembled. They were transcribing their own death decree!

Their fellow scribes, most of whom neither knew nor cared what ethnicity or religion their fellows were, also stopped breathing. This was completely alien and unexpected. An Empire-wide massacre, formalized into law during peace time, was unprecedented in their lifetimes. They simply had no way to process the evil and its breadth.

Haman's eyes scanned the suddenly still room. "Get to work, every one of you, if you don't want to meet the same fate! I expect these Edicts to be translated, written, and ready for the king's seal in five hours' time! The decrees will be rolled, sealed by my hand," — here he once again held up his hand and made a show of the King's Signet Ring—"and packed for the royal runners and express riders. They will be on their way before sunset."

Deliberately, Haman moved his right hand across his waist and laid it on the hilt of his short sword. His eyes swept the room once again, and the meaning was clear. Haman meant business, and anyone who hesitated to carry out his orders would be eliminated. The scribes got to work; even the two Jews.

That night, the royal express riders carried the Extermination Decree far and wide, while the royal runners hastily distributed the scrolls within the capital city of Susa and its nearby towns and villages. Within twenty-four hours the Death Decree, as it became informally known, had either been distributed throughout the Empire or was on its way to every province, city and town, to be read aloud as Imperial Law at each town well and in every central square, and posted for all to see. Within three short weeks all within Persia were on notice to prepare and be ready for the day of extermination of all the Jews in their midst in eleven months' time.

The Terror had begun, and the people of Susa—Persian Jews as well as ordinary folk—were swept up in the speed and momentum of the Death Decree, and were in shock.

Ten Thousand Talents of Silver

The infamous ambush and massacre by Amalek of straggling Israelite ex-slaves a millennium before Xerxes' Persia, had an analogue event four centuries later. That later battle—where a victorious Israelite King Saul was expected to defeat and slay the king of Amalek—instead became a personal debacle for Saul when he and his army of ten thousand men failed to carry out their mission.

According to ancient Near Eastern battle lore and protocol, a victorious king who failed to take the life of an enemy king in battle forfeited his own life and crown. This penalty befell not only the Israelite king Saul, but also included the ten thousand Israelite soldiers who fought the battle alongside him, and who thus shared their king's battle obligation. In Saul's case, Samuel-the-Seer admonished the Israelite king severely for failing to slay the defeated enemy king Agag of Amalek. Instead, the seer slew Agag himself, and prophesied that as punishment Saul had, as of that day, forfeited his kingdom. What's more, Saul's life as honored first king of Israel had effectively come to an end on that day, even though Saul would not actually die in battle until years later.

But that was not the end of it. That battle against Amalek had another far-reaching consequence for the ten thousand men of the Israelite army. Because *they also* had failed in their battle duty, they, too, would be called to pay a steep personal penalty as their king had done. In lieu of forfeiting their lives, each man was expected to pay one talent's weight of silver into the national treasury. And in lieu of forfeiting their "crown," their people were fated to be exiled from their ancestral land centuries into the future.

Because even one talent of silver was an unattainable fortune of money, none of the ten thousand soldiers was able to pay his debt. As a consequence, and far into the future, the Israelite nation remained heavily indebted; required to pay one talent of silver as ransom for each of the lives of the ten thousand men of Saul's army.

Centuries passed, and the debt of ten thousand talents of silver was forgotten by successive generations of Israelites.

But it was not forgotten by the fates or by the constantly warring armies of Assyria, Babylon and Persia. There was an extant ransom debt outstanding and owing from the Israelites to their conquerors. And fate would not allow that debt to go unpaid.

In the year 586 BCE — one hundred years before Xerxes' Persia — the Israelites are conquered by the Babylonians, and ten thousand of their people are exiled from their land of Judah. This number is not a coincidence. It represents an old debt come home to roost. King Nebuchadnezzar of Babylonia was within his rights to hold the lives of the ten thousand Judean exiles ransom until they paid him one talent of silver per person exiled; totaling the monumental sum of ten thousand talents of silver.

That King Nebuchadnezzar did *not* hold the lives of the exiled Judeans ransom was due, in no small part, to the intervention of a young, exiled Judean nobleman named Daniel, who became a highly trusted and influential advisor to the Babylonian king, and who prevailed on the king to forego collecting the ransom debt. The Jewish exiles — who had become productive and valued, tax-paying members of their new country — were perceived to be more valuable to the king and to Babylonia *alive* than they would have been had they been slain in lieu of the ransom.

Daniel's influence over successive kings and conquerors continued through four monarchs, first Babylonian and then Persian, ending with his service to Darius the Great, Xerxes' father. In Xerxes' time, however, there was no one in the king's inner circle to whisper in the king's ear to forego collecting the owing ransom.

As fate would have it, there was an advisor to the king by the name of Haman, son of Hamdata, the Agagite. As descendant of the long-ago King Agag of Amalek, and as a sworn enemy of the people who slew his ancestor, Haman was aware of the ten-thousand-talents-of-silver debt that the Jews owed to their conquerors. And as Haman rose higher in Xerxes' cabinet, the likelihood of that debt being called in increased.

Mordechai Bilshan, advisor at the King's Gate and titular leader of the Persian Jews in Susa, also knew of the age-old debt. He had been alerted to the danger of its falling due by Old Daniel, his mentor and secret spymaster.

Which was why, when Xerxes elevated Haman to second-to-the-king, Mordechai already was on high alert. Old Daniel had been seeing visions of blood every day for weeks, and he had told his disciple that the Terror was near.

What neither Daniel nor Mordechai could have anticipated was the speed and cleverness of Haman's plan to collect on the debt, and the ease of Xerxes' agreement to the plan.

Mordechai's bold — some would say rash — move to publicly disobey his political rival and ancestral nemesis by refusing to bow down to him may have precipitated a bloodbath. Mordechai was in a near-panic.

The Economics of Haman's Extermination Plan

Haman, knowing that Xerxes' treasury was in dire need of an infusion, had come to his meeting with Xerxes prepared to sweeten his tale of an impending threat with a covert bribe. Of course, as viceroy to Xerxes he could not very well offer the king a financial incentive outright, as inducement to issue an imperial law. Haman's bribe was more subtle. He resurrected the ancient debt, known in royal circles but ignored, the tale of which had been passed down from Amalek, father to son, for nine centuries.

And he conflated it with the ancestral enmity between Jew and Amalekite. Selectively remembering *not* that the Jews' King Saul had had mercy on King Agag of Amalek, but only that the fierce Jewish seer, Samuel, had slain the captured King Agag, Haman found an outlet for righting two wrongs. The first "wrong" was ancestral, and the second was present-day and personal. He had only to get the king to agree in principle, without revealing the pesky truth of the matter: that the people he intended to destroy was a race of people who historically were loyal, wise and wealthy, by-and-large productive and valuable citizens of the Empire. Haman concealed the truth that his personal pique against one man — Mordechai — had triggered his irrational bout of temper, and was propelling his king and country to commit a genocide.

Because Haman was only a minor noble himself, he possessed insufficient disposable riches to influence a king. So he cleverly revived, for the king's consideration, the stagnant debt owed by the Jews to their conqueror's treasury.

"Your Majesty, I will make sure that the royal treasury does not suffer a deficit of even one *daric* in this operation. In fact, if the Crown were to agree to my plan, I would pay into the royal treasury a sum of ten thousand talents of silver."

Such an enormous amount of silver, gifted to him free and clear, was irresistible to Xerxes.

Without mentioning the Jews' debt specifically, and concealing his intent to murder beneath an assumption to merely enslave, Haman knew that he would have access to collecting on the long-standing debt once the king gave his consent and issued him broad powers. Once Xerxes handed the King's Ring to Haman, collecting the silver became almost child's-play. Haman's plan was to extort a ransom in silver talents from every single Jew in the kingdom. He would allow the Jews to believe that they could buy their freedom with the payment, but in reality Haman intended to enforce the killing scheme regardless of whether the Jews paid the ransom. He would kill each Jew *after* he took their money.

Haman planned to leverage the Jews' debt. Over and above collecting the ten thousand talents of silver owed to the king, Haman intended to squeeze every *daric* and *peruta* from every single Jew in Persia. A portion of this loot would go to arm, feed and pay his army of mercenaries; the vast remainder would line his own pockets. It was a win-win scenario. The king himself would never seek to collect on the silver-debt for fear of alienating powerful Jewish ministers and local officials. But Haman had no such political constraint or compunction. The Jews would be handing over their fortunes to him by the fist-loads in their haste to avoid "enslavement," and the king's treasurer would be happy to accept the silver talents, no questions asked. Haman's Death Decree would pay for itself ten times over.

On the night after their meeting, Xerxes and Haman sat down together in private celebration. They ate and drank and congratulated themselves on their clever decisiveness in making the Empire more secure against insurrection. And still, the king did not ask Haman the identity of the people he had targeted. The king had no real interest in the particulars. He had elevated Haman to second-in-command and head of state security precisely to ensure that the king was secure, and that nothing threatened his way of life. Haman's means of doing so did not interest Xerxes.

Thunder rolled from a cloudless blue Persian sky. Shadrach was delirious with laughter. Daniel shuddered at the blood that covered his open eyes, and Abednego and Meshach held their hands to their ears.

Mordechai

Both of the king's Jewish scribes were Mordechai's agents. Within minutes of their having penned the last copy of Haman's

Decree, the two men were standing at the threshold of Mordechai's chamber at the King's Gate. They had not even bothered with a coded message. All pretense at secrecy was gone. Mordechai did not evince surprise at their coming to him. He took one look at their stricken faces and slumped shoulders, pulled them inside and locked the door. He had an instant of premonition even before they spoke.

"My friends, something terrible has happened to bring you both here in broad daylight. Tell me."

One scribe, elderly but spry and reliable, produced a copy of the Decree from the sleeve of his overshirt, where he had secreted it. Without speaking he handed it to his Control. Mordechai read it through swiftly, and then a second time.

"It was Haman who dictated it, Mordechai," the scribe said. "And Haman who sealed it. Mordechai, Haman is wearing the King's Signet Ring."

The second scribe, young and full of nervous energy, continued: "Even now the Decree is on its way to the furthest corners of the Empire. Every city, town and hamlet will know of this within twelve hours, or within weeks for the most distant regions. There will be chaos, Mordechai. Now every single Persian who has resented even a single Jew — because he was smarter, or richer, or wouldn't betroth his daughter to their son, or because he kept to himself — every one of those ordinary Persians will treat this Decree as a license. They will take a long look at their Jewish neighbor, and think, 'In eleven months I can take his house.'"

"There will be many who will not wait the eleven months." The older scribe interjected, speaking from experience. "Their eyes will become very big. They will add up their real or imagined grudges and they will take what they want *now*. Property — and worse."

The three men knew what the older scribe was saying, and what they all three were thinking. The Decree had given license to ordinary Persians, and also to thugs and opportunists, to steal whatever they desired from their Jewish neighbors. And it was not only a house, a prize camel or a pouch of hidden coins that would be taken by force. Abduction and rape would be on the agenda for sure. Haman's Decree was a state-sanctioned warrant for an Empire-wide pogrom. And because it was state-sanctioned, there would be no police force to stand for the Jews.

"We need to do something, Mordechai, and soon!"

Mordechai was ashen. His mind flooded with questions and short-term action plans. He needed to meet with Daniel right away. Also to convene the Sanhedrin Brotherhood. They needed to mount a security detail this very night. Orders had to go out to every Jewish home in Susa to keep their daughters and young sons inside and to go out and about only with a grown male escort.

Tucked away in Mordechai's mind was the question: Where was Esther through all this? Did she know about the Death Decree?

Mordechai saw that the two scribes awaited his orders. "Yes. This is big, and we cannot wait, not even a day, to respond with a plan. The Jews of Susa, at least, must present a united front. Let me convene the Sanhedrin Brotherhood. We will get word to you all by tomorrow at this time. Meanwhile, stay off the streets, and" — here Mordechai paused and fixed the two men with a steely stare — "arm yourselves."

The two scribes nodded and left the King's Gate, hurrying to their homes. The afternoon streets were preternaturally quiet.

Countdown to the Terror
Nighttime, on the Day the Death Decree is Written

Mordechai was in the empty underground room at the tanner's field, waiting and pacing the small space. The flame in the one fat candle fluttered, and Daniel, hooded and, if possible, frailer than usual, stood on the other side of the long table.

"Well, you were right, Master, you haven't lost your touch," Mordechai said without greeting or preamble. "The Terror *was* coming. All these months you felt and saw it in your mind, and now it is here, out in the open. It has a face and the face is that of Haman, son of Hamdata, the Agagite. Even now the express riders are fanning out at full speed to every corner of the Empire, spreading the word of law: In exactly eleven months' time there will be a one-day massacre of all the Jews in the kingdom.

"*One day*, Master, on which to kill us all! Just think of the size of the army of mercenaries Haman must raise to accomplish the killings in one day. But who will care, really, if the killing spills over a day or two or three? Who will care, and who will stop them?" Mordechai beat his fist once against the whitewashed stone wall.

Mordechai was angry and despairing, and Daniel, understanding and feeling his pain with a century of experience, forgave his sarcasm.

"Being right, in this case, brings me no boon," he answered. "The situation is unfortunately worse than 'just' a programmed day of massacre in eleven months' time, though such a Terror is unprecedented. Worse, still, is that in reality we face *two* Terrors; one that is immediate and the other distant.

"The first Terror begins *tonight*—watch and see—it will begin as soon as the first scroll announcing the Death Decree is read aloud and posted in the town square. From that moment none of us is safe. From that moment it is open season on every Jew. Every single Persian—whether it is the neighbor next door, a rival business owner, a foiled suitor, a bully or a gangster thug, even a woman who covets her neighbor's earrings—any discontented Persian will, as of tonight, read immediate license into Haman's Decree. License to take, torment, destroy, rape, and terrorize.

"That is why the *first* Terror for our people will be living through the eleven months preceding the anticipated butchery. There will be those among the ordinary civilian Persians who won't wait until the month of Adar to start the killing."

All through Daniel's exposition, Mordechai stood against the wall with his arms crossed, listening intently. It was as his two scribe agents had feared. He knew that his mentor spoke the truth now and always. The man had lived a long life, had been exiled twice, and had served four kings. Plus the man possessed eerily special intuitive and sensory abilities. For all these reasons Daniel's clear assessment defining *two* periods of Terror commanded Mordechai's close attention. Together they would have to conceive of—if not a solution—then a strategy for surviving the "now;" the first wave of Terror.

By nature, Mordechai was that rare agent who had both a head for strategy and the nerves and patience for field work. He was an ideal successor to Old Daniel, the secret spymaster, because not only had he been a top agent himself and seen action, he also was masterful at coordinating multiple simultaneous operations. Mordechai was a superbly skilled Control for over several hundred agents throughout Persia, moving them around and orchestrating their operations, collecting and processing their information, and maneuvering and shifting them to best effect. He acted vicariously through *them*, affecting national and local politics and keeping everything—names, locations, data—in his head. His operatives trusted him, literally, with their lives, as he in turn trusted, relied on and protected them.

Up until this infamous day of the Decree, Daniel's overriding mission—and now Mordechai's—was to keep abreast of everyday events in all areas of Persian life, thereby supporting the king and assisting local governors, ensuring as smooth and danger-free a life as possible for their adopted country. Peace and prosperity for Xerxes translated into stability and a good life for the Jews of Persia. Mordechai functioned as eyes and ears for his king, and also for his people.

With no country of their own, shunted every few decades from one regional superpower to another, and worshipping their invisible One-God, Yahweh, the Jews were without a voice and without any real power in Persia, their latest country of exile. It would be difficult to overstate the importance of the information flowing from Daniel and Mordechai's operatives. The information network Daniel created and Mordechai maintained and grew aimed to serve their king and thereby also to give their people a measure of security.

One key trait Mordechai was known for was keeping a cool head. Which was why, five years earlier, when he had lost Hadassah to the king, his new propensity to express anger or emotion surprised himself, and also caused concern to his close associates and his operatives. To compensate, Mordechai had spent the past five years working to exorcize the ghost of Hadassah from his heart and mind, focusing instead on his ministerial tasks and his spymaster duties. He was back on track now, running his network with his trademark sang-froid.

It was unfortunate that Xerxes had become overly paranoid and enamored of the evil and manipulative Haman, ancestral enemy of Mordechai and the Jews, and Mordechai's personal nemesis. The standoff between the two men over the loyalty test of religious bowing to the vizier may have given first strike to Mordechai, but with the promulgation of his Decree Haman had won the bout. The swiftness of the Decree brought to the fore — and brutally illustrated for Mordechai — Haman's superior power to influence the king. It also highlighted Mordechai's inability to slow or prevent Haman's terrifying political juggernaut.

Now, with Persia's Jews on the brink of extermination, Daniel was counting on Mordechai's cool head and strategic dexterity to devise a plan.

Daniel also was prepared to call Esther, his secret weapon, into play. This was, after all, the reason he had held Mordechai back from fighting the king's army to the death for Hadassah years ago, on the night they were to be wed. Daniel had foreseen the future Terrors, and knew that Hadassah — as Esther — was destined to be essential to his people's salvation.

The great irony, of course, was that now, more than at any time in the last century, thanks to the prescient maneuvering of Daniel, as secret spymaster, the Jews of Persia *had* seemed to be best positioned and most secure. One of their own people — though unbeknownst to more than a handful of people — was

Queen of Persia; another was a minister at the King's Gate; and still another was a roving former advisor to two Persian kings.

In reality, though, things were not functioning as the old spymaster had expected.

The Queen had been instructed to keep her Jewish identity a secret, so no one—not even King Xerxes—knew she was a Jew.

Mordechai, a trusted minister and until just days ago also a secret Jew, had, on a point of religious principle and personal enmity, exposed his ethnicity and locked horns with the vengeful and megalomaniacal Haman. The consequence was that he forfeited the power his position had afforded him, and, significantly, his access to palace secrets.

And Old Daniel, once the closest of advisors to Kings Cyrus and Darius and a prominent and proud Jew, was now an aged shadow of his former self, with neither influence nor access to the Crown.

With the day of their extermination sealed and delivered, the situation could not have been blacker for the Jews of Persia. They were alone and without either political or actual weapons to oppose Haman.

In every corner of the Empire, as the Death Decree was delivered, read aloud and posted in the town squares, Persian Jews spontaneously donned mourning garb. In an age-old expression of mourning, days of public fasting were announced, and the people, young and old, were seen about their business wearing sackcloth, their faces ashen and tear-stained. A pall had fallen over the normally loquacious and contented Jewish populace—comprised of storekeepers, housewives, grandfathers, businessmen, old women, cocky young men and doe-eyed girls; all, even the children, were silenced. Only individual cries and the one-note mourning song could be heard through open windows, as ordinary Persians went, sober-faced and perplexed, about their day.

Old Daniel and Mordechai bent their minds to devise a short-term plan of action.

Mordechai in Sackcloth

Out of options and with nothing to lose, and certain he would be first on Haman's kill-list, as a first step Mordechai took his dire situation and that of his fellow Jews to the public arena. He put on the humble and unadorned sackcloth clothing of the mourner, visibly rent his overgarment, and rubbed his face and head in ashes. In such a filthy state he paraded, barefoot, in the town square of central Susa on market day, when the streets and square were packed with people. His behavior was terrifyingly genuine, worth ten thousand words and speeches. In the universal guise and stance of one who was in deep mourning, Mordechai's appearance was calculated to both galvanize his own people and shock the ordinary Persians.

Mordechai stumbled back and forth in the public square, eyes half closed, wailing at the top of his lungs, punctuating his wails with his litany: "Woe unto the Jews! Woe unto all Persia! Blood will run in the gutters! Woe unto all of us!" His hands were scrubbing his face, tears runnelling paths in the filth that crusted his cheeks.

The people in the town square gave the raving Mordechai a wide berth. They were frightened and confounded.

The spectacle of not just a man in extreme mourning, but particularly of Mordechai, the noble and meticulous minister at the King's Gate, behaving thus, was shocking and terrifying to everyone. Mordechai's display of keening grief brought home to the Persians in Susa that their world was tilting off its secure and predictable axis.

Mordechai Mourns at the King's Gate

Mordechai's misery and grief were genuine. But he was still and always a master tactician. He knew that no number of straightforward and sober broadsides would have the effect of his parading as a mourner and crying out in public. So, acting deliberately *counter* to his lifelong, elegant and circumspect mode of deportment, he opted instead to shock the people of Susa.

So Mordechai paraded as a mourner and cried out his grief and doomsday fears not only in the town square; he also made his slow way the down the broad avenue that led from Susa's town square to the palace fortress, gathering gawkers and curious townspeople as he went. The Royal Guard, alerted by Mordechai's cries and by the churning crowd, stopped him at the King's Gate; ironically the very same gate he — as minister and eyes and ears to the king — had entered with impunity not twenty-four hours before.

"Halt! What is this demonstration?!" one of the Home Guards stood, his spear crosswise in a blocking and defensive stance, denying entry.

"Do you not recognize Mordechai, one of the king's ministers?" A local man, with no interest in the goings-on except perhaps to stir trouble and to provoke more excitement, gestured theatrically in Mordechai's direction, addressing the guard. "Make way for Minister Mordechai to enter the King's Gate!" The crowd roared with nervous laughter, eyes on the guard and on the three others who had joined their fellow, all of them armed and blocking entrance to the majestic gateway.

The first guard, now recognizing Mordechai beneath the filthy crust of ashes and torn sackcloth, was momentarily stunned. This was the dignified and unfailingly polite minister who greeted him daily. The guard was torn between obvious duty and his own humanity. He straddled his roles, and, leaning down to speak directly to this strange "Mordechai," he addressed first the man and then the crowd.

"Minister, it is forbidden for a mourner or a mourner's entourage to enter the King's Gate. Sackcloth and ashes and mourning criers are barred from the palace atrium. You may return, Master Mordechai, when you are properly attired and comported, and you will be permitted entry.

"As for all of you, you will disperse immediately! Go back to your homes and businesses and cease this disturbance!"

The four guards formed a line across the gateway to the fortress, barring entry and presenting a line of spear and power that no one had an interest in testing.

To satisfy the guards, Mordechai retreated a distance from the palace gateway, sitting instead on the opposite side of the public thoroughfare, crying out at the top of his voice and beating his chest, thighs and even the ground where he sat. He stayed that way until evening, even after his voice had given out.

Esther

The palace guards had recognized Mordechai, and were shaken by the minister's overnight transformation from elegant and polite courtier to raving, beggarly madman. One older guard in particular recalled Mordechai from six years previously, when the young courtier had haunted the Courtyard of the Women, waiting for any news of one of the captured virgin girls. He recalled that back then Mordechai had had some sort of legitimate channel of interest in the maiden Esther. The guard took pity on the "fallen" minister who had always been kind to him, once even pushing a small pouch of coins into his hands when he had overheard the guard telling his fellow that he was lacking a dowry for his marriageable daughter.

So that evening the older guard sought out his fellow in the Courtyard of the Women, and the two men decided it would do no harm to send a messenger to the queen's lady-in-waiting asking her to inform the queen that Minister Mordechai was dressed in sackcloth, covered in ashes, and raving at the entrance to the King's Gate. If the queen wished, she would take some action to assist the man. If she did not, at least they had tried.

Esther had woken with the sun two hours before, and was in her suite of chambers, coifed and dressed, ready to meet the day's duties.

"Begging your pardon, Majesty, but a message has come from the Home Guard for you." It was early morning on the day after Mordechai had been turned away at the King's Gate. Azam, the queen's chief handmaid, stood at the doorway to her mistress' apartment. Further back, at the vestibule doorway, and watched over by a giant armed guard, cowered a diminutive Ethiopian boy. And just outside Esther's chamber door ranged her six handmaidens, all of them standing ready to aid their queen. They sensed, with their sensitivity to nuance and mood, that something grave was afoot.

"Thank you, Azam." She held out her hand for the expected scroll.

"Majesty, the message has been entrusted orally to the Ethiopian boy," Azam said, gesturing toward the vestibule, "and he is quivering with duty and fear at his mission. He says he was sworn by the Home Guard to speak his message only to the queen's ears."

Esther saw the boy from afar and smiled. "Bring him in, Azam, and please stay with me as he delivers his message."

So Azam led the Ethiopian boy, no more than ten years old, into the queen's reception room, where Esther sat, awaiting the message in as unintimidating a stance as possible. Though she, too, sensed something dire, there was no point in frightening the boy to the point that he would forget his message.

Azam gently prodded the boy. "Bow to the queen and then speak your message! And be sure to recite it exactly as you were commanded."

The boy's eyes goggled at the vision of the queen. She seemed an angel, sitting silently in her small throne chair, her dress a golden yellow, her hair braided and coiled atop her head in a deep red corona, her hands folded in her lap. Her eyes stared seriously at him, willing him to calm himself and commanding him wordlessly to speak the words he had memorized. She smiled encouragingly at him, and he was certain she glowed. He roused himself and bowed briefly from the waist as he had been taught.

"Majesty, my master, guardian at the Courtyard of the Women, has requested that I tell you this: 'Yesterday, the Minister Mordechai was dressed in sackcloth, covered in ashes, and raving at the entrance to the King's Gate. The Home Guard sent him away, because it is forbidden for a mourner or a mourner's entourage to enter the palace atrium. Sackcloth and ashes and mourning criers are barred from the King's Gate.' That is the message."

The boy's spoken words echoed in the silent chamber and reached the vestibule. The queen thanked the messenger boy with a smile, signaling Azam to give him a coin before escorting him to the waiting guard. When Azam returned from escorting the boy back to the guard, there was a rustling and whispering from the handmaidens gathered at the queen's doorway. Azam moved to quiet them, but one longtime maid, Banou, spoke up.

"Mistress Azam, we also have news."

Azam turned to the queen, who beckoned the maidens to enter the chamber, and nodded to Azam.

"Speak, then, Banou."

"Majesty, the word has come just this morning from returning royal messengers. The Jews of Persia have donned sackcloth and covered themselves in ashes. They are weeping and fasting throughout the Empire."

The queen began to tremble and shake uncontrollably. Her blood running cold with fear, she rose to her feet and, gripping her hands together tightly, she paced from her chair to the latticed window and back, thinking quickly. The other handmaidens ranged before her, awaiting instructions.

She told her trusted maid, "Azam, you know of the man Mordechai, Minister at the King's Gate. You have heard the messenger and Banou. Surely something calamitous has befallen him to cause him to act thus." Addressing the other maids, she instructed them, "Gather a washing basin and cloths, a comb, a man's tunic, trousers and shirt, and proper boots. Have two sturdy man servants carry them for you outside the palace and across from the King's Gate. Use my side door; do not walk through the public corridors. Find Mordechai and tell him that the queen requests that he accept these clothes, wash himself, and comport himself properly. You will please wait while does this, and then you and the man servants will please escort Mordechai to his chambers at the King's Gate. Return to me after you have seen to Mordechai, and you—only yourself, Azam—will bring me any message he sends. Go at once! Speak to no one until we solve this puzzle."

The faithful Azam hurried away to do her mistress' bidding, ushering the agitated maidens before her. Azam had served this queen for five peaceful years, and had served another queen before her. She was attuned to palace moods and events. Something terrible had happened, and there was not a moment to lose.

Esther used the waiting time to turn the puzzle over in her mind. *What has happened to turn Mordechai into a raving mourner? To have caused him to break protocol and draw all eyes to him? He would never behave in such a fashion unless there was a powerful reason. He must be sending me an urgent message. He must intend me to hear of this!*

The Women's Compound

The House of the Women, housing the king's harem, and the House of the Concubines, its companion building where the secondary wives and royal offspring under the age of five were housed, were isolated and secured compounds within the palace fortress of Susa. There were vetted and specialized rotated units of Home Guards who policed the outside of the compounds at all times, and the houses were managed internally by utterly trustworthy eunuchs, former military, and decades-long female retainers. The cooks and laundresses, grounds men and animal caretakers were watched over and checked in a random rota by the chamberlain of each house. In addition, the women's compounds were separated from the rest of the palace by a two-foot thick stone wall standing ten feet high.

The women were important to Xerxes, as to any reigning hereditary monarch, for the reason that favored wives produced male heirs, thus assuring a loyal court and cabinet and, vitally, the succession of the crown. The women also counted for the sexual pleasure and entertainment of the king; they were an adornment; and the child-princesses raised in the House of the Concubines were valuable political coin, to be bartered to foreign kings for political gain in war as well as in peacetime, and to secure economic or military hegemony.

But regarding domestic political matters and the goings-on at court or on the international stage, the women's compounds were as isolated as the moon. Runners carried no daily news bulletins to the exclusive and guarded doorways of the women's compounds. The only way news of a political nature penetrated the cloistered women's world was through the gossip of servants.

News also traveled through the whispered messages of spies.

The queen was the only woman whose quarters and privileges extended beyond the cloister and the purely domestic concerns. Ceremonially as well as sexually, the queen was in a class by herself. The queen had access to the king that no other woman — and possibly no other person in the Empire — could duplicate. Because her walled apartments were located within the palace proper and separated only by a long marble breezeway from the king's private chambers, she was liable to overhear palace and national news and to encounter courtiers, diplomats and servants. It was also possible that the king would bring her into his confidence on certain matters as the mood struck him, or if he thought she could be of assistance.

But as regards Haman's Decree, so recently written and dispatched, and concerning such an unsavory subject, the king had not spoken to Esther, nor had she yet heard of it through the palace or servant grapevine. There was really no need for her to have heard of it at all, especially as no one in the palace had any inkling of her people or her kindred.

So it was that while the news of the Death Decree was stunning Susa and spreading to the farthest corners of the Persian Empire, Esther, Queen of Persia, was ignorant of it.

Two hours passed, and Azam returned to the queen, crestfallen.

"Tell me, Azam. Was there a message for me from Mordechai?"

"Mistress, Master Mordechai refused the fresh clothing and the bid to wash himself. He seemed quite angry and not madly raving at all. His eyes were clear and he deliberately ignored me, my man, and the clothing. I am sorry I failed you, Mistress."

"No, Azam, you have not failed completely; Mordechai's refusal is itself a message. Something extraordinary and dire is afoot. I must discover what it is." Esther paused in thought, then said, "Azam, fetch Hatach! You can send word with Abbas, who guards and serves him. Tell Abbas that it is urgent that I speak with Hatach immediately. Go now, please. Hatach will be my intermediary to Mordechai."

Azam trotted out of the queen's chambers, intent on finding Abbas.

Esther Seeks an Intermediary

The day's events jolted Esther back into "agent" mode. Automatically she analyzed what she knew, and reasoned that by refusing to dress and comport himself as a proper minister and thereby be permitted entry into the King's Gate, Mordechai's purpose must have been, first, to grab her attention, and second, to make a loud and unmistakable public statement.

By remaining outside in the public square Mordechai was deliberately avoiding communication with Esther. This is because the queen — not an insubstantial force *within* her cloistered world — was powerless to exert any influence *outside* the palace compound absent the king's imprimatur. So while Mordechai remained in the public square, Esther was unable to exert her will upon him. And Mordechai, a canny political operative, knew this. What's more, Esther knew that he knew. And her knowledge of Mordechai and her memory of his methods fueled her concern. Mordechai was deliberately holding himself beyond her reach; presumably he was not yet done making the public spectacle and statement that he had set out to make. She presumed that he would send her a message when he saw fit, but Esther the Queen was unwilling to wait in ignorance.

She was desperate to know what was happening outside the palace.

For nearly all of her life, Esther — as Hadassah, living in Mordechai's home — had relied on Mordechai to brief her on court, domestic, or national events. At first, after she had been taken into the cloister of the harem and even later, during her last five years as queen, she had received random and innocent enough coded messages through various servants or maids. She always suspected, but never knew for certain, that the messages originated with Mordechai. The messages kept Esther in the know about what was happening around the Empire; and particularly about how her people fared. Of late, during her tenure as queen, the messenger who had brought her her news had been the silent but reliable old palace retainer known to her only as Hatach.

Esther had never before initiated a communication with a person outside of the palace. But on this day, she had a great need to discover why Mordechai was mourning in public, and why her people were in mourning as well. She was sensitive and highly intelligent, and chafed at the realization that as queen she had been kept oblivious of important events. She was determined to open her own avenue of information, and she intended to do it using Hatach, the trusted and dignified palace regular who would act as her go-between. She would speak to Hatach and he would be her mouthpiece with Mordechai.

Hatach

That Hatach was Daniel was not commonly known. Esther, for instance, did not know that Hatach had nearly a century of service and an encyclopedic knowledge of royal secrets under his belt, or that he was Mordechai's control. She would find this out later. For now, Esther knew only that Farah and Hegai entrusted Hatach with messages to her, and over the past six years she had learned to trust him, too. She did not doubt that the mute giant, Abbas, Hegai's guard, would relay to Hatach Azam's emergency call from the queen.

As Daniel, Hatach knew all about Haman's Death Decree against the Jews. He knew about the precipitating act: Mordechai's public refusal to genuflect and bow down to Haman as a god, which acted as the kindling that ignited Haman's burning anger at this public snub to his rank by Mordechai the Jew. Hatach knew that Mordechai's Jewishness gave name and purpose to the hatred that Haman harbored against Mordechai, not only as a political rival and threat, but also because as a Jew, Mordechai was a visible member of the people who were sworn historical blood enemies of Haman's own people, descendants of King Agag of the nation of Amalek.

Hatach, as Daniel, had engineered placement of Esther within the palace six years before, and had set Mordechai up as her control. As Daniel, Hatach had had vivid premonitions of the coming Terrors that would affect his people, and he also had known that the day would come when Esther, his secret weapon closest to the center of Persia's source of power — King Xerxes — would be called out of hibernation to catalyze a rescue. When Abbas appeared at his chamber door that morning and spoke to him with his eyes, Hatach knew that that day had come. He dressed with care, not in Old Daniel's hooded cloak, but in the garments of a royal messenger: a long, white belted blue tunic with braided trim, leather sandals, a close-fitting turbaned hat, and an ebony leaning staff befitting his age. Gone was the slumped and invisible mien of Old Daniel. In his place stood an erect and alert Hatach, the queen's messenger.

Hatach as Messenger

"Hatach is here, my Queen." Azam bowed out of Esther's receiving chamber and closed the door.

Esther stood facing her messenger. The role of Royal Messenger, not unlike that of Royal Cup Bearer, was a more trusted and serious role than the simple title conveyed. Confidential secrets were entrusted to him, often orally, and his integrity was the backbone of his success. Hatach and Esther surveyed one another. Serious, life-and-death matters would pass between them this day, though Esther only sensed the gravity, while Hatach knew the grave seriousness to a certainty. He was measuring Esther anew on this fateful morning.

"Hatach, I summoned you to ask that you act as my trusted intermediary in a matter of urgency and diplomacy. It concerns Minister Mordechai." And she told him all she had learned of Mordechai's making a spectacle of himself across from the King's Gate, of his public mourning and raving, of his refusal of garments and comfort.

"Go out to Mordechai, and find out from him the reasons he is acting in this outrageous way. *Why* is he mourning in public, and why are the Jews mourning throughout Persia? I must know the truth."

Hatach inclined his head. "I will go now, my Queen."

"And Hatach, allow no one and nothing to stop you. Go and come directly to me and to no one else. What is said between Mordechai and myself, through you, is of the highest confidentiality. Swear this with your life."

"I swear it."

So Hatach left the queen's quarters, and hastened through the palace and into the soaring King's Gate atrium, moving purposefully through the King's Gate itself. On this day, Hatach had no use for side doors. Once outside the fortress he stopped, and saw a small crowd across the wide roadway fronting the fortress Gate. At its center was Mordechai, seated on the ground of the public square, dressed in soiled sackcloth, his face, hands and bare feet coated with ash and the dirt of the street. He was tugging at his filthy and disarranged hair, wailing in his hoarse voice the litany he had been shouting since yesterday. "Woe unto the Jews! Woe unto all Persia! Blood will run in the gutters! Woe unto all of us!"

But Hatach knew that Mordechai was not mad; to the contrary, Mordechai was hyper-aware of his audience. Surrounded by curiosity-seekers, he cried out a warning litany that blood would run in the streets. But when he saw in the crowd the receptive faces of his colleagues and fellow ministers, he interjected his cries with brief, eloquent appeals.

"*Today* it is the Jews of Persia whom the vizier is targeting for death. But who among us is safe? Who knows which of *you* will be in his murdering sights tomorrow? Perhaps it will be you, Jalil, or you, Hadwin? Once the killing starts, it will be hellishly impossible to stop it."

Hatach saw that some of the ministers nodded subtly, recognizing the truth in Mordechai's words. They, too, had seen and felt Haman's meanness and arbitrariness; his sadism and his evil nature. They dropped their eyes and walked thoughtfully through the King's Gate.

But other ministers—those who had resented the rise of this energetic young minister—who, once Mordechai had disclosed his Jewishness, sided silently with Haman, latched onto the excuse that Mordechai's rebellious Jewishness constituted a threat to the Empire. Why not take the opportunity to rid Persia of *all* the Jews, and in the process loot or confiscate their businesses and their homes, their daughters and their fortunes?

Mordechai's Command

Hatach crossed the road and with dignity and in a soft but commanding voice he dispersed the small crowd. Then he crouched down so that he was eye to eye with Mordechai. They recognized each other and both knew this was the moment of truth.

"All right, Mordechai. Esther has sent me to hear from your lips exactly why you are behaving thus. Tell me everything and I will relay it to Esther. Do not omit any detail."

So Mordechai retold to Daniel — as Hatach — everything, in more detail than he had told him at their short meeting in the tanner's secret room just days before. This time Mordechai included details that even as Daniel, Hatach would not have heard: the secret and fiendish fact that Haman had essentially bribed the king to go along with his scheme against the Jews by offering to pay 10,000 talents of silver into the king's diminished treasury if he agreed! Mordechai also gave Hatach a crumpled copy of the Death Decree to take back to Esther. Having the dates for the massacre set out in bold script and knowing that, even now, the Jews throughout the Empire were reading the same words and were shocked, terrified and hopeless, was blood-chilling. Mordechai gripped Hatach's tunic front in his strong fist and practically spat the words into his face:

"You must show this Decree to Esther. Read it aloud to her so she hears it and so that she knows it is official, and real, and deadly serious. You must command Esther, in my name, that she *must* use her position as queen of Persia to put a stop to this massacre! *Now*, before Haman's mercenaries march into Persia! *Now*, before the evil ones within Persia's own borders get a taste for the plunder they could have if they were to murder all the Jews in the Empire!

"Tell Esther that Mordechai commands her to go to the king and plead with him! Beg, if she must, for the lives of her people.

"Tell her all this, *Hatach*, and tell her I will not budge from this spot until I have her assurance that she will act!"

Hatach prised Mordechai's hand from his tunic and straightened up from his crouch.

"I will tell her, Mordechai."

Leaning heavily on his walking staff, Hatach re-crossed the boulevard from the public square to the fortress of Susa, making his way back through the King's Gate and the palace corridors to the queen's apartment. He would walk this same path numerous times on this day, and on the morrow, as well, ferrying messages back and forth between Mordechai and Esther. Alternately exhausted and energized, Daniel, as Hatach, could not rest. It struck him that *this* was the reason he had survived for the past century and had served four kings. This was the reason he had maneuvered his two star agents and in the process broken their hearts. At stake was no less than the survival of his people in their land of exile. He would succeed because this was what he was: a Jew, a diplomat, a strategist, a survivor.

Who knows if the reason I have survived this many years has been just for this one mission? Saving my people from Haman's slaughtering machine?

Hatach, speaking for Mordechai, would pose this precise question to Esther within the coming hours.

Esther in Crisis

Hatach and Esther are alone in her apartment's reception room. Hatach has told her everything, speaking to her using Mordechai's words. In fact, Hatach, in effect, *is* Mordechai throughout his messenger interchanges with the queen. Esther is holding the Decree, having read it quickly once, and a second time, more deliberately. Her face is ashen. Thoughts crowd and chase one another in her superior mind.

It is almost beyond belief. This extermination Decree has been agreed to by my husband, the king! It has been signed and sealed right here in the palace, and I did not know. There is much, much more that I do not know: How has this monster Haman become my husband's second-in-command? Why has Xerxes agreed to annihilate an entire productive population, seemingly just for the sum of 10,000 talents of silver? Can it be that Xerxes is not fully aware of Haman's intentions? Has Haman deceived even Xerxes? Could it be that Xerxes expects the Jews to pay the 10,000 talents ransom, thus sparing their lives, yet remaining enslaved to the king?

Esther has many questions, and, as yet, no answers. She is all potential energy, poised but circumspect.

Though Esther has been, ostensibly, hibernating as queen these past five years, Daniel was counting on her superior intelligence and quick grasp of politics and peoples' motivations being roused and activated by this crisis. Esther was a weapon perfectly placed. She needed to be primed and armed, and then freed to do what she was trained to do.

As Hatach, Daniel watched with satisfaction as Esther's very posture altered subtly as she reread the Decree. She stood straighter, pacing the room as she silently absorbed the crushing enormity of the situation Mordechai had thrust upon her. As Hadassah, Esther had buried her torn heart and youthful dreams of love and romance. She had secreted her Jewish self and all but forgot the girl she had been. This was her skill, and this was her duty. She was, without any doubt, the highest-placed sleeper agent in the history of the Jewish exile. Since the Pharaoh of Egypt a millennium ago, there has been no more powerful monarch than Xerxes, whose empire spanned the known world. And Esther, an exquisite young woman and a secret Jewess, had captured his heart.

Esther was a spymaster's dream come true.

Daniel watched to see if his calculated risk—his gamble on the girl Hadassah six years ago—would pay off.

The Queen as Agent

Up until this moment, and since becoming queen, Esther had allowed herself to be lulled by the ceremony and sameness, the luxury and the protection, the minor exercises of power, that being queen afforded her. She had become the most perfect agent, but as many agents before and since had done to their detriment, she had fallen so far into her deep cover that she very nearly forgot that it was just that: a cover. A mission. The irony was that it was her complete immersion in her role as Esther that had ensured her success! She *was* precisely what she appeared to be: Esther, the anonymous Persian girl who had captured the heart of a king.

And yet now, at a moment of life and death, Esther's cover was being torn away and she was being asked—commanded—to bare her true identity and lay herself down as a sacrifice. Haman's Decree and Mordechai's words acted like immersion in a bath of ice water. She became instantly clear-eyed and braced for action.

Esther absorbed and calculated the dire situation and her precarious place in the drama within moments, as she paced, after reading the Decree and hearing Mordechai's orders. And, like the prize asset she was, she began to analyze.

If Xerxes has in fact agreed to annihilate the Jews, fearing their power or having been convinced by Haman that they pose a threat to him personally and politically, and I were to reveal to him that I am a Jewess, having kept my Jewishness a deliberate secret from him, it is a certainty that Xerxes will suspect me of seeking to undermine or harm him. He will turn his back on me in an instant—regardless of our years of intimacy together. Allied with Haman, who will be filling the royal treasury with silver, Xerxes will sacrifice me along with the Empire's Jews. None of us will survive.

But—if I can hold my secret back just a bit longer, and seed some doubt into Xerxes' mind about his vizier's intentions...if I can use myself as bait...I may have a chance.

Esther, a secret Jewess and the most powerful, yet still restricted, woman in the Persian Empire, had the kernels of a plan. She had noticed — registered but ignored — Haman's interest in her over the past years. Back when she was in the harem she had had fleeting intuitions of his envy and lust. She had felt it particularly strongly in the person of his daughter, Zareen, who had been an avid competitor for the position of queen. In the course of her elevation to queen and in the five years since, Esther had several times caught Haman watching her at ceremonial events when she had sat at Xerxes' side. Her sixth sense had warned her, and she had been careful not to so much as glance in his direction, so as not to encourage his stares. But she felt his interest in her. While it chilled and repulsed her still, she was thinking to leverage Haman's desires — for dominance both political and sexual — to her advantage.

That she would be playing a most dangerous game was a given. But her back was against the wall, and Mordechai had called in his bet. Esther was refining a scheme as she paced.

The first step will be to sow seeds of suspicion against Haman in Xerxes' mind. Somehow I must encourage Xerxes to suspect Haman on two fronts: as coveting both the crown and the queen. Vizier or not, Xerxes will tolerate no encroachment to his power and sexual dominance. Only when Xerxes is already distrustful of Haman will I disclose to him my people and my kindred; not before. Because once Xerxes is suspicious of Haman, it will cast all his acts – including this killing scheme – into doubt as well.

And Esther's keen mind, now in strategic mode, went further.

Perhaps the king can be persuaded that Haman's mercenaries would not stop at killing just the Jews? After all, what is to stop Haman's blood-drunk soldiers from turning on the king himself and executing a coup?

Yes, sowing doubt will be my strategy. My challenge will be how to go about it, and with speed and dispatch, at all times allying myself completely with the king.

On the one flank I have an evil and lecherous Haman, over-confident and more than a little drunk with power and success. On the other flank is poised a suspicious and insecure Xerxes. It will not take much of a spark to set the tinders of both their tempers flaring. I must take care when I light that flame to stand well back, so as not to be burned along with them.

Esther Responds to Mordechai

Hatach was still standing at attention, awaiting the queen's response. As Daniel, he watched Esther closely as she paced, wishing he could read her thoughts.

"Hatach, here is my answer to Mordechai's command to go before the king and plead for my people. And I need not caution you to repeat my words precisely as I am telling them to you!

"You have commanded me to go and plea with the king for my people.

"Yet all the king's courtiers and ministers, even those in the far-flung provinces of the Empire, are aware of the law of the palace. Mordechai, as a minister at the King's Gate you, too, are aware of this law and of its drastic consequences: The law of the palace is that any man or woman who ventures into the king's presence — into the king's private, inner courtyard — *without having first been personally summoned, will be put to death!* There are no exceptions to this law. In fact, this law is being scrupulously kept in the wake of the recent attempt on the king's life.

"There is only one slim possibility of reprieve. *If* the king were moved to extend his golden scepter to the uninvited interloper, then and only then would that person live, and would not instantly be put to death.

"But even I, as queen, enjoy no special privilege. I am *included* within this law's proscription. Uninvited, I am courting death if I initiate an audience with the king, seeking an audience without having been personally summoned.

"And there is another consideration. I may be at a particular disadvantage right now; for the king has not called me to be with him for these past thirty days! "

Hatach bowed his head and left the queen's apartments, leaning on his walking stick.

Esther's Plan Takes Shape

Via Hatach, Esther is outlining for Mordechai the practical difficulty of following his instructions to "go before the king and plead" for her people. Such an audience cannot be undertaken casually; there is a rigid royal protocol that must be followed. Xerxes, in the wake of the recent foiled assassination attempt and other close calls, has clamped down, tightly restricting access to his presence. Always insecure and cautious, as monarchs tend to be, Xerxes — post-Biktan and Teresh — has narrowed access to personal audiences even further, keeping people away and instilling fear with the threat of summary death. No exceptions.

It is something of a surprise that even Esther the queen, who shares Xerxes' intimate space during the nights, is included in the proscription against uninvited audiences with the king. Perhaps this is the reason Esther adds the seeming postscript, that she has in fact *not* been intimate with Xerxes for the past thirty days. She is emphasizing for Mordechai that her privileged, wifely status appears to be of no use in the face of this draconian law. She is implicitly inviting Mordechai to suggest an alternative to her going before the king uninvited and risking her life. She would be no good at all to their cause if she were struck down by an overzealous royal guard.

Esther actually is quite worried that the king has not called her to his bed over the past month. She has revisited their conversations and interactions, avidly searching for the reason. Was it something she said or did? Or perhaps did *not* do? In ordinary times her concern might be attributed to womanly vanity, but the times were anything but ordinary. Esther's real concern was that if perchance the king had lost interest in her, though she would retain her title as queen, her utility as an agent would be seriously compromised.

There could be several interpretations to Esther's not having been summoned.

Perhaps the king has not called Esther to his bed for the simple reason that his interest in her—so keen for so long—had at last waned, and that he has sought other female comfort during the past month. This would not bode well for Esther's utility as a secret weapon during this crisis.

Or it could mean that the king has not indulged in his nightly and husbandly pleasures with Esther because he has been exceedingly worried and preoccupied following the foiled plot against him. Plainly stated, Xerxes has been too worried about a coup and death threats to summon energy —or Esther—for sex.

Given that in recent years Esther has been personally privy to Xerxes' very real insomnias and night fears, and absent even a whisper that another girl either from the harem or from among the concubines has drawn his interest, it is more than likely that it is the king's anxieties and preoccupation with his safety and vulnerability that have kept him aloof from her.

Hegai and Farah, who between the two of them have half a century of intimate experience serving Xerxes, keep close tabs on the king's bed partners. They had championed Esther, and they, too, are troubled by the king's lack interest in her these past thirty days. Hegai, as keeper of the virgins, and Farah, matron of the harem, had done a similar analysis to Esther's. Unbeknownst to Esther, their assessment of the situation jibed with hers. Hegai had served with Xerxes in military campaigns for three decades, and, as he confided in Farah, when Xerxes was worried or preoccupied or on eve of a battle, his interest in sex evaporated.

Esther is betting that her intuition is correct, and that the reason Xerxes is foregoing sex is his anxiety and paranoia, not disinterest. A plan is taking shape in her mind that will use — rather than avoid or ignore—Xerxes' exaggerated fears, and will further her mission.

Esther is familiar enough with the ways of Xerxes to know, with absolute certainty, that if ever she were to attempt to use "pillow talk" to gain a favor from the king, she would forfeit her leverage in an instant. Her original strategy, conceived six years ago when she was a neophyte in the harem, and executed with stunning success, had been to enhance her mystery and desirability in the king's eyes by acting in the *opposite* way to the other girls: so she *never* asked the king for anything. Instead, Esther *gave*, in a seeming endless desire to please. In this way, over the intervening years Esther had conditioned Xerxes to expect—and receive—an undemanding loyalty and compliance from her. Esther had no ulterior motives in pleasing him; she asked for nothing. Xerxes believed that Esther pleased him for the purest of motives; that her sole goal was to serve him and to bring him pleasure. Over the years, Esther had secured her place in the king's affections by fulfilling the king's fantasy.

Esther's Fears

Now, however, just at the time when she is in dire need of confidence and security in the king's attraction to her, Esther is plagued with doubt; the king has not called her to his bed for the past thirty days. Esther is encouraged only by the knowledge— whispered to her by Farah—that the the king has not called *anyone* to his bed over the past month. So in a subtle twist of the kaleidoscope, Esther is calculating that after thirty days of abstention from sex, Xerxes' passions might be easier to arouse. Esther plans to stoke not only the king's banked desire for her, but also his paranoia and his temper. Esther's plan is to nudge Xerxes to the edge so that he will act precipitately when she applies the pressure.

Esther's beauty and her calm, undemanding personality; her air of mystery; her loyalty to Xerxes — did not Esther she sit up night after night with a dagger in her lap guarding the sleeping king? — and her unquestioned personal and sexual generosity, made her the king's favorite. She was relying on Xerxes' continued trust and good feelings as she laid her plans.

But despite her rationalizations, Esther was frightened and cold to the bone. The simplest interpretation of the fact that Xerxes had not called her to his bed these past thirty days was that this fickle and demanding lothario-king had lost interest in her. Esther could not dispel the terrible suspicion that if she were to violate Xerxes' law and enter his private courtyard uninvited, he would not intervene to save her life.

Mordechai's Angry Response

Mordechai is torn. On the one hand, and buried deep beneath his own fear and anger, he is proud of his ward's success. They had sacrificed their love on the chance that Hadassah, as Esther, would capture the heart of a king. And against extraordinary odds she had done exactly that! This sheltered virgin girl, a secret Jewess, was within daily, breathable proximity to the most powerful monarch in the world. She had not only achieved the pinnacle, she had managed to stay balanced at the summit these past five years.

Even more than that, Mordechai is proud that Esther had not crumbled in the face of everything he had just thrust at her. In an instant she had had to comprehend and navigate a new reality where a love sacrificed to duty was mere child's play. In this new reality of Haman's rising supremacy and Xerxes' preoccupation and paranoia, Esther was thrust to the very edge of the chasm between a life of luxury and a certainty of the brutal death of her people.

Mordechai has noted with a measure of subliminal pride that, instead of sinking into hopelessness or inaction, Esther's response to his gauntlet to "go before the king and plead for your people!" — relayed through Hatach — was a measured one. Not for his Hadassah a descent into female hysterics! His instinct told him that Esther already was working out a plan of action. Reading between the lines, Mordechai is reading Esther's plans clearly. He sees Esther stepping cautiously, seeking to bide her time; in a softly-softly approach, she thinks she will be able to turn the king around, bend him gently to her will and then make her plea. He sees her as reluctant to risk her life and approach the king unbidden, and he counts this as a flaw.

Mordechai categorically rejects the softly approach. He is done with diplomacy, and he is commanding Esther to risk all, shed her cover, and plead with the king outright to save her people.

That Mordechai has misread Esther's plan does not enter his mind. To Mordechai, Esther is still, in her essential makeup, the Hadassah he knew: smart, yes, possibly even brilliant in her own way, but essentially naïve, compliant and eager to go along. That she could conceive of a complex, multilayered real-life chess game with the highest of stakes, practically on the spot, never dawned on him. But Mordechai has no knowledge of the woman now called Esther.

Mordechai is neither the first nor the last highly intelligent and ambitious man to underestimate her.

So Mordechai, misinterpreting Esther's words, grows angry at what he perceives is a fear and hesitancy to immediately petition the king on behalf of her people. To Mordechai, a practiced and successful do-er; a mover of men and women who *acts* and plays out his political games, Esther's strategy is dilatory. Impatient, he blows up in anger at Hatach:

"You have the temerity to throw the king's paranoid law in my face as the reason you cannot go before him and plead for your people?! Wake up, Hadassah! If fate has prevented you from working your wiles on Xerxes in private, then you have no alternative but to seek an audience with him and take the risk of throwing yourself on his mercy. There is no other way, and there is no time to lose!

"Don't hold up the king's laws as a shield, Hadassah," he sneered. "Your personal fears are of no consequence to me now. If you do have a fear it should run much deeper than concern for your own smooth skin. Being Esther, Queen of Persia, will not insulate you from Haman's butchers. Do not for a moment imagine that living in the king's palace you will be spared the fate of all the Jews! On the contrary! If you remain silent and do *not* go before the king, be assured that even so, relief and deliverance *will* come from other quarters. You are not the only asset we have in the palace. You just happen to be the best one.

"The time for silence is over, Hadassah. If you remain deaf to my pleas, and if you choose to remain mute now, when action—not passivity—is desperately needed, know for certain that you will perish along with Persia's Jews when the Terror comes. Haman's mercenaries will roll through Persia, through Susa and through the palace like a murdering juggernaught, and will sweep you, too, under its wheels. Once you are destroyed, there will be no trace left of your father's house.

"Think, Hadassah! Who knows, but that it was for *this very moment* that you were chosen queen?!"

Mordechai, still seated on the ground in the public square throughout his speech, stopped his monologue abruptly. He had been looking through Hatach as he spoke, not really seeing the man crouched in front of him who was memorizing the words he would repeat to the queen. In his mind's eye Mordechai had been speaking directly to Hadassah, now Esther. He stopped cold because he had run out of options and arguments. Esther was by far his best weapon against Haman. If out of fear or inertia she chose not to take the risk; if she refused to go before the king, Mordechai would deploy a team of others. But as a seasoned spymaster he knew she was the best—the only—person who had even a hope of intervening successfully with the king.

Esther Refines Her Plan

On hearing Mordechai's angry and bitterly sarcastic words, Esther realized anew that the Mordechai she had known and loved truly was no more. The Mordechai issuing these directives was a complete stranger to her. *Spymaster he may be*, she thought, *but he has no inkling of my life in the palace; of my six-year tightrope walk; of the dagger I keep in my pocket day and night; of the subtle and delicate strategy needed to ensnare and hold the king.*

Mordechai had misunderstood her words, reading in them her desire to *avoid* intervening with the king. How could he *not* know that she had never given up hope of being a useful agent, even after everything she had lived through? That her deep cover never reached that corner within her that was always poised and ready to heed the cryptic words of Abednego, her guardian angel, or that still, after six years, waited for a coded word from her control. That yearned to be useful and needed?

Standing literally and figuratively outside the palace, Mordechai did not appreciate that as queen, Esther's life was protected, yes, but was ruthlessly, rigidly circumscribed. At its most basic, she would have difficulty complying with Mordechai's directive—even if it were strategically sound, which Esther deemed it was not—because she was not free to walk where she wished, when she wished. Esther figured that it must be the extreme stress of Haman's Death Decree that obscured Mordechai's strategic skill. But fortunately for everyone, *she* still understood and appreciated what it would take to get her to speak to the king personally, and then, importantly, to get the king to pay attention to her petition once she voiced it. That it would take a sophisticated plan and not the blunt approach of "go before the king and plead for your people" was obvious to Esther, but lost on Mordechai.

She would not lose precious hours educating Mordechai in palace protocol and in the ways of Xerxes. She had learned much these past six years, and she decided right then to put a two-pronged plan into play. First, she would enlist her personal maids and the circle closest to her; what she thought of as "her people," drawing them into her confidence and allowing them to appreciate the dire life-and-death situation that was at stake.

Second, she would set up her plan to trap Haman in stages. From the first, Esther had been aware that the palace was a place of danger, and she had acted accordingly. For six years she had conducted herself cautiously and kept her secrets close. In that time there had been small harem and palace intrigues that she had navigated adroitly, with the help of Farah, Hegai, and her devoted maids. She knew that in this present situation, while she would keep the entirety of her plan to herself, for day-to-day execution she would again need to rely on her confidants. Some time soon they would need to be told her true identity, but perhaps she could delay even that. There was a danger in the telling, as Esther always feared a leak, but it was a calculated risk, something Mordechai had taught his agents to consider when no other alternative was open to them.

In this game of high stakes intrigue Esther was banking everything on her two advantages: the first edge was that neither the king nor Haman knew that she was a secret Jewess; and the second was the hope that Xerxes still desired her.

Esther Issues Orders

"Give Mordechai these instructions, and caution him to follow my directives precisely, neither adding nor deleting so much as a jot:

"Rise immediately from your place of mourning in the public square. And go—send out your runners and messengers with an urgency this very hour—issuing the call to all the Jews of Susa to assemble this day. At this assembly tell them that Esther, Queen of All Persia, respectfully requests that henceforth, all Jews of Persia refrain from attending any public banquets, for fear of their safety. Furthermore, tell them that beginning this very day, every

Jewish man and woman, young and old, is to refrain from food and drink, from sunup to sundown, for three days. They will fast *on my behalf*, and I and my servants and my people in the palace will likewise fast along with them these three days.

"At the conclusion of three days of fasting by all the Jews in Susa, at sundown on the third day, *I shall go to the king*. I shall go to the king notwithstanding that my uninvited entry into the king's royal courtyard and throne room is against the law. I shall go notwithstanding that the king's law demands that any person, without exception, who approaches the king uninvited risks the death penalty. I shall go notwithstanding that the king has not issued me a royal invitation or permission to approach him there—or anywhere—for the past thirty days.

"At the end of three days I shall go to the king."

Hatach receives Esther's commanding directive in silence, and for the first time in his four days of shuttle diplomacy between Esther's palace apartment and Mordechai's place in the public square, Hatach hesitates. Esther notices his slight pause.

"What is it, loyal Hatach? Speak what is on your mind."

"My Queen, Mordechai gave me *another* message in addition to the one I told you. His second message was to be told to you alone, when no one else was present. He swore me to speak his words for your ears only, and to bring back your reply."

Esther's heart stopped. She had given up any hope of reaching the true Mordechai; had relegated him to the secret treasure chest containing her deep past, and had locked it tight. *Mordechai has sent another message! Perhaps this one is personal.*

"Speak, Hatach." Esther gestured broadly, indicating her private receiving chamber, empty now except for the two of them "As you can see, we are the only ones here."

Hatach began to speak Mordechai's words.

"Hadassah, I spent my life doing my 'duty,' making no room for anything else. And while I wasn't looking, you, the child I took in out of duty, became the love force that made the duty I owed to my country and my people richer and more personal, more immediate and joyful for me.

"Then, I lost you to duty. I lost you and my heart stopped. For duty I pulled my punches and let you go. Because, in Daniel's words, our duty was greater than our love. Or so I thought.

"Now, at the brink of annihilation—and I have seen Haman's face; he is quite mad and his Decree is deadly serious—I know that my old mentor, Daniel, was right. Duty, yours and mine, supersedes our love. But it does not nullify it; it only sidelines it. We have an immediate job to do, and throughout everything, our love exists, just in another dimension. We cannot access it. Neither should we obsess about it or mourn it. I beg you to use its power to do what we have to do. Vanquish our mortal enemy, and save our people. Isn't that 'love,' too?

"Even just four days into it, the Terror is real; the killing machine has been activated. My sources tell me that the word has gone out from Haman and from the Baradari Brotherhood of Haman's sons, calling for mercenaries. *Twenty thousand* trained warriors from all over the known world are on the march, coming here, to Persia, to Susa. They will be massing in the fields and barracks that are even now being built on the sands on the city's outskirts, at Haman's orders, with the power of the king's ring.

"*You* have a power, Hadassah, in your mind and in your body, as Queen Esther, to stop this juggernaught. We have a great need of every possible instant of time if we are to fight back against such an army. Actions you take *now* will buy us the time we need. Don't squander your time on regrets.

"Duty *has* trumped love. But after we are saved, who is to say love won't find another expression? And of what value is our love, anyway, compared to the lives of an entire people? Three million hearts beating, three million souls striving. We were fashioned for this fight, Hadassah. Of this I am certain. You need to be certain, too.

"As Esther, you must go to the king and plead for our people."

Esther had closed her eyes as Hatach spoke, envisioning an impassioned Mordechai speaking to her in Hatach's stead. When he was done, she opened her eyes and stood silently. Nothing in her face betrayed her thoughts. But Hatach saw the subtle change in her posture. Watching her, Hatach thought, *Our Hadassah has become a Queen. Hadassah truly is Queen Esther, our secret weapon.* Esther—living up to her Persian namesake, Ishtar—was becoming a warrior-queen before his eyes. *It will turn out all right.* He sighed silently, awaiting her answer.

Tell Mordechai that "I *will* go before the king. But I will do it *my* way. And if I perish, well, then, so be it! I will perish as a Jewess."

Hatach left to tell Mordechai.

And Mordechai heeded Esther's directives, and readied the Jews of Susa.

Azariya—as Abednego— Esther's invisible guardian, observed the unfolding events. He flexed his sword arm when he heard Esther's last statement. As if he would let any of the palace goons so much as harm a hair of her head. But he did wonder how she planned to get past the circles of protection that the king had thrown up around him. He managed a grim smile. After six years of guarding Esther, he had an appreciation of her quiet strength. Palace politics—especially in the House of the Women—was brutal; but in all this time no one had bested Esther yet; she had not so much as stumbled. She had an almost magical ability to inspire loyalty among those around her. She had a small and silent army of women who smoothed her way and watched her back.

And then there was Azariya himself, the extra layer of protection. He had hovered close to Esther since the disastrous night of her foiled wedding. He smiled to himself at the memory of Esther's small, smooth hand resting calmly on the hilt of the dagger. Since the day six years previously that he had left it for her under her pillow, she had kept it with her always. *The woman might not know it herself,* he thought, *but she is a warrior.*

Azariya took his mission seriously, especially as Daniel's prediction of the approaching Terrors appeared to be coming true before everyone's eyes. If Daniel thought Esther was key to saving the Jews, then she was. And Azariya's job was keeping Esther safe from harm, so that she would be free to do hers.

Shadrach smiled, and when he did, the cloudless desert sky rumbled with invisible thunder. He looked forward to sitting back and watching events unfold as Haman, the human vehicle for his evil and bloodthirsty plans, took the lead. He himself might have thought that unleashing twenty thousand armed and brutal mercenaries on the Jews of Persia—most of them unarmed shopkeepers and merchants who had never held a sword in their lives—was overkill (wasn't that a laugh, too). But Haman had the bit between his teeth now, so Shadrach was content to watch an impotent Daniel, a panicked Mordechai, and a terrified and helpless populace scramble. *All in a day's work*, he thought.

Shadrach never gave even a thought to Esther.

A "New" Esther

Subtly but significantly, the command baton had passed from Mordechai to Esther. Mordechai's seemingly impossible command to Esther that she "go to the king" had galvanized her. With clarity, Esther began to see how her own plan could unfold. She was, as of that moment, a spymaster's secret weapon deployed. For six years a sleeper agent, Esther now was utterly on her own, functioning as her own control. She knew "the enemy" better than either Mordechai or even *his* control; she knew the enemy better than any other operative in the palace or in Susa. And she was perfectly placed to do what needed to be done: Entrance a king. Ensnare a murderer. Save her people.

Thus it was that, in the end, it was Esther who issued the orders, and Mordechai who hurried to put them into play. Orders he had not so much as questioned; without a qualm, he hastened to obey. And this despite Esther's order to have all the Jews fast for three days, beginning this very day. Mordechai knew, if Esther had forgotten, that this pronounced fast-day fell on the first day of the festival of Passover, when fasting was prohibited. Nonetheless — or perhaps, in some way, because of this coincidence — Mordechai immediately acceded to Esther's order and commanded the Jews of Persia to violate their own tradition and refrain from food and drink on one of their three most important holidays. So dire was the danger they faced that rules of the festivals were effectively suspended. Esther was calling the shots. The Jews of Persia fasted on the festival of Passover, their Festival of Freedom.

Esther had used the three days of fasting to think strategically and to refine her broad plan. It had become clear to her, reviewing and analyzing Mordechai's words, that even Mordechai — the most skilled control alive in Persia or likely anywhere — was woefully unaware of the personal and political motivations fueling Xerxes. Instead, it was she, Esther, an untried field operative, a relative novice and a secret Jewess, who was the only woman in Persia who understood what made Xerxes tick.

And Esther knew that Mordechai's strategy about appealing directly to the king on behalf of the Jews' lives was flat-out wrong. Xerxes absolutely would *not* be moved by an appeal to justice. Esther was certain that the king was unaware that Haman's decree was for a genocide; surely Haman had concealed his real plan, somehow leading the king to believe that the Jews were only to be enslaved. She well knew that if the king had agreed to enslave the Jews for the irresistibly high price of ten thousand talents of silver, that she would fail utterly if she attempted to change his mind by appealing to a mere principle. The very real lure of a king's ransom in silver mattered more to Xerxes than any ephemeral principle of justice.

But Esther also knew that Xerxes prized two other things as much as he prized a rich treasury: the king was near-maniacal about the security of his crown, and the inviolability of his queen.

Esther's gift was that she had an intuitive genius about people. It was this intuition that allowed her not only to survive, but to thrive within the palace, a place that was rife with rivalries, schemes, threats, and an underlying, ever-present fear of death.

Over the course of her three intense days of fasting and thinking, Esther called on her knowledge of and intuition about both Xerxes and Haman as she developed her plan. When she had worked out what she intended to do, all that was required was that she take it in carefully choreographed steps, and trust in the One-God and the Fates. Esther's plan was diametrically different from Mordechai's blunt, frontal approach ("Go and plead with the king!"). Her plan—it had become clear to her sometime during the second sleepless night of her fast—was to manipulate *both* of Xerxes' needs: his passion for exclusivity with his queen, *and* his overweening fear of coup.

To do this she needed very subtly to slip the thinnest sliver of suspicion into Xerxes' mind about his vizier, Haman. She must somehow set Xerxes thinking that his closest advisor was perhaps not as loyal to the king as he would have the king believe. She must set Xerxes to worrying that Haman had his avaricious eye on Xerxes' queen as well as his crown. Only after these shards of doubt had insidiously intruded into both Xerxes' conscious mind as well as his sleepless nights, moving in his imagination from suspicion to certainty, would she gamble on disclosing to him the secret of her people and her kindred. Xerxes must come to suspect that it was *Haman*—and not the Jews of Persia, as Haman had surely told the king—who constituted the biggest threat of all, to Xerxes as well as to his queen. Somehow, she must transfer Xerxes' trust from Haman to herself.

How to achieve these ends? Especially as Xerxes had not summoned her to his bed these past thirty-three days!

Esther had a choreographed game plan in her head. Step-one was to do as Mordechai said; she *would* go before the king! But she would do it *her* way.

Esther: Step-One

Esther's plan was extremely risky and without precedent. Though beautiful, brilliant and strategic, Esther was, at her core, still a political neophyte. She was aware that she was playing a high-stakes game, and that even if by some miracle she survived her law-breaking visit to the king, the next steps in her plan were, themselves, fraught with danger and could land her in royal purgatory at the very least, and at the end of a hangman's noose at worst.

But for now, Esther concentrated on her promise to present herself to the king. This was *her* risk to take, the ultimate test of her beauty, brains and mettle. Esther prepared herself to go alone and uninvited before Xerxes, King of all Persia.

Reprise: Esther – Alone
474 BCE
Year 12 in the Reign of King Xerxes
Year 5 in the Tenure of Queen Esther

There was no sound as she walked the marble breezeway connecting the women's compound to the king's palace. No sounds, no echoes, and no walls. The white gauze curtains hung from silver rods and draped over marble pillars fifteen feet high, pooling onto the floors. Sweeping panels of translucent fabric marked off rooms and chambers, coded by color to indicate place and station. It was a melting evening, the unrelenting Persian sun just sinking behind the palace ramparts; still, the air moving across the marble floors was mercifully cool, the lengthening charcoal shadows shifting. As she walked, Esther's own shadow appeared and disappeared on the curtains with the occasional breeze. *Like me,* she thought. *Here one moment, then who knows? perhaps gone the next.* Her soft slippers moved along honed white and gold marble floors inlaid with emerald- and sapphire-colored mosaics. As she walked, she noticed that the curtain color changed from white to blue, to, now, purple brocade of triple thickness, hanging heavily without any movement; she was nearing the Forbidden Zone.

Esther took a deep breath and uttered a silent prayer that today's sunset would not be her last. She remembered that the prior queen had displeased the king and was never heard from again. It was she whom Esther had replaced just five years ago.

She had taken great care with her *toilette.* She was wearing royal day-dress: the long chiton tunic of pale golden linen woven with iridescent gold threads, trimmed with turquoise braid and hanging down to her ankles, slit to show deep blue harem pants. Her slim waist was belted with a wide golden girdle. Her shining russet hair, thick and loose to her waist the way Xerxes preferred it, was secured with her smaller golden day-crown, a jeweled *kulah,* fashioned from the fine gold of the Ophir region. Her arms, fingers and ear lobes were bare. Normally lissome but full-breasted, on this day, her third day of refraining from food and drink, Esther stood tall but she was reed-thin, almost disappearing beneath her glistening raiment. Her face was free of enhancements, her brown eyes naturally dark-lashed and shadowed, her lips a naked, deep crimson, her skin parchment-pale. Her felt slippers were shot through with refined gold threads, sporting tassels to match her tunic's turquoise trim, but no decorative bells. She would approach the king's Inner Court unannounced.

How strange, she thought as she walked, *that on this third day of fasting the hunger and thirst have ceased to bother me.* Esther was past hunger. Her thinking was lucid, even sharper than usual; her vision was clear. She saw the tiniest, individual dust particles floating in a horizontal stripe of waning daylight. She could hear her own breaths, feel herself blink. Time had slowed for her; she was ready to face a death sentence. Or, if she was very, very lucky and blessed by her One-God and her Persian namesake Ishtar, goddess of love and war, she would have the chance to do what she had been born and trained to do: entrance a king, set a trap, save her people.

Xerxes

Xerxes sat, unusually still and pensive, virtually alone in his cavernous throne room. The day's business was done, the boring diplomats and fawning courtiers all gone to their homes or their chambers. Only the king's personal guard, standing on the dais and to the king's left, his spear at the ready; his scribe; and his personal fan-boy remained.

Some days, like today, Xerxes did not choose to exit the royal court with his entourage. Just now, with his newly built throne room nearly empty and finally silent, Xerxes relaxed marginally. He knew that his solitude would be honored, as it was the law of the land that no one could enter the throne room unsummoned, or come before the king unbidden. The penalty for trespassing in the Forbidden Zone was death.

Xerxes allowed himself to shut his eyes momentarily. He imagined that the courtiers and ministers, even the day shift of the Royal Guards, were in their homes by now, ministered to by doting wives or mistresses, secure in their attention, anticipating a night of intimacy and perhaps love. He made a small grimace beneath his carefully trimmed and oiled beard. *How the mighty had fallen*, he thought to himself. Doubtless every man in the kingdom—women, too—envied him his exquisite young queen, and his extensive harem. How they would exclaim, or even laugh, if they knew that for more than a month of nights Xerxes, King of all Persia, had slept alone. Correction: He had not "slept" more than a cat-nap at a stretch in more than a month's time. The worries of the crown weighed heavily on his head. Even the lowest stable hand was likely to be luckier than Xerxes this night. For though he had longed for his Esther these past four weeks— smooth and fragrant, smiling and understanding, fearless Esther who had guarded him while he slept—he had refrained from summoning her since the failed attempt on his life. He was secretly terrified that his preoccupation with coup and assassination would prevent him from performing his husbandly duties properly. He could stand the tension and the fear that went hand-in-glove with the royal crown and the jeweled scepter. But he would not have been able to bear the instant look of pity, quickly masked by understanding and acceptance, in Esther's eyes, if he had failed her as a man. So he did without.

But king or no, he was only human, and Xerxes fell to daydreaming a bit, thinking about Esther and about the blissful nights they had shared.

An Uninvited Royal Audience

Walking with her head held high, Esther passed unchallenged through every palace checkpoint. The guards knew her, and they privately thought the king had finally struck gold with this smiling and radiant young queen. They nodded and tilted their heads in a subtle bow, their right hands on their sheathed sword hilts and their eyes following her as she passed.

At last, Esther reached the outer vestibule of the king's throne room. This time she was halted by the enormous armed guard. He angled his seven-foot-long spear to block the entranceway. Esther could actually see Xerxes on the far end of the vast room, seated on his throne on the raised dais. She had timed it well; he was alone now, save for his ubiquitous bodyguard and his scribe, and he seemed preoccupied. His head, angled sideways away from the entranceway, rested on his hand, and his foot was tapping idly.

"Majesty, have you been summoned?" asked the unsmiling guard in a respectful tone. Recognizing Esther, he had no wish to challenge the queen, but his instructions were clear, and it meant his head if he failed to check. "You know, My Queen, that it is forbidden to enter the king's throne room unsummoned. The penalty is death." And he added, "For *both* of us."

"Yes, Hafez, I am aware of the law," Esther responded quietly. "The king is fortunate to have you as his loyal protector. I will tell him that you look out for his queen, as well. And no, I have not been summoned. But I would speak with the king."

The guard's eyes softened, though his stance remained on alert. This young queen had remembered his name. *How could anyone fail to love her?* he thought. *Surely she posed no harm to the king.* But he had his orders.

"Perhaps if the king were to see you standing here, he would invite you to enter. If His Majesty were to extend the royal scepter I could allow you to pass, My Queen." Hafez and Esther locked eyes for an instant of mutual understanding. Then the guard produced a loud cough, a booming sound that came from his enormous chest and echoed through the empty throne room. Despite her preoccupation Esther smiled subtly at him, at the same time concealing her fear.

The ploy worked. The king looked up, straight at the arched doorway where the guard's spear blocked Esther from entering. He had been thinking of Esther that very moment, and was briefly stunned to see her actually standing there. She stood tall as a reed, the gold threads of her tunic catching the evening light, so that she seemed to shimmer. He had not seen her in four weeks' time, and it seemed to him that her loveliness had only grown since their last encounter. Was she more delicate than remembered? He could not tear his gaze away from her distant form framed in the archway across the room. All his senses went on alert, and he smiled to himself. *Esther has come to me*, he thought. He was enormously flattered.

But almost simultaneous with his flash of pleasure came the intrusion of a cynical thought. *For Esther to come to me unbidden, risking death, she must have a pressing reason. She must want something.* And he sighed. Everyone *always* wanted something from him. Either a favor or a boon or a recognition of some kind. *Perhaps she does not miss me, so much as she seeks a favor.*

Then again, he thought, in the five years of their marriage Esther had not so much as asked him for a flower. The result was that he felt compelled always to gift her with surprises. There was the satin pouch containing a ruby the size of her thumb that he had left on her pillow one morning. The earrings with pearls from

Africa and shaped like tear drops that he had left on her dessert plate after a private dinner. She always evinced delight and pleasure at his gifts, but she never *asked* him for anything. Over these five years he had come to appreciate the treasure that was his young queen; she expected nothing and requested nothing, but generously gave him of herself. And her sweet nature extended to everyone she touched. Xerxes knew the palace servants were devoted to her and that there was nothing she could ask that he or anyone would deny her.

Still, after all this time, had she, at long last, come to him with a request?

If Esther has come to me, she must have a compelling reason, Xerxes thought. He was desperate to know.

"Esther, my queen!" he called out. "You are a treat for my eyes, the perfect distraction!" Xerxes extended his royal scepter toward the arched entryway and said, "Enter, Esther, and approach the throne!"

Hafez nodded his enormous head fractionally toward Esther, and withdrew his spear from the archway. Esther exhaled the breath she had not realized she had been holding, and walked slowly the length of the great room. Her heart began to beat like the tattoo of a battleship's drum. Terror, relief, then resolution rolled through her in quick succession, causing her to feel lightheaded.

By the time she reached Xerxes' throne Esther actually felt faint. The three days of refraining from food and drink, compounded by her sudden immense relief that the king did not turn her away, had the effect of causing the air to ripple before her eyes. With a force of will Esther held herself erect as she stood before the king's throne, and almost involuntarily she extended her hand, needing a moment to get her balance.

Xerxes interpreted her gesture as adherence to royal protocol: anyone bidden to enter the king's presence was expected to touch the ruby tip of the royal scepter as a gesture of obeisance. He held out the scepter to meet Esther's hand and also to symbolically draw her near.

Esther had used the few moments of her walk across the throne room to marshall her strength and focus her mind. She spent a bare instant thanking the One-God and her namesake, the goddess Ishtar, for sparing her life. It seemed she would not die this day. Watching Xerxes from under cover of her lowered lashes, she realized her gambit had worked! She knew that face intimately; Xerxes was avidly curious, wishing to know why she had risked her life to come to him. He wondered what had brought her here, uninvited, in violation of strict protocol, when she had never so much as set a foot wrong in her five years as queen. And from his stance and his facial expression Esther also realized that Xerxes was genuinely glad to see her. She sighed. He still wanted her; he had not grown bored or tired of her, or transferred his attentions to another. She would follow her plan and work with Xerxes' curiosity and possessiveness. Standing in front of the throne, with Xerxes watching her intently, Esther extended her hand toward the royal scepter. And she allowed her knees to buckle.

Xerxes, intent on Esther's movements, noticed that his always-graceful queen was slow to rise from her gentle bow. Growing alarmed, he rose quickly from his throne, leaping down the dais stairs to reach her. He wound his free arm around her tiny waist, supporting her feather-light weight, leading her to a cushioned bench. Holding her close for those brief moments, his delight at seeing her grew sharper as he inhaled her subtle scent. His kindled desire warred with his intense curiosity. *Something serious must have brought Esther to me today; she has risked her life to come to me uninvited. Never before has she initiated an audience.*

Esther's First Request

Seated within Xerxes' light embrace on the ceremonial settee, Esther straightened her spine and put some distance between them so she could look into his eyes, and he into hers. She was newly energized, her mind and being flooded with purpose. *Go slowly*, she cautioned herself. As deportment required, Esther lowered her eyes and waited for the king to address her. She focused her mind and prepared to put the next step of her intricate plan into play.

"What troubles you, Esther, my queen? What is the nature of your urgent request that you have sought me out thus? Whatever it is, you have only to ask; even if your request were for half the kingdom, it would be given to you."

Esther banked her pleasure. She allowed the seconds to tick by, strategically using time to pique Xerxes' curiosity even more. Carefully, then, she raised her eyes to his, and spoke.

"If it pleases My King, I would invite the King and Haman to a banquet I have prepared for him later today."

"That is all? *That* is your request, Esther? And invitation to dinner?"

"That is my request."

In fact, Esther's invitation that the king attend a banquet was not an idle request. It was, in fact, a key to her ultimate success. Esther had spent the past six years immersed in the customs and conventions of the Persian royal court and Crown. *She knew that a request made at a banquet was rarely refused.* There was something sacred about sharing wine and food at a banquet; it was a judgment-free-zone where a person could present his petition and, in most cases, receive a favorable response. Esther was counting on that tradition to give her an edge with the king.

Xerxes paused, searching Esther's eyes for some motive, some trick. All he read there was honesty colored with, he imagined, a tinge of desire. She was inviting him to a party; she had not asked for half his kingdom. The king broke out in a smile of masculine knowing.

"Have you missed me so, my queen?" When she said nothing, he made up his mind. "So be it! You have gone to a great deal of trouble; you have prepared a private feast, so of course I will attend. And Haman, as well." Xerxes rose from the settee, bringing Esther with him. "Until later, my Esther." And he let her go. Esther bowed her head in silent thanks and backed out of the throne room. She had survived the perilous, uninvited incursion into the throne room, and she had put the first part of her plan into play. The king had taken the lure.

Thoughtful now, Xerxes watched her go. He tapped his golden scepter against his open palm, then turned to the small doorway behind the dais, where he knew his personal chamberlain stood listening, ready to attend to his every wish. Xerxes raised his voice:

"You have heard Queen Esther's request! Go, alert Haman to the queen's wishes! And be sure to stand by to ensure that Haman stops whatever he is doing and hastens to heed the Queen's command. He and I will attend a banquet this night in the queen's quarters. Make haste!"

Esther Plans the Next Step

Walking back along the same marble corridors she had trod not an hour before, Esther allowed herself a brief moment of incredulity, then quickly reverted to her purpose-driven mode.

Her near-faint forgotten now, she strode into the kitchen/pantry that comprised part of her private quarters, checking that all was in readiness. The three-day fast having ended, her cook and faithful handmaids were following her orders. Servants dressed in white tunics ranged about the kitchen preparing platters of cold meats sliced thin as parchment, succulent sliced and sugared fruits, and bowls of nuts. In the "cool room" a girl was arranging vases of flowers; some tall and stately, others squat desert roses and water lilies, their wide, fragrant blossoms set to float in shallow bowls. And most important of all, the royal wine steward was standing by at the prepared table in her private salon, the carefully chosen bottles cooling in earthen crocks mounted in brackets on silver pedestals. Cushions were plumped, milky-white tapers were ready to be lit. That there were to be only two guests other than herself at the evening's banquet did not affect the elaborate and precise preparations.

Assured that her stage was set, Esther hurried to her chambers to ready herself. She stripped off her day clothes. Her personal maid helped her to bathe in perfumed water and to dress once again, but not before urging her mistress to drink a tall glass of chilled apricot juice mixed with pomegranate essence, her own concoction. It was necessary to revive and hydrate the young queen, coming off a three-day fast.

The few hours before the banquet passed quickly. Following the instructions she had heard Mordechai issue to his agents hundreds of times, Esther reviewed and re-reviewed her plan, and reconsidered her tactics, imagining all possible outcomes. For the first time Esther keenly appreciated the gulf between merely observing and actually *doing*. She thought, *this is my test, my riskiest assignment yet*. This time, she was not merely a backup player watching as others conducted an operation or collected a secret message. This time, she was key. This time, Esther was pitted against the king and his vizier, and the stakes could not have been higher. Could she do this thing? she thought. Could she capitalize on the seeds of doubt she would sow, and manage to turn her husband, the king, against the man who had his trust and would butcher her people—women and men, grandmothers and youths, virgins and suckling babes?

As if in answer to her unvoiced ruminations, she heard words echo clearly in her head: *Be subtle and go slowly, Esther! You have planted the seeds of curiosity. Now let them sprout.* So real were the words that she turned completely around, expecting to see someone standing there; Abbas, perhaps. But of course she was alone. She smiled to herself. *My invisible guardian,* she thought. And she smiled. *Yes, I hear you, and I will proceed slowly.*

Esther, trained by a master, knew that the king was all impatience, all curiosity, all haste. For the first time in Esther's life she would be departing from her life-path of *going along* with the person in authority. This time, she would be taking a bold step in direct *opposition* to that authority. This time, with the stakes as high as they could be, she would *act* the agreeable woman rather than *be* the agreeable woman. Because this time, her victory lay in *delay*; her strategy was the direct antithesis of the king's.

Esther had devised an audacious and provocative plan, and like a good agent, she was prepared to alter it on the spot if she needed to.

As part of her plan, she dressed with care as befitted the queen she was. She was bathed and scented; her magnificent hair was oiled and curled, partly hanging down her back like a silk curtain, and partly braided and coiled like a coronet atop her head. Her royal diadem fitted perfectly around her braid, glinting in the light of the torch sconces. She dressed in royalty: in a deep blue tunic almost to her ankles, piped with braided silver and gold thread. Her bloused trousers were palest gold, almost transparent. Her slippers were also golden, with deep blue felted soles. She wore the tiniest cord on her right ankle, adorned with a bell the size of her pinky nail. When she walked she created the subtlest of sounds, like a provocative, heralding whisper-song. She stood alone in the banquet room, waiting. She was ready.

Haman

Haman was in a hurry. He had gotten the summons via the king's personal messenger just half an hour before, informing him that he was invited to a banquet this very night, to be given by the queen. He assumed he was to be one of several guests along with the king, and he was flattered. He hoped the queen would seat him at the king's right hand, which would send a powerful signal to any diplomats or ministers attending that he—Haman, son of Hamdata, the Agagite—was second-to-the king, and was so favored that he was a "regular" at the queen's private banquet table. He had just enough time to hurry home, bathe and dress, and hasten back to the palace, where he strutted about in the palace atrium, hoping to catch any ministers who happened to still be about. He was eager to boast to them that he was dining and drinking that night with the king and queen, in the queen's private dining salon.

Haman breezed through the various palace checkpoints on his way to the queen's compound, the royal guards nodding him along. But once he reached the special walled wing, he was stopped and searched, quickly and thoroughly, by a giant guard who did not know him, and who could have cared less that he was "Haman, viceroy to the king!" despite his loud and outraged protests. By the time he had been stopped a third time, at the outer doorway to the queen's private suite, Haman was seething, taking it all as a personal affront. *Search me, indeed! This woman Esther has better security even than the king! She is watched more closely than the crown jewels! We will see if the guards don't change their tune when I become a more familiar figure around here.*

At Esther's outer vestibule her dignified chief handmaiden nodded and bowed her head, according Haman the respect due the king's vizier, graciously welcoming him inside. *This is more like it!* She treated him like an honored guest, and ushered him into the small but exquisite private dining room.

In an instant Haman took in the scene. The candelabra were lit, and the long table had only three place settings, laid out at one end. Esther and Xerxes were already seated on two plush divans near the table. They were smiling at one another, and the king was holding his wine goblet. Servants were silently bearing trays of tidbits of meats and fruits, and the royal cup-bearer and wine steward stood discreetly off to the side. The queen's giant personal guard, whom Haman recognized because the man accompanied the queen to every banquet and public appearance, stood by, watchful and silent as a statue, his spear in hand.

Why, there are only three of us here tonight! Haman masked his astonishment and deep pleasure as he was announced. He approached the king and queen, bowed his head and bent his knee.

"I am honored to join you, My King," he said, addressing Xerxes. The king barely inclined his head and took a long drink. And then, facing the queen, Haman directed a separate acknowledgement. "It is my distinct pleasure, My Queen." Haman flushed with pleasure as the young queen greeted him with a soft smile before lowering her eyes.

Haman stood a little taller, filled with masculine fantasies and flushed with success and power. He thought he had never been so happy. *And why not?* he thought. *Didn't he deserve it, after slaving day and night for the king? Hadn't he earned this special treatment? It was only too bad no one else was present to see how high Haman, son of Hamdata, had risen. But no loss. He would make sure the word got out on the morrow. And how they would all talk. Well, let them. They would envy and fear him, and they would trip over their own feet hurrying to do his every bidding! Proximity to power was a power unto itself. It was a step closer to the crown.*

All the while, as these thoughts flew behind Haman's fiercely ambitious forehead, Xerxes watched Haman.

Esther's Second Request

As the two men drink and eat, Esther plays her role of beautiful and gracious chatelaine. While she is careful to signal to the wine steward to refill both mens' wine goblets, she treats the king with particular attention. She fills his plate herself and anticipates his wants. The king expects this, and he preens at her small attentions. Esther's actions are calculated; she is playing a dangerous game, and the last thing she wants is the king to suspect *her* of deliberately attracting or inviting Haman's attentions. She wants the king's qualms to focus only on his ambitious vizier.

Esther cannot help but notice from Haman's grandiose manner of speech and his erect posture that he is delirious with pride and flushed with power. His eyes are in constant motion, taking in every detail of her private apartment, as if he is memorizing it. To Esther's feminine eye Haman is not only dangerously ambitious, he also is inappropriately lecherous. *Perhaps both of his hungers are part of the whole,* she thinks. Her highly attuned antennae have detected Haman's close gaze raking her from the top of her plaited corona to the golden tassels of her slippers, staring at her dress as if willing it to dissolve, revealing her body to his eyes. His attentions cause her to shiver slightly with revulsion and foreboding. She resists the impulse to raise her arms in front of her as a shield.

Esther had seated the king and Haman directly across the table from one another, in hope that the king would pick up on his vizier's inappropriate attentions. But Xerxes seems not to notice, and Esther is worried. Will Xerxes catch the bug of suspicion in time?

The king — though drinking steadily — is thoughtful. From under lowered lids Xerxes watches Haman, whose eyes are bright, and who in turn is watching Esther's every move. But Xerxes does not give the slightest hint that he is aware of where Haman's gaze is fixed. The king has let Esther have her head, but he is impatient now. He shifts slightly so he can see both Esther and his vizier. His hearty voice sounds loud in the room. He will discover Esther's reason for this private party.

"Well, Esther, we have come to your banquet, as you requested! Now I will ask you again: what is your wish? You have only to tell me and it shall be granted. And what is your request? Even if you were to ask me for up to half my kingdom, your wish would be fulfilled!"

Xerxes' question was not a surprise. Esther had expected that the king — accustomed as he was to instant gratification — would not be able to restrain his curiosity for very long. But Esther had hoped for a bit more time, sufficient to give the small kernel of "why" that she had planted in Xerxes' mind by inviting Haman to her intimate dinner party time to sprout. She had been moving the party along slowly, hoping the alchemy of the flowing wine and the relaxed atmosphere would work on both men. She hoped to loosen Haman's tongue and his inhibitions, allowing Xerxes to pick up — in the absence of any political distractions — on the vizier's covetous designs on her person, and on his normally well-concealed, over-weening ambitions. At the same time, Esther wished to relax the king and gladden his heart, so that he would be receptive to her coming revelation about her people and her kindred.

But either the wine had dulled Xerxes' suspicions, or the king was a master at masking them. While Esther found she was able to read Haman's face and body language quite easily, she could not detect any awareness on Xerxes' part of Haman's unspoken designs — on either the crown or the queen. Plus, she saw that Xerxes was impatient. She had played her part of undemanding queen so well, that now Xerxes' curiosity about her first-ever request was at its peak. She feared the king might lose his famous hair-trigger temper if she demurred a second time, putting off disclosing her request. Yet revealing her secret before the king was prepared to help and champion her could backfire. In a frustrated state, and feeling embarrassed in the presence of his vizier, the king might side with Haman, upholding the Death Decree to save face. She would have played her trump card in a losing hand, and she and her people would be four days closer to annihilation.

What to do? Dared she reveal her people and her predicament *now*? Her instincts screamed *NO!* Xerxes was not yet sufficiently wary of Haman to side with her against his vizier. He was not quite there. She needed more time; even one more day might be enough. Delaying her announcement even just twelve hours could possibly be all the time she would need. It was nearly midnight now, and sending both Xerxes and Haman away from her table wanting and anticipating *more* would allow a dreamless night to work its own magic on the men's imaginations. Haman would boast and dream grandiose dreams. And Xerxes would worry.

So Esther took another gamble. On the spot, she decided to put the king off for an unprecedented second time. She knew she was risking having the royal temper blow, with its power directed against *her*. She also instinctively knew if she tried putting Xerxes off with smiling, coy confidence it would explode in her face. She must not exhibit self-assurance or a whiff of power. Only an *in*secure and hesitant Esther had a chance of arousing the king's protectiveness and his desire to indulge his queen. And his consenting to a delay.

In an instant, Esther reverted to her original harem-persona of six years ago: that of a slightly insecure beautiful woman wielding her womanly skills at the will and behest of a powerful man. Such a woman made no demands. Instead, Esther improvised; she handed the power to Xerxes, and it was a brilliant maneuver.

The king was waiting, watching Esther closely, his seated stance a mixture of imperious demand and husbandly indulgence.

Haman waited, too, enjoying being a spectator to what promised to be the revelation of a royal secret. Esther turned in her seat and faced the king as she spoke.

"My wish, my request..." Esther replied slowly, haltingly, echoing the king's precise words. She raised her eloquent doe-eyes to Xerxes' face, allowing him to read her entreaty. "If I have found favor in the King's eyes, and if it is the King's will to grant my wish and accede to my request, as the King has graciously offered..." And here, again, Esther hesitated, with her repeated use of her husband's formal title acknowledging that he held all authority and license. Esther's senses were so keenly attuned that even without turning her head she felt Haman lean forward on his couch, anticipating her next words. "Let Your Majesty — and Haman — come to *another* feast that I will prepare for them *tomorrow*. And you have my word, My King, that *tomorrow* I will do Your Majesty's bidding and will reveal my request."

Esther allowed her eyes to hold Xerxes' for a second or two after she had stopped speaking. It was as if, just for those brief seconds, she held him in thrall. She had held out a plea and a promise she hoped he would read and accept. She held her breath. Had she gone too far? Would an impatient Xerxes feel that she was playing with him? Would the king's already short fuse blow at this second delay?

Xerxes searched Esther's face and in her eyes he read only sincerity. He could detect no gamesmanship. Perhaps she was shy of revealing her first-ever request to him, and needed a few more hours to gather her courage. He could afford to be generous. Esther had never yet disappointed him. By now he was intensely curious, but he would agree to her brief delay.

"Let it be as you wish, Esther. We will return tomorrow to hear your request."

Haman listened, and watched the exchange between king and queen with fascination. He had never before heard Esther speak and interact as much as she had on this night, and if possible, his secret infatuation with her that had been banked as other political issues took precedence, increased many-fold. Her beauty had flowered, he thought, and her poise and quiet smile were deliberately intended as a lure to him, he was sure of it. He was a handsome and virile man of much experience, and he could not be mistaken in this. She welcomed his attentions. She had glanced at him once or twice in that certain way... And, too, she had invited only himself along with the king to her private feast! She was ripe for the taking, and with some maneuvering she could be his, along with the crown. Patience was never his long suit, but Esther was a treasure worth waiting for. He would not rush this. He would return tomorrow and let the fates take him on this ride to the top. He was second-to-the-king, and now he also was a favored member of the king and queen's inner circle. He was invincible, a hair's-breadth away from the Crown.

The king rose from the couch, bringing Esther with him, and Haman jumped to his feet a tad reluctantly, an instant later.

"Until tomorrow, my Queen," said Xerxes. Esther lowered her eyes and inclined her head, raising her eyes fractionally to respond silently to Haman's slavish thanks and farewell. The king strode out, and Haman bowed out for part of the way, then turned and, straightening to his full height, strode hurriedly after the king.

Esther stood where she was, her right hand in the hidden pocket of her turquoise tunic, holding fast to the small sheathed dagger which she thought of as her protective talisman. All at once she realized she was utterly exhausted and she sank down on the divan, taking a moment to acknowledge her good fortune. *Last night at this time I was preparing to die, but I have come this far and still I breathe. I have sown some seeds of doubt and I have bought some time. But will the next twelve hours be enough? I will pray for the night to work its magic. Perhaps my namesake, Ishtar, the Star Goddess,*

will be watching over me and my people this night. Perhaps the One-God will lend some power. Who knows what night terrors Xerxes will experience tonight? Who knows what fantasies will embolden Haman? With luck and a little push from me, perhaps their fears, suspicions and ambitions will collide. And who knows if I will still be standing after the collision?

With a sigh, Esther rose and summoned her steward and her chief handmaiden. She had another party to plan.

Haman

Haman strutted through the darkened palace halls, ignoring the giant guards as was his wont, through the nearly deserted atrium, where, in just a few hours, would be heard the buzz of political deals being negotiated, and the din of mens' voices echoing beneath its majestic archways. Haman felt a rush of proprietary pride about the palace. *Soon. Soon it will be mine to command.* As he walked, he passed the pillar where just days before Mordechai the Jew had stood tall, defying him to his face, and he stopped still. And in that instant of remembering, Haman's euphoria came crashing down. In its place, the humiliation and anger that had filled him that noon bloomed anew. He actually felt his blood running first hot, then cold as he stood staring at the pillar and reliving Mordechai's defiance. Haman clenched his fists, breathing hard, and wondered where he could go for an hour or two. Not to crow about his new status with the king and queen, but to vent his anger. Perhaps to one of his sons' brothels? He could work off some of his energy on one of the girls. He badly needed the release.

He quickened his pace, leaving the huge gateway of the palace behind, and crossed the quiet boulevard, intending to short-cut across the deserted marketplace on his way to his son's establishment on a shadowed side street. He imagined he saw, in the dim light, on the edge of the market square across from the palace gate, the bulk of a seated man. In his mind's eye he saw

Mordechai, who had been rooted at that exact spot, his head and face covered in ash, wearing his mourning clothes and ranting.

Haman blinked his eyes. The man Mordechai was becoming an obsession. *Did the man even sleep there? Was there no law against his filthy public display, night and day? Well, if he, Haman, had his say, there would soon be a law making such behavior punishable by flogging and imprisonment. Let any other Jews get the idea to follow in the man's footsteps and they would all rot in the dungeon – that is, until the day – in a year's time, but not soon enough – when the streets would run with their blood and the kingdom would be rid of them all.*

How dared the arrogant creature ignore him even now? He was Haman, viceroy to the king! Mordechai had surely seen and recognized him – he was certain – yet he did not bestir himself; he actually ignored him! Haman could actually feel Mordechai's eyes boring into his, yet the Jew did not rise or stir so much as a muscle in obeisance! Mordechai was defying him still.

Haman impulsively changed direction and strode over to the corner of the market square, prepared to kick the huddled, watching figure. But of course, when he drew closer there was no one there; the ground was empty, and Haman's shoes touched only air and dust.

Haman's gorge rose instantly in his throat. He had to swallow the hot and burning bile, the remnants of the royal wine he had drunk, turning to acid in his stomach. He stood stock-still in the deserted square, trembling. He had been on the verge of jumping on the huddled man, pummeling him bloody. But he had imagined it all.

The Jew has cast a spell over me. He has invaded my mind! How will I be able to stand this for eleven more months?

Haman changed his mind, redirecting his steps toward his home. He no longer wished to fantasize about the queen's soft limbs while in the bed of a *jendeh*, or even to beat her senseless. More pressing was his need vent and to plot. He needed the adulation of his close friends and associates, and the advice of his wife, Zeresh. Despite the fact that she no longer shared his bed, he could count on her; she was still one of the sharpest political strategists he knew. She would reassure him, tell him what to do about this canker, this humiliation that was Mordechai-the-Jew.

As Haman seethed and Mordechai worried, the nighttime sky roiled with thunder and flashed with streaks of heat-lightning. Some swore they heard maniacal laughter.

Zeresh

Haman fished for the key among the many on his personal key ring. He unlocked the thick wooden door to his wife's home, bulling his way in, slamming the door into the wall in a fit of temper. Years earlier, in a pretentious imitation of royalty and an exercise of domination, Haman had installed his wife in a separate, walled house nearby to his own. He alone, and a hand-picked major domo, held the key, and Haman limited access to a limited number of vetted servants, even excluding members of their family from visiting Zeresh unless he granted permission.

Haman was practicing what he saw as imperial habits, seeing himself as monarch-in-training. He went to the considerable expense of housing Zeresh in a conspicuous walled house, at the same time keeping a separate house for himself. Zeresh was, in essence, a prisoner in Haman's gilded cage. She wanted for nothing material, but she could go nowhere unaccompanied. Haman's hired servants were her wardens.

Strangely, the arrangement suited Zeresh. Her political observations and her advice to her husband kept her alive and well and left alone. Zeresh had become so valuable to Haman that the higher he rose, the more paranoid he became that she might transfer her loyalties elsewhere, or that she would reveal his plans and secrets to his enemies. So Haman kept her cloistered, seeking her out for advice only, taking his pleasure with mistresses and exercising his perversions with the *jendeh* in his sons' brothels.

Zeresh, watched over by Haman's warden, was never alone, except in her bed. And again, this suited her. For the past ten years she had surreptitiously been trading small and valuable items on her weekly trips to the crowded bazaar on market days. She deliberately exaggerated her uninteresting negotiations for fruits, vegetables and meats, lulling her "watcher," who busied himself with a pipe and a gossip nearby. That she also traded goods for cash was her secret. Her watcher was never the wiser. Thus, over time, Zeresh had put aside a small treasure of coins against the day she would silently and expertly kill her watcher and simply disappear from her prison. She could ride, she could cipher, and she could speak several dialects. The Persian Empire was vast, and Zeresh knew how to take care of herself. Most important, with her secreted *khanjar*, her razor-sharp dagger always on her person, she was not afraid.

Wives in Xerxes' Persia were expected and required—by social mores and also by imperial fiat—to bear sons, and to honor and obey their husbands without demur. So Zeresh's virtual imprisonment and servitude were unremarkable and went unchallenged in a land where harems and cloisters were common among the upper classes and royalty. Zeresh had borne Haman numerous sons and a daughter, and lived out her days within her walled house, venturing out only if accompanied by either a manservant or a maidservant of Haman's choosing. Nothing about this was unusual.

The loud *crack!* of the door against the entryway wall roused the dozing Zeresh from her seat in her chamber, and she came running out to see what was wrong. She was still dressed, and had been listening with one ear in case her husband chose to pay her a visit after the day's doings at the palace. She was privy to his invitation to the queen's feast, and had read it as a breakthrough demonstration of his favored status as second-to-the-king. She was anxious to hear all that had gone on that evening.

Every detail and nuance of political and social doings of courtiers, diplomats and ministers was of utmost interest to her. Zeresh was a rare Persian creature: she was a wife with a keen analytical mind and a nose for political nuance. Her father had been a lifelong merchant and sometime-courtier, and listening to intricate discussions about business dealings in faraway ports, and palace doings here in Susa, were things she had been silent party to for nearly four decades. Political intrigue was in her blood. Haman's political maneuverings provided Zeresh with vicarious intellectual entertainment and challenge, and made her quite valuable to her husband. In this, at least, if not in the bedroom, she had no rivals. Haman's advance within the palace ranks was due to his unscrupulous maneuverings, but also, in no small part, to Zeresh's clever counsel.

"Husband! What has happened?" she asked as she moved quickly to close and secure the door against the night and the neighbors' ears.

"Bestir yourself, woman! Send for my sons and my cousins, my special team of advisors. Summon them *immediately*, to come tonight to an urgent gathering in my salon. You are to come, as well! Send out the couriers at once, and be sure they understand that I will not tolerate anyone's absence.

So Zeresh hurried to do Haman's bidding, her thoughts flying, imagining and discarding numerous scenarios. She was eaten up with curiosity. What had gone on at the queen's party to stoke Haman's anger so?

The Plot to Kill Mordechai

It was quite late by the time all Haman's coterie had gathered in his salon. Haman stood at the center of the crowded room, his wife and sons seated at the large rectangular table, with the rest of the men standing behind, against the walls. They all had come in response to Haman's nighttime summons, arriving in various states of dishabille. Some had already been abed; others had hastily left drinking parties or the arms of lovers. None dared to offend or anger the vengeful vizier.

Haman paced and raged and boasted and ranted aloud. All were intensely curious and none said a word, or even stole a glance at his neighbor. They waited for Haman to get to the point.

"It is no secret that I have been marked for greatness by the gods and by our king. I have much wealth; my private store house is crammed to the roof with gold and silver and precious jewels. I have houses and fields spread across the Empire, numerous servants, stables of horses, unworn luxurious clothing. I have more of everything than anyone can wish for; more, even, than all of you here combined!

"I live like a prince. And like a prince, I have sired many strong and healthy sons, and my sons, in their turn, are themselves siring sons. The dynasty of Haman, son of Hamdata the Agagite, is numerous and ambitious, and will be immortal. I am invincible!

"Our king has wisely recognized my talents and my worth, and has elevated me above all the slavering courtiers, the sycophantic royal family, and the entitled, seated ministers. The king recognizes that I have ideas he can rely on for advancing the monarchy, and for securing his power. The king trusts no one above me! For this reason, while the king continues to retain the ultimate power—controlling the keys to the treasury and the royal army—he has granted me the freedom to control the laws of the land. He has given me his royal Signet Ring to wear as a sign of his trust! I am the king's idea-man and his strong right arm. I *am* the law in the Persian Empire! I am second-to-the-king! I have no peers!"

Haman by turns shouted, gesticulated, pounded the table and his own chest, and thrust his left index finger, bearing Xerxes' signet ring—the undisputed sign of delegated imperial power—in the faces of those gathered around his table. Drops of spittle gathered at the corners of his mouth. He barely paused to take a breath. Haman was in a tirade; his ego and ire under full sail.

His gathered audience watched and listened, rapt. They wondered what had angered Haman this time and why they were called out this late at night. Haman is such a state was dangerous.

"What is more, this very day the queen herself gave a wine feast for the king, and she invited me to attend! And lo! When I arrived at the queen's private banquet, other than the king I was the only guest in attendance! Think of it! Not only that, but at this evening's feast the queen also called upon me to attend her — along with the king — at yet another private wine feast tomorrow! The honor to me is unprecedented!"

Here Haman paused while the assembled group muttered sounds of agreement.

"I have achieved all this. And yet, these honors are worth nothing to me. Nothing! Mordechai the Jew sits in the dust across from the King's Gate, railing against me. Or he stands in the palace atrium and smirks, refusing to genuflect to me. The man is a curse! He defies the king's law and pays me no fealty. Eleven months' time is too long to wait to be rid of him!"

As Haman wound down, it became clear to all in the room that he had called them all there for what amounted to a hurried council of war. Haman wanted their advice about what to do — *now* — to neutralize this man, Mordechai, whom Haman despised not only as a political rival, but also as a hated religious and ancestral enemy, and a symbol of defiance.

Only one person in the room detected still another potent reason for Haman's red-hot ire. Zeresh, his wife of two decades, was astute at picking up verbal and bodily cues. She understood well her husband's character, his weaknesses, his grandiose visions. And as a woman, she also was privy to some of his fantasies, which her own woman friends, acting as her eyes and ears with their own husbands in their own homes, had confirmed for her: rumor had it that Haman was harboring sadistic sexual designs on the young Queen Esther.

And Zeresh alone had just now picked up on Haman's sexual fantasy from words he spoke moments ago in this very room. Buried in Haman's telling of the queen's dinner invitation had been his characterization of it. He had said, "…the queen also *called upon me to attend her* — along with the king — at yet another private wine feast tomorrow!" Haman's slip of the tongue — he interpreted the dinner invitation as an invitation to "court" her — had revealed his own fantasy: by including only himself as the non-royal guest at *both* private wine feasts, the queen was extending a cautious beckoning hand to Haman *to attend to her.*

Haman saw the queen as intending to invite him to cuckold the king!

Nothing if not a realist, Zeresh thought that whatever else the young queen was, she was no fool. The girl had been sufficiently clever and desirable to win the crown and the heart of the king over every other beauty in the Empire, including Zeresh's own daughter. Zeresh would have bet a day's freedom that a woman with such prodigious abilities would be extremely unlikely to transfer her allegiance from the reigning Xerxes to his vizier, right in front of the king's face. *No,* she thought. The queen doubtless had something else in mind. Perhaps Haman was being used by the young queen as a tool to further her own secret plans.

But it would have been worth more than Zeresh was willing to gamble for her to suggest such a thing. Haman in his present state would be incapable of objectively considering such a possibility, and would doubtless lash out violently at her for suggesting that the queen was using him.

Besides, if her suspicion about Haman's hidden fantasies concerning the young queen were correct, there would be no point at all in suggesting to her husband that the queen might be enticing him in order to facilitate her own objectives with the king. Haman was blinded by desire and ripping with anger to boot. Zeresh knew she would make no headway taking that tack.

Zeresh concentrated, instead, on the urgent problem of Mordechai.

Zeresh, always quick to assess a situation and propose a solution, quickly factored in her husband's hatred of the Jew, and, despite his boasting, her husband's deep insecurity. She rightly assumed he would be unwilling to consider anything other than a swift and draconian resolution, and she intended to be the person to propose the solution he would implement. After all, she had her own sadistic embellishments to suggest. Keeping in mind her own precarious position with her volatile husband, Zeresh spoke up first.

"Husband." All eyes turned to her. The gathered advisors were more than happy to cede to Zeresh the first salvo. Better *she* should be cut down and humiliated by the hot-tempered Haman than they.

"This Jew Mordechai is a threat; not only to you and your authority, but also to that of the king. He is out of control and there is no question but that he must be stopped. A Minister at the King's Gate railing in public across from the palace against a royally sanctioned decree is more than a pointed insult to the dignity of the Crown. It is a treasonous act. The fact that he also thumbs his nose *at you* by refusing to obey the law of the land and prostrate himself before you, is but another unlawful act against the Empire.

"What Mordechai is doing is calling out to his fellow Jews and to anyone who will listen, literally inciting disobedience and dissent. This man Mordechai foments treason! It cannot be tolerated. The penalty for fomenting treason is death."

All in the room nodded and murmured their agreement. Zeresh continued, and Haman was listening.

"Until the Jew is eliminated, neither you nor the Crown is safe. There is only one way to neutralize the Jew's opposition to you; *one sure way* to stop him once and for all. And *you* must be the one to take the initiative, striking a bold blow for the king. Incidentally, of course, you will avenge the dishonor the Jew has shown *you*, and you will rid yourself of his threat to your own authority. Understand that every day that Mordechai sits in the marketplace in a place of public prominence, or stands in defiance at the King's Gate, he is an affront to *you*." Zeresh paused, looking pointedly at Haman and then at everyone in the room.

"You must have him killed. And you can do it legally. Have him hanged for treasonous acts, for inciting dissent, and for posing an imminent danger to the Crown."

Choruses of "Yes! The Jew must die! It is the only way!" flew around the table and echoed in the closed room. Haman stood silent at the head of the table, considering what Zeresh had said. She was encouraged to continue, fleshing out the details.

"It is not enough for you to permanently silence the Jew; you must ensure that you make him into an example of what happens when a citizen of the Empire resists the authority of the king. His death must be a swift and *public* one. It must send a strong message to everyone: As long as Haman wears the King's Ring, the king's law will be enforced. Anyone who resists Haman will meet a similar fate to Mordechai's!

"So this is what you must do, Husband. You must order a tall wooden stake to be constructed in the courtyard of your residence. Order it to be built fifty cubits high. At the height of seven stories, when your stake is hoisted it will be the tallest structure in Susa outside of the palace. Then, while Mordechai is still alive, you will order that he be impaled on the sharp end of your stake. Your soldiers will use pulleys to raise the stake, bearing the Jew's live body aloft and securing it for all to see. His bloody body will be visible from any point in the capital city. The carrion will feed on his eyes and his entrails. Everyone in Susa and for kilometers around will hear his cries for mercy as he dies. No one will ever dare defy you again."

Zeresh knew she had hit on the perfect solution. Haman's eyes lit up, and he smiled. All his family and advisors chimed in, offering suggestions honing Zeresh's plan, but it was unanimously agreed. Haman's course was set. All that remained was to secure the king's imprimatur. Even the vizier could not accuse, try and execute a Minister of the King's Gate without the approval of the king. Zeresh had an answer for this, too.

"If you give the order tonight to build the stake, by tomorrow all will be in readiness. In the morning, you will tell the king of your plan. He will surely agree; you will order Mordechai impaled on the stake, and afterwards you will cheerfully accompany the king to the queen's private wine party. Problem solved."

Haman nodded slowly. He felt relieved and a little magnanimous. He addressed the room: "My wife does me credit, does she not? All of you who have come here tonight have served me well with your advice. It pleases me. Let the stake be built!"

Haman

Haman's advisors—his sons and his cousins—rose from the table and, after taking leave of Haman and sending a nod to or making brief eye contact with or ignoring Zeresh, they filed out into the night. Zeresh rose and faced her husband in the empty room. Haman stared at her, thinking he did not know her, even after they had been married for two decades, and despite her having borne him many sons. She was brilliant and ruthless. And—he was certain of this after hearing her advice tonight—she was a dangerous woman to cross. Too much like himself for him ever to turn his back on her.

Xerxes–That Same Night

The king could not sleep. It was already into the second watch of the long Persian night and he was wide awake. He had abandoned his bed, wandered into his throne room, and sat on his throne. In deference to the time of night, he wore his informal, loose white linen robes, trimmed with blue and gold piping. His oiled hair was unadorned and instead of his gold crown he wore a headband sporting his crest: a rampant lion. At his right hand, as ever, was his royal scepter.

Despite the hour, on the dais with him was his personal bodyguard, and at the bottom of the stairs sat Shimshai, the chief scribe, busy scrivening into the royal record, the king's Book of Days. A locked chamber adjacent to the vast throne room was lined, floor to fifteen-foot-high ceiling, with leather-bound volumes bearing the hand-written records of everything that had transpired in the king's world, every day, for the past twelve years. The scribe himself was all but invisible, his hand poised over the sheet of parchment, gripping his reed-pen in ready position. The scribe's head was slightly bowed over the page, his small cap askew from his hasty dress when the king's valet had knocked peremptorily on the door to the sleeping chamber that served the royal scribes. They took it in turns to sleep in the palace near the king's personal servants. It was the law of the land that everything that transpired in Xerxes' palace must be recorded. There was always the possibility that the king would rouse himself during the night; the scribes had to be nearby.

Xerxes could not settle. He had coup and sexual frustration on his mind. Because he feared that his anxiety would hamper his sexual performance, he chose to abstain rather than risk that age-old sleep potion resorted to by virile men the world over. So, wide awake, he had come to his throne room, which never failed to give him a jolt of satisfaction. He had built this room, this entire grand palace, rivaling even his father's and grandfather's building projects.

But tonight, his cushioned throne and the opulent room failed to calm or distract him. Xerxes was worried. Ever since those two traitorous gatekeepers had plotted to assassinate him he had been unable to sleep. Granted, their plot had been foiled, but he was plagued by the fact that they had gotten as close as they had, undetected! Did they have accomplices? Were these accomplices even now plotting to continue where their hapless fellows had left off? It had been pure luck that one of his ministers had overheard their plotting and that he had understood their arcane dialect. And Xerxes was too good a soldier to trust in luck or coincidence. He knew a king's life was ever at risk, but lately his unfailing soldier's instincts sensed a gathering threat. He could not rest, worrying from where the next threat would strike. Was it—or he—even now lurking just beyond his throne room?

Side by side with this worry was his yearning for his young queen. He had kept her at bay for his own reasons for over thirty days, but being in her presence twice today had rekindled his desire. Xerxes, concerned with his ability to perform as a man, was secretly enormously pleased at his body's familiar reaction to his queen. Perhaps his worries would be mooted now. Esther had come to him unbidden, and seeing her after his self-imposed celibacy — unprecedented for him — had been sweet torture. He had feasted his eyes on her like a young groom. He had contrived even to hold her briefly; he inhaled her special fragrance, and watched her soft lips as she spoke, drank and ate. Now it was nighttime, and he was restless, desiring her.

But Xerxes was a canny veteran campaigner and monarch, and in the solitude of the night he admitted to himself that it was not only the fear of coup or his frustrated desire that kept him from his bed this night. He trusted his instincts, and so allowed the additional thought to surface that had been niggling at him most of the day.

What was Esther thinking, inviting Haman to a private wine feast?

She had never done such a thing before; adding a third person to their private dinners. Why had she included the vizier to what he, Xerxes, had thought would be a kind of reunion dinner-à-deux in the queen's private apartment? She could have revealed her request to him, he could have granted it, and their dinner might have ended in the bedroom, had Haman not been present.

The troubled king further wondered how Esther had even come to be acquainted with the vizier. After all, she was not present in the royal court during daily discussions of politics or state security; the vizier's prime roles. Neither was she present when the king and Haman privately discussed sensitive matters of state. Xerxes added all this onto to the custom that it was highly irregular for a sitting queen — or any married Persian woman, for that matter — to encourage private friendship with a man not her husband. The queen was cloistered away in her private apartment, and was at all times in the presence of maids and trusted attendants. In essence, she was kept from all harm, but also denied contact with the world outside her compound. The reality was that the queen was corralled by a velvet rope.

Haman would have had to seek Esther out rather than the reverse, since *he* was the one with the freedom to move about. The inevitable next thought snuck into Xerxes' head and lodged there.

Did Haman have designs his queen? His Esther!

That Esther was exceptionally beautiful and would be attractive to any man with breath in his body was not of concern to Xerxes. After all, a monarch often chose a beautiful queen precisely in order to stimulate envy and awe. But a beautiful queen was a double-edged sword. In the culture of the ancient Near East one well-known way to dishonor a reigning monarch or clan chief was to sleep with his wife or concubine — either willingly or by force. What burned Xerxes' gut as he sat in the quiet of his empty throne room, then, was the possibility that his vizier was seeking, first, to curry favor with, and ultimately to seduce, the queen. Or, in a more sinister vein, to gain her unwitting confidence and then surprise and overpower her. Xerxes became alert to the possibility that his vizier might be taking the first steps on his march to seizing Xerxes' Crown.

The King is Worried

Xerxes pondered this possibility. Perhaps he had granted his vizier too much power too soon. The king resolved to be on the lookout from now on whenever his vizier proposed a course of action. No longer would he automatically give the man approval to his various requests and schemes. He would ask himself first, *Is this for the good of Xerxes and the Empire? Or is it for the good of Haman and his cohorts?* Perhaps he had been precipitous, cutting himself off from his various cabinet ministers and placing his confidence in only the one man.

It came as a revelation to Xerxes that he was utterly without protection if his vizier turned against him. What, after all, did he really know of the man? His face was a familiar fixture in the palace, but was he truly loyal to the king? And how could he ever really know? And then the idea struck: Would it not be preferable to have as his second-in-command a person who had *proven* his fealty under fire? Xerxes was not ready to open himself up again to pluralistic decision making, but maybe it was time for him to take things in hand, to shake up his vizier.

Since he was awake anyway, he thought now was as good a time as any to get started. He would make good use of the quiet nighttime hours. He called out to his chief personal servant, who at all times waited out-of-sight but within earshot, just behind and to the right of the throne. He stood behind a hanging *arras* tapestry that concealed a secret door to the king's private apartment.

"Bring me the royal diary, the Book of Days, the volume covering the past two months, and have it read aloud to me here!"

His man trotted off, and in no time returned carrying the large leather-bound volume, followed by a tall bearded man known as the Royal Reader, and several of the king's servants, roused from their beds. The Royal Reader, accustomed to the king's requests, bowed his head respectfully before Xerxes, waiting for the king to let him know what he would have him read aloud.

"Go back to the day of the recent hanging of the two treasonous royal gatekeepers. Read to me of that entire incident, from detection to punishment. Do not omit anything."

And in his clear and rounded orator's voice, the Royal Reader read aloud of the entire affair: the secret treason of Biktan and Teresh, keepers of the gate and officers of the Crown; Minister Mordechai's having overheard the plotters planning to assassinate the king; Mordechai's prompt disclosure to the queen of what he had overheard; and the swift and successful apprehension and punishment of the two traitors. And here the reader paused and looked up at the king. All who had gathered in the now-silent throne room stood fascinated. They had lived through the event itself and its furious aftermath, and were curious as to why the king wished to relive it now. They hoped the happy ending to the story of the foiled coup would calm the king and send him—and all of them—back to their beds.

The king sat, thoughtful. Then he addressed the room.

"Remind me. What special honor, glory or elevation was conferred on Minister Mordechai to express the Crown's gratitude for his heroic part in all this?"

There was a low mutter as the king's servants conferred with one another and even with the scribe. After a few moments the chief servant replied, "Why nothing at all was done for him, Your Majesty." A surprised murmur rippled through the throne room.

At the time, in the immediate wake of the foiled assassination plot, all the king's personal servants — including the guards presently at the throne room doorways, the scribes and the Royal Reader — had watched the king's explosive reaction from the sidelines. Shocked, angry and feeling vulnerable, the king had lashed out, instituting an immediate and wholesale dismissal of palace personnel. He had suffered a crisis of trust; everyone was now suspect in his eyes. The remaining servants were grateful they had escaped the palace purge, but lived in daily fear that the king's vizier, who wore the King's Ring and struck out at the palace staff at his whim, might arbitrarily cut them from their jobs, substituting his own cronies, and sending *them* to the dungeon. They had watched, helpless, as Haman had exercised his new power in ways calculated to humiliate and crush their spirits. The result was that all the servants present in the king's throne room on the night the king could not sleep had a fear mixed with a secret loathing for Haman.

At the same time, most of the palace servants and guards recognized and appreciated Minister Mordechai. He was not part of the king's inner circle of courtiers, but whenever his business of state brought him into the palace, or he spoke at court, upon entering or leaving the various palace chambers he was unfailingly courtly and polite. Undoubtedly Mordechai had been the tool of a benign Fate when fortune placed him within earshot of the plotting curs, Biktan and Teresh. All those within the palace not owing their positions to Haman had sent up words of thanksgiving to the gods that the coup attempt had died at Mordechai's hand. They could only imagine the terror their life would have become in the event of a successful coup. As loyal servants of a deposed Xerxes, they would all have surely lost their heads, their houses would have been confiscated or burned, and their wives and children enslaved or worse.

For all these reasons, Minister Mordechai was well liked by the palace servants and guards. They murmured at the revelation in the throne room. Why had Minister Mordechai *not* been recognized and rewarded? It was an unpardonable oversight!

Xerxes Suspects Haman

At that very moment, there was a discreet cough from the main archway leading to the throne room. Hafez, reluctant, this time, to disturb the king, but wary of angering the vizier, kept his spear across the doorway and waited for the king to take notice. Despite the king's wakefulness, it was still the middle of the night. The loyal guard was wary of allowing anyone entry.

The king, still pondering the news that Mordechai's heroic part in saving his life had gone unrecognized, turned to face Hafez. He was long attuned to the guard's signals.

"Is someone waiting out there?" *Who would be in the court at this time of night?* he thought.

Hafez moved his bulk to the side of the archway, allowing the king to see the figure standing expectantly in the inner courtyard. When the king saw that it was Haman, he sat back in his throne and smiled to himself.

Really, the night was devolving into an interesting circus. For what possible reason could his vizier be pacing the courtyard during the second watch of the night? He had parted company with the man just hours before, in the courtyard outside Esther's royal apartments. What was so pressing that it could not wait until morning? And another thing: how could Haman have anticipated that he would be awake at this time of night? Does the man have spies even in my royal bed chamber? Xerxes resolved to make his own discreet investigation into his vizier.

The King continued to give his thoughts free rein. *If Haman, who is second only to me, and is responsible for royal security, may in fact have secret designs on my queen and crown, who, then, will stand in his way if he stages a coup?! Whom can I trust?*

It was at that precise moment of existential doubt and suspicion that the king had heard the small commotion in the outer vestibule, inquiring of Hafez, "Who is in the outer court at this time of night?"

After Haman had dismissed his hastily-convened midnight "cabinet session," and after he had roused his own servants and ordered them to construct a fifty-cubit-high wooden stake in his courtyard and to be quick about it, he had shunned his own bed. He was too focused, too impatient, too full of venom to sleep. He could actually see and taste Mordechai's grisly end, so anxious was he for Zeresh's plan to be enacted. While pacing his own bed chamber Haman actually imagined that he heard Mordechai's agonized screams. *I really need to be rid of this loathsome Jew. It must be a favorable omen that I can so vividly imagine his miserable death.*

And so, heedless of the hour, Haman abandoned any thought of sleep. Much better, instead, to make his way back to the palace, so as to be ready and waiting at the door to the throne room when the king emerged to conduct his morning duties. He intended to be the first person the king would see. He would tell the king of his plans for impaling Mordechai on the wooden stake he had prepared specifically for that purpose. He would make it easy for the king to approve the Jew's execution. He considered it as good as done already. Haman was quivering with anticipation. He did not expect that the king would be awake and holding nighttime court.

"It is Haman who stands in the outer court, Your Majesty."

"Let him enter," commanded the king.

Hafez looked down his great height at the arrogant vizier, and slowly and deliberately raised his giant spear from across the arched doorway.

The impatient Haman sneered at Hafez. *This hulking dolt will be among the first to go when I get royal permission to replace the king's security detail. The man is big, for sure, but he must be a mental pygmy; he moves as if he is under water.* Wearing a feigned expression of apology for disturbing the king at this late hour, Haman strode across the throne room to stand at the base of the dais steps. Though impatient to be heard, protocol demanded that he allow the king to speak first. He restrained himself, briefly inclining his head in the barest gesture of respect to Xerxes.

But Haman could not quite conceal his arrogant impatience from the king's sharp eye,. *This is still my throne room and I am still in charge. Let Haman wait. I will test him; I would see if he rises to the bait.*

Notwithstanding the hour, once it became known that the king was in the throne room with his scribe, almost magically and one by one members of the king's entourage appeared in the throne room. If something was afoot they wanted to be on hand to witness it.

Dispensing with a greeting, the king began speaking, almost in a musing fashion, ignoring the few spectators, directly addressing Haman.

"Tell me," mused the king, addressing his vizier, "what should be done for a man whom the king desires to honor?"

Haman was distracted and momentarily disarmed. The king, his senses sharpened by his suspicions, and with his own unfolding agenda, had rolled right over Haman's obvious impatience to be heard. Xerxes knew his opening gambit — this red herring — would temporarily divert the vizier, hopefully causing him to reveal his true ambitions. Xerxes was betting that his own passivity over the past weeks would play to his advantage here, as Haman would be utterly unsuspecting.

The king was setting a trap to snare a traitor.

The king's instinct hit a bull's-eye. Haman, his own urgent concerns temporarily forgotten, was easily drawn into the king's trap. The narcissistic Haman immediately cast *himself* as the intended royal honoree. *Who but myself would the king desire to honor?* he thought. So Haman replied in kind to the king, unknowingly casting himself further into suspicion:

"For the man whom the king wishes to honor, let him be glorified in the following manner: Let royal *clothing* that the king himself has worn to his coronation be brought out. Also a *horse* upon which the king has ridden at his coronation."

Warming to his theme, Haman took no notice of the communal gasps that sounded in the great room among the hastily gathered courtiers at his mention of the king's coronation robes and coronation steed. Everyone present in the throne room that night—and anyone who has ever lived or worked with Near Eastern royalty—knew that for anyone other than the reigning king to wear the king's robe was a serious taboo. The royal robe physically represented the kingship; in fact, it was a stand-in for the king's authority. Wearing coronation garments was the sole province of the king, and he passed the mantle only to his chosen successor. As for riding the king's steed, the gold-inlaid saddle on the ornately decorated royal horse was, likewise, a proxy for the king's throne. Absolutely no one sat on the king's throne but the reigning king. To do so was tantamount to treason.

For Haman to have proposed, in one breath, that a royal honoree don royal robes and ride the royal horse, was unheard-of. He was effectively suggesting a symbolic succession to Xerxes' throne while Xerxes still sat on it! And all those present in the king's throne room that night knew that Haman's preening stance during his monologue left no room for doubt that he was certain it was *he* whom the king desired to honor. Haman was arrogating to himself, in open court, the right to step into the shoes of Xerxes, a dynastic king who was yet hale and vigorous, and who had no intention of stepping down.

The king's servants were dumbstruck, and in the ensuing silence all turned to watch the king's reaction. He sat stone-faced.

But Haman, oblivious to the undercurrent, was not finished. Feeling confident, Haman spread his arms in a grandiloquent gesture and continued.

"And thirdly, for the man whom the king desires to honor, let the royal *crown* be brought, which has sat upon the king's head at his coronation, and let it be placed on this man's head."

Haman did not notice the king's brow rise fractionally at the last suggestion, while he otherwise remained still as a statue. Haman continued, voluble and almost breathless, painting his vision of coveted honor.

"These royal garments in purple and trimmed with gold, and the king's horse, adorned with a golden bridle, golden threads and silver bells woven into his mane, should be placed in the charge of one of the king's most noble courtiers, whose responsibility it shall be to dress the man whom the king wishes to honor. So royally attired and mounted upon the decorated steed, wearing the king's crown, this man shall be paraded ceremoniously through the city square. The king's most noble courtier shall lead the king's horse, all the while proclaiming for all to see and hear: '*Thus* shall be done to the man whom the king wishes to honor!'"

Haman wound down his recitation, and stood tall, smiling, as he waited for the king's revelation; that *he*, Haman, was the man whom the king desired to thus honor.

There was not a sound to be heard in the throne room. The third element proposed by Haman — that the man so honored should wear the king's crown — was an unprecedented arrogation of the ultimate symbol of power.

Haman's obvious glee at his hubristic recitation had captivated the imaginations of all present. None in the throne room — except, perhaps, the royal scribe and the reader of the Book of Days — doubted for a moment that it was, in fact, the vizier whom the king intended to honor. And they all secretly dreaded the effect that conferring this additional royal honor would have on the already-tyrannical Haman. With the vizier's power already virtually unchecked — he wore the King's Ring, after all — he would become even more arbitrary and ruthless, essentially unstoppable. The tense situation in the palace would become unbearable. So the servants' and courtiers' mood in the throne room that night was solemn, their expressions grim.

Only the scribe, hunched over his small desk, wore a small smile as he wrote. He had been a scribe for Xerxes for the past twelve years, and his ears had heard every conversation; it was *his* fingers that had memorialized them. He knew the king's behaviors and moods; he alone sensed a reversal.

Xerxes tapped his scepter against his thigh and took his time. He scanned the room, his eyes returning to Haman. Holding his vizier's gaze, and enjoying the drama of the moment, the king dropped his bombshell. In a strong and clear voice that echoed through the vast chamber he issued his command:

"Quickly, now, Haman! It shall be as you say. Go and gather the royal garments and the royal steed, and do *to Mordechai the Jew*, incumbent Minister at the King's Gate, *exactly* as you have just said! Omit nothing from all you have proposed! You, as the highest member of my court, will do the honors."

In point of fact the king made sure, through express instruction to his valet, that wearing the ceremonial royal crown was *not* to be included among the honors. The king never intended this display to imply succession; simply a public expression of the monarch's gratitude. No, the king's crown stayed with the king. It was telling, though, that Haman had specifically included placing the royal crown on the honoree's head, and that fact was not lost on Xerxes.

The moments following the king's announcement seemed literally frozen in the air; all those present were to remember and retell the story for months afterward. The king wore a thin, enigmatic smile, and tapped his scepter against his opposite palm. His servants were smiling hugely, some hiding their schadenfreude behind their hands and lowered lids. As for Haman, he remained rooted to his spot at the base of the royal dais. His face had first gone pale as alabaster, then had immediately become suffused with blood. His breath came in pants, and his mouth was a terrible rictus; a horrified, twisted smile. His hands clenched and unclenched at his sides.

He managed, barely, to get a grip on himself, and, still unable to speak, inclined his head in the king's direction, then turned and walked the distance of the throne room. He actually pushed past Hafez, who chose to ignore the affront.

Mordechai is Honored

As dawn broke over the fortress of Susa, a friendly runner from among the palace servants quickly made his way out of the fortress gate and through the streets of Susa to Mordechai's house. Ever since Esther had agreed to go before the king and had ordered the three-day fast, Mordechai had abandoned his public demonstration in the market square and had thrown himself into work, using his home as his headquarters.

Poupeh, about to begin breakfast preparations, hastened to open the door a crack and to *shush* the messenger.

"What is your business? Speak softly, if you please, so as not to rouse the Master."

"I am sent from the palace, and my message is for Master Mordechai."

"Wait here; I will fetch the Master." And Poupeh closed the door, leaving the messenger standing outside on the step. She felt no compunction about doing so; a dawn summons did not bode well, and she refused to give courtesy to a messenger of bad tidings.

Mordechai, who had not been asleep in any case, and had heard the knock and the exchange, came into the hallway.

"Let the man in, Poupeh. I will hear what he has to say."

So Poupeh led the palace servant into the salon, and the man, eager to convey his message and be gone, began speaking at once.

"Forgive the intrusion, Master Mordechai, but the king's head attendant has asked that you present yourself at the door of the royal bath house. I am to escort you there." He must have sensed that Mordechai was about to refuse to budge, so he rushed on. "His Majesty King Xerxes has just today decided to honor you, Master Mordechai."

As Mordechai said nothing, the servant continued.

"For your part in saving His Majesty's life and uncovering the plot of those nasty gatekeepers. You must come quickly, if you please, to bathe and ready yourself for the ceremony."

For once, Mordechai was caught by surprise. *I am to be honored? What timely stroke of good fortune is this?* If it were true that he was to be honored, perhaps it would afford him the moment of opportunity he needed to ask the king for a boon; perhaps he could save his people yet. Mordechai agreed to go with the palace servant.

As Mordechai was bathed, oiled, dressed and plied with fresh fruit and juices, the excited and sympathetic servants chattered away, retelling to one another—and to Mordechai—the amazing story of the king's sleepless night. Of his reliving the event that had saved his life; of his realization that he had overlooked expressing his thanks to the man who had saved him; of Haman's attempted opportunism; and of the king's swift and effective snub.

Everyone loved an underdog story, and the night's doings were just the thing to lighten the dark and threatening atmosphere that had pervaded the palace since the foiled assassination plot. Haman's cruel and arbitrary hand had touched almost every area of daily palace life. Each guard and servant knew another one or two former comrades who had "disappeared" or been summarily sent away by the cruel vizier. Likewise, the servants and guards all knew about the refusal of the Minister Mordechai to prostrate himself to the arrogant vizier. By itself, Mordechai's defiance had provided thrilling palace theater, with everyone taking sides. Though most in the palace liked and admired Mordechai and feared and despised Haman, there was swift wagering going on behind the curtains over who would come out on top.

So by the time of Mordechai's palace bath, the essence of the past night's events in the throne room—the put-down by their king of the unpopular and feared Haman, and the command that the arrogant vizier personally honor the very same minister who had dared defy him—had spread quickly and gleefully from the throne room to the palace kitchens to the royal bath house. Haman would be taken down a few pegs, and Minister Mordechai would get some revenge as well as an overdue public acclamation, at Haman's expense.

Mordechai absorbed all this news, and held his own counsel as he was fussed over, bathed, dried, and dressed in the prescribed royal robes. Fortune was a fickle woman, he thought, and she had decided, for her own purposes, to smile on him this day. But Mordechai had a realistic sense of his evil adversary, and he knew as surely as the sun had risen that Haman would be ignited with a dangerous anger at this latest humiliation. Doubtless he would redouble his determination to bring humiliation and painful death not only to Mordechai, but also to his people. Mordechai secretly worried that out of spite Haman might somehow even move up the date of the genocide! This morning's parade would be public torture for the vizier. Mordechai resolved to stand on his dignity; if it were at all possible, he resolved neither to speak to nor interact with Haman on this day. There was nothing to be gained by fueling Haman's temper; more essential than scoring a personal coup off him would be if he, Mordechai, were somehow to rise in the king's estimation. This turnabout could potentially inure to the good.

Mordechai could not have predicted what the rest of that day would bring. And the turnabout would be wrought not by himself, but by none other than Esther the Queen, his prized sleeper agent.

The Parade:
Mordechai's Acclaim and Haman's Humiliation

The two sworn adversaries faced each other in the royal stable yard without deadly weapons. Each was aware that this day's event was a significant confrontation, and one that put Mordechai — at least temporarily — on top.

Had Haman been less of a venomous and insecure narcissist, he could have brushed off this regrettable, mandatory honoring of Mordechai as only a glitch. After all, the man's death warrant was already signed and sealed. In less than eleven months Persia would be in the throes of a civil war of Haman's making, with his own army of mercenaries slaughtering all the Empire's Jews, Mordechai included. All Haman had to do was wait. But waiting was not his strong suit. As he draped the king's deep blue coronation cloak over Mordechai's squared shoulders, Haman's hands trembled with suppressed rage. He actually envisioned his powerful hands throttling Mordechai and choking the breath out of him. The vision was so real he had to blink his eyes several times to bring himself back to the present. He was racking his brain for a way to make the Jew pay for this public humiliation. Haman was on the verge of doing something rash.

As for Mordechai, he stood to his full height, carrying the royal garments with a noble dignity. The man was, after all, a scion of the royal house of Saul the Benjaminite, first king of Israel, and as a matter of pride he was determined to present the people of Susa with an imposing image of an honored citizen of Persia. By his silent dignity he intended simultaneously to give a boost both to the king's beneficence, and to the Persian citizenry's desire to perceive that theirs was a just empire where loyal citizens were acknowledged and rewarded. And, not insignificantly, also to give a boost to his own people, who were at the edge of despair, living in the shadow of Haman's Death Decree.

So Mordechai graciously accepted the assistance of the king's groom and servants, mounted the royal steed—itself draped in colorful parade regalia—and sat tall in the saddle. As Haman led the horse and rider out the palace gates and into the sun-washed main square of Susa, Mordechai looked right and left, nodding his turbaned head to the people of Susa who came out to watch and cheer. He recognized his friends and Sanhedrin Brotherhood comrades, Eliezer, Shimon and Pinchas and his brothers. Eliezer and Shimon nodded at him, while Pinchas and his brothers glared daggers at Haman. There were included in those cheers some audible jeers—directed at the unpopular vizier, but also at Mordechai, a now-visible and vulnerable Jew.

The feared Baradari, Haman's sons' "enforcers," were seen circulating in the crowds wielding their wooden cudgels; anyone caught jeering at Haman was quickly subdued and beaten. Soon enough the jeering subsided.

For three hours Haman led the king's horse, with Mordechai tall in the saddle, at a sedate pace on a circuit through the main streets of Susa. Practically choking on his words, Haman followed the king's instructions and proclaimed as he walked, "*This* is what is done for the man whom the king wishes to honor!" Afterwards, a hoarse and irate Haman led Mordechai back through the fortress gates and into the royal stable yard. He dropped the reins as if they were studded with thorns, and stalked off without a word.

The royal groom helped Mordechai to dismount, and once inside the side vestibule the king's servants fussed over him as they removed the royal clothing and exchanged it for his own. Feeling like himself once again, Mordechai made his way through the familiar palace corridors to his chamber in the King's Gate, to the smiles and hails of many of his fellow ministers.

Haman is Warned

As he hurried from the stable yard and through a side gate to the street, Haman pulled his cloth cloak up over his head. He had suffered a bitter defeat this day in his "war" with Mordechai. The Jew was no longer dressed as a beggar, squatting in the dust in the public square; Haman had this day ceded to the hated Jew his place at the King's Gate while he, Haman, had lost ground.

Haman used the folds of his cloak to hide his face and his defeat from curious eyes. *That I am reduced to this!* he fumed. He hurried along side alleys, avoiding the main avenue, his face in the shadow of his cloak, hoping to pass unnoticed. He was alternately hot with anger and cold with a sick feeling of humiliation. Mordechai had publicly bested him this day! *How can I bear to show my face?* Granted, it was the king and not the Jew who had engineered his shame, but Haman felt the personal defeat none the less keenly. He headed to his home, as a wounded predator makes for his lair to lick his wounds.

He burst through the door, shouting for his servant to hurry and gather his wife and friends. "Find them, wherever they are, and tell them that Haman demands that they come to my house immediately for an emergency meeting! Tell them I will accept no excuses!"

When they all had gathered once more, they stood around in Haman's salon an agitated bunch, no longer the unified family and friendly-disposed advisors of the previous night. Through fast-moving gossip all had heard of, or had witnessed themselves, Mordechai's honor and Haman's mortification of that morning. His wife Zeresh, and especially his sons, were filled with an unaccustomed dread. That they should all have so misread the earlier signs!

In the wake of today's public embarrassment of Haman loomed a shame-by-association. Because their fortunes rose and fell with Haman's, Haman's family and advisors they sensed *their* heyday was come to an abrupt end as well, and they grew afraid. Try as they might to see today's fateful reversal of the fortune of Mordechai the Jew at Haman's expense as only a singular event, they saw in it instead an augur of the future. In their Zoroastrian view of the binary nature of the workings of Fate, once Mordechai's unexpected rise was begun, Haman's precipitous downfall was inevitable. As Haman recounted for them all that had befallen him since their meeting last night, they became even more fatalistic and worried.

When Haman had finished his recitation, the room stood quiet for a moment; but this time the silence was not expectant. Zeresh and his family and friends had no optimistic advice to offer. And knowing Haman's volatility, they hesitated to speak aloud what they feared or foresaw. Eventually, first Haman's counselors and then his wife Zeresh—who had, in past days, accurately predicted the future—spoke in turn, relaying the same message:

"This morning's events tell a new and different story, Husband. Even a blind man can see that the Fates have turned against you; there is no winning against the powerful pull of the destiny of the Jews. If you have begun this day your precipitate fall in the face of Mordechai, who is himself of noble Jewish blood, your end is inevitable. You will never recover; you will never best him. On the contrary, you are doomed; in the end, it is *you* who will surrender to *him*."

Haman's wife and counselors had barely finished speaking when the sound of chariot wheels was heard in the street, followed immediately by a loud pounding on the street door. Haman's wide-eyed house servant hurried to answer it, and when he opened the door he saw the king's chamberlain on the door step, flanked by two armed guards. They did not come in.

"We are here for Master Haman!" announced Harvona—the king's chamberlain and, when it suited the king, as now, his trusted messenger—from the doorway. When Haman had hurried into the vestibule, Harvona continued:

"Master Haman, the king has dispatched us to escort you and hurry you along. You will accompany me immediately to the queen's wine feast."

His mood switching instantly, a sneering Haman turned to his gathered advisors and said, in an angry bluster, "You see! Even as you predict a downfall, I, *alone*, am summoned to drink with the king and queen! You will all of you eat your words and choke on them! I will see to it!" He turned his back, and stalked out, flanked by the king's men.

Ironically, unbeknownst even to Haman's wife Zeresh and his soothsaying advisors, their predictions of doom were soon to come true. But at that moment everyone who had hastily assembled in Haman's salon could only hope that despite Zeresh's intuition and their grim forecasts, perhaps it was yet possible for Haman to effect another turnaround.

Of all of Haman's friends, sons and advisors, only Zeresh knew the game was over. She prepared her traveling bag and her hoarded treasure cache, secreting it behind a loosened stone in the wall behind her toilet. She would be alert and would choose the moment of her escape.

Esther Switches Tactics

Late in the morning on the day of her second wine party, Esther paused in her preparations to think back to her first move, a mere five days before. Then, she had been prepared to sacrifice her life — provided she could take the evil Haman with her.

Her original plan had been to subtly flirt with Haman in Xerxes' presence over the course at least one private wine party, stimulating the king's jealousy. She was relatively confident that — given Xerxes' heightened preoccupation with and fear of assassination — he would see what Esther wanted him to see: betrayal by queen and vizier — and possible coup — playing out under his nose. She had hoped that in a fit of jealousy and outraged temper Xerxes would condemn *both* his queen and his vizier to immediate death.

Mordechai's admonishment had echoed in her head: *Who knows, but that it was for this very moment that you were chosen queen?* Esther took his words seriously, and thought that acting as a live lure might be the only way to rid Persia and her people of this evil and murderous maniac. *As usual,* she thought, *Mordechai was right: she* was *the perfect person for the job. I have no husband, no children, no parents who would mourn my death. I would leave nothing and no one behind. And if I perish in my attempt, well, then, so be it; I will perish. My life would have been well spent,* she thought, *if I were to die while also sending Haman to the fires of hell.*

The irony — completely lost on the king, of course — would be that in the process of trapping Haman she would probably also save Xerxes' life. Her intuition screamed that the king's vizier had designs on his throne. She even suspected — there was no proof, but her intuition was at work again — that Haman had been the brains behind the foiled attempt by Biktan and Teresh.

With Haman dead, she had thought, *Mordechai would be left with a clear field; he could certainly convince the king that the double-dealing vizier had tricked him into approving a decree that would annihilate a people who overwhelmingly supported the king, and who were mainstays of his economic success, besides.*

The morning's events had changed everything. Improvising yet again, Esther moved seamlessly to her alternate plan. With a secret smile she acknowledged that now there was no need for her to die in order to assure Haman's death. Apparently, overnight, Xerxes' fears had worked their subconscious magic; by his own hand Xerxes already had taken the arrogant vizier down several pegs. And in public, no less! The palace grapevine had worked with lightning speed, so that Esther had been kept apprised of the overnight doings in Xerxes' throne room. She knew that Haman was, at this very moment, leading Mordechai—his hated nemesis—through the main square of Susa, praising him at the top of his lungs as an honored hero! Esther shook her head in wonderment.

But she knew that the danger was far from over. A "wounded," humiliated Haman was unpredictable and, if it were possible, even more dangerous. Who knew what lies he would tell the king to save his skin, at her or Mordechai's expense? No, her new plan was to distance herself from Haman and align herself openly with her husband, the king. While her ultimate goal was to have the king rescind the killing decree, her first step was to discredit Haman.

But how to achieve this? Esther's mind returned to the unexpected excitement of Mordechai's overnight reversal of fortune.

Unless I miss my guess, Esther thought, *the king has caught on to his vizier, or at least he suspects him. But what about me? Will Xerxes tar me with Haman's treasonous brush?* Esther knew that to have even the slimmest chance of convincing Xerxes to rescind the genocide decree, first and foremost the king had to trust and desire her. If he even suspected she had invited Haman's advances, all would be lost.

For the past four days Esther had been fueled by adrenaline. Even on the day of her second wine feast—a day after her imposed three-day fast had ended—she was still so tense and intent with purpose that she found it hard to swallow even a morsel of food. She took a moment now to take stock. She had passed the first crisis when the king had extended his scepter to her; she had passed the second crisis when, despite Xerxes pressing her to reveal her request, she had convinced him to accede to a one-day delay.

Now, on the verge of her second wine feast and for the first time in five days, Esther allowed herself a sliver of hope. Perhaps she would survive this day, as well. Perhaps she could help nudge a volatile Haman to the edge, and open Xerxes' eyes wider to his vizier's subversive ambitions. Perhaps she could do this without throwing herself on her dagger. She squared her shoulders and switched tactics yet again.

Esther Prepares

This time, Esther chose to hold the wine party in her apartment's "small" reception room. It was a lofty but still private chamber, opening onto a wide rooftop balcony, its arched porticoes extending over the lush private gardens of the house of the women. She timed her banquet to coincide with dusk, so that the soft and fragrant Persian sunset would project the magical, moody tone she sought. This was the most important play-act of her life, and the stage setting was vital.

She dressed with extreme care. Her tunic was of layered, diaphanous sapphire silk shot through with gold threads. Her pantaloons, cropped at her ankles and exposing two inches of milky-white skin, were of flowing bronze silk trimmed with saffron-colored braiding. This time there was a miniscule silver bell, the size of a pinky fingernail, sewn onto the bottom trim of each pant leg. She wanted an almost undetectable melody to accompany her when she moved. Her hair glowed the deep color of the persimmon wine, and she had dressed it specifically to please Xerxes: the sides were braided and coiled atop her head, and the rest was left to hang behind her back in a shiny, undulating curtain. The royal diadem—a rose-gold band studded with cabochon emeralds, sapphires and rubies—sat nestled atop her braided head. Tonight she dressed to project both seduction and strength.

Esther's hands were cold as ice, her mind utterly focused. Tonight she would again be gambling with her life. But this time, for the first time since she was brought to the king's fortress six years ago, she would stand unprotected, stripped of her cloak of secrets. In a matter of hours at most, all would be revealed: her secret identity as a Jewess; whether the king's desire for her could survive that revelation; whether Xerxes valued and trusted her over Haman; and whether the king's emotions could be maneuvered so that he would sacrifice his vizier to save her.

Esther knew her husband's character, and expected that Xerxes would be punctual to the minute. He was consumed with curiosity about her request. It had taken on added mystery for the very reason of her coyness and her delay at revealing it. *Xerxes' curiosity will be one of my tools*, she thought.

She stood surveying the room one more time, assuring herself that all was exactly as she had instructed. There was a semicircle of three low couches upholstered of golden velvet and draped with intricately woven and deeply fringed silk scarves. Centered in the semicircle was a low table, upon which were laid three large golden wine goblets, two large laden crystal compote pedestals overflowing with fruit so plump and fresh it glistened with moisture, and two filled wine carafes. A third, sealed wine carafe waited on its own pedestal near the king's ubiquitous Cup Bearer, who stood, still as a statue, at a nearby pillar. Three servants, one for each guest, stood ready at the room's perimeter holding platters of thinly sliced spiced meats. All awaited the signal from their mistress the queen.

The golden couches faced onto her private rooftop balcony, screened on three sides by a waist-high stone balustrade and by trellises heavy with flowering vines. The queen's balcony had been built strategically. It was deliberately the tallest protruding structure around, so as to prevent prying eyes perched on nearby rooftops from glimpsing the exquisite queen as she walked or sat at her leisure. But at the same time, anyone standing on the queen's balcony and looking outward would have been able to see clearly in three directions, and watch the sun's majestic circuit over Susa.

Right then, the sunset's glow limned everything in the room with gold, casting the balcony in shallow pink and purple shadows. The atmosphere was luxurious, mysterious, and sensuous; it was also intentionally private.

Esther stood at the archway to her reception room, her smile fixed, and her posture regally straight. As she waited to greet the king and his vizier, out of habit her right hand found the secret pocket beneath her tunic. She felt her dagger there, as comfortable to her as her jewelry. Esther momentarily toyed with a third possible plan: she was prepared to run the dagger through Haman's heart herself if worse came to worst. One way or another, she was determined that he would not walk free to do more damage. Ending Haman was only the first stage of her mission to save her people.

Abednego

Abednego, guardian of Ishtar, namesake of Queen Esther, hovered, invisible, just inside the doorway to Esther's reception room. He nodded fractionally to himself when he saw the queen touch the dagger he had left for her six years ago. She was a warrior-queen, and he was her guardian-at-arms.

Shadrach

It was all going better than he had expected. The evil stars were perfectly aligned and nothing would stand in his way. He had waited and watched, nursed his grievances and planned for over a century, and he was closer now than he had ever been to

achieving his objective. He was on the verge of besting the One-
God of Israel, by destroying his favorite sons, Daniel and Mishael,
and by watching Haman's army annihilate Daniel's precious
Jews. Nothing and no one could stand in his way now. There was
a royal death decree hanging over Daniel's precious people;
Daniel's protégé was hiding behind a woman's skirts; and
Haman's armed and impatient mercenaries were massing
throughout the Empire. Shadrach laughed maniacally, causing
thunder to roll overhead from the cloudless desert sky. After a
hundred years of waiting he was gleeful, anxious for the
bloodletting to begin.

Unable to see into the future, Shadrach could not know he
would achieve only part of what he had planned.

Esther: Step-Three
The Second Wine Party

Xerxes and Haman arrived at Esther's apartments, and, as
instructed by the queen, the royal herald tapped a trill on his
small, indoor trumpet. Her longtime guard, alerted by the
trumpet sounds, listened to the approaching footsteps and kept
his eye on the distant archway. As soon as he glimpsed the king's
robes he announced, as practiced, in a booming voice, "My
Queen, His Majesty King Xerxes, King of All Persia, And his
vizier, Haman, Son of Hamdata!"

The king was in his element. He strode swiftly into Esther's
apartments. He had walked this marble walkway hundreds of
times over the past five years, always with anticipation, and never
once had Esther disappointed him. He strode confidently, leading
his small retinue. He saw his queen in the distance, waiting for
him, as was her wont, under the archway to her reception room.
His royal bodyguard was slightly behind him, matching the king
step for step, ever watchful. The king's hands were loose at his
sides, his sword hand habitually free, his favored mace hanging,

as always, from his belt's right-hand side, his dagger sheathed and secured to his belt on the left.

Behind the king's bodyguard walked Haman. He had never been to this wing of the queen's apartments, and his eyes were everywhere as he tried to memorize every golden detail. He would have slowed his step, the better to savor the moment, but he was obliged by protocol to keep up with the king.

Last of all, behind Haman walked Harvona, former comrade-at-arms during Xerxes' Babylonian campaigns, royal chamberlain throughout Xerxes' twelve-year reign, and sometime royal messenger in sensitive personal situations. Harvona accompanied Xerxes to every state dinner and party, and traveled with the king on military and diplomatic tours. He and the king had shared combat and peacetime for more than half their lives. Comfortable in the shadow of his king, Harvona melted into the background but was always alert, and always in attendance.

In fact, Harvona had recently redoubled his vow of loyalty to his friend and king. He had been approached by one of Haman's sons, who struck up a friendship as a screen to asking too many questions about the king's daily schedule, which was a closely held secret. Harvona had only his instinct to go on, but he was virtually certain that he was being scoped out as a potential turncoat or spy. Certain people would pay fortunes in gold and jewels for accurate information that would lead to the king's kidnap and death. Harvona could certainly use the extra gold, and he might even — only momentarily — have wondered at the life he could lead if he were to accept the veiled bribe for allowing the fellow brief access to a portion of the king's schedule. But it was only a mind-game for the loyal Harvona. Oh, he had his grievances to pick with the moody and volatile — sometimes cruel — monarch after more than two decades together, but he was a practical man and he also knew that turncoats had short life-spans after a coup. Who could trust a turncoat, after all? A man who would betray his king once could betray his successor just as easily.

So to atone for his having wavered — only in his secret fantasy — in his loyalty, Harvona chose the most demanding guard detail; he watched over Xerxes at all parties and banquets, when people with no-good on their minds might take advantage of the loosened protocol and try to harm the king. He also nurtured a steadfast dislike of Haman, the king's vizier. Harvona had no proof, but his instinct told him that Haman had had a hand in the Biktan and Teresh plot, and that he had engineered his son's attempt at "friendship" and recruitment.

Harvona did not trust Haman one bit, suspecting treason was just beneath the surface of the wily and sadistic vizier, and he tried never to leave the man alone with the king. He saw it as his duty to attend to the king and to stay physically in the background, but actually to be one step ahead of the deceiver.

The king and his small entourage arrived at Esther's threshold. She bowed her russet head and half curtsied in respect to Xerxes, who was inordinately pleased at the pains she had obviously taken, and was proud of her beauty. She gestured a welcome to the king and his vizier; and the royal bodyguard and Harvona, knowing their place from long experience, fanned out about the room to stand behind the golden couches.

"My King," Esther said, locking eyes meaningfully with Xerxes, "and Haman," she added, with her eyes cast down. "You do honor to my humble table. Please come and enjoy what I have had prepared especially for you." Esther led the way into the lofty and gold-tinged room, alive with the scent of cut flowers, the queen's own subtle perfume, the tantalizing food aromas, and the bouquet of the night-blooming jasmine vines in the terrace garden. Only the absence of traditional lute music — at Esther's express direction — signaled that the wine party hid a business agenda. She gestured first to the king and then to Haman, leading them to their orchestrated places at separate couches, and leaving the couch closest to the terrace archway for herself.

From their cushioned seats Xerxes and Haman watched Esther move about the room and settle herself opposite the king and cater-corner to Haman. Each man dwelt in his thoughts: Xerxes, intrigued by his queen and missing her acutely, worrying the problem of his ambitious vizier and his inclusion in the invitation to the queen's private party. And Haman, his nose up against the window, so-to-speak, coveting what was the king's, his lust for what belonged to the king clear in his eyes.

Harvona and the royal bodyguard also watched, but it was Haman, not Esther, who was the object of their attention. In Haman they sensed a predator, and not for the first time. Over the past weeks since his promotion the two had had their suspicions about Haman, but tonight they were particularly uncomfortable. In their minds the vizier had overreached his station one time too many. He lounged, now, in the queen's reception room; he wore the King's Ring; he stalked about the palace giving orders; he spoke with the king's authority. Now, watching him intently, they could see that he was very close to stepping over the line from subject to suitor with the queen. They were on alert as they attended the trio at the wine banquet. Who knew what scheme Haman might have up his sleeve? Thus far they had no actual proof of treason, but they distrusted the king's new vizier; he was becoming too familiar with the queen. They intended to be ready if he made any move they could construe as a threat to Xerxes. They would relish the opportunity to put the man in his place.

Esther's Request

At a subtle signal from the queen, the royal Cup Bearer unsealed the king's wine carafe and, after tasting the wine, filled Xerxes' golden wine goblet. Next, the queen's unobtrusive servants served her and Haman, then retreated to the room's perimeter to await Esther's signal. The king drank deeply, a sign that the wine feast had begun. He replaced his goblet on the low table and leaned back, spreading his arms on either side of his couch. Esther took a breath, anticipating his words and readying herself.

"And now, Esther my queen, at your bidding I have waited these two days, and I am come to your two wine banquets. Once again I bid you to speak. You need only tell me, Esther my queen, what is your wish, and it shall be granted to you. Tell me your request! For even if you were to ask for up to half my kingdom, your must know that your request would be fulfilled."

Xerxes fixed his dark eyes on Esther, seated directly across from him. Neither paid any heed to Haman, the fascinated observer on the third divan. Esther understands that Xerxes is *commanding* her to answer him; he will brook no more delays. This is her moment. She remembers everything she has so painstakingly rehearsed and revised; the substance of her appeal as well as her precise method of delivering it.

Leaning forward on her couch, her golden crown glistening as she moves, her posture erect, she is the very image of a desirable queen. With her eyes on his, Esther speaks directly to Xerxes, beginning slowly, in the quasi-shy and subservient manner he would expect from her. In her introduction she follows royal protocol, speaking the familiar and disarming phrases she has used before.

"If I have found favor in your eyes, O King, and if it pleases Your Majesty." At her pause Xerxes nods his head in assent.

Esther continues in a clear and measured voice. She does not want the king to misunderstand.

"My wish is that you allow my life to be granted to me; and my request is that you do the same for *my people*." She pauses strategically, watching the king's face register his perplexity. He has just caught on that her requested boon is a serious one. She has never before, in the past five years, so much as alluded to her people. She had his full attention now.

"For we—I and my people—have been sold out. We are to be destroyed, massacred and exterminated!" Esther paused here, allowing her eyes and her voice to display her unfeigned emotion.

Reaction to her Request

At first, more than a reaction to Esther's bombshell message, the king was transfixed by this new aspect of his hitherto placid and unruffled queen. Esther was unaware that her heightened color, her eyes bright with intense emotion, served only to highlight her beauty. And he would not have been a man if he had remained unaffected by her extreme upset. She shed no tears—he did not expect that, as a queen, she would do so—but her agony was easily readable. The king listened, rapt, leaning forward in his seat toward his queen.

Esther continued, her words carefully chosen, spaced to synchronize with Xerxes' ability to process not only the surprise information about her people, but also the additional revelations.

"Had my people only been sold as slaves and bondwomen, and our lives spared, I would have kept silent, My King. The trifling troubles of one people would not be worth distressing Your Majesty. I would have dealt with the matter through lesser channels. But a plan to murder your queen *and* her people is a matter of highest urgency, and therefore is surely for the king's ears, as it constitutes an outright threat against the King himself."

Such was the completeness of the ensuing silence that Esther could actually hear Haman breathing hard. She dared not turn her head to look at the evil vizier. She was focused intently on the king's face. Was he "with her?" In the pause, Esther's mind raced, going over the strategy she had orchestrated.

Esther's Strategy

When Esther had acceded, five days before, to Mordechai's demand that she go to the king and plead for her people, she had faced a tactical dilemma. She knew that if she did as Mordechai urged, and issued a *direct* appeal to the king — pleading the injustice and barbarity of Haman's genocide decree — her plea would inevitably fail. The king would resent her intrusion into matters of state, and besides, she was certain that Xerxes was unaware of the extent of Haman's decree against the Jews. She was not sure how she knew this, but her intuition told her that Haman had deliberately misrepresented the decree to the king, his offer to deposit an exorbitant amount of silver into the king's treasury blinding Xerxes to the small print. Haman had known that his offer would at least momentarily divert the king from what his vizier was "purchasing:" a free hand with — as Haman surely had represented the situation — an uncooperative, rebellious people spread out over the Persian Empire. Once the king had acceded to the deal, leaving the pesky details to Haman, Haman had refined his true plan: to utterly obliterate Mordechai's people.

Esther knew that the king could easily turn against her if he felt she was challenging an edict of state that he had personally approved. She had seen this happen to others. Plus, the ten thousand talents of silver deposited into the king's treasury was a serious incentive for him to allow the "deal" to stand. The delicate trick would be for her to present the king with a threat that was so real and serious that it overshadowed everything else. And, she reasoned, there was nothing to prevent the king from keeping the ten thousand talents of silver.

She intended to present Haman — not herself — as the immediate threat to Xerxes' authority.

To accomplish this, Esther favored a different tack than Mordechai's. She would approach the king *indirectly*. Her experience with the king these past five years taught her that her only chance at success would be to present the facts in such a way that Xerxes would perceive Haman's genocide plan as a blatant power grab; as an unauthorized arrogation to himself of sovereign powers. If she could do this — if she could, by force of her personal appeal and her oratory — lead Xerxes to see that Haman had lied to him; had, in fact, played him for a fool; and that it was Haman — not the Jews — who posed an imminent personal threat to Xerxes besides, then *all* Haman's actions would become suspect. Xerxes would, at the very least, banish the man on the spot. He had done exactly this with Vashti, his prior queen, when she had defied him. The king would not now abide a daily reminder that he had been conned by his vizier.

What's more, Esther saw Haman's hired army — already fanning out across the Persian Empire ostensibly to "enslave" the empire's Jews — as a direct threat to Xerxes' rule. In her eyes it constituted a thinly veiled act of sedition. She intended that Xerxes would see it that way, too, and that he would appreciate that with armed mercenaries infiltrating his kingdom, answering to a man who was not the king's general, his sovereignty was in jeopardy, and time was his enemy. She intended to help the king realize that keeping Haman in his post was a risk he could ill-afford if he wished to keep his neck and his kingdom. On the contrary, the king needed to act fast to quash the threat. She would play to Xerxes' impetuous streak.

Knowing Xerxes as she did, Esther planned to feed the incendiary combination of the king's pride and anger. Once Xerxes realized that his vizier had pulled one over on him, Esther counted on his emotions taking over. First would come embarrassment that an experienced monarch such as he should have failed to catch Haman's sleight-of-hand, presenting the genocide as something less, something acceptable. His pride would not tolerate the deliberate deceit against himself. Next would follow anger at the vizier's audacity. Esther wanted, above all, for an angry Xerxes to perceive Haman as the threat. When angered, Xerxes was capable of anything. She only hoped his anger would not overflow onto herself and her people. After all, she well knew that no one gave medals to the bearer of bad tidings.

Esther has one ace up her silken sleeve: contrary to the *public* nature of the Vashti affair, where the king was humiliated at a feast attended by hundreds of noblemen and courtiers, *this* meeting in her royal apartment was to be tiny and private. She deliberately decided against having musicians present for just that reason. Any embarrassment or betrayal the king might feel here today would stay inside this room. The king would be able to go forward, stronger than ever, with no one the wiser about the subject of the queen's disclosures. But this would hold only if the betrayer were eliminated. Only two people would emerge from today's wine feast. Esther intended it to be Xerxes and herself.

Which was a prime tactical reason she chose to disclose Haman's perfidy to the king *with Haman present*. She could easily have met with Xerxes privately and exposed the vizier's lies to the king's ears alone. But Esther knew enough about Haman's methods and his snake-pit morals to know that if the king had confronted the vizier with the queen's accusations but without her present, Haman would have concocted some slick lie to cover and defend himself, and would have managed to slither from beneath the suspicion of treason. No, Esther needed the king to watch Haman's face as she accused him of plotting to murder her people in the king's name, and of raising and arming a huge fighting force under the king's nose that reported only to Haman. Let Haman sputter and deny and plead! This was what she wanted Xerxes to witness, and to feel the deep cut of betrayal by his vizier, the very person who should have had the king's back.

As a strategist, Esther was coming into her own. She intended Haman to be blindsided. He did not know it yet, but in Esther Haman has met his nemesis.

Throughout the preceding night Esther had imagined what she hoped would be Xerxes' thoughts, if her strategy at her wine party was successful. He would think:

Does Haman think me a dolt, so easily gulled? The sheer nerve of the man, to think he could get away with bringing an entire army of mercenaries — answerable to him*! — into Persia under my nose. What other lies has he told me? What other schemes is the man up to that I have* not *caught? This man is not to be trusted with my personal safety* *or with the safety of my queen. He is not the man to wear my ring of command! I will eliminate him, neutralize the danger, and give my ring to another, more loyal and worthy than he!*

Now, at the moment of truth, Esther employs the power of the pause. She allows her words to hang in the air and her distress to show in her face and posture. Xerxes has not spoken, and Haman is breathing hard. She restrains any smile of relief and triumph at the king's eventual words, spoken directly into her eyes and with a deceptive calm masking his growing surprise and awareness. Here was an awakened Xerxes coming to grips with Esther's veiled accusation of an act of treason:

"And who is this man who dares to threaten *you* — Queen of Persia — and also your people? Tell me, Esther, where is this cur, this creature who is so filled with arrogance that he would plot to do you harm?"

Esther knew that the king would be putting two and two inexorably together. First, he had been narrowly saved from an attempted assassination and a coup. Within weeks his queen is now threatened, and, apparently not content only to plot against her, that same someone is planning to move against her people, as well. The calculus was obvious: Xerxes had a target on his back and his queen and monarchy were under siege. But still Esther drove the point home. Any foe of the queen was by definition also a foe of the king. Any threat to *her* translated into a threat to the monarchy.

In a slight departure from protocol, highlighting her deep agitation, Esther deliberately rose from the edge of her seat while the king was still seated. Standing tall and in a confident voice, she responded to the king's question.

"My enemy, O King — *our* adversary" — and here she pivoted part way in Haman's direction, and, looking down at the man sitting motionless on the third couch, she pointed and accused, "is *this* evil monster of a man; this Haman!"

No one moved. The king switched his penetrating gaze from his queen to his vizier. He would think later how curious it was that he had not doubted for an instant that Esther's accusation was true. Hadn't he, overnight, felt suspicion at Haman's power lust and pretensions first-hand? Esther's revelation confirmed the king's own judgement.

Haman

As for Haman — who had ordered men killed on a whim; who enjoyed using his knife on human flesh to torture men slowly; who himself had abused and severely beaten girls barely out of their teens in brothels he financed; who had thought nothing of condemning an entire population of three million people — all the Jews in Persia — young and old, children and women, to a butchered death, all in one day — the tables were now turned. This man/monster sat immobile on Esther's golden couch as she stood and pointed her regal finger at his head and accused him of treason.

Haman was stunned; he never saw it coming. He still could not believe his eyes and ears. To be accused, taken completely unawares, and by a woman! Two pairs of royal eyes focused aggressively on him: in the king's eyes Haman read a dawning knowledge and a fierce anger; in the queen's Haman read challenge and triumph. Haman cringed at the open hostility, pushing himself further into the couch as if to escape the force of the royal pair's enmity. His wife Zeresh's words just hours before replay in his mind now: "…the Fates have turned against you; if you have begun this day your precipitate fall in the face of Mordechai, your end is inevitable. You will never recover against him. You are doomed."

Haman grows cold, and experiences an emotion he has not felt since his childhood, when facing his sadistic father's fist or whip: raw fear. He smells the terror on himself and is disgusted.

Xerxes

Xerxes is lit with anger. He does not trust himself to speak. So shocked is he by Esther's revelation and accusation; so protective is he of his young queen; and so disgusted with himself for falling under Haman's spell, that he, too, stands up, his fists clenched at his sides, his right hand reaching instinctively for his sword, which of course he is not wearing. But a king is never without a weapon, whether actual or symbolic. He tears his eyes from the figure of his cringing dog of a vizier—bespeaking guilt as clearly as if he had confessed aloud—and, without even glancing at Esther, he stalks from the room, through the arched doorway, out into the terraced garden.

He needs air, and he needs to think. He paces back and forth along the far balustrade beneath a leafy vine, staring ahead, his eyes unseeing. He is looking inward, lost in thought. *There is no one to advise me now, no vizier to lean on. I am on my own, like in the old days, when I was a young commander on the battlefield in Egypt and Babylonia. I relied on my wits then. I can do so again, and I must decide. How shall I deal with the whoreson vizier?*

Feelings of energy and excitement layer over Xerxes' fury. His guardian star is surely protecting him; the dangers swirling around him have been turned on their heads and intercepted just in time. The thought came to Xerxes that *Esther* was *his* "star!" Hadn't she broken her own precedent and come to *him* with her concerns? She was a courageous warrior-queen worthy of her name to have taken the riskiest path of accusing his second-in-command to his face. Xerxes felt no need to send a minister to check on Esther's claims. He knew her to be honorable and truthful. Though he did not consider himself to be either of those, he recognized and admired the qualities in his queen.

Despite the risks to herself, his Esther had spoken the difficult truth: his vizier, Haman, son of Hamdata, had betrayed him. Haman had pulled the wool over his—Xerxes'—eyes, and had engineered a plot to massacre the queen's ancestral people.

Further, under pretense of a dragnet for slaves and bondwomen, Haman had unleashed a dangerous threat into Persia by amassing a division of murderous soldiers answerable only to himself. The king's soldier's heart shrank with shame and rage that, partially due to his own blindness, his own vizier controlled a fifth-column of armed fighting men who were, at this very moment, spreading out across *his* Empire!

Esther was right; her words had hit the target like arrows shot by an expert archer. *She* recognized in Haman's mercenaries a coup-in-the-making.

And, truth be told, hasn't Esther's revelation come at the perfect time? Hadn't he already begun to be suspicious of Haman? At yesterday's wine party Haman had seemed entirely too enamored of the queen, and then just last night the man had practically salivated for the king's crown to be placed on his own head. It was past time to neutralize Haman.

The king turned his back on the garden and headed back into Esther's reception room. He had made up his mind.

Haman is Desperate

Watching the king stride angrily from the room, Haman breaks out in a cold sweat. He knows Xerxes' moods, and what he has read on the king's face and in his demeanor — underscored ominously by his uncharacteristic silence — is a resolution to destroy him. The king absolutely believes Esther's accusation. In an instant Haman knows that the king has found him guilty, and will see him in hell. Even facing that certainty, Haman recovers enough to muster some bravado, thinking he might be able to plead some leniency from the queen. *Queen or not*, he thought, *she was only a woman, and an easy mark.*

When the king had stalked from the party room, Esther had resumed her seat on the edge of her own couch, her back straight, her hands in her lap, her implacable face turned toward Haman, watching him closely. She watched him for the simple reason that she resolved to herself never to turn her back on Haman ever again. In a fatal miscalculation, a desperate Haman — his judgement clouded by a combination of terror and a deep contempt for women — interprets Esther's aspect as potentially sympathetic, even inviting. He has never met a woman he could not dominate, so again he underestimates Esther. This time, Haman's error in judgement is fatal.

Haman pushes himself up off his couch and stands before the queen. He *must* convince her to recant her accusation, even in part, or he will hang for treason. In a macabre parody of the law that began his ill-fated confrontation with Mordechai, Haman throws himself down at the feet of the seated queen, his forehead touching the marble floor. His only course is to plead with the queen to intercede to save his life.

Xerxes

Returning to the party from the sunny patio garden, Xerxes' eyes are momentarily unaccustomed to the room's shadows. The king stands under the archway and stares at the scene before him, the suggestive nature of the two figures on the queen's couch enhanced by their indistinct outlines. In a matter of seconds he can clearly discern Haman clutching at the queen's tunic, even now groping in her lap to grasp her hands. The two do not appear to have seen him enter, and the king cannot tear his eyes from the tableau.

Of course Esther *has* seen the king return. At all times Esther has been hyper-aware of Xerxes, even when he was on the terrace. Seated, now, on her low couch, Esther is energetically pushing Haman away with her slippered feet, and slapping at his hands. The king's bodyguard, who had accompanied the king into the garden and even now stood at his side, moves to intercede. So does the surprised Cup Bearer, who is already hurrying across the room, intending to come to the queen's aid. It is forbidden for any man to touch the queen except for the king!

Only the chamberlain Harvona stands off behind a pillar, his presence all but forgotten. He knows the queen is not in any real danger with the king and his bodyguard standing by. Still, he flexes his right hand on the shaft of his spear just in case. He had been hoping the king would return in time to discover Haman half stretched out atop the queen, and would jump to the obvious conclusion. If he knew his king, the vizier was finished.

But Xerxes stays his men with a gesture of his muscled arm and a shake of his head. He commits to memory the prostrate form of Haman lying across the queen's slippered feet, his forehead now almost at her gowned knees, his arms outstretched and his tanned hands clutching at the pale silk of her lap.

The king snaps.

"On top of everything else, does the man intend to defile the queen right here in my palace?!" An outraged Xerxes thunders the rhetorical question. "It is broad daylight, no less, and I am standing not twenty feet away!"

Haman's Downfall

The words have barely left the king's mouth when Haman freezes, allowing Esther to slide away from his now-slack hands. She straightens her clothing and positions herself in the far corner of the couch. Her posture is straight and her eyes are on Xerxes, her liquid look grateful. She has not spoken a word this past quarter-hour, since accusing Haman of treason. She is a virtuoso, and having played the king's emotions — jealousy, desire, possessiveness, surprise, betrayal, outrage, and hot anger — she is wise enough to stay silent now, and to let the king take the lead.

Silenced by the king's outraged exclamation, Haman slumps to the floor, beaten. He realizes that his pleas to the queen are bootless, as the king has interpreted his desperate posturing to be an unforgivable act of seduction. Haman's swarthy face shows white beneath his carefully trimmed black beard; his once-sharp eyes are alternately hopeless or round with terror. Better than anyone else, Haman appreciates the savage determination of Xerxes in a righteous fury. In a flash Haman realizes he is a dead man, and almost instantaneously with this realization his face takes on the appearance of a death mask.

The king's bodyguard and Cup Bearer, responding to some wordless signal from the king, move to flank the fallen vizier, their muscular arms lifting his unresisting body off the floor, his head hanging slack, below his shoulders.

"Majesty, what would you have us do with him? Shall we take him to the dungeon?" asks the Cup Bearer.

The king appears to hesitate, on the verge of agreeing. Esther holds her breath. She desperately does not want Haman to sit in the palace dungeon; she fears the possibility that the king might reconsider his suspicions of the vizier once his anger cools, regretting his rash action and releasing him. After all, a similar sentiment had swamped Xerxes after he had banished Vashti in anger six years ago. Esther wants Haman over and done with.

Harvona

As if in answer to her unspoken wish, Harvona — who had moved from the sidelines into the room when the king's servants had lifted Haman from the floor — speaks up.

"My King," he begins, with the accustomed familiarity of a longtime adviser to the king, "it could not be more perfectly suited if we had orchestrated it. At this very moment, a giant stake stands in Haman's courtyard. You can see it from the terrace!" Harvona pauses and, one hand holding his spear, points with the other behind the king, through the open doorway. All eyes turn to look, and in fact the point of the super-sized wooden stake is as visible against the cloudless sky as a minaret. Harvona, appreciating that he has the king's attention, continues.

"The vizier had the stake built last night, in order to impale the body of none other than Mordechai, the minister who disclosed the plot against Your Majesty's life, and whom the king has recognized and honored." Almost as an afterthought, Harvona adds, "The stake is more than fifty cubits high, and would make a fine display."

It is not lost on Xerxes that Haman had had the stake built specifically to impale the man who had saved his life, mere hours after Haman had paraded him throughout Susa, proclaiming him a decorated hero to the throne and the Empire. It could not be clearer: Haman had plotted to dispose of this courageous man who had proven loyal to the king! In politics, the hoary calculus was true enough: *my enemies' enemies are my friends.* If Haman sought the death of the man who saved Xerxes' life, it was Haman who became dispensable. Because he held his own interest above the king's, he was not to be trusted. Worse, he had deliberately deceived his king, whom he had sworn to serve and protect. While *appearing* to do the king's bidding, Haman had schemed to undo or sabotage matters to suit himself, at the king's expense.

To Xerxes, the propitious confluence of Esther's revelation and Harvona's suggestion are nothing short of a sign from the gods.

The sooner Haman is disposed of, the better — and safer — for the safety of the king, his throne, and his family. The king decides on the spot.

"Impale *him* on it!" he commands.

The bodyguard and Cup Bearer move swiftly to comply with the king's order, marching a limp Haman none-too-gently from the room.

Esther exhales in relief, but otherwise she displays no emotion. She keeps her elation at Haman's death sentence to herself.

The king has not moved from the arched doorway, relishing his command position. His hands clasped behind his back and his feet apart in parade position, he stands tall, seemingly relaxed, as he watches his guards manhandle an unresisting Haman between them. Unconsciously, Xerxes takes a relieved breath and rolls his shoulders.

Only the king, the queen and Harvona remain in the banquet room. The queen's attending servants had scurried into the hallways and kitchen when they heard the king's angry outbursts. Harvona, having said his piece about the tall gallows, retreats back to the perimeter, but stays close to the king. In the absence of the royal bodyguard, Harvona is detailed to protect the king with his life.

Esther wisely keeps her own counsel. She has achieved her first objective: Haman has been exposed and neutralized, and is on the way to a traitor's death. She plans her next move. Rising from the couch, Esther moves toward the terrace doorway and Xerxes. She bows deeply, one knee to the floor and her head bent, her eyes on the king's shoes. She is paying the king his due obeisance, and it is clear that she is prepared to demonstrate her gratitude.

In the hush after Haman's removal, Xerxes' many thoughts continue to jostle for attention. Twice, now, in a matter of weeks, he has escaped attempts on his throne and his life. Now, apparently, the life of his young queen has also been in peril. He realizes that his most pressing need is to find a new second-in-command. But this time he is taking no chances. This time he would select someone whose loyalty has already been tested and proven.

But for now, he thinks, what we have accomplished here is sufficient unto the day. The wine was waiting, and his exquisite and appreciative queen had doe-eyes only for him. His world once again had righted itself. Politics could wait until tomorrow. He extends his hand, lifting Esther up to her full height. The king and queen smile at one another. At that moment they feel closer to one another than they ever have. Together they have weathered an acute threat and have neutralized a foe.

Haman Hangs

Things moved quickly. As the queen toasted the health of her husband, the voice of the king's herald on the streets below could be heard through the open terrace doors.

"*This* is what is done to the man who threatened the life of the king and queen! His possessions are forfeit and his family is shamed! It is forbidden to remove his body from the wooden stake; it will remain there for three days at the king's command! Let the name of Haman, Son of Hamdata, the Agagite be stricken from the record books!"

There was no trial. The king had found Haman guilty of treason by virtue of Esther's revelations and Haman's tacit admission. His pawing of the queen on her own couch as he pled for mercy compounded his offenses and sealed his guilt in Xerxes' eyes. Xerxes had already begun to suspect his vizier's overweening craving for imperial power, and this, added to the king's recent awareness of the man's lustful admiration of the queen, had spelled the end of Haman. While such qualities and behaviors might be tolerated in a monarch, in a second-in-command they spelled danger, verging on the treasonous.

The king had pronounced the Haman's death sentence by impalement ("Impale *him* on it!") in the presence of witnesses, and the bodyguard and Cup Bearer had moved with dispatch to subdue and escort the condemned man. The king had walked over to the ashen-faced Haman and had held out his hand in mute request; Haman was finished, and the king sought return of his signet ring. As Haman twisted the heavy ring off his left index finger, a black shadow momentarily covered his hands. The shadow was gone in an instant, though, and as soon as the king took possession of his ring, the ring warmed.

In ancient Mesopotamia, capital offenses — those calling for the death penalty — such as crimes against the state, treason, some murders, sexual offenses and crimes during wartime, were punished via a most gruesome public mode of execution: death by impalement. This involved complete or partial perforation of the doomed prisoner by a pointed stake, bringing death instantly or slowly, depending on the skill and desire of the executioner. In an ironic turnabout, the royal executioners impaled Haman on the very stake that he had prepared and built for Mordechai. Instead of the unjust hanging of the man who had uncovered the plot to assassinate the king, it was Haman's limp body that was stuck atop the 50-cubit-high stake. The grisly banner could be seen from the king's chambers, and from all points in Susa.

There was no mourning for Haman. Over the years, hardly a family in Susa had not suffered from his sadistic cruelties and those of his sons. Haman had learned knife skills as a boy, perfected them as a man, and grew to enjoy inflicting pain. Many a Susan man and youth had yielded to Haman's extortion at knife-point, too many losing eyes and tongues, fingers and ears. Haman had institutionalized and personally enjoyed and profited from rape and abuse of their daughters and sisters, and he openly supported enterprises that engineered kidnap and forced prostitution of boys and virgin girls. Others who had labored for Xerxes for years in the palace had suffered summary dismissal at Haman's hand, and, blacklisted from further work, they were forced into penury. At his whim he ordered homes and businesses of those he and his sons disliked or envied vandalized, torched or confiscated. His name and that of the Baradari was synonymous with random cruelty, extortion, beatings and threats. Unchecked, during his brief tenure as vizier, Haman's sadistic tyranny had mushroomed into a regional reign of terror.

So it was with sober eyes that the people of Susa watched as Haman's body twitched high above them atop his wooden stake. Perhaps they wondered what had been the catalyst that had tipped the king from chief proponent to arch-enemy of the once-invincible vizier.

Aftermath

After Haman's execution, the king's fury abated, and he doubled his security detail.

That same day, in the age-old exercise of eminent power of the king to distribute the property of his defeated enemies, Xerxes deeded over to Queen Esther the house and holdings of Haman, traitor to the crown and nemesis of the Jews.

In her own house in Susa, Zeresh prepared to escape, with her hoarded treasure, to a distant city with her two servants.

In the House of the Women, Zareen, Haman's daughter, was caught in the wave of girls and women who surged into the cloistered courtyard to view the spectacle of the hanging. Hegai and Fatima, knowing the girl's parentage, felt pity for her, but could not shield her from this. The next morning the palace gardener found Zareen's lifeless body crumpled at the base of the palace wall. The girl had either jumped or been pushed from a parapet.

On the outskirts of Susa, in one of their secret houses, Haman's sons seethed. They had gone underground, where they planned widespread, targeted revenge on everyone: on the king, his queen, his children and his concubines; on the keeper of the women, on Mordechai, and on all the Jews. Their father's enemies were their enemies now, and the sons vowed to be his avenging arm reaching out from hell to wreak havoc on one and all. Now the king had one more life to account for, they thought; that of Zareen, a sister they cared little for in life, but now used as an excuse for their planned campaign of violence and bloodshed. *Let the king sit and drink in his palace. Let him think himself safe; with his guard is down he and his queen will be that much easier to kill.*

Shadrach, taken by surprise at the swift turn of events, shrugged. Haman had been a convenient vehicle, but not a necessity. Even without Haman as a conduit for his evil schemes, Daniel, Mordechai and their precious Jews were still doomed. The killing machine that Haman had financed and unleashed on Persia had a life of its own now, and could not be called back without spilling rivers of blood. The petty heroisms of a beauty queen, the desperate maneuvers of a spymaster and his heir, and the insignificant magical powers of two old men were as nothing to one who had banked his hatred and perfected the black arts over the course of a century. There was no remnant left of the friendship that had once been stronger than the tie between brothers. It — and the young man named Hananya — had been incinerated in the furnace of Darius all those many years ago. In his place stood Shadrach, a twisted and powerful sorcerer whose own blood ran black. Shadrach laughed, thunder rolled in the clear evening sky, and bolts of heat lightning crackled overhead.

Esther Presents Mordechai to the King

The sun is past the meridian and moving toward evening. Much had happened this day, and by rights Esther should be able to exhale. She had brilliantly maneuvered the curious king and his unsuspecting vizier into an intimate and relaxed situation, their hearts made happy and their egos stoked. Projecting a balance of vulnerability and strength of character, Esther had revealed her ethnicity, cornered the king's vizier and exposed him as a conniving traitor. And she did this in such a way that the king was compelled to believe her. What's more, Haman — throwing himself onto her feet and clutching at her hands and clothing while begging for mercy — had breached an inviolable boundary of royal protocol, whipping the already suspicious king to a froth of anger. The revelation of Haman's political treachery had been momentarily eclipsed by what the king now perceived to be the man's making a sexual play for the queen in broad daylight under the palace roof! Suffering an incendiary mixture of protectiveness, jealousy, embarrassment and fury, the king had pronounced the death sentence on Haman and ordered it carried out immediately.

It is still daylight, and after having been plied by his queen with several goblets of his finest wine, the king is relaxing for the first time in a day of surprises. In addition to discovering that his second-in-command had deceived and betrayed him, Xerxes also learned that his beautiful young queen is a Jewess. Xerxes harbored no ill-feeling toward her people; he and his father and grandfather had relied on the wisdom and counsel of Jews to their benefit for decades. Xerxes' present thoughts are centered on the fact that Haman had used the power of the King's Ring to seal an edict declaring this people's destruction, thereby also ordering the murder of the queen!

It is at this point that the king's day is about to become more complicated. He has just noticed that his beautiful Esther — instead of being relaxed and demonstrably grateful, as he had expected — is distracted.

"Esther, my queen, you are sitting here by my side, but your mind is far away. A frown mars your forehead and you have barely touched your wine. Tell me what else is troubling you."

"My King, you are correct, of course. Something is weighing on my mind. You know now that I am a Jew, but you do not know that I am an orphan, bereft of any family save for one kinsman who raised me. I would dearly like to present this kinsman to you. His name is Mordechai Bilshan, and is a trusted Minister at the King's Gate. And he is not unfamiliar to you. Your Majesty surely recalls the name of the man who uncovered the plot against the crown, saving Your Majesty's life. That man Mordechai is my kinsman! He is loyal and wise, a man of many languages, and he has a quick political understanding. Would Your Majesty do me the honor of granting him an audience so that he might express his fealty to you?"

At the king's assent Esther dispatched Hatach to summon Mordechai to a royal audience. Dressed, now, as befits a dignified Minister of the Crown, Mordechai wears a fine tunic and trousers, a flat turban, and has oiled his hair and beard. He stands tall and dignified at the entryway to the imposing throne room, waiting to be given leave to present himself to the king. Esther has her eye on the doorway, her facial expression inscrutable, her thoughts rioting from past to present.

From her throne on the dais, Esther watched the man who, when she had been a girl named Hadassah a lifetime ago, had been her almost-groom. Now he waited to approach the dais and stand before her and the king. And while her heart briefly fluttered the remembered tattoo of six years ago, her steely resolve dutifully tamped down her clamoring emotions. She clenched her fist in her lap and repeated her mantra. *I am Esther, Queen of Persia. Hadassah is dead, and my young love is buried with her.* With the same strength of will that had served her as she faced a murderous enemy and bested him, Esther closed off her heart. *I will look at Mordechai and I will see only a kinsman, not a lover and almost-husband.*

In truth, it stunned the young queen to recall that the sheltered girl in white lace that fateful night years before had been she! Calling up the memory now, Esther felt as if she were looking at the narrow neck of a bottle from the far end. As if her abduction by the king's guards had happened to another. *This*—living in the palace as wife to Xerxes and Queen of Persia—was her life now. She had no other fate. She had taken her guardian angel's advice to heart years ago, and had trained herself only and ever to live in the present and face the future. Looking, now, at the face of the man whom she had loved all her life, Esther's vows and resolutions, her principles and her integrity—cost her. She actually felt the moment that a piece of her heart finally broke off. Despite her personal desolation, she steeled herself to live in the present.

Waiting in the vestibule for his audience, Mordechai was perfectly placed to see into the throne room. He could not tear his eyes away from the vision that was Hadassah. He knew he would have only these few moments to look his fill. Once he was called before the king, and henceforth, he could relate to her only from the platonic distance of a minister of the king, and a kinsman. Even to entertain anything more was not only treasonous and a death wish, it was unheard of for a son and daughter of royal Benjaminite blood. Besides, they were both on a mission that allowed for nothing besides focusing on the survival of their people.

But he was a man, after all. His hopeless love for Hadassah burned hot within him, and only the One-God could see into his heart. She was a grown woman now, a married woman who shared a bed with the king of the greatest empire on earth. She was as distant from him as the stars, and as inaccessible. This was the private torture the fates had dealt him.

He schooled himself not to look at her as he walked to greet Xerxes. He called up reserves of will and almost visually pushed shut the door to his most private yearnings. Seeing Hadassah there on the dais, seated to the left of the king, in her crown and majestic robes, the last rays of day slanting from the skylight onto her glorious braided hair, turned the key and locked down his youthful hopes and memories for all time. The click of that lock on his heart was practically audible. For the last time he heard his own disciplined voice reciting his mantra: *This is my kismet. I was never fated to know a great love.*

From this moment he would look upon Esther and see only a queen and an ally. Nothing more. He would channel his energies into serving his king and his people.

Xerxes Gives Mordechai his Signet Ring

A sobered Xerxes watched closely as Mordechai the Jew approached the dais and bowed his head respectfully.

The man has a presence and a noble bearing. He looks neither to the left nor to the right. His shoulders are squared and his eyes are lowered, showing proper respect. Though he must be filled with pride at seeing his ward sitting on the throne, not by the flicker of an eyelid does he allow this to show. I am in dire need of a chamberlain, but this time there can be no mistakes. What better chance will present itself than this? To appoint as vizier the kinsman of my queen, a man who has proven his loyalty to me and who very nearly went to his death for keeping to his principles. The wise and kindly fates have placed this man before me.

The sonorous voice of the king's palace herald booms through the court and interrupts the king's reverie.

"Mordechai Bilshan the Jew, Minister at the King's Gate, Your Majesties! He is come to pay his respects to the King and Queen of All Persia! You may stand fast, Mordechai Bilshan, and await the king's pleasure."

Xerxes stood and, in an unprecedented move, stepped down off the dais and extended his scepter to Mordechai's right hand. Mordechai and Xerxes locked eyes, taking one another's measure. The warrior king, fourth in a line of fierce and powerful monarchs; and the Jewish spymaster, a citizen of Persia descended from Israelite royalty. A political partnership was forged in that instant.

"You are welcome to my court, Mordechai Bilshan. And there is another here who would welcome you, too."

Xerxes turned toward Esther, nodding his permission.

So Esther, Queen of Persia, rose from her throne and stood on the dais, smiling at the king's minister. And Mordechai Bilshan bent his knee and knelt before his queen, familial pride and respect flowing between them. The king watched his queen's face closely, and knew he was about to make a correct and politically brilliant move.

"Arise, Mordechai! For your proven loyalty to your king and to the people of Persia, and in deference to my queen's confidence in your wisdom and abilities, I hereby appoint you King's Vizier, Chamberlain to Xerxes, King of all Persia."

Xerxes removed his signet ring from his right forefinger and held it out to Mordechai. The ring glowed purple for a brief moment as it left Xerxes' hand. Mordechai extended his left hand to the king, allowing the king to choose whether to place the ring in his palm or on his finger. Xerxes appreciated the man's respectful gesture and slid the signet ring bearing the rampant lion of Persia onto Mordechai's left index finger. The court broke out in spontaneous applause, and shouts of "Hail Xerxes!" No one noticed that the ring warmed and glowed gold on Mordechai's finger.

Esther was satisfied. Now Mordechai would have unlimited access to the palace. No longer would she be the solitary agent of her people within Xerxes' fortress.

Sensing that a concomitant gesture of public moment should now flow from her to her elevated kinsman, Esther looked at Xerxes and spoke up.

"With My King's permission, I would like to add my boon to that of the King's."

Xerxes nodded, and Esther spoke aloud so that all at court could hear and note the significance of her action. It would soon be spoken about in the corridors and in the marketplace.

"All the property—real and personal—belonging to Haman, son of Hamadata the Agagite, which King Xerxes has this day gifted into my hands, I hereby transfer to Mordechai Bilshan, a man who is loyal and wise and more worthy than Haman. Henceforth, let Mordechai serve Xerxes, King of all Persia, as royal vizier in Haman's stead, and in all things."

Xerxes was pleased, and he confirmed Esther's gesture.

"So be it! Let the scribes record it in the royal chronicles."

So Mordechai rose and at the king's gesture he took his place at the bottom of the dais and off to the right, where he would stand every day at the king's will, witnessing events at court and providing advice and counsel to his king.

In the corridor, Old Daniel, shadowed by the watchful Abbas, pauses and listens to the goings-on in the king's throne room. He nods to himself. *It is fitting that Mordechai should move into Xerxes' circle. Raving in the public marketplace is not the proper spot for a spymaster. Esther has engineered events expertly until now, but for this next crucial stage she will need Mordechai and the network he commands. Xerxes has made a good choice for the continued well-being of the Empire and also for the Jews of Persia.*

As for Xerxes, for the first time in weeks he relaxes, congratulating himself on a most satisfactory outcome to a fraught and difficult day, and resumes his seat on the throne. With a hand gesture he invites Esther to sit beside him on her smaller throne.

Though outwardly calm and regal, Esther is on edge. With Haman's disposal she has achieved only the first part of her plan. Though the evil mastermind was now gone, the death apparatus he had set in motion remained in effect, and it continued even now to permeate the Empire. Haman's Death Decree was still extant, still the law of the land, and his enormous army of mercenaries remained at-large.

But knowing Xerxes as she did, Esther appreciated that he would not be receptive to another plea. He had taken more drastic action this day than he had been accustomed to doing in past months. The immediate threat was quashed, and as for the larger, more pervasive threat, Esther intuits that the king has closed his mind to it. He is at the end of his patience. For now, he will simply not hear any additional bad news or even conceive of dealing with another crisis. So Esther retreats. The most important part of her mission will have to wait. She slips back into her accustomed passive persona, choosing to watch and wait. Will the king, of his own volition, move to dismantle Haman's army and rescind the Death Decree? Or—and this fear plagues Esther—is it possible Xerxes has even now forgotten about the rumor of an armed threat, dismissing it as an artificial danger inflated by an anxious queen?

Mordechai

Mordechai paced the length of his new chamber adjacent to the throne room,. He disagreed with Esther's waiting strategy. From the very first day of the Death Decree's dissemination he had advocated a direct approach. He was slightly mollified by Esther's quick success at exposing and defusing Haman, but now that that danger was past he chafed to attack the remaining one. He was a man accustomed to moving the chess pieces himself; not to watching the game from the sidelines. In his new post as vizier to Xerxes, he was certain he could convince the king to retract the Death Decree that had been sealed with his ring. Only a secret message delivered to him by Hatach stopped him from going before the king the next morning and requesting the Decree's retraction.

Esther had known Mordechai was impatient to press the king harder. She sent cryptic word via Hatach that very night.

"You must trust me in this, cousin. Make no moves with the ultimate arbiter. I know his character and beg your restraint. I have succeeded once and will do so again. I will not let this rest and will move when the time is right."

So against his instincts, and desperately worried about his brethren in Susa and throughout the Empire who were even now suffering the abuse unleashed by Haman's Decree, Mordechai acceded to Esther's directive. But he would not wait long.

Old Daniel

It was during the quietest and darkest watch of the next night that Mordechai met his old mentor in the underground room at the tannery on the outskirts of Susa.

"Heed her advice, Mordechai. The girl has her finger on the king's pulse. In just *one day* she managed to get the king to to what we could not have done short of killing Haman ourselves. And you are now a close confidant to the king instead of a minister with a limited life span." Daniel nodded his hooded head at the king's signet ring, glowing dully on Mordechai's left index finger. "Esther has a strategic brain and she has courage. And though she does not wear it on her sleeve she, too, feels keenly the brutalities against our people. You trained her well, and she is the very best there is. You must trust her to watch and know the right time to plead with the king."

"But every day of delay brings another score of reports of vandalism, beatings, and intimidations!" Mordechai slapped his palm on the scarred wooden table, and the flame from the single fat candle on the mantle quavered at his intensity. "My spies send daily accounts from their posts throughout the Empire. Shimon and Eliezer are mapping the incidents so we can track them. Pinchas and his brothers are impatient and vocal. So far the hoodlums have stayed away from them and their families—they don't want to end up with their necks broken—but how long will that last? Already Pinchas and his brothers are arming themselves. They have told me they are prepared to break from our Brotherhood and go on the offensive as independents, defending their neighbors if we do not implement an action plan, and soon.

"There is much anger, Daniel. Pinchas and his brothers will take many of our members with them if they break away. You must understand our impatience. You and the very few who are left from your generation have known only exile. You were exiled from Judah, and then again from Babylonia. You are accustomed to being passive, laying low in order to stay alive, to survive the next deportation.

"But our generation is different. We do not see ourselves as exiles. We are Persians, and have been so for four generations. We have fought in the Persian army. We are not accustomed to lying down when we are attacked; we fight back! We do not cower and wait for a beneficent king to decide whether to send his troops to save us. We were born into freedom and plenty, and we are prepared to take up arms to save ourselves. There are many among us who will not tolerate being bullied and terrorized. They will join with Pinchas and we will have uncontrollable bands of vigilantes. Then we'll really have trouble—on two fronts! The Home Guards will join the bullies and will beat our people to a pulp.

"Daniel, we cannot wait much longer."

"Urge Pinchas and his brothers to hold back for just a short while longer. Tell them to trust Esther. She is one of them, of *your* generation, and she has proven that she will do what she promises, even at great peril to herself. Esther will not let them down.

"And in the meantime *you* can do what you were trained to do. Gather the Sanhedrin Brotherhood and formulate a battle plan. One way or another our people are facing a war, Mordechai."

Two Months Pass

Esther had had no conception of what it would be like having Mordechai so close-at-hand, working within the king's circle every day. She had been worried that she would see him too often; likely in passing several times in a week, or at a meal, sitting at the king's side. What was surprising was that she only caught glimpses of him: as he hurried along the palace corridors or momentarily as a door was gently closed on a private cabinet meeting. This was a relief to her.

Esther's prime concern now was the still-in-force Death Decree; she was sleepless at the implications and practical effects on her brethren of the king's not having rescinded the Decree as yet. Perhaps she had even thought that, despite her request to Mordechai to leave the matter in her hands, now that he was installed as second-to-the-king, Mordechai might have taken advantage of an available moment and moved the king toward rescission. But no, the Death Decree still stood, and Mordechai was preoccupied with the king and pressing affairs of state from early morning until late into the night, every night.

After Haman's execution and Mordechai's installation, the king had moved quickly to re-establish himself as the person in charge of the political and practical running of the Persian Empire. This meant that within a short time Mordechai had had to apply his quick mind and prodigious memory to grasping a dizzying array of affairs of state, including dealing with neglected and angry diplomats, quelling a work stoppage on a critical roadway, and recalculating budgets and reassessing tax revenues. For the first time in years Xerxes had at his side the perfect viceroy, and the king relaxed, and the Empire began to blossom as a result.

But Esther realized that regarding the matter of rescission of the Death Decree, for their own reasons neither Xerxes nor Mordechai was available to help her! So with great effort she reined in her anxiety and impatience, and bided her time. In such a fashion the weeks became a month, and then one month became two. By now Esther was distraught. She realized loweringly that the king had quite simply forgotten about the danger facing her people and his early assurances to her. She feared that the momentum of the day of her second wine banquet had slipped away. She felt the weight of responsibility on her shoulders and resolved that propitious or not, tomorrow she would go to the king.

In fact, Xerxes had not forgotten about the Decree. But right now he was reluctant to take a step backwards to deal with a matter that was certain to be an extreme embarrassment to him. Since ridding himself of the dog Haman, Xerxes felt he was in a politically advantageous spot, riding a tide of public approval. He was optimistic; he had foiled one assassination attempt and uncovered a sophisticated grab for power. Public sentiment and that of his ministers appeared to be on his side. He had gotten back on the track of ruling his empire, attending daily to affairs of state through a new, efficient and loyal viceroy. Dealing with the knotty problem of the still-valid Death Decree that had been slipped by him but that nonetheless was sealed with his Signet Ring and thus bore the force of his authority, was low on his list of priorities. He did not care to be reminded of his bad judgement in elevating Haman. And the force of Persian law reinforced his inertia. The law of the land was that *even the king cannot alter an imperial law once it has been decreed.*

Also, the niggling question still in Xerxes' mind was whether Haman was perhaps not all wrong about the Jews. While they were tax-paying and smart and loyal subjects, and were high-level advisors to the crown, were they not also well-placed and formidable? What if one day they were to grow displeased with his policies? Would they pressure his ministers? Would they pressure his queen to influence the king? *Was* there a grain of truth to Haman's caution of the threat the Jews posed to the monarchy? Xerxes was not sure. As long as his queen and new vizier remained quiet about the Decree, Xerxes was happy enough to leave it alone. If push came to shove he, Xerxes would personally issue a new decree exempting Esther and Mordechai from the planned killing. He and they would remain untouched by it.

So the Decree stood. Without some kind of intervention or extraordinary recission, Persia's Jews were facing a sanctioned, brutal death in ten months' time.

Even Mordechai, as he labored night and day to do the king's bidding and to gain his confidence, had to admit to himself that he could not be the one to approach the king and lodge an appeal for Persia's Jews. Esther had the best chance at success. *Her* action would be critical.

Esther — In Peril

Sixty-six days—two months—have passed since the afternoon of Esther's fateful wine banquet, her exposé of Haman, and his public execution. Esther has counted every one of those days, and has grown thin agonizing. The king has called for her only once since that day—on the night that he had ordered Haman impaled on the stake meant for Mordechai—and, attuned as she was to Xerxes' moods and needs, she had seen to it that the night was a success, and she had been hopeful that it would mark a renewal of their former closeness.

But now, two moons had come and gone, and the king had not called for her again. In her precarious world, this signaled trouble. Esther catalogued excuses, and at another time she would have accepted the status quo, as each or all could have been the reasons for the king's aloofness. Perhaps, despite its truth—or, perversely, because of it—Xerxes was embarrassed by her revelation of his vizier's treachery. What king would *not* be somewhat shamed to have his queen—and not the captain of his security guard, for instance—divulge a serious threat to his monarchy? And what king would then not seek to reassert his sure hand on the tiller of the ship of state, to the exclusion of distractions? And finally, could there be a small corner of the king's mind that perhaps bore anger toward his queen? After all, he had selected Esther as queen on the basis of her exceptional beauty, not for her political acumen. Perhaps the king resented Esther's intrusion into the politics of his all-male inner circle, especially as her revelation had turned out to be prescient. Esther's spectacular success inadvertently cast everyone else in Xerxes' inner circle into shadow. These were all good reasons for Esther not having been called to Xerxes' bed.

Esther was not so self-centered that she failed to appreciate that Xerxes would be extremely busy dealing with backlogged matters of governing. She appreciated the need to give him time. But she had expected that Xerxes' confidence would surely have resurfaced over these two months, and that any embarrassment he felt at her part in events would soon fade away. She had expected that his need for her would return, and that they would resume their intimate relationship. She waited anxiously for this to occur; life and death truly hung in the balance.

But as time passed it became clear to Esther that she had miscalculated, and that for any or all of the possible reasons—or for reasons known only to him—Xerxes was spurning her.

With the king preoccupied and Mordechai working through the daylight hours alongside Xerxes and then personally overseeing the administration of the government until all hours of the night, she was once again on her own, again facing two crises: First was the looming death threat hanging over the Jews of Persia, with the prescribed day of their massacre drawing inexorably closer. Second was that absent an invitation from the king—and her despair grew daily—Esther would well and truly be placing her life in danger if she initiated an audience with him. Whatever personal peril she had faced ten weeks ago when she had first agreed to go before the king unbidden was multiplied now. *This* time she could not play the innocent or issue a banquet invitation to pique the king's interest. She was out of options and her people were running out of time. Esther needed to act, and soon.

She racked her brain for a strategy that would give her the best chance at success.

Esther paced the length of her reception room, deep in thought. Daylight poured into the room from the wall of arched doors leading out onto her private garden, but today she did not see the flowering vines; today her focus was inward. Unconsciously, her right hand found its way to the pocket in the seam of her blue linen harem trousers, underneath her dun-colored day tunic. She gripped the hilt of her small and deadly *khanjar*, the dagger she had found beneath her pillow six years before, on her first night in the harem. She drew strength from it then, when she was alone and heart-sick, and had done so ever since. It had been a gift from her guardian angel, and magically, she thought, whenever she was in despair or in need of guidance, the dagger's force-field asserted itself and warmed or hummed gently at her touch, calming and focusing her.

Esther gripped the hilt now. And as before, she felt the responsive buzz. She stopped pacing and closed her eyes, attuning her thoughts and listening to her heart-center, concentrating on the vision she kept in her mind's-eye for just these moments: of a bright, pulsing star in an inky-blue pre-dawn sky. Standing very still, she breathed slowly and deeply for three measured breath-cycles. So focused was she, that she did not hear her servant knock and enter, prepared to serve the mid-day meal. The servant backed carefully out of the room; she had served her sweet mistress since the day Esther had been brought to the king's bed five years ago, and the servant girl respected the queen's deep silences. The servant personally thought of her mistress' standing silences as trances.

The servant was not wrong. Starting back when Esther was just a girl called Hadassah growing up in Mordechai's house, she had felt small surges—call them hums or buzzes—of thought. A lone girl, without mother or sisters, she spent much time on her own, thinking, and so she had learned to pay close attention to the special thoughts that came to her unbidden, and she had wondered endlessly about them. Over the years, she trained herself to be adept at "hearing" what was being told to her. And she discerned a pattern. Whenever she was in a state of indecision, or sadness, or at a personal crossroads, the unbidden thoughts would simply appear in her mind, as if spoken by a voice; but it was a voice only she could hear. The most amazing aspect of the visions and voices was that they spoke to her of *events that had not yet happened*. And inevitably, these visions would come to pass! She told no one of this, and had been looking forward to finally telling Mordechai on their wedding night. But alas, that was not to be. The inner voice that had clamored and buzzed when she had confessed her love to Mordechai had sounded, too, on the evening of her aborted wedding night, but then it had gone terrifyingly quiet after her kidnap to the king's harem. Slowly, as the woman known as Esther grew out of her despair and the blackness coating her heart had begun to fade, she began again to listen and to hear the soft buzzes in her mind—especially when she held the hilt of her *khanjar*.

Had Esther lived a thousand years before, she would have heard of others, like herself, who heard and saw what others did not. And she would have understood what peoples have known since the dawn of time: that there lived a special few in every generation who had the gift of "sight," and who could intuit more keenly and see more clearly than anyone else. In certain times they were known as "wise men" or "wise women," "shamans," "magi" or "prophets." But as Esther had no mother, sister or aunt to confide in, she kept her abilities to herself as she navigated her solitary life. It was only now, as an adult living the improbable existence of queen to the most powerful king in the world, that she came round to paying close heed to her voices, and to drawing strength from them.

Millenia into the future she would be known as one of the Seven Prophetesses of Israel. But right then, alone in her chambers with the weight of the souls of three million of her people on her shoulders, she was just a young woman with fears, responsibilities, and a gift of insight.

As she stood in her focused trance, her hand on the hilt of her *khanjar*, the thought came to her, as if spoken clearly, in her own voice: *I will throw myself at Xerxes' feet and plead for my peoples' lives. I will allow the king to see me as he has never seen me: as a woman at the limit of my abilities, reliant entirely on him to countermand his signed decree. I will appeal to Xerxes the King, and his desire to be seen as the supreme arbiter in his Empire. And after all, really, I have no choice. Either I will be condemned to death on the day I appear before him unbidden and undesired, or I will join the ranks of the doomed in less than nine months' time.*

Esther opened her eyes, and eased her fist from the hilt in her pocket. *I will prepare myself; and then one last time I will go before the king to plead for my people, though he has not summoned me.* Esther called for her personal maid and spent careful time at her toilette. She would go before the king, but this time she would go when he was holding a full court. This time her plea would be made in public. If Xerxes had a thought to withhold extending his golden scepter, consigning her to death, then let him do so in the light of day and in the court of public opinion.

Again, Esther Goes Before the King Unbidden

Standing at the same arched doorway as she had ten weeks before, Esther was struck by how different the setting was this time. Before, it had been Persian springtime, with fragrant breezes sweetening the air and nudging the draperies. The king had been alone in his throne room, which had fitted her desired approach to him. She had been able to engage him personally, female-to-male, wife to master, in a manner that both king and queen were familiar and comfortable with.

In contrast, this time the season was ripened Persian summer, and if there had been a breeze earlier in the day it was long gone now. The air in the corridor where she stood was tolerable, but standing on the threshold she could feel the heat and smell the sweat of the crowd in the throne room despite its score of open archways.

She could not have chosen a busier or more packed afternoon for her appeal. The colorful costumes and different languages and dialects created a subdued bazaar-like atmosphere. Standing in the arched doorway next to the familiar guard, Esther surveyed the various groups, kept in strict order by a system of velvet ropes closely manned by other armed members of the king's Palace Guard. The head of each petitioning group clutched a stamped letter of royal permission, duly vetted earlier that morning by the Guardian of the King's Gate, without which permit they would not have gotten into the palace or the throne room, or within fifty yards of the king.

Standing in the first rank behind the first velvet rope was a clutch of foreign diplomats obviously on an official mission. Next in order, milling about in a carefully corralled area and watched over closely by a member of the Palace Guard, were two dozen local and far-flung petitioners from various points in the Empire, dressed in colorful local costume, talking and gesticulating excitedly. Then there were queues of individual subjects, commoners, their ranks patrolled by watchful guards, each person patiently awaiting his turn, each clutching his stamped permit, each with a request, and each bearing a gift for the king. Finally were the king's own ministers, more subdued than the rest, unguarded and arrayed by seniority, either seated or standing, flanking the raised dais where Xerxes sat in state. The king's hulking bodyguard stood to Xerxes' right, his fan boy to his left and slightly behind the king. The ubiquitous royal scribe was at the bottom of the dais but closest to the stairs and the king.

And, relatively new to the court scene and in closest proximity to the king, stood Mordechai, the king's vizier. He was stationed on the dais at the king's immediate left, forward of the fan boy, holding a raft of documents listing the day's petitions and the named petitioners. Despite its casual appearance, nothing around the king was random or left to chance. Security was high, and access to Xerxes was limited either to requested or permitted persons.

Esther noted that from time to time Mordechai would lean down and whisper in Xerxes' ear.

Taking emotional stock of herself as she surveyed the action in the king's throne room, Esther was pleased that she remained unmoved romantically at the sight of the man she had once loved and lost. Since becoming queen she had schooled herself to think of Mordechai only as her cousin-guardian, and after five years as wife to Xerxes she had mostly succeeded. It was the recent development of Mordechai's daily presence in the palace that had given her a jolt, and thrust her mind and heart back to the last time she had seen his face on their foiled wedding night. On seeing Mordechai for the first time since that fateful night—as he stood before Xerxes two months ago on the day he received the King's Ring—Esther could not block a wholly female thought: *How he has aged! I wonder if I have aged in his eyes.* But the stray thought was eclipsed by her unrelenting preoccupation these past months with somehow preventing the looming massacre of her people. She had called up her core of iron and focused her disciplined mind on political strategies, approaches, and possible choices.

And in the process, without her being aware of it but to her intense relief, her heartsore had magically receded! Esther gratefully embraced the relief from romantic angst and heartsickness. Standing on the threshold now, with the palace guard's long spear drawn across the opening to the throne room, she only felt relief.

The atmosphere in the king's throne room was expectant, businesslike, and, Esther noted, meticulously choreographed. She was about to throw the formal court dance into disarray.

Esther Risks Her Life in Open Court

The familiar guard of the threshold looked down at the serene and beautiful young queen standing patiently at his side. She had come to petition the king, but had not been summoned. He never for a moment doubted that the king would extend his scepter to her, but orders were orders. And as he had done two months ago in almost the same situation, he prepared to cough loudly or to give one resounding pound with his spear handle on the marble floor to get the king's attention.

But this time, the queen did not wait for his signal. This time she startled the guard, the king, and everyone at court. This time there were gasps in the great hall, followed immediately by shocked silence, as Esther did the unprecedented. In a blink, she slipped beneath the guard's drawn spear, strode across the floor, and threw herself down upon the crimson runner leading up to the dais and the king's throne.

All speech died abruptly. The king's courtiers had thought the drama done and over with months ago, but evidently they had been mistaken; for here was fresh theater. Courtiers and guards alike were struck dumb at the sight of he queen's body prostrate in supplication, her turquoise skirts billowing out around her onto the white marble and the deep red of the carpeted runner. Her legs and hips were on the floor at the foot of the dais steps, her waist propped on the stairs, and her hands reached up to touch the king's feet and ankles in an age-old posture of petition to a superior entity. The sleeves of her pale gold silken blouse rode up to her shoulders, displaying her slender arms. Their unexpected slim whiteness somehow underscored her vulnerability.

Though her day-crown circled her forehead and anchored her flowing hair, it is only the top of her head that is visible as she bows. Her forehead is touching the top step, and though her face is hidden from view, from her stance and her precipitate behavior it is obvious to all that the queen is distraught.

Esther's prone figure presents an eerie echo of Haman's beseeching posture of two months earlier, when he had begged her to intercede on his behalf at her private wine banquet. *Will they share the same fate?* she wonders a bit wildly. Her own eyes remain shut tight, and she registers the soft silkiness of the rug against her forehead, and the sudden silence. She counts her heartbeats as she awaits her fate. At almost the tenth count, with still no movement of the king's feet or arms or word from him granting her an audience, the potent mixture of anxiety and fear bubble into her chest and she finds herself sobbing silently. Not a sound is heard from the crowd, so the ministers, scribe, bodyguard, Mordechai and Xerxes and all those closest to Esther watch in horror as her shoulders begin to shake. In the silent chamber the sounds of her choppy breathing are terrifying.

Esther cannot see what happens next, but as one, all eyes in the throne room switch from staring at the quietly sobbing queen to the stone-still king. Will he extend his scepter to Esther? What is he waiting for? Sympathy is palpably in favor of the gracious young queen.

The guardian of the threshold stands pat. He will not touch even the hem of the young queen's skirt. She knows what she is about and he is as fascinated by the tableau as everyone in the throne room. Will the king extend his scepter to her? Or will he—a secretly adoring guard—be forced to pick her up bodily and escort her to the dungeon to await execution? The thought had not yet dawned that he, too, could be in line for execution for dereliction of duty if the king withholds his scepter.

Looking down, Mordechai watches Esther's shaking shoulders with mounting alarm. What was the girl doing? Only hours ago he had broken with his own men and had specifically opposed pressuring Esther into a second unsanctioned audience with the king. Xerxes' mood was hard to read these past weeks; Mordechai was intent on establishing a backlog of trust with the king so that when the time was right Esther could privately entreat him to revoke the Death Decree. But this! This was a *public* display, and unless he missed his guess Esther was about to make her case in open court! That is, if Xerxes ever came out of his distracted fugue state to extend his scepter to her! Mordechai clenched his papers in one fist and gripped a nearby pillar with the other.

Xerxes never expected this public spectacle. He had been avoiding his queen unforgivably, and was aware that his withdrawal was surely causing her agonies of insecurity and worry. He still had not responded to her impassioned request to countermand Haman's Death Decree.

The truth was that he had inquired of his legal minister if an exception could be made for the queen and her people in this one case, but the man had confirmed that Persian law was firm: once the King's Ring had sealed a decree, it remained in force forever, and was impossible to revoke, even by fiat of the king himself. Xerxes had needed some time to think the matter through and to get his political house back in order after Haman's betrayal and execution. He thought that his legal aide might finally have come upon a workable solution. But all this had taken weeks to engineer.

And additionally—it was lowering to admit—the fact that it had been his queen, who spent her days in a cloister—and not one of his guards or longtime aides—who had uncovered the vizier's perfidy, was a nagging embarrassment to him, however founded or unfounded. He had reminded himself repeatedly these past two months that only Esther, himself, and a handful of trusted aides were aware of the specific events that had led to Haman's execution. Since neither he nor Esther would have gossiped about her role in the affair, he really had no need to feel any shame. No one was the wiser! As far as the court was concerned, it had been his own executive acumen that had saved the day.

It had taken awhile, but his own military practicality had reasserted itself, so that now, two months later, he had begun to feel that—contrary to feeling residual embarrassment—he should instead take his good fortune in stride, from whatever quarter it was offered.

The thought even occurred to Xerxes that he should probably have rewarded his young queen for her steadfastness and courage rather than shunned her. Well, hadn't he awarded to her Haman's houses and all his properties? Those constituted a princely fortune all by themselves! Yet what had she done? She had turned around and gifted them over to her cousin Mordechai. She had not profited from Haman's execution in any material way.

And as far as her cousin Mordechai was concerned, the man was quite simply an administrative genius. Why, in a matter of weeks he has become as familiar with matters of state as a veteran chamberlain. The man has excellent judgement, a natural but not overbearing authority, and he wears the cloak of the vizier lightly, deferring to the king's prerogative. Xerxes thought that if he were honest with himself he owed Esther an additional boon, then, for introducing him to his new vizier! But he knew the character of his queen. She would neither expect nor accept gifts of jewels or property.

Yes, he had much to be thankful for in his wise choice of queen. Though he had kept himself aloof from nighttime pleasures of late, his Esther was not lacking in ability and desire to please him. Added to that, she has had a part in saving his life *twice* now! He smiled to himself that his young queen was not just a beauty; she also had the special gift of inspiring affection and loyalty in those around her. Esther was so well-liked by the palace staff, his guards and even his hard-boiled ministers, that he would not have put it past the guardian of the threshold to countermand a royal order denying the queen her audience at this very moment! They would give their lives to protect her.

How much was he willing to give her to keep her safe and happy?

On that thought, the king leaned down and extended his golden scepter to gently touch Esther's glowing hair. He had a need to see her face, and he was moved to be generous. He would hear her out; what has his queen risked her life to ask for this time?

Esther Pleads with the King

After what seemed an eternity lying prostrate on the dais steps, Esther is lightheaded with relief to feel the touch of Xerxes' scepter. If Xerxes had wanted her gone, he would have kept his scepter by his side and ordered her removed and executed. Instead, he is curious. She rises gracefully to her feet, and stands tall at the bottom of the steps. Looking neither to the left nor to the right, Esther makes pointed eye contact with her king. She makes no attempt to erase the signs of anguish from her countenance; she wishes the king to see them and to be moved to grant her request. One way or another she will save her people this day.

A prime difference between this appearance and her first one two months before is that this time both the king and she are under no illusions about her considerable ability to perceive and affect political events. So Esther uses this knowledge. This time, when she addresses the king, she does not hesitate or sugarcoat her appeal. She speaks clearly and with feminine majesty. She also works with the fact that she is bearding the lion in his den, so-to-speak. This is no private audience like last time; this time, while she is appealing to the king, indirectly she also is addressing everyone at court. Everyone present in the vast throne room is eager to hear what she has to say, if only for the diversion value. But more than that, Esther correctly senses that she has an audience that is overwhelmingly sympathetic to her. The psychological advantage is Esther's. Does the king sense this, too?

Esther begins speaking, slowly and clearly. She opens with her familiar polite introduction.

"Your Majesty." Esther inclines her head out of respect, and her hair and the jeweled, golden crown glint in the shaft of sunlight from the skylight. Some of those present will later say they were sure they had seen a flash of lightning, and they took it as an omen.

"If I have won your favor, and if my proposal is deemed correct to Your Majesty, and if I am pleasing in your eyes—" here Esther pauses for dramatic effect and the entire throne room strains to hear, "I beseech the king to let dispatches be written *retracting* those that were written by Haman, son of Hamdata the Agagite, ordering the annihilation of the Jews throughout the king's provinces."

There, she had said it outright. Her request was bold and unambiguous, almost a pronouncement or a demand, skillfully couched as a request. The king knew precisely what she was saying. This time, she would not allow Xerxes to tip-toe around her need for a royal retraction. And because she was arguing in the court of public opinion, she went further, using a skilled bit of oratory and the time-worn tactic of a rhetorical question to explain her deeply personal connection to the decree, and the reason for her urgent appeal to retract it.

"For how can I bear to witness the disaster that will befall my people? And how can I sit by and witness the destruction of my kinsmen?"

This is explosive news to virtually everyone in the throne room. While the Persians standing behind the velvet ropes no doubt knew, first-hand, about Haman's Death Decree, it is certain that no one knew that Esther, Queen of all Persia, was herself a Jewess. This revelation cast Haman, the Decree, and the queen in a whole new light. The diplomats and ministers quickly made their inferences. They figured that Haman's decree against the Jews must have been the reason for his precipitate execution for treason. Anyone who targeted the queen's people and kindred for murder was by definition setting his deadly sights on the queen, as well, and this constituted outright treason against the monarchy and was punishable by death.

The King Responds

Xerxes is prepared to give Esther an additional reward for saving his life and exposing Haman. But he has a bit of a problem accepting orders or even a strong suggestion from a woman. That she has asked for a retraction of Haman's extermination edict takes the momentum out of his own intentionality. He thinks, sulkily, *What else can I do for her, really, other than what I have already done?* Extending his arm toward the assembled court as if expecting everyone in the throne room to agree with him, Xerxes directs his words to Esther, but intends for his new vizier to hear him, too. Mordechai the Jew is listening closely.

"Esther, my queen, have I not already met your request? In truth, for the very reason that Haman set in motion this killing scheme against the Jews of Persia, two months ago I ordered that Haman be impaled on the very stake he had had built for his enemies! And after Haman's death did I not give you his house and holdings as your very own to keep or to gift away as you chose? What can be left to give or do? Your enemy is dead and you have inherited his wealth."

The king's words to Esther were staged polemics. In fact, Xerxes was acutely aware that he had fallen short of granting his queen's clear request two months before. In truth, while presenting a controlled and authoritative face to his court, with the assistance of his most trusted generals and the advice of Mordechai, Xerxes had spent the past two months secretly girding for war. From the moment Esther had revealed, at her second wine party, that Haman had raised an army of 20,000 mercenaries that was at that very moment massing and dispersing throughout the Empire, Xerxes had known that he faced a coup at the least, and likely a bloody revolution. Ridding himself of the brains behind the scheme had done no more than cut off the head of the serpent. There remained the serpent's newly regrown heads and deadly tentacles to outplay and rout. A division of a rogue army answerable only to Haman was abroad in his land! And because they had already been paid, they were content to bide their time, waiting to unleash their violence on the pre-appointed day as they had been commanded.

But what to do with the army afterward? Their blood lust having been satisfied, and flush with certain victory against an unarmed populace, it did not take a military genius to foresee that the mercenaries' commanders would see the Persian Empire itself as an easy target, and its vast treasures theirs for the taking. It chafed him to admit the truth of it, but the mercenaries' commanders would think it child's-play to redirect their battle-tested soldiers against the weak king who had foolishly invited them into his country in the first place. In a country so vast, they could easily roll over unarmed and unsuspecting scattered civilians to stage what would appear to all to be a civil war, but which in reality would be a hostile coup d'état. And Xerxes knew that even with the protection of his Home Guard and a quickly deployed army of his own, he, his family and his countrymen were no match for vicious mercenaries. A brutal and violent death were the best fate he and Esther would be facing. The reality facing Esther and his concubines in fact did not bear contemplating. If he could not think of a way to successfully oppose Haman's mercenaries, he would do better to send Esther away while there was still time. Of course the woman would wish to stand fast, but there were ways.

Esther knew that Xerxes was jousting with her. King and queen—and Mordechai, too—were aware that a prime reason the king had been avoiding her was that while he had fully expected her to reiterate her appeal, he had been stalling until he had an answer that would satisfy her as well as himself. And in truth Xerxes had used the two months to confer with his military and civilian advisors, to devise not only a politic and face-saving way to rescind the Death Decree, but also a strategy for defeating the mercenaries.

Mordechai had been present at the king's right hand, privy to his secret deliberations. Armed with the knowledge of what the king was planning, but unable to disclose it, Mordechai had urged his Sanhedrin Brotherhood to wait just a little longer before going vigilante. He preferred to have his agents act *within* the law if possible. And there had been no need for him to risk all to confer with a distraught Esther. Unless he missed his guess, if Esther was not already was aware of the king's plan, she would intuit it soon enough. He would not underestimate her ability as a strategist ever again.

Esther stood her ground and waited. She had said her piece; the next move was Xerxes'.

The king had decided. The moment Esther had slipped under the guard's spear and glided across the throne room to lie prostrate at his feet in open court, Xerxes had known that he would grant her request, but he would do so *his way*; at the same time winning popularity points by appearing magnanimous. On this day he would disclose to the court the first part of his plan to rid the Empire of Haman's army.

Xerxes addressed Esther, glancing at his new viceroy to include him in the conversation.

"Esther, My Queen — and Mordechai, you will confirm this — it is an immutable law of the land that an edict of the king, once it is issued and sealed with the King's Ring, *may never be revoked*. Despite my personal desire to grant your request, I am unable to do so. Even I — king of the entire Persian Empire — am legally prevented from altering Haman's edict; it is immutable, as it was sealed and authenticated with the King's Ring."

At his words Esther paled, and stood very still. If the king would not or could not revoke the killing edict — there was no effective difference to a Jew of Persia — her people were doomed and she would perish with them in nine months' time. But almost at the same moment, she had an instant flicker of understanding. *Why does Xerxes appear so cheerfully unmoved by my situation? Surely he can't have grown to hate me so much in these past two months that he now welcomes my death. Perhaps he is holding something back.*

Then the solution struck her, infallible in its simplicity.

Why, there is *a way out of this legal quicksand! If the king is forbidden to* revoke *a sealed decree once it is issued, then the antidote is to issue a* new *decree precisely countermanding the first one and sealing it with the King's Ring!* She knew she had hit upon the answer and her body became instantly energized. She thought, *Does Mordechai know?*

Esther lowered her flashing eyes to her shoes, and then, under her lashes, she stole a glimpse of Mordechai's face. Mordechai was watching her intently. In that shared instant both Esther and Mordechai knew that each had independently come upon the same key to the deadly puzzle. This was the way out of Haman's murderous trap! All that remained was to encourage the king to agree and authorize it.

"Then the solution, My King, as surely you already have divined, is for Your Majesty to cause to be written a *new* edict, countermanding the annihilation decree that is currently on the books." And Esther smiled at Xerxes as she said it.

Xerxes' young queen, whom he was coming to realize was an excellent strategist, had played into his hand. With her words she placed the resolution of her request squarely in his lap. In open court he could not now back down from saving her people in such an elegant and reasonable way. All this worked well for his own ends. The king nodded.

"Mordechai!" the king used his proclamation voice. "You will do as we have discussed, and together we will save the Jews of Persia. I charge you to work with my queen and to compose a new edict for my signature countermanding Haman's decree. Compose this new edict in my name as you see fit, and seal it with the King's Ring. For an edict that is written in the king's name and sealed with his ring may not thereafter be revoked!"

The court erupted in applause.

Xerxes leaned back on his throne and smiled to himself. He had set his plan in motion, and was content to watch it play out. Mordechai and Esther were supremely competent. What's more, they were personally motivated. They would now compose a new edict that would *allow Persian Jews to defend themselves* against any and all enemies and aggressors on the assigned day of Haman's planned massacre. This was the key to his strategy. It would become the new law of the land, and would countermand and supplant Haman's annihilation decree.

Of primary importance to Xerxes was that he could count on his new vizier to devise a scheme whereby the Jews of Persia would rise up and defend themselves against Haman's mercenaries. *Xerxes would be using the Jews* to solve his two most pressing problems in one blow: They would conveniently annihilate the vicious army that quietly had taken hold of Persia, and they would save themselves in the process. With any luck, he, Xerxes, and his trained militia, would not have to lift a finger or put themselves in harm's way to be rid of Haman's army. This exiled people would fight his civil war.

It was a perfect solution, and by authorizing it, the bonus was that he kept his queen and his vizier loyal and beholden to him.

Xerxes was content.

Esther sighed with relief. She knew, as did Mordechai, that while ostensibly granting her a boon to save her people, Xerxes was in practical terms passing onto the shoulders of the Jews of Persia the burden of eliminating the looming threat that Haman's army of mercenaries presented to the monarchy. But the king's dual motives did not concern her. If the king sought to use the saving of the Jews to simultaneously suit his own ends, she had no quarrel with that. For she, in turn, had played the king's own game to achieve *her* own ends, as well! She had skillfully used Xerxes' strong fear of a coup to move him into a corner where his only way out was to give the Jews permission to fight back. And her strategy had worked. The king had "bitten," grabbing onto the lifeline that saving Persia's Jews had afforded him.

Esther and her people had passed another hurdle, but both she and Mordechai were grimly aware that their work was just beginning.

The New Edict

As the business of the court swirled around them, Esther and Mordechai lost no time. They bowed away from the King's presence and immediately got down to work, writing a new edict in the king's name. The date was the twenty-third day of the third month of the year, known as the month of "Sivan," when Mordechai summoned the royal scribes to the cavernous but well-lighted two-story chamber in a marbled corridor nearby to the king's throne room. There were upwards of fifty scribes, present at their tilt-top desks, their quill pens poised and the ink wells filled. Mordechai and Esther had decided to use Haman's own Death Decree as their model. They would counter each and every one of his macabre entitlements with a corresponding authorization to fight back.

Of utmost importance to Esther and Mordechai at this stage was to get the word out to the 127 provinces of the Empire that first, the might of the king of Persia stood behind the kingdom's Jews; and second, that on the coming day of reckoning — the thirteenth day of the twelfth month of Adar — the empire's Jews would not sit idly by and allow themselves to be killed. They would fight back with a vengeance. In and of itself this fight would entail a complete *volte-face* or turnaround from the reality that Haman's decree had set in motion. And Esther and Mordechai did not underestimate the difficulty of changing the prevailing mind-set not only of the three million far-flung and fearful and beleaguered Persian Jews, but also of the millions of Persians. Haman had set loose a poison-clawed, fire-breathing dragon. Xerxes was counting on the equivalent of a callow boy with only a bow and arrow to slay it.

The first step in this war — for make no mistake, a war was what Xerxes had authorized — was to write and then dispatch the new royal decree countermanding Haman's Edict.

So with an original copy of the Death Decree in hand, and with Esther standing by on the elevated platform at the head of the scribes' room, Mordechai began to dictate. And the scribes, simultaneously translating Mordechai's words into each of the many languages and varied dialects of the Persian Empire, bent their heads and wielded their pens.

~~~~~

EDICT of the KING
On This 23rd day of the Third Month of Sivan
in the Twelfth Year in the Reign of Xerxes

~~~~~

By the ORDER of Xerxes
Supreme King of All Persia, from the Indus to the Elephantine
and all the World

~~~~~

NOTICE
Is hereby given to the Jews of Persia,
to All Satraps, Governors and Officials
In every Town and City
In all of the One-Hundred-and-Twenty-Seven Provinces
in the Empire
From India to Ethiopia
In the language and script of every People of the Realm,
And to the Jews in their own script and language.

And
EDICTS Are to be dispatched with haste
on This Day via Royal Mounted Couriers
To Every Province in the Realm
So that All may Know and Obey this, the King's Edict.

~~~~~

These Orders are Hereby issued in the name of King Xerxes,
And are Sealed with the King's Signet Ring.
And are This Day hereby enacted into
IMPERIAL LAW
As Follows:
On a single day, namely, on the 13th day of the Twelfth Month,
this is Adar
In all the Provinces of the Persian Empire
1.
The Jews of every City, Town and Village of the Realm
Are Hereby Permitted to
Assemble and Fight for their Lives,
To Defend themselves against Any People, Person or Province
that attacks them.
And
2.
The Jews are Hereby Permitted To Destroy, to Massacre
and to Exterminate
Whatever armed forces attack them,
Including Women and Children.
And
3.
The Jews are Hereby Further Permitted to
Plunder the Possessions of their attackers.

~~~~~

Bi'anjam.
So Be It.

~~~~~

Mordechai and Esther's intention was to write and then
publicize the new law of the land: Authorizing Persia's Jews to
arm and prepare for the fateful day on which Haman's Death
Decree was to take effect. On the thirteenth day of the Twelfth

Month of Adar, this new law allowed and encouraged the Empire's Jews to defend and avenge themselves against their enemies.

Every single one of the Letters of Decree that was scribed that day and late into the night was personally sealed by Mordechai using the King's Ring as he sat at the long table on the raised dais in the scribes' chamber. Esther ran the operation like a well-oiled machine. Each document was handed to her as the ink dried, and each decree was laid out on the long table, preparatory to being read twice: first by Esther and again by Mordechai, both of whom were fluent in not only Hebrew and Aramaic, the languages of their people, but in many of the languages and dialects of the realm, as well. The four-part process of reading, vetting, sealing and tying was laborious, and Esther had pressed into service four of her trusted servants to tie each scroll. No one even thought about taking a rest; urgent haste was the byword, and speed was essential. The clear objective was to get the word out. As soon as was humanly possible Esther and Mordechai expected the new edict—authorizing the Jews to mount a defense—to be posted on every marketplace stall, at every village well and in every town square. The "law of the land" needed to reach Persia's three million Jews and also forty-nine million general Persian citizenry for it actually to become effective.

Though Haman's killing edict was not to take effect for eight more months, the Jews already had begun to feel the whip of the opportunists, thugs and general troublemakers who had taken advantage of the edict and had jumped the gun, beginning their torment early. And because the coming pogrom was state-sanctioned, the Jews had found themselves without police protection. Their unarmed and vulnerable state only served to embolden the bullies, feeding the spiral of the Jews' despair. As a result, if they had the means, many Jewish Persians were either trying to leave the country under cover, or they were splitting their families and sending children and wives out with friendly merchant caravans or bribable ships' captains. Those who left, left all their worldly goods behind, taking only what they could carry easily, so as not to draw attention to themselves. They held private nighttime sales in their homes, turning the content of their treasured homes into cash or jewels, in order to finance their escape.

Esther and Mordechai were counting on the early publication and distribution of the new edict to bolster the depressed Jews who feared the coming state-sanctioned butchery, and also to stem the exodus of the best of Persian Jewry. An equally important effect was to serve as a warning to the underclasses and thugs to step back from their harassment and worse.

An Additional Letter

To accompany the new edict, Mordechai dictated an additional message addressed only to the Jews of Persia. It was a personal message designed to rouse the Jews and to urge them to take heart. It stressed that under the new law the king was giving all the Jews in the Empire permission to fight back, and to that end they should begin to arm themselves and train for the fateful battle in under nine months' time! It was signed by Mordechai the Vizier and Esther the Queen, so that the Jews would see and recognize two of their own, and believe them.

This additional letter from Mordechai and Esther, directed at Persia's Jews, was strategically brilliant. Esther and Mordechai knew that over the next nine months they would be consumed with organizing, mobilizing and preparing an overwhelmingly non-military people to train and ready themselves to bear arms in their own defense; something the Jews had never in their history of their exiles been allowed to do. In fact, picking up arms in the host country would normally have been considered an outright act of rebellion, punishable by death!

Even a millennium ago, just the fact of the Egyptian Jews' unified social network and their sheer numbers had been enough to send Egypt's Pharaoh into a paranoid panic, fearing a possible fifth-column action by the country's Hebrew population. The result of his unfounded fear was more than two centuries of brutal enslavement masking the Pharaoh's true goal: nothing less than a genocide, erasing the Jews utterly from Egypt's midst.

So over the centuries it was bred in the bone and seared into the social conscience of all Jewish exiles not only not to rile their host government; but rather to actively support and enrich the host country in any way possible. That strategy afforded the Jews their best chance of living peaceable lives among people who viewed them as "strangers" despite decades of assimilation, and who likely mistrusted and perhaps also envied them their successes.

The additional letter to the Jews of Persia that accompanied the new edict gave Mordechai the very real boon of using the king's own couriers to jump-start Mordechai's coming paramilitary campaign. It would have been impossible, otherwise, for Mordechai to have gotten the word out *in time* to Persia's Jews — spread out in villages and towns across the Empire — that not only were they permitted to do so, but they were exhorted by their king to arm themselves and stand up in their own defense. And because of its unprecedented nature, without Mordechai and Esther's signatures, the kingdom's Jews and everyone else would likely have thought to new edict a hoax.

Esther and Mordechai had a three-fold mission: to inform the kingdom's Jews that they were expected to prepare for the coming battle; to spur them to organize, arm and train themselves; and, perhaps most important, to let the Empire's Jews — and their tormenters — know that all these actions were endorsed and protected by the king!

Distributing the New Edict

When the hundreds of scribed original copies of the new edict were sealed and tied, they were distributed to waiting couriers wearing cross-body pouches who were lined up by region in the long palace corridor. To reach the nearby cities and towns it was not necessary to enlist the fleetest messengers or the steeds. The messengers to Susa and its outskirts, for instance, were runners on foot or riders with ordinary mounts. But to reach the vast distances of the Empire — from the closer regions of Babylonia and Medea, to Ionia and Parthia in the north, further to Bactria and India and the Indus mountains at the Empire's easternmost borders — special steeds were required. For this reason all long-distance couriers were mounted, riding horses bred of the royal stud and used exclusively in the service of the king. It was times like these that tested the brilliant prescience of the Empire-wide postal roads laid down by Xerxes' father, Darius the Great. When the recognizable livery of the king's steeds and couriers were sighted speeding along the treated highways, woe to anyone who got in their way.

The administrative task facing Mordechai and Esther of organizing, vetting, recording and checking up on the small army of couriers was enormous. Esther was in close communication with the royal stable master, who was charged with breeding, raising, training and exercising the royal mares and stud that comprised the teams of horses used by the royal couriers. The stable master was also charged with supplying the hundreds of speedy but reliable mounts used by both the royal postal system and the king's special messengers. The accustomed riders and mounts were familiar with the roads and the Empire's terrain.

Sprawled over 7.5 million square kilometers, the terrain of the Persian Empire ranged from alluvial riverbed to desert wilderness to mountainous and almost impassibly rocky and geographically hostile landscape. Despite Persia's network of postal roads it could take upwards of three months for a royal message dispatched in Susa to reach all points of the Empire!

Esther and Mordechai were counting on that delay. It had been nine weeks since the day that Haman's original killing decree had been written and dispatched, so it was still possible that the his runners had not yet arrived at the farthest reaches of the Empire. This time lag could work in Esther and Mordechai's favor. They impressed the royal messengers with the need for more-than-usual speed, hoping their new edict would *overtake* the old one. Because the king's edicts were instantly respected and obeyed everywhere in Persia, even an hour's advance notice could mean lives saved.

Royal couriers were trained and vetted for long-distance riding. They switched mounts as well as riders almost daily, at designated posts along the way, where, at the king's expense, they replenished their saddlebags with food and lightweight, makeshift shelter. Before they headed out with the new edict, Esther and Mordechai made it clear to the messengers that speed was paramount. Everyone understood that failure to reach their geographic targets was not an option.

In addition to following the strictest instructions concerning speed, each courier also was provided with mallets and nails. Not only did they *carry* the king's legal pronouncements; they also were briefed in detail about where and how each letter was to be publicly *displayed*. It fell to the couriers to post the new law in every public gathering place across the realm. The final stage of their mission was to make their way back to Susa, where each courier was then checked off in Mordechai's great ledger. Once checked-in and paid off, each courier was detailed either to rest up and be dispatched once again, or to return to their billets or homes to await new orders.

A Revolutionary Edict is Announced in Susa

The new edict that Mordechai and Esther wrote at the king's behest was a revolutionary one. Understanding, as they did, Xerxes's true, driving motivation—to rid himself of Haman's army of mercenaries while shedding a minimum of Persian blood—they wrote and then codified into law the unprecedented order that one race of Persia's citizens could *and should* take up arms *within the boundaries of the Empire,* and kill and plunder any aggressors! The new law did not distinguish between local Persian aggressors and mercenaries. Under the new law, ANYONE—Persian or mercenary—who took aggressive action against the Jews in Persia was, by this new stroke of the king's pen, fair game for lawful, aggressive military retaliation.

At its essence, the new law encoded and encouraged a civil war. Yet this was the law Xerxes sought, in order to quell Haman's army; this was the law the Persian Jews desperately needed, so that they might defend themselves against annihilation; and this was the law that Mordechai and Esther dutifully and brilliantly wrote.

A Companion Message

Simultaneously with sending out the scribed letters or edicts via courier, Esther and Mordechai instructed that both the edict and its companion message to the Jews of Persia were to be *read aloud* inside the palace fortress, in Susa's market place, and at designated public posts along the King's Road radiating outward from the palace gates. Esther and Mordechai understood that it was not sufficient just to write the new edict; nor was it sufficient even just to post it throughout the Empire. It was additionally imperative that the king's support of the Empire's Jews be made known publicly within the palace and its nearby environs as soon as possible. Any credence given to Haman's killing Decree, or damage done to Mordechai's reputation among the fellow ministers and the people of Susa from the days he had sat ranting and covered in ashes, had been neutralized when he was elevated to vizier. But Esther had a separate concern. She did not wish anyone to think that Mordechai the Jew enjoyed protection from the killing decree only because he happened to hold a high post in Xerxes' cabinet, or because he was cousin to the queen. She wanted every Persian in Susa — non-Jew and Jew alike — to appreciate that the new law was a sweeping imperial announcement of support for *all* the Jews in Susa, regardless of station, and also for those at the Empire's far-flung edges. Reading the new edict aloud would reach everyone, including those who could not read.

More, the new edict codified a reversal; a transfer of power from those throughout Persia who had either been opportunists or supporters of Haman's bigoted and sadistic ways, to the Jews of Persia themselves. Esther wanted all those within the corridors of power and in the fortress city to get the message that the tide had turned, and that there would be quick and serious consequences in response to both outright and subtle persecution of the Empire's Jews.

To this end, professional criers or announcers, whom Esther supervised in rehearsal, were dispatched to the various prearranged "news" spots within the palace fortress and in the capital city of Susa. The new edict was read aloud all throughout that day and the next, and a political balance or sorts was restored in Susa.

A Resplendent Mordechai

Once Xerxes decided to side with his queen, his new vizier and the Jews authorizing the recanting of Haman's killing edict, at Mordechai's suggestion the king made the strategic decision to do so with much fanfare. He would turn a diplomatic reversal—the betrayal and execution of his corrupt vizier—into a populist triumph. Esther's celebrity was at its height, and as his home guards, his soldiers and his ministers reported, Empire-wide the king and queen enjoyed the highest level of approval and acclaim. Xerxes would capitalize on this. Following his instinct and without consultation with anyone, the king crooked his finger to an aide and spoke into his ear. The man hurried from the throne room, returning soon thereafter, carefully balancing a small woven crate covered in a cloth of purple and gold velvet. Trailing him were two Ethiopian servants carrying large parcels and what appeared to be bulky, folded fabrics. At the king's nod the aide and his small retinue exited the hall and hurried to the scribes' room, intent on finding Mordechai.

After a day-and-a-half of working at peak speed and urgency, Mordechai and Esther finally dispatched the last of the couriers bearing the last scroll, containing the final translated and sealed copy of the New Edict. Esther sat, unmoving, on one of the scribes' benches, her hands in her lap. Mordechai stood, leaning heavily against the dais table. They had done it! Haman's Death Decree was now officially past history; they had achieved the all-important first step towards saving their people. The coursing, urgent excitement that had fueled them was now spent, leaving them both exhausted.

At that moment the king's aide and servants appeared at the doorway of the lofty room.

"Your Majesty," he said, nodding and bowing to Esther. "I have an urgent message for Master Mordechai." At Esther's assenting nod, the king's aide—his cap bearing the royal tasselry and carrying the king's authority—addressed the new vizier courteously and reverently. The aide was laden down with the small, covered crate, and standing by were the two servants carrying thick parcels.

"Master Mordechai, I bear gifts from the king: there is a crown, given into my hands by the king himself." The aide looked down and nodded at the woven crate in his arms. "There are also turbans, royal robes, a girdle, linen mantles and boots. The king bids you to clothe yourself in these garments, and to return to the palace wearing them." The servant inclined his head briefly, awaiting Mordechai's assent. No one turned away the king's gifts, especially when they included an implicit command.

An exhausted Mordechai acknowledged the gift. "Thank you, Salim. If you would accompany me the short distance to my home you and your men can leave your parcels there and take some refreshment before you return to the palace."

"A thousand pardons, Master Mordechai, but the king expects you to change into these clothes forthwith. The king expressly wishes you to exit the palace wearing the crown and robes, and to return dressed in them, as well." After a pause, the man continued. "I can help you dress, Master, and then we will be happy to accompany you to your home with the rest of the garments."

Mordechai understood — as did Esther, who had heard the interchange — that this gift of crown and royal robes, and the command to wear them henceforth, was another measure of their success. It spoke both of Xerxes' desire to please Esther by elevating her cousin, and also of Xerxes' need of his new vizier. Mordechai recognized Xerxes as a clever tactician; the king was using him not only as a close advisor, but also as a strong public face of his renewed grip on the monarchy.

Esther sent a speaking look at Mordechai, appreciating the symbolism of the gift and the implicit demand. She rose and, nodding at Mordechai and at the aide and his servants, left the room, leaving Mordechai to the aide's ministrations.

Soon thereafter, a gloriously attired Mordechai exited the palace, accompanied by his small retinue. It was evening, but there were many people about to note and acknowledge the vizier's magnificence: ministers, guards, and ordinary citizens. All made way, affording the erect and dignified vizier due respect. It was a deliberate choice on Mordechai's part to walk the short distance to his home rather than to ride on horseback. He wanted the difference in posture between himself and his predecessor to be visible, allowing everyone to note that Mordechai the Jew was a world apart from the arrogant and terrifying Haman, son of Hamdata. He also wanted to get a sense of the energy of the people, and of their affinity for the new political order. Mordechai nodded at whomever he passed, acknowledging them and accepting their gestures of respect as his due. In fact and in everyone's eyes, Mordechai the Jew had risen to the position of second to the king.

Mordechai stopped before the door to his home. It opened without a knock. Old Poupeh had been waiting, having been warned in advance by a young runner that "Mordechai is coming! He is dressed like a king!" Even his housekeeper was awed.

Early the next morning, after bathing, sleeping and eating, Mordechai was able to make a closer survey of the contents of the clothing parcels that Poupeh had arrayed in his private bed chamber. The king had sent several changes of clothing fit for royalty. Laid out on the bed and couch were three-quarter-length robes of finest white linen and blue damask; heavy tunics of four-layered, brocaded wine-colored silk; tan-colored linen trousers bordered with purple threads; deep magenta woolen overshirts; a woven sash with gold braiding; and soft, sueded short boots that fit him exactly.

Most magnificent of all was the crown or head ring of heavy, gleaming gold. Though obviously precious, it was modest and even plain by royal standards, which was a relief to Mordechai, who picked it up and examined it. He had no desire or need to wear an ornate crown, and would have politely refused to wear a gem-encrusted crown signifying royalty or quasi-royalty. This plainer crown — which the king considered a necessary and critical part of his new costume — was better suited the man and his station. It was small by royal standards, really just a circle of heavy chased gold, devoid of gemstones. It bespoke royal authority without making a pretense at royalty, as befitted Mordechai's notion of his role as royal vizier. Mordechai knew that despite the fine trappings, he was still only a servant of the king, albeit a high and trusted one wielding special powers. But he was a servant nonetheless; his status could change at the king's whim. Haman, his predecessor, had worn a taller crown covering his entire head and encrusted with precious stones, but such a thing was not for Mordechai. It pleased him that Xerxes had known that.

The next morning, intending to return to the palace, Mordechai dressed himself in the king's robes, taking special care with his new garments. The tall, black-bearded minister-turned-vizier cut an impressive figure standing at inspection before his lifelong housekeeper.

"Master Mordechai, you look like a king!" she said, her voice serious.

"Do not be fooled, dear Poupeh. It is still just I, Mordechai the Jew, beneath these royal clothes. The same man I was before I put them on. Let us see if these clothes will aid me in my mission to save our brethren from Haman's filthy decree. I will need to bring much strength and magic to bear if we are to prepare our people in time to fight back against Haman's army."

Then he put his hands on Poupeh's shoulders and spoke softly the words he knew she waited to hear, but was reluctant to ask.

"Your Hadassah is well, dear Poupeh. She is known to one and all—yes, even to me, *especially* to me—as Esther, Queen of Persia. But she bade me to tell you that *Hadassah* thinks of you daily and sends you her love and blessings. She is still beautiful and unspoiled, Poupeh, but she is also strong and smart and courageous, as a good queen must be.

"But she is altered. When she addresses me there is no personal spark, no innuendo or added personal meaning to her words. Neither are there any small touchings. She is in all things a true queen of Persia and wife of Xerxes. We neither of us looks upon the other as a former betrothed lover. It is as if *those* two people existed in a dream, in another life, and are unrecognizable to the people we are now. Now, between us, there is no emotion; there is only duty." Mordechai spoke with conviction for

Poupeh's benefit; the deepest truth within himself was of course quite the opposite.

Mordechai encircled his strong arms about his old friend, nurse and housekeeper in a mutually comforting embrace, and in turn she placed her gnarled hands atop his, gripping them. As she did she felt the gentle pulsing of King's Ring and her eyes flew to Mordechai's. Poupeh began speaking softly but intensely with the familiarity, license and wisdom of nearly eight decades of service and mutual love and respect.

"The truest heart is buried deep in both of you, Master Mordechai, and there it must remain. Fate has bigger plans for you. Do you not see it? A Jewess is crowned Queen of all Persia, and a Jew is elevated to second to the king! It does not take a prophet to divine that both of you were chosen for great things. Not for you the ordinary life and loves of the likes of us. Your duty is all, and it is a great mission you have before you: you must save the lives of the Jews in exile. It is this duty that has become your life. Do not let us down, Mordechai. Do not set one foot wrong with Hadassah. She is queen, and you are vizier. Nothing else. Help each other to rule. *This* is your fate."

When she concluded her uncharacteristically long speech, Poupeh held Mordechai's gaze. The King's Ring glowed gold and purple, and pulsed like a heartbeat. Mordechai felt it and so did Poupeh. It was a confirmation of the truth of her words. It was also a pact, a silent promise that Mordechai made as he stood in the vestibule of the house where he was born, holding the gaze and the hands of the woman who raised him.

"I swear to you by the One-God that I will do my duty to our people and that this duty will be my standard. For me, Hadassah is no more; there is only Esther the Queen. Together, she and I will save the Jews."

Poupeh nodded and Mordechai stepped outside, dressed like a king.

So it was, that seventy days after Haman had written the decree proclaiming the annihilation of Persia's Jews and sealed it into law, Mordechai the Jew appeared before the king and his court, crowned head to sueded toe, and dressed in royal raiment. Though Mordechai's nemesis, Haman, was no more, Mordechai knew that the powerful, evil force that the man had deliberately unleashed was very much alive, and was, even now, abroad and spreading throughout Persia. Mordechai was under no illusions. His impossibly daunting task was about *to begin*: he must mobilize, arm and train a scattered, diverse and overwhelmingly peaceable population, so that on the day ordained by Haman for the extermination of the Jews, they would instead fight for their lives with deadly physical force—and win! And he had just under nine months in which to do this.

The City of Susa Rejoiced

When the people of Susa—non-Jew and Jew alike—saw Mordechai dressed like royalty and accompanied by the king's retinue as he walked through the city to the palace, they followed him in an impromptu parade, cheering and dancing in a spontaneous outpouring of relief and happiness. Everyone had heard the royal criers announcing the new edict, and the message was clear. Haman and his Death Decree were supplanted, and Mordechai and Esther had saved the day. Though the two heroes well knew that the rejoicing was premature—the truly difficult work was yet to begin—they also appreciated that it served as a legitimate release of tension. Haman's reign as vizier, though brief if counted in days, had been brutal and terrifying, and the people of Susa were eager to embrace the new vizier and, hopefully, a return of the reign of their familiar monarch.

The city, no stranger to parties, took Mordechai's elevation to vizier and the announcement of his new edict as a sign for serious merry-making. Perfumed spices were burned in street stalls and in open windows, and dancing and singing broke out in the streets and marketplace. The rejoicing Susans spread myrtle branches on the roadway as Mordechai made his way through the city to the palace, the trampling feet beating the leaves so that, citywide, their distinctive fragrance rose into the air. To the peoples of the ancient Near East the flowering myrtle plant represented victory and rebirth, and its pliable branches, soft with essential oils brought out by the heat of the sun, were woven into celebratory wreaths and worn as crowns. Mordechai's elevation to vizier and the new edict were hopeful harbingers of victory over their enemies and a rebirth for all the Empire's peoples.

So it was, that in the city of Susa on the day after the announcement of Mordechai's new edict, it was a time of great feasting and joy, and no one celebrated more sincerely than the Jews of Susa in the privacy of their homes. They interpreted the turn of events as a sign that their own Queen Esther had brought about the beginnings of a victory of the forces of light over the forces of darkness. The Jews of Persia gave themselves over to a new optimism; somehow, they thought, Esther and Mordechai would figure out a way to thwart the Haman's Death Decree. They embraced a future that just yesterday was scheduled to end in under nine months' time, on the thirteenth day of the twelfth month of Adar. They began to believe that they would live and not die.

And as the days passed and official word of the king's new edict spread further afield, through villages, towns and cities to the far reaches of the Empire, many Persians who had either embraced Haman's sadistic hatreds or who had cowed to them, once they saw that the full force of the crown supported the Jews, now hurried to disown their abusive behaviors and to publicly embrace the very people whom they had vilified. Some reasonable souls who had privately rejected Haman's edict but who had felt powerless to resist the pressure from the Baradari thugs, now openly sided with their Jewish neighbors, expressing their approval of the *new* law.

Other Persians went even further, renouncing Zoroastrianism, seeking to become members of the Jewish religion. These Persians, having seen the turning of the tide and desiring only to be on the side of the winner, and regardless of whether they truly respected the Jewish faith, went so far as to accept Jewish circumcision. They were practical people, and they deduced that in the present regime — with their king flanked on the one side by a Jewish queen and on his other by a Jewish vizier — their fortunes were more secure if they proclaimed themselves as Jewish. They and other Persians had listened again and again as Mordechai's new law was read out in the streets and marketplace. They feared the inevitable Jewish reprisal that was authorized by the new law.

It was an ecstatic but confusing time for the Persian Jews. They who had recently suffered theft, beatings, abuse, burnings and rape at the hands of fellow Persians, were now being showered with honor. The Jews could be forgiven if, in these heady first days, their public smiles and embraces of their neighbors concealed secret worry, fear, distrust and yes, residual disdain for people so easily turned from longtime friend and neighbor into mortal enemy, and then back again into friend.

Turning Shopkeepers into Soldiers

Mordechai let himself into his sleeping house. It was past midnight and he was exhausted. The whipsawing of events and emotions, on top of his prodigious administrative duties, had depleted him. In the familiar darkness of his bed chamber Mordechai removed his crown and the tunic given to him by Xerxes. At the same instant, he sensed a presence and the wick of the fat candle on his writing table spontaneously sputtered into flame. Mordechai closed his eyes, resigned to a meeting with his hooded mentor. He seized the initiative.

"Daniel, this is not a good time. It's late and I am so weary I can't see straight; I have great need for a few hours sleep. I have spent days on end working to emasculate Haman's killing decree. I have written a new law, and I have personally signed, sealed" — Mordechai held up his left hand, brandishing the King's Ring —

"and dispatched nearly one thousand letters to all points of the Empire."

At Daniel's silence, Mordechai continued. Had he not been so exhausted he probably would never have admitted what was in his heart.

"And I am condemned to a purgatory where I have been given back my lost Hadassah to see and to speak to every day, but where, as Esther, she looks at me but sees not her former betrothed, she sees only her cousin, the vizier. She is untouchable! She is also stronger than I am.

"I am only a man, Daniel. I thought I had grown resigned to living without her, but now this. Seeing her in the palace every day is my personal rack of torture. 'You must save our people, Mordechai!'" bitterly, he mimicked his mentor's words of months ago, and shook his head. "It is not enough to expect me to fight an army of mercenaries with nothing more lethal than spoons and forks. Oh, no, not for the great Daniel. Daniel expects miracles. Daniel expects me — using a network comprised of a scant one hundred agents — to figure out a way to turn half-a-million shopkeepers into a viable fighting force, and in the process to give the three million Jews of Persia back their future." And here Mordechai pounded his closed fist on the nearest wall. "Assuming we are even *alive* at sundown on the thirteenth of Adar, I will still have to face my life without her. I will need to learn how to grow a heart of iron."

At the end of his anguished monologue Mordechai sank into a chair, his head in his hands.

Daniel, feeling his age along with his protégé's pain, moved across the room and rested a gnarled but powerful hand on the shoulder of the man he had taught for three decades, and had come to love.

"Yes, Mordechai, you will grow a heart of iron. For some of us Duty is our one true love."

And Mordechai, sleep deprived and heartsick, laughed aloud without mirth. "You sound just like Poupeh. She said the same thing."

"The old woman has seen much and she is wise," Daniel replied, and he patted Mordechai's shoulder as if to put an end to their discussions. Daniel was better equipped to talk spycraft and strategy for a political or a military campaign than he was at displaying emotion. He only hoped that Mordechai was strong enough to close off his heart and focus instead on the enormous task at hand. Daniel needed Mordechai to function as the general in the coming campaign. In turn Mordechai needed to select captains who would appoint sergeants who would spread out within the Empire and mobilize and train every single Jew — man, woman and able-bodied youth who could hold a sword or a knife or a slingshot, or who could shoot an arrow with accuracy. In under nine months' time the Jews would be facing a fighting force of fabled skill and strength. Daniel knew first-hand that there was more to winning a battle than brawn alone. When, as here, strength of numbers or weapons or swordsmanship were lacking, a wise general prepared by employing the power of his mind, and he used other less direct tactics. Mordechai was an expert at tactics, strategy and games of the mind. Daniel had some ideas, but for this important meeting he needed Mordechai to be clearheaded and sharp.

"Mordechai, outside the palace fortress and all over the Empire, The Terrors have already begun! We need to get started on our counter-offensive at once. Call a mandatory meeting of the Sanhedrin Brotherhood for tomorrow night at the tannery. I will be there. In the meantime, get some sleep." And Daniel vanished back into the night.

Mordechai's last thought before falling into a dreamless sleep was not of Esther; it was of women and youth fighting hand-to-hand combat with muscled mercenaries.

The Terrors

The period of Xerxes' reign that came to be known as The Terrors ultimately lasted about eleven months. To those innocents living through it, it seemed like one unending period of escalating horror. But looking back, the Terrors could be divided into two distinct epochs.

The first Terror began on the day Haman wrote the Death Decree and dispatched his messengers throughout Persia. Once the Decree hit the streets, it provided license in cities and villages both urbanized and primitive, to go after the person and property of the Empire's Jews. Some evil and avaricious Persians saw no point in waiting until the thirteenth of Adar—the Decree's effective date almost one year hence—before beginning the pogrom. In this first stage, then, though at first many Persians intervened, defending their Jewish neighbors, friends, and family, they were no match for Haman's advance guard. The fierce and conscienceless Baradari, led by the ten sons of Haman and comprised of the worst thugs in Persia, instigated and inflamed the thievery, destruction, beatings, killings, and rape of Jewish Persians. During this first Terror the Jews by and large did not fight back.

The second Terror began at about month-three after Haman's Death Decree, on the day Mordechai and Esther wrote and dispatched the New Decree, permitting the Jews of Persia to fight back and defend themselves against their enemies. Once it became known throughout the Empire that the King of Persia had authorized—via new legislation—an edict all but encouraging the Empire's Jewish Persians to fight their enemies to the death on the thirteenth day of the month of Adar nine months hence, the nature of the Terror altered. Now the thugs and bullies enabled by Haman's edict went underground, still abusing, extorting and terrorizing the Persian Jews, but not doing so openly.

The advent of the New Decree was a game changer. The Empire's Jewish queen and new vizier had brought the power of the king's legal writ to bear supporting the kingdom's beleaguered Jews, so that now the Jews of Persia felt legally justified to fortify and arm themselves, even if they did so secretly. They were not legally authorized to pick up arms and fight back until the effective date of Haman's Decree nine months hence, but nevertheless Jewish vigilante groups in every village, town and city formed protection corps. As a result, morale of Jewish Persians cautiously increased, though the targeted abuse and thievery of Jews, their homes, families and businesses went on largely as before. The reality was that in a vast empire covering 7.5 million square kilometers and spanning three continents, policing and protecting the kingdom's Jews would have been impossible. Many far-flung towns never even received the New Edict until weeks after it was promulgated. In this way, impatient mercenaries and local thieves and bullies still ruled the day.

This second period of Terror lasted for the better part of those nine months, culminating in a fierce two-day battle that was to leave more than seventy-five thousand dead. During those intervening months the Persian Empire was in effect engulfed in a *de facto* civil war, pitting mercenaries and enlisted Persians against Persian Jews; a senseless and sadistic conflict fueled and encouraged by Haman's sons and his well-paid army of twenty-thousand soldiers — Nubian, Roman, Greek, Assyrian and Egyptian killers-for-hire — one of the fiercest fighting forces ever assembled in the ancient Near East.

The story of how the overwhelmingly nonmilitant Persian Jews were roused and mobilized, armed, and taught to fight and kill, is the story of heroism and teamwork, desperation and genius, and luck, or providence. The men and women who mobilized, created and trained a guerilla force from nothing and largely in secret, causing a military turnaround that would be retold and sung about for millennia, is the extraordinary untold coda to the story of Esther and Mordechai.

Preparing for War

Mordechai awoke early, refreshed and with a plan already forming in his mind for the training and preparation for battle. Before heading off to the palace, he sent out trusted runners from the Sanhedrin Brotherhood to the pre-assigned surveillance points, issuing the Serah code, calling for an emergency meeting that night.

Later, with the appearance of the first star, Mordechai, dressed unobtrusively now in his ordinary tunic, trousers and turban, lit the candles set out around the underground room beneath the tannery on the outskirts of Susa. One by one the familiar faces of his boyhood friends and other tested and trusted operatives of various ages appeared, first in the narrow, stone stairwell and then seated on benches ranged around the long, scarred table. Shimon, Eliezer, Gidon, Natan, Levi, Pinchas and his six burly brothers, and at least a dozen more. Each man with a strong opinion that likely differed from that of the man sitting on either side of him. Only a single mission united them all: to keep their exiled Jewish community safe and strong.

Mordechai scanned the faces and took a mental roll call. When all had arrived except for Old Daniel, he decided to begin. There was much to cover, and Daniel would arrive on his own timetable anyway.

"My brothers, thank you for coming tonight."

"You issued a Serah code. We couldn't very well stay away, given the situation." This from Natan, the perpetually anxious wine dealer.

"Besides, now that you're a great man you haven't had much time for us. We're missing you," quipped Eliezer.

"And we're curious," added Pinchas.

The banter eased some of the tension and Mordechai allowed the men the moment to relax. He knew they had been working flat out these past ten weeks putting out local fires, instilling hope and strength where there was precious little of each.

On a daily basis, in their respective precincts, the men of the Sanhedrin Brotherhood dealt with the thieves, thugs and worse; the sadists who had become aggressively abusive, treating Haman's edict as a license to go after their Jewish neighbors, taunting and humiliating them, desecrating their homes and businesses and targeting their daughters and sons. Nearly every man present had heard some version of the taunt, "I will be living in your house in eleven months' time, Jew!" Or their wives and daughters had been improperly touched or pressed against in the marketplace, their robes or veils tugged off or torn away, to the tune of the vile threat, "How many of us will have you before we slit your throat, Jew-*jendeh*?"

For the past ten weeks, Jews throughout the Persian Empire had been subjected to the psychological torture of their enemies; a sort of terrifying pre-killing. Those Persians who hated the Jews as a race or who imagined a grievance against any single Jew, used Haman's edict as official permission to vent their evil fantasies and plant their poisoned darts. And thus far the Jews' enemies' campaigns had been wildly successful. In the wake of Haman's killing edict the Jews of Persia were individually and collectively isolated. Most were powerless to defend against taunts, abuse and thefts. A miasma of hopelessness had begun creeping through every Jewish heart. Many ordinary people surely thought, *Why even bother to put up a fight against them? After all, aren't they correct? My life, my home, my business, my wife, daughter and sons, all will be forfeit to these animals, and we will be butchered before the year is out.*

The men of the Brotherhood tried as best they could without formal weaponry or official backup to champion their fellows and to circumvent the effects of Haman's edict. But they were a pitiful few, and by now they were weary and worried, with good reason. Mordechai thought that they would be needing every bit of group camaraderie if they were to achieve the impossible — a military victory over Haman's mercenaries — which was exactly what he planned to present to them tonight.

At that moment there was a cool draft, the candle flames flickered, and the tall and hooded figure of Old Daniel appeared in the room, seated on a stool off to the side. The old spymaster's presence sobered everyone. Mordechai began to speak.

"My Brothers, as all of you know by now, two days ago Queen Esther prevailed upon the king to allow us to write a new edict to counteract Haman's killing decree. The new law, which even now is on its way to every precinct in every corner of the Empire, throws the weight of the crown behind the empire's Jews. If and when anyone — Persian or mercenary — raises sword or fist to harm any Jew in Persia, then, on the thirteenth day of the twelfth month of Adar, the day chosen by Haman as the day of the mass murder of all the Jews in Persia, the king's order permits the Jews to fight back, to defend themselves aggressively against their tormentors."

"Not soon enough, if you ask me," muttered Pinchas. His six brothers nodded and murmured.

"This is all well and good, Mordechai," added Shimon, "but what are we supposed to do in the meantime? Look away as they steal from our businesses, abuse our sons and daughters and threaten to cut our throats if we resist?"

"We can't wait nine months!" cried another man whose family lived farther away from Susa. "We can't just sit back and do nothing between now and the thirteenth of Adar! Our wives and daughters can't leave the house. And even then, they need an armed escort. We need strong men to police our homes, so that we can sleep securely in our beds. As it is, one of us sits guard throughout the night in every house. Just last week Joseph's front door was doused in lamp oil and set aflame in the middle of the night. If his old grandfather hadn't had to piss every hour and sounded the alarm in time, all ten of their family would have been burned by morning."

" So we do it in turns," continued another. "During the day, when we husbands and fathers are out, we need to feel that our homes and families are safe. If the king's men will not guard us, then I say we need to arm ourselves!"

"We need our own militia!" Cries echoed in agreement in the underground room, and fists pounded the tannery table.

"What we need," said Eliezer in his measured tones, cutting through the raised voices, "is an army." Eliezer had cut to the essence.

Mordechai listened without expression, understanding their anger and frustration. If they defended themselves with weaponry without express authorization from the king, they could be considered outlaws and would be subject to prosecution. And if they stood by and did nothing, they ran the risk of losing not only their homes, businesses and families, but also their self-respect. There was no way to win. And Mordechai knew each of these men; they were his hand-picked operatives. He knew how far each man could be pushed before he fought back or broke. He knew from experience the way each of them thought and reasoned, and had, on many occasions over past years, relied on each man to keep a state secret or to relay one, or to save a life in danger. In matters of life and death there was not one of them he would not trust utterly. He spoke now.

"All of you have the right of it, and this is the reason we are here tonight. Eliezer is correct; what we desperately need is an army. We Jews are presently in an undeclared war with Haman's mercenaries and with every Persian who threatens every one of us. And the decisive battle will be fought on only one day, barely nine months from now.

"Starting right now, each of you men here tonight is designated a captain in this new army; you will be responsible for the safety of your precincts." Mordechai reached back and retrieved a long, rolled scroll that he had leaned against the wall. He flattened out a large rolled map onto the table, overlaid with a sheet of thinnest papyrus, covered in hand-written columns of names and numbers.

"I have here a map of the Persian Empire, divided by precincts. Wherever Jews reside, even into the remotest mountains of the Indus, we must identify, gather, arm and teach them to fight. Many of you have served in Xerxes' army, and certainly others of our people across the Empire have done so, too. The first order of business after each of you accepts his assignment is to travel overnight, over land or over water, quickly and secretly, if possible, to each of your assigned precincts. Most of you will be far from your homes. This cannot be helped; all of you have undertaken dangerous and secret distant missions before. Rest assured that we here in Susa and nearby precincts will form small brigades that will watch over and protect the homes, families and businesses of those of you who are serving our cause farther afield.

"Any questions so far?" No one said a word. Most eyes were fixed on the map covering nearly half the tannery table. The scope of the task before them was impossibly huge. But there was a current of excitement in the room; at last, they were doing something. Mordechai continued.

"Now to the details. Upon reaching your assigned precincts, each of you captains will poll the local Jewish populations and will deputize any and all men who have served in the military in any capacity, and additionally, anyone—even men who lack direct military experience—who has facility with sword, mace, knife, and the like. Use those men to gather others from among the locals who have strength and skills that can easily be turned to combat: farriers, stable hands, wheelwrights, builders, stonemasons, butchers, farmers, reapers. The local men will know who is available, who has skills, and who can be counted on. Draft a local woman or boy who can write and cipher to keep records of everyone's name, skills and prospective use in the precinct's army.

"You are tasked further, to identify those among us expert in the various modes of traditional combat: hand-to-hand, archery, swordsmanship, knife, slingshot, catapult. We need to find these experts because every stone and every arrow loosed by our army must find its target. We will have no ammunition to waste.

"And, importantly, you must also seek out those who have experience in *non*-traditional modes of combat. Here, game hunters will be of use, as they are experts at laying traps for foes that outweigh and can outrun them, or can tear them to bits in seconds if they get within striking distance. It is these practiced hunters who will be invaluable to train our new army of Jewish guerilla fighters.

Mordechai was relentless, and the Brotherhood listened, rapt, as he continued.

"Each captain must keep a daily countdown of every day until the thirteenth of Adar. Training time is ridiculously short, so we must make every hour of every day count. Our task is monumental, but nothing we have ever done will mean more than this. We need to use the daylight hours to forge weapons and to train. You will erect pavilions to shield the men from the sun and to camouflage what you are doing from prying eyes. And when the sun sets you will drill in storage sheds by candle light. Use every hour.

"Recruit the local women to act as your eyes and ears. All of you are experienced at spycraft and disinformation. Set up a local information network. Let the women, mothers, grandmothers— even young girls who are discreet and who understand the gravity of what's at stake—listen at the marketplace and pass on what they hear to your designated guardians or other trained receivers. The women are always in a position to identify troublemakers because they are the most vulnerable and are the objects of threat, intimidation and harassment. Use them as couriers. No one ever suspects the grandmothers. They are excellent conduits for spreading intentional *dis*information. The women agents can casually pass to waiting ears whatever information you feed them, and women are useful at distracting or diverting the enemy at strategic moments.

"Identifying the local thugs and troublemakers will allow you to pick them off and dispose of them in advance of the thirteenth of Adar. The more of the enemy we can secretly eliminate before the designated day of battle, the better it will be for us.

"I don't have to tell any of you men that as essential as manpower is to our new army, so, too, is weaponry. Every soldier in our army must carry a weapon he—or she—is confident they can wield. We will be facing the fiercest fighting men in Mesopotamia. No Jew will go into battle on the thirteenth of Adar unarmed. You must build—if necessary steal—and stockpile an arsenal of weapons that can be honed and sharpened for use in hand-to-hand combat. When you arrive at your precincts you must identify nondescript locations that can be used for arsenal storage. It is important that the weapons be easily accessible, especially on the day of battle, but that until then, they remain in secret storage. You will assign watchmen in shifts, safeguarding your arsenals at all times. A cardinal rule is never to leave our weaponry unguarded. All the training in the world will be for naught if we meet our enemies with a fistful of nothing.

"And finally, there are those among you who are members of the Brotherhood's special forces. You are the commandos in our army; our super-soldiers. You know who you are. And you know many of your fellow commandos, some of whom are absent tonight because they are already at their posts in distant precincts. You are our army's prime guerilla fighters, street fighters, desert fighters, and mountain fighters. You are trained to engage the enemy any- and everywhere he appears. You will dig pits at strategic points in the road, you will line them with sharpened stakes, and you will camouflage them. You will use local men and women to lure enemy fighters into redoubts and dead-end traps.

You will not hesitate to ambush mounted mercenaries from rocks and sand dunes, and to kill them on contact, with your bare hands if need be. And, of course, to save their weapons and ammunition."

Mordechai paused here, his gaze moving from man to man, gauging their responses, and willing them to attend to his every instruction. Breaking into the silence, Daniel spoke in his rasping voice for the first time since Mordechai began his briefing.

"Let me emphasize what Mordechai is saying. Make no mistake about the seriousness of this struggle. You must gird yourselves and every one of your people against hesitating even for an instant when engaged with the enemy, be he mercenary or Persian. This is a war for the very survival of the Jews of Persia, and you can be sure your enemy will not hesitate to cut your throat and those of your wives and children. The enemy is first and foremost a division of twenty thousand mercenaries from Babylonia, Assyria and Egypt, armed to the teeth and mounted on trained and battle-seasoned horses. These men have been paid handsomely by Haman and have but one mission: to massacre each and every one of us. And they have an additional incentive to kill us: Haman declared that any possessions belonging to the persons they kill are *theirs to keep.* This incentive has motivated even ordinary Persians — unfortunately, hundreds of your neighbors — to earmark, torment and provoke your families in advance of the thirteenth of Adar.

"You must all be ready to strike back instantly against mercenary or Persian, wherever they attack our people."

The men were respectfully silent when Daniel finished speaking. Pinchas, the head of his small clan of special fighters, addressed urgent words to Mordechai.

"We will need hundreds of horses, and we will need to train and drill in fields — horses and men — until our troops respond instinctively to commands, like an army. Where will we get the mounts?"

"Wherever you can," responded Mordechai. You will commandeer and convert farm horses into military mounts, and you will purchase mounts a few at a time in the open markets. Make up a cover story if anyone is overly curious. What you will all need to do, as captains of your precincts, is to find one true and capable man at each outpost who will serve as your quarter-master. It will fall to him to acquire, secure and store what you need, and to enlist local people in this quest.

"And I cannot stress strongly enough that you must not neglect to enlist and befriend the local Jewish women. This is key! You will need willing cooks and laundresses. And on the subject of women, you will instruct your men to keep their hands to themselves regardless of the temptation. Whether Jewess or Persian, the women are off limits to our troops. For the next nine months, starting tonight, we are all in strict training, and all violators will be summarily punished, no questions asked. This means total abstention from physical pleasures."

"Including wine?" asked Natan. And everyone laughed.

The men around the table looked at one another tellingly, but no one said a word. Mordechai was right. It was serious business—very nearly a suicide mission—creating a fighting force from nothing. Mordechai continued.

"As for financing, I have prepared pouches of coins, silver and gold, and letters of credit stamped and sealed. You will pick these up in the covered shed adjacent to this room as you leave tonight, and you will sign for them. You will not want for the means of funding our struggle, I can promise you this. I have requested a voluntary tax from every single Jewish household in the Empire according to every family's ability to pay, and already runners are collecting the monies—more than I have asked for—and are secreting them in predetermined locations. We are all of us in this to the end. Our lives, the lives of our wives and children, and all that we have, are in your hands.

"It falls to you, my friends and brothers, to create order where there is none, to transmit the sense of urgent mission to every single person in your precincts, and to make an army out of ordinary citizens.

"You can communicate with me and with each other through our system of secret messaging. Use the signal fires that we have used for years when affirming the new month or calling for a special tribunal. The ciphers have changed, of course, given this crisis. I have a key to them here, and before leaving here tonight you will each of you study the key and memorize the new ciphers.

"Ask any questions now, or hold them and wait until you arrive at your new quarters."

No one moved. It was Shimon who spoke up.

"Mordechai, our secret army must have a name! Have you thought of one?" The men raised their eyebrows, some even smiled at their comrade.

"You are absolutely right, Shimon." Mordechai answered his lifelong friend. "Our secret army should have a name. And no, I have not thought of one. But I can tell from the look in your eyes that you have one in mind. Tell us."

"Our mission to create a secret army should be known as Operation *Dashneh Jahood*; Operation Jewish Dagger." Shimon sat back in his seat and looked around at his comrades. For the first time in days, Mordechai smiled.

"*Dashneh Jahood*. I like it! What say you, brothers? Shall this quest be known as Operation *Dashneh Jahood*?"

There were muted calls of "*Dashneh Jahood!*" from the men in the room, and those closest to Shimon slapped his back or patted his shoulder. Even Old Daniel seemed pleased.

"It is settled, then," said Mordechai. "And well said, Shimon. I will read out your assignments now, for Operation *Dashneh Jahood*. Understand that wherever possible I have assigned precincts to coincide with each man's language facility and ability to blend in. Here are your assignments."

Consulting the unfurled map and his secret list, Mordechai read out loud. "Shimon, you will head to Persepolis, and will also cover the cities and outskirts of Pasargedae and Borazian. Eliezer, your precinct is Aria and Parthia. Natan, you head to Basra and Gandara. Levi, to Hyrcania. Pinchas, you and your brothers and ten special forces of your choosing are bound for Babylonia and Assyria, the most dangerous tract. Thousands of mercenaries are already encamped between Susa and Assur."

Mordechai continued calling out names and precincts as the men filed forward, studied the cipher keys—committing them to memory—then climbed the stone stairs on their way to pick up their pouches of coins and letters of credit.

The sky was still dark and star-studded, but the moon was half-way to morning when the members of the Sanhedrin Brotherhood headed home, most for the last time, some perhaps forever. But they were an optimistic and hardy lot, and would train their focus on succeeding at their mission. If they could create a functioning army, then with luck and surprise they could wrest an improbable victory from the killer army left in place by Haman. With luck, there would be time to return to their homes and their beds then.

Esther

That same night, standing at a window in her apartment at the palace, Esther reviewed the situation. *How time had telescoped itself!* she thought. Only ten weeks had passed since Haman had sealed the fate of the Jews of Persia, condemning millions of innocent people to a butchered death in a year's time. Ten weeks since Mordechai had sent a message to the palace exhorting her to go before the king to plead for her people. Ten weeks since she had walked the long, lone walk from her apartment to Xerxes' throne room, risking her life on the likelihood that the king still desired her. Ten weeks since she had conceived of a desperate and dangerous plan to play simultaneously on the king's fears and on Haman's lust, acted the coquette and trapped the vizier. Ten weeks since revealing to Xerxes and all Persia that she was a Jewess, a secret she had kept, waking and asleep, for six long years. Ten weeks since Haman was executed and Mordechai was elevated. And mere hours since she had genuflected to Xerxes once again, begging him to allow queen and vizier to write a new document neutralizing the Death Decree.

It felt much longer than ten weeks to Esther. Every moment had crawled, weighted down with consequences. She was exhausted from the unrelenting tension and the play-acting. True, she had spent the past six years play-acting, first in the harem and then in Xerxes' bedroom. But that had been easier for her, somehow. Once she had shut off her old life—Poupeh, Hadassah, and Mordechai—her sole raison d'être had become surviving and succeeding *as Esther*. Her present play-acting, oddly enough, was much, much harder for her. Now not only did she play queen to Xerxes by day and by night, but she also was faced with the daily presence of the man whom she had loved all her life, lost, and then regained, but only as platonic cousin and associate.

Esther smiled ruefully to herself. No one who knew her would call her a killer, yet that's in effect what she had become, was it not? Since the moment Xerxes had invested Mordechai as vizier, Esther had known what she must do. Her survival and that of Mordechai and her people required a true sacrifice. Though not even by the lift of her eyebrow had she displayed her inner turmoil, the closed door of her imagination was no bar to her surging feelings upon seeing Mordechai daily, close-up, as equals. By night, when she was alone, Esther literally felt her heart shredding. Just when she thought that she would not be able to sustain this additional taxing split between her deeply-held emotion and her duty, the solution came to her, clear as the dawn: *she* was to be the lamb on the altar!

Not as Esther, but *as Hadassah*. And the laughing Fates had decreed that *she* must be the one to perform the sacrifice, to "kill" Hadassah.

In one important way Esther was the perfect person to have been chosen as queen and to have kept all her people's secrets. Her lifelong orphaned state, her ineradicable, existential aloneness—certainly a source of personal sadness growing up—paradoxically prepared her perfectly for her future trials. As a girl, Hadassah had been trained to think through any problems on her own, and to draw comfort from her inner strength. She grew up relying on her own resourcefulness, honing her instincts and her analytical abilities. All this was excellent preparation for the next stage of her life, when, as Esther, she had no choice but to keep her own counsel while stepping carefully and appearing confident. The essential precept of "being Esther" was that "Hadassah" had had to disappear forever. And she had done her job brilliantly, moving from abducted orphan girl to harem favorite, and then to Queen of Persia.

For all these reasons, facing this present impossibly difficult practical and moral personal crisis alone, was not an alien state for Esther. She could not very well discuss her dilemma of love and loss and searing pain with Mordechai. And after all, wasn't "aloneness" one of the spymaster's prime precepts? How many times had she heard him tell other agents to tell no one anything? If you told no one, you did not have to worry that your secret would be betrayed. Only if more than one person knew a secret could you no longer rely on its being secret.

And as fate would have it, the solitary girl who grew up to be Esther, Mordechai's prize pupil in the intricacies of spycraft, was the one person in all Persia destined to play for the highest stakes of all: she must close herself off forever to love, and must succeed at the duty thrust on her by fate. She must literally save her people from genocide.

So it was that Esther, who lived by the credo "Tell no one," wrestled alone with her heart-wrenching dilemmas.

Esther knew what she must do to save her own sanity. The solution had become clear to her when she fancifully thought of herself as a "killer." But now, when the Esther-Hadassah split was all but tearing her apart, and she thought seriously about it, it was not fanciful at all. Keeping "Hadassah" — and the hope that she had represented — alive, albeit buried away, was eating away at Esther. In her own mind she knew her survival depended on steeling herself to envision, in all ways but actually, doing away with the girl she had been. There was no longer any hope for the girl Hadassah. Too many souls now hung in the balance if that girl, with her dreams and desires, ever were ever to resurrect herself. For just by *being*, the girl Hadassah would betray Esther the queen. As an experienced agent Esther knew better than most that even one small, romantic "Hadassah" slip could nullify everything she had built as Esther. She could not risk it. At stake was not just her own life, but literally the millions of innocent souls of her people, too. Much better, and cleaner, Esther thought, to sacrifice just the one girl that she had been, letting go once and for all of her former self and her hibernating hopes for future happiness. The calculus was morally compelling, if personally tragic.

So Esther—brilliant, disciplined and brave—did what needed to be done. She meditated and visualized; until by force of will she figuratively exorcised the girl Hadassah from her heart and memory. Standing before her window gazing at the crystal-studded dark bowl of sky, an exhausted Esther actually felt the first eighteen years of her life molt, like a chrysalis. Already they were no longer clear and bright in her memory; they were out-of-focus, as if behind a gauze scrim. With prodigious effort Esther closed her eyes and her mind to the girl Hadassah's loves and dreams. For Esther, wife to Xerxes and Queen of All Persia, and a woman whose life was all Duty, the girl she had been died that night, as surely as if she had fallen on a dagger.

Thus, it was solely *as Esther* that she stood before her window the same night that Operation *Dashneh Jahood* was born. She stood as a queen, envisioning the speeding messengers and the lathered steeds carrying the life-saving decree she and Mordechai had written, to every corner of the Empire.

Taking stock, she counted this a victory, with immediate palpable, positive, and practical consequences. Esther expected that as the New Decree became known near and far within Persia, the Jews' morale would surge. Her people would view the New Decree as evidence that the queen and the new vizier, Jews like themselves, were strongly advocating on their behalf with the king. And hopefully they would come to view their king as an ally rather than as the royal enabler of their destruction. As for the Persians, in wake of the New Decree the tormenters, opportunists and sadists among them should, to some small degree, back off, and quiescent supporters of the Jews among their Persian neighbors might be emboldened to stand by the Jews.

The vital consequence of the success of her recent bold and risky gambit with the king was that—because of her and Mordechai's newly visible Jewishness—the Jews had, overnight, become publicly legitimized at the highest levels of the social and political structure in Persia. The expected trickle-down effect of this was that the Jews' enemies should begin to feel isolated and outlawed rather than the reverse.

Abednego

In an exhausted sleep, Esther dreamed. She saw the figure of Abednego, her guardian angel—her guardian warrior—standing by her open terrace door, dressed and ready for combat, wearing leather breast plate and shin guards, his short sword and dagger pendent from his belt. In her dream she was standing next to him. Esther could feel his reassuring presence. He began to speak, instructing her.

"The coming battle will be fierce and bloody, Esther. Many will be slain, of the enemy but also of our people, as Haman's army of mercenaries know more of butchery than Mordechai's Brotherhood can teach in nine short months. But know this, Esther: there is a great need for *your* skills. Our guerilla army will need to strike swiftly and strategically, in many locations and before the enemy even knows what has hit them."

"*My* skills? But what knowledge of warfare do *I* possess?"

"Ahh. Your knowledge is not of swords and armies, but is *within* you. Have you not felt it? Have you not "known" things before they happened? Throughout the ages, some very few humans who are pure of heart have been gifted with this "sight," and you are one of them. Some call it intuition or woman's wisdom, prophecy or premonition. Most people with this gift dismiss their visions as ordinary coincidence. It helps them to live among the ordinary and unsighted. But not you, Esther. You know I speak the truth. Have you not felt and known things? As a girl, as a maiden, and even living here in the palace? Your ability to sense *me* is evidence of it."

Esther responded truthfully, whispering her assent. And for the first time, she addressed him by his name, which he had never disclosed to her, another proof of the truth of his words.

"I *have* felt things, and I have known things, Abednego, since I was a girl. I have told no one. Sometimes it was almost an infinitesimal knowing just a bare moment before something happened or before someone appeared at the door. As a woman I used this knowing, harnessing it, so that as an agent I was able to warn Mordechai, or another of our Brotherhood, moments ahead of danger, to move to safety or to expect a maneuver. The knowing also allows me to feel the needs of other people. It is as if I am hearing their secret yearnings, and I can respond to them." After a thoughtful pause she continued, understanding dawning about precisely what her guardian was asking of her.

"You are telling me I will need to harness my visions, even call them down preemptively, so that I can see where the enemy lays in wait, preparing to attack. I can then relay this information secretly to our army, enabling our people to strike *them* first, catching them unaware. Surprise, strike and retreat. This is the only way our dispersed and amateur soldiers will be able to defeat a professional enemy."

Abednego watched Esther as she worked out what she must do. It was a desperate time, and it was the first time in her life she had had to put a name to her power; the first time she had been asked to consider controlling it instead of waiting passively for the visions to visit her. But Abednego had faith in this slip of a woman. She had risen to every situation thrust upon her by a capricious Fate, this girl who was orphaned at birth and who led a solitary girlhood until she had been torn from all that was familiar and thrust into a gilded nightmare. Yet she had adapted, doing what no other woman and few men were equipped to do: she had soldiered on despite a shattered heart. She possessed strength as well as beauty, and wisdom to match her kindness. She was a born queen and warrior, like her Persian namesake. Watching her closely, Abednego saw her right hand move, unconsciously, to her hidden pocket, to grasp the dagger he had given her seven years ago. The girl had needed a champion then. The dagger was a comfort to her, a reminder of a protective power stronger than the five senses. Watching her, Abednego knew the moment Esther steeled her spine to accept what he was asking of her. Satisfied, he willed himself to disappear.

Still in her dream, Esther looked over to where her guardian angel had stood. He was gone now; only the night sky was visible, outlined in the pillared opening. She sighed.

Esther stirred in her sleep. She would awaken infused with a purpose, and would not question where the thought and the intention had come from. She would be poised to use her power to serve as the Jewish army's secret weapon.

Mordechai Faces a Threat from Within

The next evening, Shimon and Eliezer, Natan, Pinchas and his six brothers waited impatiently in Mordechai's salon. Poupeh had brought them refreshment and assured them that they might have a long wait, as there was no telling when Master Mordechai might return from his duties at the palace.

"We'll wait, Poupeh," Shimon had told her kindly.

Poupeh sensed an undercurrent of anger buzzing among the men, and hated that her Master could be walking unsuspecting into a volatile situation. She had just determined to send him a message at the palace via the butcher's boy when she heard the door close and Mordechai entered the hallway. An agitated Poupeh bustled to greet Mordechai, but before she could warn him he saw Shimon standing in the archway to the salon and the others ranged about the dimly lighted room. Placing a reassuring hand on Poupeh's shoulder, Mordechai removed his crown and cape, handing them off to her as he walked into the salon. He had been worn out when he had opened the door, but at the mere whiff of trouble his tiredness vanished and he was ready for anything.

"Well, brothers. Peace to you, and greetings. I sense this is not a social call. I was expecting that all of you would have been on your way or preparing for your precinct assignments. Eliezer, what's the trouble?"

Ever-loyal Eliezer came straight to the point.

"Mordechai, there is some serious dissent among our people here in Susa and beyond. Simply put, some see you as a traitor to your own people. These people are vocal and are gathering support opposing you. They are saying that it was your fault that Haman came down like a fury on the Jews; that you incited him when you refused to bow down to him and even flaunted your refusal. They are saying that the command to bow down applied only to persons at the King's Gate or to those at court. So had you just gone along and been quiescent like everyone else at court, the Jews of Greater Persia would not even have come to his notice! They are saying that the Jews have *you* to thank for Haman's killing edict, promulgated in angry retaliation for your disobedience. That you made us *all* look bad; that because you acted *as a Jew*, you made *all* Jews look like potential dissenters or, worse, traitors to the king. And that now, *all* Jews in the Empire — not just those within the King's Gate or at court — will be made to pay the ultimate price."

"They are out for your blood, Mordechai," said Shimon. "We fear that, if the situation goes unaddressed, these men will send a delegation *to Xerxes* registering their loss of confidence in you. They could declare a formal break from recognizing you as our community leader, and propose one of their own in your stead."

"If they do this now," injected Pinchas, "at this vital and sensitive juncture, it could sink Operation *Dashneh Jahood* just as we are getting started. Simply put, we cannot allow this! We cannot allow any inkling of dissent to reach the palace and hamstring your influence with the king."

"There is something else, too, that complicates this," explained Natan. "Other than the people in the immediate vicinity to the palace who know that as vizier you are pushing back at Haman's edicts, many of our people do not yet see you in that light. They last saw you being led around on the king's horse by that bastard Haman. They view you as having been won over to the enemy. Most are not privy to the fact that Haman had targeted *you* to hang on his fifty-cubit stake. Or that it was *you*, along with Esther, who wrote the New Edict countermanding

Haman's death orders. Or that between you and Esther we Jews are in a stronger position to win out against Haman's army than we would be without you. And finally, as of right now, because of legitimate security concerns, precious few of our people have any idea that we are mounting Operation *Dashneh Jahood*, raising an army that *you* are commanding!"

"Despite your speedy royal messengers, it will take weeks, perhaps a month or longer, for your New Edict to reach, and be read," and here Shimon ticked off on his fingers, "by the people, by the satraps, by the governors and by the local Jewish leaders of every precinct in the Empire. We need to quash this anti-Mordechai movement *now*, while it's still containable, before it does real damage."

"And the damage is not just to *you*, Mordechai. With all due respect, it is damage to our mission that concerns us. We *must* stop them, and *now*." Pinchas and his brothers, ever practical, always angry, were ready to bash heads, even Jewish heads, for the greater cause.

Mordechai, understanding the threat and its origins, was grateful the men had come to him with this rather than handling it on their own.

"Thank you, Pinchas, and every one of you for coming to me with this. We will handle it strategically, and will try to channel some of these men's forceful energy for our own purposes." He smiled as he spoke, looking pointedly at Pinchas. The others muttered or were silent, prepared to hear Mordechai out. Pinchas paced.

Mordechai stood at his desk and considered. He knew the men standing before him and trusted that their word was true and that, notwithstanding any differences, they were loyal to him in this mission.

"The people are terrified. They would push me into the furnace because it is something they think they can do, as they are helpless against the terrorizing Baradari and the impending massacre. I'm an easier target. The question is, how to defuse this campaign? It would splinter our people and would siphon off unity and energy that is desperately needed elsewhere.

"Shimon, do we know who the leaders of this movement are, and where they are concentrated?" At Shimon's nod, he continued, on his feet as he paced and thought out loud. "How far has it permeated? If you've caught wind of it early enough perhaps we can head them off. Here's what we will do. Pinchas, you and your brothers fan out and bring the leaders of this 'Mordechai is a traitor' movement to me. Shall we say, midnight tonight at the tannery?" Mordechai looked around at the men in his salon.

"What's your plan?" asked Eliezer.

"My plan is to try and turn them! Any of you not involved in actually bringing these men to the rendezvous tonight will meet me there. We'll see who these men are. We will swear them in a blood oath to secrecy, tell them of Operation *Dashneh Jahood*, and enlist them as soldiers."

"Ha! And you think they will agree?" This from Pinchas.

"None of us here is a fool. We will gauge their sincerity. My aim is to avoid tearing each other to bits. But neither will I swear a loyalty oath to them. I don't have the time it will take to convert them to our cause if they are dead-set against me. We will give them this *one chance* to see what we are about and agree to join forces to fight the common enemy: Haman's army and the Persians who are Hamans themselves. If they do *not* agree to train and fight with us, or if any of us senses that regardless of what they say they will nevertheless betray us to the king, then they will not be sleeping in their own beds tonight. They will be blindfolded and on their way before morning aboard a ship bound for Athens. We will have our brothers there hold them in a safe house up in the mountains, unharmed but incommunicado, until after the thirteenth of Adar. We cannot afford to risk our mission, but neither will I authorize silencing them permanently. However misguided they are, Pinchas, they are our brothers.

"What do you say? Pinchas? Eliezer?"

"We will see you at midnight," said Eliezer, and the others nodded.

"We will try it your way first, Mordechai," said Pinchas. "Let's get moving so we can bring them — voluntarily — to the tannery tonight." Pinchas and his brothers smiled the smile of predators, gripping Mordechai's forearm in a gesture of support on their way out.

In the end, of the twenty anti-Mordechai agitators corralled and brought to the tannery that night, all but three enthusiastically agreed to be a part of Operation *Dashneh Jahood*, and they swore a holy oath to support the cause and to train and fight Haman's army. It turned out they were good men, fearful for their families and frustrated at the inaction. They were eager for the opportunity to strike a blow against their enemies, and to do so as part of an organized force. As for the three angry holdouts, within hours they were bound and under guard and on horseback headed overland on the Royal Road from Susa to Sardis, and from there as "guests" of a merchant ship owned and operated by Natan's family, bearing wine casks and animal hides to Athens.

And Mordechai himself swore to all in the tannery room that night that their cause would supply funds and other support to the families of the three who had "disappeared." They would be told their men were on a mission.

Haman's Secret Lists

As the heir to Old Daniel's mantle as spymaster, over the course of two decades Mordechai had collected, catalogued, processed and issued orders based on literally tens of thousands of bits of information he received from his network of agents. And one of Mordechai's unique strengths was that he was able to keep every tip and bit of information in his head. He wrote nothing down, taking seriously the teachings of Old Daniel. *Leave nothing for anyone to find, even accidentally. You or your agents cannot be hanged for what exists only in your memory.*

One vital but elusive trove of data that Mordechai craved was Haman's lists. Though no one had ever reported seeing any such lists, both Mordechai and Daniel felt certain that such lists existed; Haman, known within the palace as a compulsive record keeper, would surely have kept a written record noting each of his sons, their local supporters, their secret hideouts, and the locations of arms caches throughout the kingdom. Haman would have wanted and needed to keep a close track of his cells of Baradari and other paramilitary supporters.

But though Mordechai and his men searched everywhere — including behind the walls and beneath the floors of Haman's house—now Mordechai's house—they had come up empty. Even his undercover agent within Zeresh's house, a longtime "maid," had secretly searched the small house from cellar to roof, but come up empty.

Mordechai barely slept, working and reworking the problem of where Haman's lists could be. He had a vital need for them *now*, in the desperate, hectic weeks of preparation for war. What his Jewish army lacked in military experience, arms or blood lust, they could make up by taking their foes by surprise. To do this, he badly needed information of the Baradari whereabouts. Mordechai had counted on recovering Haman's lists in order to save literally thousands of Jewish lives.

But where were the lists? A few of Mordechai's men even voiced their opinions that to spend any more time and manpower searching for them was a waste. After weeks of fruitless searching they were convinced the lists did not exist. Perhaps Haman, too, had kept it all in his head.

The Scribe's Story

Early one morning in the week following the creation of the *Dashneh Jahood*, one of the royal scribes — one of the many who had hand-written the New Edict, and *not* one of Mordechai's agents — approached Mordechai in a deserted palace corridor, and, inclining his head and standing at a respectful distance, sought the viceroy's attention.

"A thousand pardons, Master Mordechai, but if I may have a private word with you." A surprised Mordechai ushered the man into his chamber off the hallway leading to the throne room, closed the door and sat behind his large desk, piled with scrolls and covered with the administrative paraphernalia of governing. Mordechai had been in the game long enough to sense the man's nerves. Perhaps the scribe had some information for him. By keeping silent he allowed the man the courtesy of speaking when he was ready. The scribe looked directly at Mordechai as he began.

"Master Mordechai, I have been a scribe in the king's service for ten years, and I am a loyal subject and citizen of Persia. I have no grudges against your people, the Jews, and I was happy to be of service scribing the New Edict."

Mordechai wondered where this was leading.

"I have been troubled these past three months. I have been burdened with a secret that I was forced to keep at knife-point, but I have decided that a forced oath does not bind me. I feel conscience-bound to disclose to you what I know. It might be of assistance to you and your people as you defend yourselves against Haman's edict."

Mordechai felt the air ripple around him. His instincts told him this man held the key to something vital.

"What is your name, my friend?"

"I am called Ahmad, Master."

"Tell me, Ahmad."

And the man, more at ease with copying words than with speaking them, painstakingly told his story.

"Some months ago I was taken aside to a secret room in the cellar of the palace by Master Haman"—the man mimed a spitting motion over his left shoulder—"and I was instructed to scribe eleven copies of a pile of lists and columns of hundreds of names and places. At all times I was watched over by a guard and I was not permitted to leave the room for three days and nights until I had completed the scribing, the checking, and the rechecking of the lists. I slept and ate and even relieved myself—begging forgiveness, Master—under guard. When I was finished scribing, I bound the lists with thread into eleven separate volumes. Master Haman himself, and one servant, a cousin of the vizier, collected the completed volumes from my hands.

"Afterwards, the vizier stood in front of me as I sat at my desk, with the armed guard at my back, and he asked if I knew what I had been scribing. I looked him in the eye and said 'words and names, Master.' He continued to probe, but I feigned stupidity. I stammered and told the vizier that I have a skill to copy and scribe, but that I possess no memory for such things. I was shivering in my shoes, Master Mordechai, as I am a coward and I expected to be killed at any moment.

"I thought the vizier must have believed me, as he dismissed me to my home, but before I could get up from my seat he held a knife to my throat, and leaned into my face. Spittle from his lips splashed onto my cheek. He said if I ever spoke of what I had copied in that room, he would personally cut out my tongue and make me eat it, and he would kill me slowly and painfully. Then he cut me, Master Mordechai." And here the man opened the top button of his white tunic to reveal a two-inch-long livid scar.

"Almost passing out from the pain, and with blood seeping through my fingers, I did not cry out. Again I told the vizier that I had no memory. And as I was shaking with fear and appeared a pathetic as well as a stupid creature, the vizier must have gauged me harmless, and he dismissed me."

"And why are you telling me this now, Ahmad?"

"Master Mordechai, I am a peaceable man, and want nothing more than the chance to do what I was taught to do, and to enjoy a peaceful and long life surrounded by my children and their children and my wife, and to sip wine in my garden. I bear no ill-will toward my Jewish neighbors. Haman was a sadistic madman, and I do not owe such an evil man the honor of a promise made at the point of his knife.

"Until coming to you today I have told no one about what I scribed for Haman. But I have spent my nights thinking, and after vizier Haman's death I concluded that the Fates surely spared me from the evil man's knife for a reason. It was as I sat scribing hundreds of copies of your *new* edict over these past two days that the reason came to me. I thought perhaps the information I knew could assist those he had condemned to death.

"I thought that coming to you with this information would be fitting, as it was *my* hand and *my* pen that scribed his Death

Decree! It is this guilty knowledge of my part in scribing Haman's decree that gives me no peace. I would like to make amends."

Ahmad paused and gathered himself for his final game-changing words.

"Master Mordechai, in actuality, I have an excellent memory. After scribing the first set of lists and columns of names and places, I was able to scribe the remaining ten from memory, though I did not allow Haman to see this. I recall the names and places clearly, as if they are words and stanzas in a familiar song." The man finished his story, and looked pointedly at Mordechai.

"Could you reproduce those lists now?"

"I could."

Mordechai blinked. Then, rising, he asked Ahmad to have a seat at his own desk. He pulled several clean parchment sheets from a shelf, readied pen and ink, and signaled the man to proceed.

As the morning sun streamed brightly into the chamber, Ahmad wrote steadily, methodically filling lines and columns, and page after page with names of persons and corresponding place names. Mordechai did not interrupt him and in fact gave instructions that he was not to be disturbed. He placed a goblet of cool water at the man's disposal, and once or twice over the next three hours he leaned over the man's shoulder to peer at the words as the ink dried.

Mordechai was quivering with excitement. As if in answer to his secret prayer, this man Ahmad was handing him the information he and his confidants in the Brotherhood had speculated about but had begun to fear did not exist. Ahmad was reproducing the list not only of the secret hideouts of Haman's ten sons, but also of the entire feared Baradari confederacy, of their local associates and supporters, and of the locations of their arms caches in every province of the kingdom!

Armed with this trove of information, Mordechai's generals and their amateur army could, in surprise and in secret, coordinate simultaneous lightning raids emasculating every cell and unit of Haman's fierce Baradari fighters. With minimal exposure to their own men, the Sanhedrin Brotherhood could orchestrate the execution of the heads of Haman's poisonous fighting hydra serpent, thereby crippling one section of the enemy's offensive beyond repair. Tens of hundreds of lives would be saved!

Eventually, Ahmad laid down his pen and flexed his fingers. Mordechai stood where Ahmad had stood earlier that morning, feeling, in every fiber of his being, that he had just been the recipient of a miracle.

"Ahmad, my friend, words are insufficient to express my deep gratitude for what you have done this day. Many innocent lives will be saved thanks to your God-given skill, your bravery and your good conscience. Your family will never want for anything as long as Mordechai walks on this earth, and they will be protected with our lives. You have my oath on my eternal soul. You are now one of us."

Ahmad rose, and, facing Mordechai, bowed his head. The two men clasped forearms and stood thus for several moments.

"I will explain that I have been about the new vizier's business this morning, so as not to arouse the curiosity of the other scribes." With these words Ahmad exited the chamber soundlessly.

Mordechai sat down at his desk and stared at the pile of newly penned sheets. *More precious than gold,* he thought in wonder.

Planning Simultaneous Lightning Strikes

Mordechai knew that the success of his planned commando raids depended on secrecy, speed and surprise. His personal tactical preference was to execute operations against an unsuspecting enemy target in absolute silence, or as near to that as was possible and practicable. He began to see how it could work.

With Ahmad's lists in hand Mordechai wasted no time. He issued a Serah code, calling the local generals who had not yet departed for their precincts to one last midnight meeting at the underground room at the tannery. Hearing the news of the discovery of Haman's lists and seeing Mordechai's barely controlled impatience and excitement fired the men. What had seemed a near impossibility just days before — a clean defeat of any of their foes — now seemed achievable.

Throughout that night the men worked with a purpose, encrypting the lists and sending out coded fire signals ordering immediate and secret military preparation in every one of the assigned precincts where Haman's Baradari or collaborators were, including those in the Empire's farthest outposts. Levi's prized carrier pigeons were dispatched at first light, miniature cipher scrolls tied to their legs. The reliable winged messengers bore the portentous message encoded by Mordechai himself, in a double-blind cipher, saying that eight months hence, on the night of the *twelfth* of Adar — the *eve* of the day of Haman's planned massacre — the Jews' army would stage simultaneous, surprise commando raids against the feared Baradari.

The concept was a stunning one, even for a trained military force. Not so much the surprise attacks, or even the fact of executing them simultaneously. Such concurrent attacks were militarily possible. But that they should be carried out with precision and surprise at scores of strategic points across the entire Persian Empire — an area of nearly eight million square kilometers — was grandiose and smacked of folly. And that it should be carried out by an army of largely untried and underarmed men! Not even seasoned generals would attempt such an undertaking.

Yet Mordechai's proposed lightning operation appealed to the leaders the Sanhedrin Brotherhood. Desperation had made them even bolder than they might otherwise have been. "Go big, and go in smart." This was the bold mantra of Pinchas and his brothers, and with the scribe's information, and Mordechai's eyes shining with excitement, the men in the Brotherhood sensed the potential for victory.

Xerxes Authorizes his Army to Join with the Jews

The days merged quickly into weeks, and Mordechai, though restricted by his duties as vizier, received daily and weekly reports from his generals throughout Persia on their recruitment and training progress.

His current worry, now that he had a strong handle on routing the Jews' *Persian* foes, was how to vanquish their *foreign* foes, Haman's bloodthirsty mercenaries. Even employing surprise, ambush and guerilla tactics, he was under no illusions; at best, the Jewish army would only slow down their paid executioners. Even if the mercenaries lost dozens or hundreds of their soldiers, they still had the Jews vastly outnumbered, out-armed and out-classed. Mordechai desperately needed to enlist professional allies, and he was nursing another plan.

Just the day before, Mordechai had received an emergency coded dispatch from his agent in Parthia, describing new, escalating barbarous behavior on the part of the Baradari and their collaborators. The agent reported that in an obscene and sadistic move, the thugs enlisted by Haman's sons were ordered to meet a daily quota of dead Jewish babies! Months ahead of the thirteenth of Adar the butchers had already begun house-to-house searches, grabbing babies from mothers' arms and either smashing them into stone walls or running both baby and resistant mother through with their swords. Not only that, but while they were at it the murdering thugs attacked and raped any available girl or woman who caught their eye, their confederates holding the girls down and laughing.

The field agent described hysteria, panic and chaos in his precinct, reporting that Jewish men and boys were engaging the Baradari in hand-to-hand combat with disastrous results for the unprepared and outmanned Jews. Jewish blood had begun to run in the streets, and the agent was desperate for help.

Mordechai, distraught but displaying his trademark calm, understood the gruesome Baradari tactic. With no one to oppose them, the lawless butchers had begun terrorizing the locals, both Jew and indigenous Persian, ensuring no meaningful resistance. And they were trying out the obscene tactic of baby-killing far away from Persia's cities. In the outer reaches of Parthia the likelihood of encountering serious resistance and outside help was nil.

Mordechai had shot back a coded response that he would send help. And over the course of that same night he authorized the immediate dispatch of men and arms to Parthia to stand by its Jews.

Throughout his sleepless night Mordechai searched for a solution. As the sun rose, he hit on a possible answer.

What if the king were to offer, on his own initiative, some of his Royal Militia to assist the Jews on the appointed day of the massacre? Mordechai thought that having the king's soldiers at his disposal and on the side of the Jews would give the Jews better than just a fighting chance. It could give them a victory.

Mordechai became obsessed with this new idea. Pitting the Jews against Haman's professional killers — both local and foreign — was nothing short of authorized butchery. But using the king's own elite troops to augment the amateur Jewish army would level the playing field.

Subtly, and throughout the next several days, Mordechai maneuvered conversation with the king to include scheduled updates on the two edicts. He calculatedly allowed the king to think that the Persian Jews had no need for any additional assistance on that fast-approaching, fateful day; that in fact, the Jews had lines to various *foreign allies* with substantial trading interests with Persia's Jews, and that the Jews had been assured via informal business and diplomatic channels that these foreign allies would lend troops to aid their Jewish trading partners.

Mordechai could see that the prospect of *more* foreign troops fighting on Persian soil, even to aid the Jews, whom the king supported, did not sit well with Xerxes, who had been strategizing and fighting wars since he was a young prince, and who knew the danger of inviting foreign troops — even temporarily — onto domestic soil.

The king sought Mordechai's counsel.

"Mordechai, tell me, what would you advise in this situation? Right now we have twenty thousand foreign mercenaries in Persia, poised to murder Persian citizens in six months' time. If these *other* foreign princes send even a few thousand troops apiece to aid their Jewish trading partners, in the end Persian soil would be overrun by armed foreigners, and likely soaked in Persian blood. And how would we rid ourselves of these foreign soldiers *after* the thirteenth of Adar, once they are armed and flushed with success in battle?!"

"You are right, Your Majesty, on both counts. Having legions of foreign soldiers on our soil who are not answerable to Your Majesty's command would be a grave tactical error, and would make us vulnerable to a coup. You seem to be implying that it would be better for Persia if we aided the Jews ourselves, obviating the need for allowing more foreign soldiers within our borders, no matter how well-intentioned. I would agree with Your Majesty."

The king slapped his hand on the arm of his throne, punctuating his decision.

"We *cannot* allow more armed foreigners onto Persian soil! Our prime objective must be to roust these mercenaries. Confer with my general, Mordechai, and tell him I have authorized him to muster ten thousand armed soldiers from our royal militia to be deployed to assist the Jews against the foreign mercenaries on the thirteenth of Adar. You will see to it that the royal troops work together with Persia's Jewish citizens, defending them against all aggressors, and repelling any and all foreign troops who threaten them. See to it this very day, in the name of Xerxes, King of All Persia!"

So Mordechai had his solution to the looming two-front war against Persia's Jews, which only days before had seemed hopeless. To combat the *Persian* aggressors, the scribe's information would allow the Jewish commandos to surprise and neutralize the Baradari and their supporters, and access their weapons stores. And to counter the *foreign* soldiers now massed on Persian soil, Xerxes' authorization of his militia to aid the Jews would balance the odds, and hopefully rid Persia of that threat, too.

The Night of the Twelfth of Adar

The months of preparation for war flew by. The distinction between day and night became blurred for Mordechai's agents, officers and soldiers. The Jews of Persia — the vast number of whom did not live in Susa or its suburbs — had worked themselves into exhaustion not only repelling the brutal Baradari and their confederates almost daily, but also arming themselves and training relentlessly for the fast-approaching "official" day of battle. All Persia's Jews lived in a state of unrelenting tension. Would the thirteenth of Adar bring their utter destruction, as Haman's edict decreed? Or would they be able successfully to defend themselves against their enemies and so survive as a people? The consensus of Mordechai's generals was that the Jews were as ready as any amateur fighting force could be. Lacking formal armaments, they were using sharpened tools, farm and kitchen implements, and their ingenuity. Honed scythes, pitchforks, shovels, kitchen knives, slingshots, wooden stakes sharpened to knife-points, cauldrons of boiling oil and boiling water, buckets of rocks and home-made catapults. Everything was a potential weapon in the hands of Mordechai's Jewish army.

Added to the might of a half-division of the king's Royal Army, the Jews were ready for the thirteenth of Adar.

But it was on the evening *before* that legally prescribed day of battle that Mordechai's logistical genius and sheer luck — never discounting the Jews' determination and courage — changed the face of the coming larger battle.

For the past six months, since the scribe's revelation of Haman's lists, the Sanhedrin Brotherhood commandos in three score locations across the Empire had been planning and training for synchronized raids on the Baradari strongholds. This was no small undertaking, as the short- and long-distance planning was accomplished in extreme secret lest even the smallest hint of their raids leak out, damning all of them and finishing the Jews' war before they had had a chance to defend themselves. The extraordinary reliability of Mordechai's established spy network, built and refined over decades, and the redoubtable men and women who comprised it—most of whom did not even know their counterparts at the other commando stations—laid the groundwork for the Jews' resolution and stubborn optimism despite the grim odds.

In Susa, Mordechai paced his salon throughout the night. Over and over he reviewed his plans and the refinements instituted by his resourceful generals and captains, searching for a flaw. He imagined his trained commandos, dressed in black, wearing soft-soled felted slippers, faces blackened with dirt, armed and lying in wait at sixty locations across Persia. At the second hour of the second watch of the black Persian night—the darkest hour of all, when men, women and even animals are at their lowest level of wakefulness and are into their deepest sleep—his commandos would move simultaneously and silently to surround, surprise and disable each Baradari command center.

In the palace, a restless Esther did not even attempt to sleep. To ensure her solitude that night, she had gently encouraged the king to drink the potent wine that Natan had purposely supplied to the king's Cup Bearer. In addition to wanting time to concentrate her thoughts on Mordechai's commandos, she had other matters on her mind.

The fact was that Esther was magnificently large with her first pregnancy, and even at two weeks from her time she had barely slowed her pace. Try as she might to ignore her body and focus on the high-stakes drama unfolding for her people this night, the babe within her was active, and she was frequently compelled to stop in her tracks and hold tight to the nearest table or chair back. She was secretly thrilled at the life growing within her. An orphan herself, she hand a fount of untapped love for her unborn child. This child would know its mother. Still, she thought, her one small birth event was trivial compared to the thousands of life-and-death dramas daily affecting her brethren throughout the Empire.

Old Daniel had not slept a night through in at least ten years, and this night was no different; he could not rest. He had planned and overseen hundreds of operations over the course of his life as advisor to four powerful kings, but standing by the window in his chamber in the palace annex, Daniel admitted to himself that this ambitious commando raid was at once the riskiest and the most significant in his long life.

He had reconciled himself to a sideline role, and was more than proud of his protégé's — Mordechai's — strategic genius, his ability to foresee and map every detail, his prodigious memory, and, perhaps most essential, his ability to command willing obedience and loyalty from every agent in his service. Still, it was so very hard to stand in his chamber and fret when he knew his brethren were facing their most serious test.

Daniel imagined what each of the four hundred and twenty Jewish soldiers was thinking as they crouched or lay, barely breathing, in alleys, sands and grasses, awaiting the moment of silent attack. Each man and woman involved in the operation had, by great force of will, forced from their minds the reality that on their shoulders this night rested nothing less than the future of their people. If tonight's simultaneous ambushes were successful, then the Jews would have struck a preemptive blow ending the reign of terror of the Baradari and their cohorts, and gained access to their weapons caches.

There was that, of course, and it was a critical objective. But the incalculable added effect of a victory this night would be on the morale and confidence of the other tens of thousands of ordinary Jews who were poised to engage a brutal and inexorable military machine on the morrow, the thirteenth day of Adar. A victory tonight could show the Jews what dozens of rallying speeches could never do: that they had a better-than-even chance at dealing their foes a death blow. A victory tonight could signal to the Jews that discipline, desperation and, yes, sheer luck could carry them to victory. The thirteenth of Adar would not be the day the Jewish people ceased to exist in Persia.

It was an unfortunate fact that, even if tonight's simultaneous raids were successful, news of the rout would not reach all the Persian Jews in time to give them a morale boost. Still, many of the Jewish fighters *would* know of the victory, and the news would travel swiftly. But in addition, given the vastness of the Persian Empire, news of a surprise victory by the Jewish commandos would also fail to reach the *mercenaries'* generals!

Which was too bad, really, thought Daniel. It would be delicious to watch those cocky musclebound animals pale at the news that the unarmed Jews of Persia had in one brilliant stroke destroyed the fearsome Baradari. The news might crack the confidence even of the hardened mercenaries.

The thought of lending a hand in the battle via an injection of his personal brand of *psychological* guerilla warfare was very appealing. But Daniel knew that a general's toughest job was to be patient and allow his men to do what they were trained to do. So he throttled back his keenness to act. He would wait through the night for Mordechai's commandos to do their job; Abbas would let him know when the operation was done. *Then,* Daniel thought, he might just go to work planting doubts in the mercenaries' minds. It wouldn't harm the Jews' cause if some of Haman's mercenaries had second thoughts and deserted before battle.

Shadrach was not concerned. If he had needed sleep like ordinary creatures did, he would have slept like a newborn. After all, why should he worry? Granted, when Haman had been executed he had lost his perfect instrument for evil. But the man had done one thing right: he had put in motion the fiercest single-minded mercenary army in history. The soldiers only awaited sunrise on the morrow before they would commence to systematically and mercilessly annihilate Persia's Jews. The Jews' pitiful maneuvers tonight would only serve to cull out their best soldiers, making tomorrow's battle bloodier and quicker.

As Shadrach could not read the future, he could only figure the odds; and the odds were overwhelmingly against a successful outcome to Mordechai's nighttime commando operation.

Come morning, Shadrach would be struck a figurative body blow when news of the commandos' overwhelmingly successful surprise operations would reach him.

Simultaneous Raids

At the prearranged time of the silent stroke of the second hour of the night's second watch, in cities, villages, desert huts and remote mountain redoubts throughout Persia, one by one and at the exact same time, Mordechai's commandos took down sixty Baradari hideouts.

In the end, the simultaneous hits went more smoothly than anyone had dared hope. Haman's ten sons, though insulated and protected by bodyguards and hundreds of Baradari, thugs and sadists, were taken completely by surprise. Though some tried to keep the secret even years later, when stories were retold of the amazing nighttime raid, the truth of it was that the enemy were caught and bound *while still in their beds*! Most never knew what had hit them until they awoke, hours later, in a holding pen or cell guarded by Jewish soldiers.

The Commandos' Secret Weapon

Years later, minstrels and bedouins alike would be singing of the "magic" of the Jews' nighttime raids.

The overwhelmingly bloodless raids were executed successfully thanks to the commandos' first-stage weapon: a lowly sponge, saturated with a potent concentrate of soporific aromatics.

One of the Sanhedrin Brotherhood, an older medical man with an encyclopedic knowledge of herbs and plants, had proposed to Mordechai, at an early stage of the operation's planning, a better way of defeating the Baradari than through hand-to-hand combat. One advantage of his proposal was that it would enable older men, and some women, too—those not necessarily best skilled at conventional soldiering—to augment the complement of Jewish commandos. Two-thirds of each team assigned to a particular hideout were skilled soldiers ready for combat; the other third of the team—call them "noncombatants"—would be armed with what the medical man termed their "secret weapon."

Though every commando on the lightning raids carried a sharpened knife at their belts, the ones who were designated fighters were armed to the teeth, and also carried rope and strips of cloth to be used to bind and gag their quarry.

In contrast, each of the designated "*non*combatants" was armed, instead, only with a skin of water slung across his body. A second pouch, slung across the body from the other shoulder, contained dried sponges that had been seeped in a boiled solution: a combination of hasheesh; of *afiun* or ground poppy seeds; and of *sit al huscin* and *zo'an*, a wheat infusion. The pre-soaked and then dried sponges retained the potency of the active soporific ingredients even after the water had evaporated.

Like magic, when the dried, "loaded" sponges came in contact with small amounts of water, the soporific was instantly reconstituted. All that was required was that the dampened sponge be held tightly over the enemy's mouth and nostrils. The same potent combination of herbs had been used for centuries by ancient healers and surgeons as an effective and instant plant-based anaesthesia.

So between soldier and noncombatant — the teams having practiced the mock maneuver hundreds of times over the past months — the actual raids were nearly automatic. To everyone's delight and surprise, most of the snoring Baradari were disarmed and neutralized without a sound and with no loss of life.

The Thirteenth of Adar

As dawn broke on the thirteenth of Adar, a preternatural quiet lay upon Persia's Jewish households. No one had slept the night before. Within their homes and at pre-set vantage points, the Jews held their collective breath and waited. Would the day be their last? Most tried not to focus on the near-impossibility of their objective and the likelihood of a hideous death. Instead, they awaited the inevitable first violent volley from Haman's mercenaries. Would the armed and armored soldiers march through their villages in phalanxes, slashing and bludgeoning every living soul? Or would they crouch just outside their small city and send thousands of poisoned arrows into their homes and streets?

Of course, in the end the mercenaries' mode of attack varied, depending on the size of the target community and on the terrain. The mercenaries engaged in all forms of violent combat, seeking to finish off Persia's Jews in the fifteen hours of daylight on the allotted day.

Particularly terrible, and striking fear into every Jewish heart, even those who were seasoned fighting men, were the dreaded and impregnable war carts. The equivalent of a modern-day tank, the mercenaries' war carts were drawn by teams of magnificent armored horses seventeen hands high. The carts had lethally spiked wheels taller than a man, and were manned by soldiers wielding fire-arrows and catapults aimed in all four directions.

These carts rolled heedlessly through town, village and field, leaving behind swaths of burned destruction and bloody death.

A Defensive War

It had been drummed into the Persian Jews, soldier and non-soldier alike, by Mordechai and by his generals and sergeants, that on no account were the Jews to strike the first blow against their enemies. The language of Mordechai and Esther's New Edict was clear; it had mirrored the language in Haman's killing edict: permission was given to the Jews to do unto Haman's men what he had authorized the mercenaries to do to the Jews. The mercenaries had been given the order "to destroy, to massacre and to exterminate all the Jews in Persia, young and old, children and women, and to loot their possessions." To counteract that edict, at Esther's behest, with the second edict the king had given the Jews in every city in the Empire permission *to strike back*; to defend themselves, and likewise to destroy, to massacre and to exterminate all those who attacked them, or who sought to do harm to their young and old, children and women, and to loot their possessions. The New Edict was clear: this was to be a *defensive* war only. Thus, every Jew expected to see blood shed that day, either his own blood, or of someone he knew.

The mercenaries were to have first volley, and people would die.

The Jews Fight their Enemies and Take No Spoils

Their arms ached; their hearts were heavy; they were exhausted and disgusted and terrified of dying, but were afraid to ease up even to rearm and reload. The Jews, unaccustomed as they were to waging war, were nevertheless a disciplined lot and, tamping down their revulsion in order to repell this existential threat, fought back against Haman's mercenaries with every bit of strength and cunning they had. Using the guerilla tactics outlined by Mordechai and practiced over the past nine months, the Jews — supported by the king's soldiers — killed five hundred of their enemies in the city of Susa alone, on that single day, the thirteenth of Adar.

On the day that was to have been their last, and which their enemies had marked as the day they would overpower and murder them all, the Jews surprised everyone — even themselves; it was *they* who had out-fought and overpowered their enemies instead of the reverse! But it was not only the fact of the extraordinary military victory that buoyed the Jews. Jews everywhere began to notice that after the one-day battle, ordinary Persians — the Jews' neighbors and erstwhile friends — instead of avoiding them, as had been their recent wont, now afforded them marked respect. It was a shock for the Jews to realize that what they were witnessing was the expression of profound *fear* that their improbable victory had instilled in their Persian neighbors. Word had gone out swiftly, from the highest satrap ministers, to the local governors, and thence to the king's stewards, that the Mordechai's Jewish army was a fierce and fearless adversary. The terror that the Jews had been feeling for the past eleven months was now visible in the faces of every Persian they encountered, whether ordinary citizen or high official. Contempt and pity had been replaced with a palpable fear and grudging respect.

Seventy-Five Thousand Dead
Including Haman's Sons

After the sun set on the thirteenth of Adar, Mordechai's network sent and received hundreds of coded fire signals from across the Empire, reporting all casualties. The number of enemy combatant dead throughout the Empire tallied at seventy-five thousand. This number included the ten sons of Haman, who controlled the feared and sadistic Baradari. Mordechai had instructed his generals that searching out and eliminating the sons of the mad Haman—the sons who carried out their father's genocidal vision with relish and evil perversity—was a strict priority. So it was with grim satisfaction that he read the special dispatch identifying their bodies and naming them individually, as he had requested: Parshandata, Dalphon, Aspatha, Poratha, Adalia, Aridata, Parmashta, Arisai, Aridai, and Vaisatha. The dispatch confirmed that the ten bodies were being sent directly into Mordechai's custody in Susa from all points of the Empire, as he had requested.

The seventy-five thousand dead included not only Haman's mercenaries, but also the casualties from the private armies that had been raised by the scores of Haman's patronage appointees. These private fighters had ranged against Persia's Jews and had sought the Jews' annihilation for no reason other than that Haman had decreed it. These wealthy, patronage satrapies were, in effect, armed enclaves spread across the Empire, loyal not to Xerxes, but to the corrupt vizier to whom them owed their political lives and considerable fortunes. Any of these smaller, provincial armies that had made the political and tactical error of failing to declare themselves unambiguously on the side of the Jews, were treated as outright enemies. It was these recalcitrant, hostile soldiers who swelled the death toll.

Only when the number of casualties was known to the king did he begin to appreciate what a close call he had had. If Esther had not risked her life and exposed Haman to the king eleven months before, it was a virtual certainty that by the end of the day on the thirteenth of Adar, Xerxes—and likely Esther, as well—would have been toppled and dead, and Haman would have been installed as regent.

In stark contrast, the number of Jewish dead was in the low hundreds. And it was a mark of pride and character that the Jews' army—in deliberate contravention to the king's blanket *permission* to loot and kill given to Haman's army—took *no* spoils, and also refrained from in any way harming the enemy's helpless, including their women and children.

Late that night, the exhausted Jews wondered thankfully that they had survived the brutal day that was to have been their last. As they gathered their dead for burial and wiped their weapons clean, preparing to consign them either to a cellar room or to the community storehouse, word came via messengers from Mordechai reminding everyone that laying a hand on any of the enemy spoils was expressly forbidden. Ordinarily, taking spoils from a defeated enemy was considered the victor's right, and often the spoils of war were a soldier's sole compensation. In fact, for Haman's mercenaries, the promise of looting the Jews after they had annihilated them was an enormous financial incentive.

But as regards the Jews' one-day victory over Haman's army, the mercenaries were so detested and reviled that it was generally felt that whatever they possessed — with the possible exception of their weapons — was cursed, and was ill-gotten gain which the Jews had no desire to touch or possess in any case. Mordechai and the Sanhedrin Brotherhood were adamant — and the Jews agreed wholeheartedly — that they not be enriched in any way by looting Haman's soldiers. All their energies were concentrated on ridding themselves and Persia of these sadistic mercenary parasites who had sought nothing less than the Jews' annihilation. The Brotherhood leadership wanted no physical memory of the army they had repelled. The victory itself was enough, and would be talked and sung about for generations.

The mercenaries' horses were stripped of their armor, corralled and earmarked for transport to Susa, to the king's stables. As for the mercenaries' corpses, their armor and personal effects, all was to be carted outside the cities and villages and piled up as the unwanted detritus of war. Details of men — Jew and Persian — across the Empire were assigned to dispose of these corpses on the outskirts of the provinces that Haman's mercenaries had cold-bloodedly and confidently attacked only hours before.

The Night of the Thirteenth of Adar
Mordechai as Master Strategist

The Jews were not to know this now, on the night after they fought for their lives, but Mordechai's stock as vizier and as a commander of men had risen exponentially as a result of the one-day war. From members of the king's court to the local town officials and the ordinary Persians on the street, everyone — including the princes, satraps and governors — either openly supported and sympathized with Mordechai's Jews, or else they stood in fear and awe of them.

Six months ago, not one of them would have given a boot-lace for the chances of Mordechai's Jews to survive the thirteenth of Adar. And yet, here it was, sunset on the day Haman had appointed for their annihilation, and Mordechai's Jews were still standing, while Haman's army and the armies of his supporters were badly damaged and on the run.

Mordechai had envisioned and engineered a two-pronged defense: in addition to feverishly preparing the Jews to repel their enemies *militarily*, he also undertook a broad *diplomatic* campaign. Mordechai, in his role as vizier and second to the king, shamelessly parlayed the power of his office in his quest to save the Jews of Persia. Mordechai's diplomatic strategy was to personally appeal to every one of the local provincial dignitaries either to remain neutral in the coming war, or, much preferred, to openly support the Jews. He had lobbied, cajoled and begged — via summons to the palace; via dispatch of a royal envoy; and via letters bearing the king's seal — for local support throughout the Empire.

Mordechai had convinced the leaders of the provinces of two things: First, that given the king's open support of the Jews, their victory over their enemies — local and foreign — was inevitable. And second, that it would therefore be to the provinces' distinct political advantage to throw their support behind the Jews and alongside Xerxes.

One way or another Mordechai had gotten the support he sought. As royal administrator and military strategist Mordechai had no equal in the kingdom of Persia.

At Mordechai's House in Susa

On the night of the surprise defeat of Haman's armies by the Jews, though the streets of Susa were relatively calm, in stealth and quiet hundreds of surviving mercenaries — many of whom were wounded but still extremely dangerous — searched the city for temporary hiding places. Haman's mercenaries were stunned. The Jews had proven fiercer fighters than anyone had predicted, and in a turnabout for the ages, they had routed a division of trained soldiers! The surviving mercenaries' only thoughts were to find a place to rest, eat and drink, clean their wounds, and plan their escape from Persia as expeditiously as possible. They had planned to fight a passive and unarmed foe, and had reckoned they would be returning home with their saddle bags laden with booty. Instead, most of their comrades were dead, and those who survived were wounded and hunted.

Poupeh, alone in Mordechai's tightly shut and secure house, had relaxed her rigid vigil when, just an hour before, she had retrieved a coded message from Mordechai via carrier pigeon at her bedroom window saying that the Jews had won the day, and assuring her that he and Esther were safe and unharmed.

Into her eighth decade and craving rest, Poupeh left her window ajar to catch the cool night breeze, then she stretched out on her bed with a sigh, instantly falling into a relieved and exhausted sleep. Light from a small shielded candle illuminated the chamber.

Two bloody and wounded mercenaries, desperate for a place to rest and hide out, were crouched in an alley adjacent to Mordechai's house. They had watched as Poupeh opened the heavily shuttered window and retrieved the messenger bird. It was a stroke of luck for them that she had neglected to pull the iron shutters closed afterwards. Hearing no sound from the open window after several minutes of waiting, one soldier climbed onto the other's shoulders and, peering inside, took in the silent room and the lone, sleeping old woman.

Losing no time, they boosted themselves into the room and stayed crouched, waiting to see if the old witch would waken. Even one scream from her could rouse the household and spell disaster for them. They were not to know that the place was empty. Realizing their luck as the old woman snored gently, the first soldier mimed with his finger across his throat and pointed at Poupeh. The two seasoned soldiers weren't taking any chances. The second soldier pushed himself up and, with his filthy dagger in hand, he calmly slit Poupeh's throat, wiping his knife on his torn trousers.

In that obscene instant, the faithful old woman who had never harmed so much as a centipede became a slaughtered innocent noncombatant in the Jews' defensive war. Poupeh died without waking, believing that her beloved charges were safe and that they had saved the day. She had served her people faithfully for all of her life, meeting her end at the hand of a blood-caked mercenary who would not live until morning.

Mordechai let himself into his house soundlessly. He knew Poupeh would have gone to her bed only after learning that Esther was safe, and he did not wish to wake her. He wanted only to wash and catch a few hours sleep. He removed his crown, placing it on a table, and he toed off his soft boots. Though the hour was not especially late, the sky was dark and starless and the entryway windows tightly shut, letting no light into the house.

Knowing his way in the dark, he was slipping off his cape as he walked, soft-footed, down the hall.

Some sixth sense had Mordechai dropping to a crouch. He stopped cold to listen, the hairs on the back of his neck tingling with danger and anticipation. He closed his eyes for an instant to better locate the sounds, and realized there were snores coming from Poupeh's chamber. Rough masculine snores. Instantly his dagger was in his right hand, balanced lightly and ready for anything. He flipped his cape over his other forearm, and rising silently, put an eye to the hinge-crack of Poupeh's slightly open door.

Taking in the scene, he acted on instinct with a spurt of rage. Roaring out atavistic, guttural sounds, Mordechai crashed into the room.

The soldiers, who had stretched out on the carpeted floor as Poupeh's life blood soaked her bedclothes, and had counted themselves lucky, woke instantly and were already reaching for their weapons. Technically, the advantage was theirs, for even though they were wounded and surprised, they were trained killers, and were two against one.

But Mordechai was possessed. The instant before the mercenaries awoke, when the door had cracked like a gunshot against the wall followed by their momentary confusion, was all the advantage he needed. Mordechai stepped close to the armed man on his right and, in an experienced move, shoved his dagger upward into the man's throat with enough force that the man was thrown backward. With a hard pull, Mordechai yanked out his knife. Simultaneously, he crouched and pivoted, tossing his cape into the face of the second soldier moments before the man's knife would have sliced off Mordechai's ear. With the first soldier rendered useless or dead, Mordechai focused on the second, thrusting his dagger through the cape and into the man's chest, piercing his heart and killing him instantly.

It was all over in less than a minute. The room—a good size for Poupeh alone—was crowded now with violence and death. Mordechai checked that the two soldiers were in fact dead, posing no further threat. Stepping around the pooling blood, he knelt by Poupeh's bed and placed his fingers to her cold neck, checking automatically for a pulse. Her lips were blue and her homely and loved face was already a death mask. He lowered his forehead to hers and closed his eyes. Straightening up, he pulled the cover over her face and murmured goodbye in the language of their forefathers.

Haman is reaching out to me from hell, he thought, ineffably sad. *This day of killing is not the end of it.*

At the Palace – The Same Night

Esther, very nearly at her term, sat heavily at the table in her sitting room, laid her head on her forearms, and wept silently and copiously. Her two maidservants stood close by, concerned for their very pregnant mistress. Over the past six years they had seen her by turns intuitive, generous, submissive, silent, thoughtful, determined, and angry. But never had they seen their beloved queen cry in their presence. They worried now that in her grief Esther could bring on the birth contractions.

As it was unheard-of for any man except for Xerxes or Hegai to walk in the corridors of the queen's palace apartments at night, Mordechai had sent the news of Poupeh's murder to Esther via her longtime personal maid. He had added an urgent post-script: *We* must *have a second day to finish off Haman's mercenaries!*

Esther understood Mordechai's implicit request. So she dressed hastily but carefully, in a turquoise underslip topped by a diaphanous golden tunic edged in persimmon and gold braiding. Her magnificent russet hair was anchored at the sides by two golden clips, and it fell free down her back. In fact, as she walked, slowly, by virtue of her pre-natal girth, but gracefully down the corridor connecting her apartments to the king's wing, it was impossible to tell from the back view that she was nearly nine months along with child. And from the front, one saw a pale but lushly beautiful, regal woman who embodied the female power of the crown.

The marble mosaic floor was the same one Esther had walked alone a year before. Back then she had been terrified but determined to try to win over her husband, the king, and foil a madman. Back then, she had had virtually no hope of success, nor even of a future. Now, on the day, one year later, that her enemy had predicted he would be dancing on the graves of her people, she carried not only the king's child within her, but also the knowledge that her strategies had helped save a nation.

This time, Esther walked confidently, though secretly bereft, toward Xerxes' throne room, followed by her anxious handmaidens. This time, as she approached the great Hall of Pillars, as the throne room also was known, the king's bodyguard announced her presence almost before she had stepped into the arched doorway. This time, Xerxes rose and stepped down from the dais, extending his hand and scepter to a woman and queen who virtually glowed with power, confidence and ripe beauty.

One year after Esther had first walked that marble mosaic path to the king's throne room, the spell that she had woven to entrance her king was still in evidence as she watched him watch her. Ever intuitive to nuance, Esther was surprised to detect something extra in the king's face and posture. *Could it be respect? Surely it could not be fear*, she thought.

Esther Requests A Second Day to Fight

The frenetic daytime atmosphere of the throne room was nowhere in evidence. Flanking the king at this time of night were only his bodyguard, his scribe and his fanboy, and of course

Mordechai, his trusted vizier. Esther barely noticed anyone but Xerxes, so intent was she on her mission: to secure the king's permission to go after the retreating but still lethal mercenaries. She reflected briefly that she had come a long way from the passive harem girl of seven years before, who had made it a habit not to request even an extra bar of soap from the harem master. Now, as queen, she was about to present her fourth request to the king, and this request, like the others, had life-and-death consequences.

The king welcomed Esther and led her solicitously toward a seat on the dais.

"Esther, my beautiful Queen! Come sit by me. I was just receiving the report of today's battle." Xerxes was privately shocked as well as terrified, in the way of men, that his very pregnant queen had come to him unbidden. He rose to escort Esther to her seat and he glanced towards his vizier, who was standing nearby, holding a sheaf of lists. "Your people have acquitted themselves well; in the city of Susa alone they have killed five hundred men in addition to the ten sons of Haman! Are you not pleased? We can only wonder what they must have done to their enemies in all the *other* provinces of the realm!"

Esther might have inclined her head slightly at the king's comment; but when she remained silent, the king—before whom no one ever came just to sit and chat about the day's events—correctly assumed that she had come to him, as she had in the recent past, in order to pose a request.

"Ah, Esther, but you must already be aware of all this. You have not come to hear me exult in your people's success; you have come to ask a boon of me. What is your wish now? Ask and it shall be granted to you. Any additional request you have will be fulfilled!"

Seated on his throne, the king had turned toward Esther, seated off to his right side, as he asked her to reveal her request. Esther watched Xerxes carefully, assessing whether he was actually pleased with the day's events or merely tolerant of his Jewish queen and vizier. Xerxes' present state of mind could cue Esther in to how best to broach her request. Watching the king, she sensed something extra under the surface—was it impatience? Was his offer to fulfill her request *before* she had uttered it merely formulaic and polite? Had he already granted all the largesse he was going to bestow on her and her people? If so, she was out of luck, and the Jews might have to continue their battle on the morrow, but as outlaws.

Or could the king's preemptive offer signal something else entirely; something extraordinary? Could the king perhaps be nervous, feeling surrounded, so-to-speak, by his Jewish Queen and his Jewish vizier, in a kingdom that, just today, has seen the Jews win a resounding military victory? To a king who in the past twelve months has executed three traitors who sought his crown—one who had risen to the second most powerful position in the land before he was brought down—it was not impossible to imagine Xerxes' discomfiture at realizing that his own army was not the only military force in Persia.

But could Esther once again use the king's insecurity to her advantage?

Mordechai had taught her, many years ago, to use illusion to create the effect of reality. Hadn't she done just that nearly a year ago, when she had allowed the king to think that Haman was prepared to cuckold Xerxes in his own palace in order to have her? Yet even then she had not created a sham "reality;" Haman had indeed intended to betray the king, and either kill or subdue her by brute force. She had merely encouraged the king to see Haman for what he was, rather than as the illusion that the villain had allowed the king to see.

And now? She would attempt to allow the fact of *today's* Jewish victory create the *illusion* of *enduring* Jewish military power. The king would back the Jews *only* if he perceived that their power was unstoppable. The king would grant her request because he always backed a winner. Also, Xerxes knew that after the battles were done and Persia returned to business as usual, he would need the formidable political and economic support that Mordechai and the Jews could offer him.

Esther had her wedge. It was the king's fear of coup and his desire always to be on the side of power.

"If it please Your Majesty, I would request that tomorrow, as well, should be given to the Jews of Susa to do battle as they have done today. For though the enemies of the Jews and of the Crown have largely been destroyed, many of the mercenaries are wounded, and renegades are still at-large in the city, armed and dangerous. They rove the streets, preying on Jewish and non-Jewish Persians alike."

Here Esther paused for effect before continuing in her soft, clear voice.

"There is nothing to keep them from infiltrating our homes and even this palace, as well-guarded as it is. It is a terrifying prospect.

"Just this past hour, My King, I have received reliable intelligence that wounded mercenaries have tonight broken into the home of a prominent member of the king's court, and have murdered an innocent old woman in her sleep."

She had the king's undivided attention.

"Your Majesty, I implore you — to allow the Jews to finish the job they have so ably begun. Give them a second day to fight Persia's enemies."

The king was silent, considering. He was no fool. Esther had read him correctly, and he would, indeed, back the Jews, who had defied all military odds and were now a force in Persia. But he also was a fierce military campaigner, and as such he knew first-hand the serious carnage defeated, retreating and angry soldiers could wreak, fueled by desperation. The resident population was at high risk; the weak or old, children and women, commoner or king, all were fair game. The sole objective of a retreating army was to survive and get out, and they would burn a path to the nearest border if need be. It seemed that this was what the mercenaries were about now, and Susa was their last enclave. The Jews would have their second day to fight; Xerxes would give them a chance to finish the job.

"So be it, Esther. Let it be decreed that the Jews of Susa are hereby permitted to take up arms and fight their enemies tomorrow, as well."

"There is one thing more, Your Majesty. All the citizens of Susa are terrified, first with the day of bitter fighting outside their doors, and now with the horrors of the escaping soldiers. They need to see a sign from their king that he is in control, and that no resistance to his rule will be brooked. The ten sons of Haman..."

"...Who have already been killed, according to my report," interjected the king.

"This is so, Your Majesty. Their corpses are even now labeled and stored in the Susa prison. But the Persian people do not know this. Recall how Your Majesty used Haman's execution and impalement as a public symbol of the consequences awaiting *anyone* who betrays the King of Persia. It was Haman's impalement eleven months ago that marked the beginning of your taking back the reins of power from a rogue advisor intent on a coup." Here Esther paused and assessed Xerxes' demeanor. Had she gone too far, reminding him of his lapse of judgement? She forged ahead.

"Your Majesty is in need of a similar public symbol to mark the end of the terror reign of the Baradaris. One that the people of Susa will see and remember for always." Here she paused again to let the concept percolate. The king was always interested in flexing his power arm.

"If I may suggest..." Esther hesitated.

"Speak, Esther," prodded the king. "What would you have me display as a symbol of my control?"

"Let Haman's ten sons' bodies be impaled on ten stakes in the public square just outside the palace walls. Have the Royal Crier call out a periodic announcement similar to when Haman's body was on display, drawing attention to all in Susa to take heed of what befalls enemies of the Crown. At the end of three days and nights, have the bodies removed and buried in a common grave outside the city with the rest of the enemy combatants."

Esther placed her hands placidly in the small bit of lap she still had, signaling she was done, and she watched Xerxes closely. The king was likewise watching Esther, and he saw the strategic sense in her words. He also appreciated what she did not say: that while the move would be a visual assertion of his imperial power, it also would bespeak the Jews' victory. He admired Esther's strategic advice. King and Queen could both benefit.

"Let this all be done exactly as Esther the Queen has said! Do it under the King's Seal!" Xerxes announced in his proclamation voice, the words echoing in the vast, empty chamber. The king turned to Mordechai, and wordlessly and quickly the vizier left the throne room to pen the decrees, mobilize the royal messengers for the continued fight on the morrow, and order the ten stakes to be erected in the market square. There were still more than six hours until dawn, and much to prepare.

The Fourteenth of Adar

And so, in the royal city of Susa, at dawn on the day *after* the thirteenth of Adar—the day that Haman had decreed all the Jews of Persia were to be massacred—the bodies of Haman's ten sons—who had been hunted and killed by the *Dashneh Jahood*, the Jews' army—were impaled on wooden stakes in the public market square. And all the people in the city of Susa, Jew and non-Jew alike, sighed in relief that their king had brought imperial justice back to the Persia they loved.

The bodies, which could be seen from all points of Susa, bore gruesome witness to the second day of intense fighting. On this second day, the Jews' search parties, in a coordinated operation, simultaneously entered the fortress city from its seven gates, effectively closing off all above-ground avenues of escape. Jewish fighters, joined by the king's troops, swept through every street and alley in armed phalanxes, blocking off and then entering every house, cellar and shop. The Royal Guards, armed to the teeth, formed a protective ring about the perimeter of the palace wall, ensuring the king and queen's safety.

One hour after sunset on the second day of fighting in Susa, Mordechai read the death tally. There were three hundred enemy dead this day, the vast majority of whom were caught inside Persian homes and businesses, holding innocent children and helpless grandmothers at knife point. Every one of the slain enemies in Mordechai's body count was hard-won, and his Jewish soldiers bore the scars of the fight.

As on day-one, no Jew took so much as a boot lace in war booty. Their war was in defense of every Jewish soul in the vast Persian Empire; it was not fought for profit or gain.

Esther Gives Birth to a Prince

Amid the terror and excitement, the death and triumph of the thirteenth and fourteenth of Adar, immediately following Esther's fourth petition to the king, she went into labor, giving birth to a healthy son, a boy who would be Xerxes' heir. The jubilant king, ever conscious of continuing his dynastic role, named their son Darius II after his father, and Esther was content. She had fulfilled her mission to save her people, and in bearing a son she had fulfilled her roles as a woman and as as a queen. She was a busy and ecstatic mother, tending to her newborn and planning his future, as all new mothers do. She thought of all she would teach him; of how she would love him and watch him grow. She never allowed her thoughts to dwell on her lost love. As for her dreams, they remained her own.

Two Days of Celebration

The Jews celebrated their improbable and spectacular military victory against their enemies on the day immediately after the cessation of fighting. There were, in fact, two distinct days of celebration, depending on where in Persia the Jews had fought. In the outer provinces, which constituted the vast majority of the territory of the Empire, the Jews celebrated on the fourteenth of Adar. In the city of Susa, where the king's fortress palace was situated, the Jews celebrated one day later, on the fifteenth of Adar, the day following their second day of routing out the retreating mercenaries.

Being Persians, the Jews celebrated like Persians. They cooked feasts and served wine and invited their neighbors—Jew and non-Jew alike—to share in their great relief and joy at their victory. The jesters pranced, and the poets sang of the heroic military victory, ever-after to be retold in stories and song. They told the tale of how the weak triumphed over the strong, and the few triumphed over the many. And, most amazing of all, that the Jews emerged strong and whole from the jaws of a certain and brutal death.

The celebrations were healing in nature. Neighbors who had remained silent—or worse, those who had acquiesced to Haman's vile decree, or even who had aggressively harassed their Jewish neighbors—all came forth on the days of feasting bearing small gifts and tokens of apology and reconciliation. And the Jews, emotionally ready to spread their joy and largesse in the wake of their victory and hard-won escape from massacre, welcomed their neighbors to their tables and lifted a glass of wine in peace with them.

But the Jews went further. Mordechai was near-maniacal about ensuring that the Jews behave in exactly *the opposite way* to

Haman's rapacious men. The Jews took *no* spoils, they protected even their enemies' women and children, and, simultaneously with their victory celebrations, they were expected to share their food and drink with those less fortunate than they. While Mordechai recognized the need to celebrate the extraordinary military victory—he shared in their jubilation—as the Jews' communal leader he also held them to a higher ethical standard. He impressed upon his people that every citizen—especially those who themselves had just survived a close brush with death—was obligated to contribute to the commonweal. So at Mordechai's instruction, every Jewish household prepared packages of cakes and wine, fruits and cured meats. The parcels were bound by the Jews, collected in wagons, and delivered on their feast day to the poor and needy Persians of their districts, regardless of religion or ethnicity. It was a unique expression of humanity and solidarity with their Persian neighbors.

A Holiday for the Generations

Mordechai did not stop there. Seeing a folk myth in the making, he dispatched official letters to the Jews in every province of the kingdom, near and far, outlining the days of celebration of a new holiday—to be celebrated on the fourteenth of Adar in the unwalled, outlying provinces, and on the fifteenth of Adar in the fortified city of Susa—and its requirements, echoing the events of the past year: fasts and lamentations followed by joy and gladness—in perpetuity. Adding the royal imprimatur to Mordechai's instructions, Esther, Queen of Persia and daughter of Avichayil, a Persian-Jewish nobleman, wrote and dispatched a second letter to all the Jews in Xerxes' kingdom officially confirming Mordechai's words certifying the new holiday. She added her imprimatur to the official scroll that created and codified the special day: *A new holiday is hereby instituted to commemorate the deliverance of the Jews of Persia, and it*

shall hereafter be celebrated for generations to come, spreading words of honesty and integrity, peace and truth, for always.

The Festival is Called "Purim"

As the annual holiday was important and evocative both of the Jews' vulnerability and their resilience, it acquired a name. The joyous holiday of the fourteenth day of the twelfth month of Adar became popularly known throughout Persia and in lands beyond as *Purim*. It was named for the *pur*, or "lot," that Haman, son of Hamdata the Agagite, had thrown when he was selecting the day on which he would crush and annihilate all the Jews of Persia. Thus, the very name of the holiday itself proclaimed the folly of the Jews' mad enemy; because ironically, the very means of the Jews' destruction was now evermore a testament to their victory.

And as the years passed, on the anniversary of their unexpected victory over Haman and their enemies, the Jews hewed faithfully not only to the joyous and merry aspects of the celebration, but also to the community obligations that Mordechai had instituted.

Over time, every Persian citizen looked forward to the fourteenth and fifteenth of Adar and the holiday of Purim. It mattered not that it was the Jews themselves who were saved from death that day. For on that day people throughout the Empire and beyond retold the story that *every* man, woman and child loved to retell: the simple tale of Esther, the beautiful commoner-queen, who risked her life to come before the king to petition him to save her people from Haman's murderous plot. They told the tale of the king who heeded his queen's requests and commanded a decree to be written that would turn the death decree on its ear, and who ordered that Haman and his evil sons be impaled on stakes for all to see and remember. And it told of the Jews' improbable and brilliant military victory over their enemies. For the Jews' victory over their enemies saved not only their own lives, but no less than Xerxes' Persia, as well. And the Persians celebrated that, too.

Aftermath

It was fascinating that while the holiday celebrating the Jews' victory was destined to be kept for millennia, Esther's strategic brilliance and Mordechai's prescient and formidable organizational and military role in the victory were downplayed, eventually disappearing from the story entirely. Both the queen and the spymaster were content to have engineered the victory—an undertaking of enormous political, diplomatic, logistical and military consequence involving millions of people and pieces of materiel.

Life went on, for the Jews of Persia, and in the palace of the king.

Shadrach

On the day after the victory of the *Dashneh Jahood* over their enemies, the skies remained a cloudless blue and were free of heat-thunder. Shadrach sulked and brooded in silence. Somehow, Daniel's people—the people who had borne him and from whom he had broken faith—had annihilated the armies he had been certain would have butchered and eliminated *them*!

Too late, he realized he had fatally miscalculated. He had placed his store in one human, and had ignored the abilities of others. Haman had shown promise as a man of unbridled evil, a lust for power and a blinding hatred of the Jews. But both Shadrach and Haman had discounted Mordechai's strengths, his spy network, and his ability to rally and to mobilize men and make alliances.

And everyone had completely overlooked Esther. The girl possessed a potent arsenal of weapons: her physical beauty and a softly irresistible, magnetic attraction masked her brilliant mind. When she focused herself on an objective, she was like an arrow loosed by an expert archer; inevitably, she found the heart of her target.

And last of all, Shadrach mused, he had grossly underestimated the Jews' fighting ability and their resilient ingenuity.

Shadrach frowned, but he shrugged philosophically. *Haman wasn't the only Amalekite in the world. Unlike Daniel, Esther and Mordechai, Mishael and Azariya, I am not bound by human time. After they are long dead I will have other chances to end the Jews, and they won't have Esther or Mordechai to save them. Eventually I will win.*

Old Daniel

Old Daniel had died quietly during the night after the Jews' victory. He had lived for over a century, had served four kings, and had built the spy network that Mordechai had inherited and commanded so well. He had lived through two exiles and had seen his people triumph over a powerful arch-enemy. He had been as close to a father as Mordechai had had, and Mordechai mourned Daniel for thirty days.

Abbas, Daniel's mute shadow, attached himself and his personal loyalty to Esther. Wherever the queen was seen, the giant Abbas was somewhere nearby, watching and guarding.

Xerxes

The king was satisfied; his plan had worked well. As he had intended, the man Mordechai had saved his kingdom by engineering and fighting a war on Persian soil that rid Persia of the foreign army put in place by Haman. Xerxes reflected that it had been a combination of sagacity and providence that had allowed him to detect Haman's lascivious designs on his beautiful queen, affording him the perfect reason for executing him. It was well known that the path to a successful coup was often through the queen, and Haman had thought to conquer Esther and move from there to the throne. Well, he had nipped *that* in the bud! Just twelve months ago his crown had been under siege, and he had not slept a single night through, worrying about the prospect of assassination. But now, his enemies were dead; the Jews were saved; his queen, his vizier, and an entire people were beholden to him; and his queen had just presented him with a healthy son. Xerxes slept just fine these days.

A New Tax

There was, of course, the troubling matter of the king's depleted treasury. Fighting wars was a costly undertaking, and not just in terms of lives lost. More pressing, Xerxes mused, as his Minister of the Purse had explained emphatically only yesterday, was the cost in basic monetary terms. Feeding and arming a division of soldiers, not to mention housing them, their cooks, caretakers and surgeons; and stabling, feeding and caring for their horses over the course the past year, had drained the royal treasury like an open spigot on a cask of wine. The Empire was nearly out of money. And other than waging a war and invading a country with wealth to spare—an age-old method used by kings to distract the populace and replenish their own treasuries—given his unsuccessful campaign in Greece just a few years ago, Xerxes had but one recourse. He would institute a new tax across the Empire.

Gone were the days of tribute forgiveness, which he had granted so open-handedly in the first years of his reign, currying favor with various special-interest groups. Gone were the bacchanalian feasts lasting half a year. Sobered by the latest close call with Haman, a maturing Xerxes, with an heir, a beautiful queen, and confidence in his right-hand man, had a renewed sense of his role as ruler. So he flexed his power and set about replenishing the royal fisc.

Epilogue
465 BCE

Eight years passed. It was the twentieth year of Xerxes' reign, and Persia had settled into a satisfying routine. The kingdom was prosperous, its borders secure, and the many populations comprising the Empire were productive and peaceful.

It was in the spring of that year that the king authorized his purser to relax his hold on the royal treasury sufficiently to allow a weeklong, Empire-wide celebration and a work-holiday, marking the twentieth anniversary of his reign. Modest by his previous standards, the celebrations were local, with wine and delicacies provided by the king with his compliments, but were extremely popular among the Persian people. Roving jesters and poets, snake charmers and magicians skilled in sleight-of-hand, traveled from city to town to village spreading the good cheer.

Notwithstanding the Empire's renewed prosperity, his confidence in his hardworking vizier, and the outward show of merrymaking and conviviality, Xerxes was ever-fearful of coup — a state of constant insecurity shared by most monarchs. This last peaceful stretch merely enhanced his worry that someone with sights on the throne might take the opportunity of his anniversary to make his move.

It turns out that Xerxes' fears were well founded.

On the last day of the anniversary holiday, when Xerxes' own bodyguards were a bit relaxed, Artabanus, an ambitious and disaffected captain of the royal bodyguards seething with time-worn frustrated pretensions at higher office, managed to catch the king's personal bodyguard by surprise, slit the man's throat, and then drive a dagger through the king's heart.

The assassin had chosen his moment well. It was the early evening, in the lull preceding the dinner hour, the great hall had emptied of ministers, ambassadors and supplicants, and Xerxes was alone, enjoying the quiet. On the dais with him were only his fan boy and his personal bodyguard of three decades. The day's business conducted, the scribe had just retired with his scrolls and his ink, and the king had sent Mordechai to his home. Artabanus, aided by a bribed eunuch who momentarily distracted the king's armed bodyguard, committed the double murder quickly and with scarcely a sound. The king's guard, a loyal fellow-soldier and campaigner, had recognized Artabanus, but in a fatal lapse had failed to challenge the man's unannounced presence. Xerxes, his warrior reflexes still good, managed to jump up from his throne, his hand just drawing his long-bladed dagger when the better-positioned and viciously intent Artabanus made his kill shot. The fan boy stood frozen, literally quaking in his shoes, ignored by the murderers.

The boy, unnoticed, crept backwards and soft-footed, using the hanging arras tapestry behind the throne as cover; then he turned and ran for his life. He sped out of a side door of the palace, following a familiar back-street path to Mordechai's house, where he had been sent with messages countless times in the recent past.

An ever-calm Mordechai, hearing the boy's news, instructed the boy to return immediately to the palace but to run secretly to Hegai at the harem with the emergency command to guard and hide both the queen and the crown prince with his life. Speed was of the essence. Determined not to allow Artabanus and his supporters to take possession of the fortress, within the hour Mordechai had mobilized his own men and was back at the palace himself, armed and accompanied by two hundred of Xerxes' own soldiers. One thousand loyal soldiers soon surrounded the palace wall, and two hundred others of Mordechai's network, working with their army comrades, painstakingly searched and secured every inch of the palace and the fortress.

Within twelve hours the coup had been suppressed, but not without casualties. Artabanus was slain, his eunuch captured, and his guards and soldiers either captured or killed. The white marble floors of Xerxes' throne room, the vaunted Hall of One Hundred Pillars, were slick with blood. It had been a faction of the royal bodyguards who had backed Artabanus, with the promise of a quick fortune and the favor of the new ruler. But Mordechai was able to rely on his friends within the established army, many of whom were now captains; men who, as soldiers, had allied themselves and fought alongside the *Dashneh Jahood* during the civil war eight years before.

By the time dawn broke over Susa the coup had been suppressed, and the palace servants were about their duties scrubbing the palace down and putting things to rights.

Esther and the crown prince were safe, having been hurried out through the kitchens by Hegai and Farah and escorted, together with longtime handmaidens Banou and Azam, to a secret safe-house outside Susa that Mordechai had kept for just such an emergency. Through it all, Abbas never left Esther's side, or the side of young Darius.

Mordechai

Mordechai had not elected to play the role of champion to Esther and her son; Destiny or Fate had given him that responsibility. And really, no one could have guarded them better. As spymaster and heir to Daniel's secrets and skills, Mordechai had been trained to do just that since he was old enough to decipher code. For the past three decades Mordechai had been applying his prodigious memory and his ability to organize people and inspire loyalty to covert operations for the good of his adopted country and of his ancestral people, the Jews. So when Haman had risen to kingly heights and plotted the genocide of his people, there had been only man in Persia with the moral, intellectual and physical courage and strength to oppose Haman *and win*. That person was Mordechai, and win he did, in true heroic style, but not without the assistance of his allies, his armies, and, of course, Esther, Old Daniel's priceless secret weapon.

And not without great personal sacrifice.

Now, with Xerxes' anniversary celebration having ended with his murder, once again Mordechai was more than just a witness to an agonizing turn in the cycle of life. He was a reluctant hero. Mordechai had ensured the safety of the queen and her son — Xerxes' heir — which, together with the show of military support by Xerxes' militia, broke the back of the coup. Following a month of national mourning for Persia's slain king, again it was Mordechai who oversaw a smooth transition of power, arranging the elevation of Xerxes' and Esther's young son, Darius II — not quite nine years old and under the tutelage and protection of Esther, as Queen Mother — to be titular king.

The Persian people were calmed and pleased that the ruling dynasty begun by Xerxes' grandfather, Cyrus the Great, would remain in power. Under the rules of Cyrus, Cambyses, Darius and Xerxes, Persia had seen itself grow into the largest Empire in the known world, enjoying advances unheard-of even by their geographic neighbors: a unified and stable monetary system, a vast complex of roads linking the corners of the Empire, a swift and dependable postal system, and — most important of all — nearly a century of peace. Give or take a two-day civil war or the occasional coup.

And thanks to Mordechai, the dynasty of Cyrus the Great was fated to continue its reign for another century.

Esther as Queen Mother

In the weeks and months following the coup, Mordechai was young Darius' steward, guiding him in ways of statecraft, and overseeing, with Esther and Abbas, the boy's training in all things: politics, history, geography, poetry, music, literature, and of course, all modes of soldiering.

Esther's stalwart watchman, the faithful and sometimes-invisible Abednego, had, at Esther's urging, transferred his loyalty to young Darius, becoming the boy's guardian and sergeant-at-arms. He and Abbas, comrades from the old days, worked together to fashion Young Darius into a strong soldier and a compassionate, worthy king.

As for Esther, she remained a presence in the court at Susa. For the first ten years after Xerxes' death she was to be found at her young son's side always. But once he reached the age of eighteen and fully assumed his role as king, she stepped back. She was prepared to sit proudly on the sidelines near the dais during royal court sessions, in the special seat reserved for the Queen Mother. Esther was in all ways a wise, trusted, and beloved advisor to King Darius II.

Her private sorrows remained her own.

Esther and Mordechai

But what of the two former lovers?

Was Esther-the-woman — the beautiful, brilliant, and courageous queen — fated to live and die loveless, serving Duty first and only? At forty-one years of age and still a fabled beauty, would she live out her life as widow to one king and mother to another, with the buried memory of her young love nothing more than a shadow on her heart? Was she fated to live and die without knowing her lover's touch?

And was Mordechai—vizier to the king of the largest empire in the world—fated to wear a king's ring, but never his lover's? Was he fated forever to be Esther's chaste champion, mentor to her son from another man, serving Duty first and only?

As it happened, Esther's star was bright enough, and her life force strong enough, to overcome the Fates and forge a new life for both of the unlucky lovers. And it happened, as many life-altering events do, during a moment of prosaic sameness, and without warning.

In the palace chambers reserved for Darius' schooling, Mordechai had just finished giving the young king a lesson in political governance, and had his hand on the young man's shoulder in affection and camaraderie. Darius had turned his face to his mentor's, a look of trust and hero-worship in his eyes. It was at that exact moment that Esther entered the chamber. She was about to ask her son if he would like to ride with her for an hour, just mother and grown son, though of course their ubiquitous bodyguards would be riding beside them. But she stopped stock-still in the arched doorway. She could not take her eyes from the strong, patient hand of the man, and the serious face of the young king—the two people she loved more than her own life.

From her vantage point across the room the afternoon light spilling through the window behind the table limned the older man's still-straight shoulders and her son's proud profile, so that optically, the two figures merged into one. Esther blinked her eyes. It was a trick of the light that she should imagine Darius and Mordechai as one. And in that instant, Esther—orphaned daughter of a Jewish nobleman—resolved that the two—man and boy—would *both* be hers. There was nothing to stop her remarrying! In fact, it was not uncommon for a widowed queen to marry her dead husband's close advisor. A widowed queen with a fatherless son was just as much in need of a protector and champion as was any other similarly situated woman of any caste in the ancient Near East of the fifth century BCE. *More* in need of one, truth be told. She and young Darius were prime targets for adventurers or predators, men — Persian or foreign — with their eyes on the throne and the royal treasury. Men who thought either that they would woo and win her and rule alongside her, or that they would kill both her and Xerxes' heir and take the kingdom by force.

Esther resolved instantly that she would approach Mordechai and make her pitch. If he no longer loved her — and he gave no inkling that he did; who could blame him after all that had transpired — then perhaps she could appeal to his protective instincts. She would point out that she and young Darius would be safer, and the monarchy more secure, if she were Mordechai's wife, and if Mordechai were the young regent's protector.

So she entered the room and, breaking the spell that had held the men for that instant, she did what she had not done for twelve years. She looked Mordechai directly in the eyes and smiled a true smile.

In the play of light on her still-luxuriant hair, Mordechai saw not Esther, but his young Hadassah. He closed his eyes for a second and shook his head. When he opened them Esther was still standing in front of him, one hand on her son's other shoulder, the other resting lightly on his own on the large table. He couldn't breathe. She had not touched him for nearly thirteen years.

Then, all three of them, man, young king and vibrant queen-mother, began to speak at once.

"Mother!" said Darius.

"Mordechai...," began Esther.

"Your Majesty," said Mordechai, his eyes never leaving her face.

Things moved quickly after that. Before the month was out, Mordechai and Esther were wed twice.

The first wedding was a small, private ceremony, known as the *aghd*, held in Mordechai's house in Susa, attended by the members of the Sanhedrin Brotherhood and officiated over by a holy man of their people. This private wedding was most meaningful to Esther. For it was here, in the salon she had been torn from thirteen years and a lifetime ago, that she would finally wed the man she had loved for all of her life.

As before, there were lit candles, blue and white nigella herbs, and clusters of flowers set out everywhere, scenting the crowded room. As before, Esther was adorned in the waist-length lace veil as a bride of her people. As before, Esther and Mordechai stood together, this time on the fragment of Poupeh's cashmere wedding *termeh*, the special cashmere floor-spread that the old woman had salvaged and repaired after that long-ago nightmare. This time, two old neighbor women, friends of Poupeh, stood in for her, gifting Esther with a bridal wreath of twined red roses, jasmine and calendula. She bent her head as they placed it reverently about her neck and gently kissed her cheeks. The scene was reflected in the gilt-framed mirrors on the walls: Esther and Mordechai's faces, their eyes on each other, Esther's son Darius standing to Mordechai's right. Esther saw Abednego against the wall, watching her. She knew no one else could see him, but she smiled at the man who had been her guardian angel through years of misery, danger and many dark nights. He nodded imperceptibly, his hand on his dagger, his glance settling on young Darius.

As for Mordechai, he had eyes for no one but Esther; his Hadassah-Esther-girl-woman-queen-warrior-mother-bride.

And then a second time, later that evening, the couple stood together in formal court dress, at a more stately and purely official wedding ceremony in the Palace at Susa, held in the Hall of One Hundred Pillars that Xerxes had built, and ringed by armed guards. The Royal Crier pronounced them wed by virtue of the law of Persia, and in the eyes of the people of the royal court and the Persian Empire they were hailed as husband and wife.

At both ceremonies young Darius gave his mother's hand into the hand of a man whom he trusted with his life and worshipped as mentor and hero; the statesman and tactician who could wield sword and dagger like a warrior.

Esther smiled at the two men who defined her life, daring to allow her heart to float free within her. She was a true bride at last.

Over the next decade, and until their deaths, Esther and Mordechai loved fiercely, as only two who had once lost one another could do. And they helped Darius rule Persia and govern their people. They were quite a match; the stuff of legends. Scrolls and songs throughout the centuries and of numerous faiths were fated to tell their story: of the queen and the spymaster who saved Persia.

THE END

ACKNOWLEDGMENTS

I grew up alongside the Bible's characters, first as a student, and then later as a scholar, teacher and author. The Bible's characters were there millennia before I discovered them, of course, but it seemed to me that each character was alive and waiting expectantly, ready to whisper their secrets. This listening ear and deep empathy for the Bible's characters made the writing of three non-fiction books of biblical interpretation a pure pleasure for me. My goal in writing those books over the past seventeen years was to retell the Bible's exciting stories through the lenses of *midrash*— the Bible's legend literature—the Talmud, and my own unique viewpoint, in the process giving voice to the Bible's women and men.

While I loved writing those books, I confess that I chafed a bit. Often there were corners of the heroine's or hero's personality, or slices of their lives or experience, that were unexplained in the spare Bible text or even in the exhaustive commentaries. Or else— and this happened frequently—my intuition simply felt something extra, saw something different. I could imagine the additional details and feel the simmering emotions as clearly as if I were walking alongside the biblical character, an unseen fellow pilgrim on a rocky mountainside; or sitting beside them as a nonjudgmental friend or confidant. And while my capacity to imagine doubtless aided me as I interpreted and wrote about *midrash* and legend, I was constrained in my retellings from giving my imagination full rein, by the frame of the genre.

My subconscious was patient, biding its time.

Some years ago I researched and wrote a series of lectures on Megillat Esther, the Bible's Scroll of Esther. I had been studying that small book — the last to be added to the Hebrew canon — at varying levels of academic intensity for decades, and as I prepared these scholarly lectures I let myself go a little, injecting sidebars such as "Just imagine what Esther was thinking and feeling as she walked that 'High Noon' walk from her quarters to the king's throne room." And people — lay people as well as clergy of various faiths — invariably came up to me afterwards saying, "You should really write a book about this." And "You made me *see* every detail for the first time." And "You have a unique perspective, an exciting story to tell that I want to read."

So I began amassing notes and ideas.

My chief cheerleader in this new endeavor was my grown son, Ben, who was in the audience one evening when I delivered my Esther lecture. He listened intently, to the lecture and also to the audience reaction, and, proud and thoughtful, he came away determined that I should write "that book." After that day, Ben's emails appeared regularly in my in-box. *You have something new to say, and a passion to tell it your way.* And he encouraged me, relentlessly, to tell it. Eventually I gave in, because it was the logical next step for me, and because I really wanted to write the story. I felt I *understood* every character in the Esther narrative and I wanted to retell their stories my way.

After clearing the decks and taking a sabbatical from teaching, I lined up my books, gave myself a reading period, then began to write. Building on the legends in the Talmud and *midrash*, and letting my imagination fly, the story flowed through my typing fingers; the unexplored corners of the familiar characters' hearts and minds lay open to me. I could clearly imagine details not even hinted at in the biblical story: the characters' ancestors, their friends, enemies, lovers, teachers, even their guardian angels; the housemaids, cooks and stable hands; the generals, palace guards, harem girls, eunuchs, scribes and messengers on horseback. I smelled their sweat, trembled at their ambitions, felt their sorrow and terror, pined for their lost loves, celebrated their victories. And I created new characters, weaving them all — old characters and new — into a gripping, multi-generational saga taking place in the dangerous and mysterious ancient Levant.

In addition to the encouragement of my son Ben, my husband Sam and my daughter Sarah comprised the other two "legs" of my sturdy support stool. I read aloud all or most of this book to all three, watching their faces and hearing their reactions at the story's dramatic new dips and twists. As a first test audience they couldn't be beat. My husband Sam, especially, invariably remembered a relevant detail I had read aloud weeks before and would call my attention to it fifty pages later. Sam, Ben and Sarah, your eagerness to enter my world and your steadfast confidence in me helped me to sing as I wrote. Thank you, Ben and Sarah, for bringing Amanda and David into our lives. And finally, another very special thank-you to Ben for, once again, creating this book's beautiful cover.

We none of us can go it alone, and I must thank my sweet and loving friends — Ilene Nechamkin, Gaby Weinreich, Irene Kofman, Cora Kirschenbaum Lessner, Faanya Rose, and Debbie Taub — for being test audiences as well as supportive and impatient boosters. Your love of a good story, for the Bible, and, humbly, for me (it's absolutely mutual) have made sharing this writing project enormous fun. Thank you all for making time for me and for this story.

I extend a special thank-you to my publisher, Moshe Heller, new owner of Ktav Publishing House. Moshe's sharp mind, amiable nature, enthusiasm, and eloquent encouragement of me and this new book venture were key to helping this book become a reality. Thank you, too, to Shira Atwood, Moshe's able and tireless assistant.

Speaking of publishers, I owe a debt of thanks to Bernie Scharfstein, my friend, mentor and redoubtable publisher of my first three books. Thank you, Bernie, for your generous advice throughout this new book project. The word "retirement" takes on new meaning as applied to you.

And finally, thank you to Steve Siebert. You have remained steadily patient and professional through four book projects and thirteen years of working together. Thank you for once again formatting this beautiful book.

And to the reader, the result of this writing adventure is before you. *The Queen & The Spymaster* is my fourth book—my first novel. It has incubated in my mind and heart for years, and I am exultant to share it with you. Hang on to your seats. This is an Esther you never knew, a Mordechai you never even suspected, and a score of new characters besides. I hope you enjoy reading *The Queen & The Spymaster*.

Sandra E. Rapoport
New York City

ABOUT THE AUTHOR

Photograph by Manning Gurney

Sandra E. Rapoport is the author of the award-winning book, *Biblical Seductions,* and coauthor of two other books that weave together biblical text and legends, or *midrash,* to tell the untold stories of the women and men in the Bible.

Before turning full-time to writing and teaching, Ms. Rapoport was a litigating attorney handling cases of sexual harassment and employment law. She became adept at reconstructing complex fact patterns into riveting stories in preparation for trial, a talent she brings to her writing. Her essays and articles have appeared in scholarly law reviews as well as in general readership publications including *Commentary* and *The Jewish Week,* and the *Wall St. Journal* has quoted her as an expert in her field. Sandra continues to write and lecture, and lives with her husband Sam in Manhattan.

SCYTHIANS

R. Danube

BLACK SEA

MACEDONIA

THRACE

PAPHLAGONIA

GREECE

Aegean Sea

Sardis

LYDIA

P'HRYGIA

CAPPADOCIA

COLCHIS

ARMENIA

CYPRUS

MEDITERRANEAN SEA

Tyre

SYRIA

ASSYRIA

Euphrates

Tigris

BABYLO

ARABIA

EGYPT

Nile R.

RED SEA

PERSIAN EMPI

Under Darius, About 5

with principal Satra

The Persian Er

Grecian Territo

Royal road fro

SCALE OF MILES

0   100   200   300   400